AF437349

Aine

INVI WRIGHT

COMPLETED WORKS
by Invi Wright

***

STANDALONE

The Nanny

Aine

The Professor

Lord of Dread

THE FEMALE SERIES

The Female

Her Males

Their War

Chev's Mate

Rock's Bully

TRIGGER WARNINGS CAN BE FOUND ON:

inviwright.com

THANK YOU

***

The largest thank you possible to my husband. You gave me the confidence and support to pursue writing, and none of this would be possible without you.

Also, to my Patreon subscribers: Brianna Kathleen, Lexie Terry, Lindsay, Leilani S., Vanessa Turpin, Kimberly Belbot, Sharon H., Gigielle, Lora Beth Farmer, Bhavini, and Patience Isch. Your support is the sole reason I'm able to do this, and I can't properly convey in words just how much you mean to me. I hope you enjoy this story!

Chapter 1

AINE

IT SEEMS THE entire village has gathered to witness my execution, the first one in years.

My father's voice cracks as he begs our leader for mercy, and I stare at the dirt as he offers himself instead. My mother's teary pleading makes its way to my ears shortly after, but her words are almost entirely drowned out by the jeers of the crowd.

They shout foul curses at me, and the more daring of the bunch go as far as to throw rocks in my direction. I try to dodge a particularly large one, but my toe catches on the dirt and upsets my balance.

I stumble, and the crowd releases a massive cheer as I fall.

It hurts, and I fight to remain silent as my wrist twists painfully beneath me. Nobody cares to hear what I have to say, and any noise from me will only make things worse.

Vik steps forward after dismissing my father. His brown shoes enter my line of sight, and I swallow past the lump in my throat as I look up at him.

I hope to see some sort of forgiveness in his eyes, but there isn't any. His face is cold, and he looks at me as if I'm nothing more than a stranger.

It's a sharp change from the friendly smiles and polite greetings he's given me for most of my life.

My wrongdoings outweigh any semblance of friendship we once had.

"Aine Ladhe," he starts. His voice is loud to ensure everybody can hear. "You are being sentenced to death as a result of capital murder."

He takes another step toward me, and I accidentally let out a panicked cry as I kick the dirt and scramble back. I don't want to die. It was an accident.

"I'm sorry," I beg, ignoring the angry shouts of the crowd. "Please. I'm sorry."

Vik shakes his head, his eyes trailing from the bloody soles of my feet to my dirt-covered brown hair. He then turns toward the bloodhounds, and I choke back a sob as I eye the large animals.

They're sitting patiently at the feet of their handlers, but I know it's not for long.

They'll be released in five minutes to hunt me down. It's almost a guarantee the beasts that live in the forest will kill me, but in the odd chance they don't, the bloodhounds will.

I'm sure they've been starved these past few days, making them desperate for the meat surrounding my bones.

One snaps its jaws in my direction. It knows I'm dinner.

"Please," I beg again, not caring how weak I look.

Vik circles me, his movements slow and calculated as he rounds my body. He looks at me with hatred, but I still find myself hoping he will forgive me.

He has to know it was an accident.

We've known one another our entire lives. He knows my character better than anybody else. He has to know.

"Please, I—"

My words are cut off as our leader slams his foot down on my arm. The bone cracks underneath his weight, and I let out a bloodcurdling scream as my arm buckles beneath me.

I've never felt a pain like this, and I struggle to think clearly as he grabs my bicep and pulls me up off the ground.

"Go!" He pushes me in the direction of the woods.

I scramble to regain my balance as I lock eyes with my father. He looks awful, his clothing tattered and his brown hair uncombed. We must look identical right about now, and I ingrain the image of him into my memory as I turn and take off into the woods.

My broken arm hangs limply by my side and tears blur my vision, but still, I run. Objectively I know it's useless, but fight or flight takes over.

The bloodhounds are loud as they wait for the command to come for me.

I have only five minutes to find the beasts.

Nobody has ever encountered a beast and lived to tell the tale, but it's rumored they kill quickly. The bloodhounds will take their time, and I don't want to suffer.

That thought alone is what drives me forward.

I jump over a small log, and my knees buckle when I land painfully on a bundle of sticks. The soles of my feet are already injured from my time in confinement, and the landing has the dry skin ripping open.

I ignore the pain and continue running.

I'm sure the beasts have heard me by now or, at minimum, have caught my scent. It won't be long before I'm surrounded.

My lungs burn, and my breaths come out in pained gasps as my body begs for rest. I can't give it, though. I need to find the beasts before the bloodhounds are released.

The beasts kill any human who ventures too deep into the

woods, the animals territorial and aggressive.

It shouldn't be hard to find them.

I know I have when the forest around me grows quiet. The small wildlife disappears as they sense the beasts, the tiny critters running to safety.

Movement on my left captures my attention, and I turn just in time to see black eyes disappear behind a tree.

The beasts are here.

Another one appears, and it takes everything in me not to spin and run back to my village.

The beasts look identical to wolves, but they're significantly larger.

There's more movement to my left. They're quickly closing in, and one even begins to run parallel to me. Its long legs push its massive body forward, and I realize it's herding me toward the others.

My legs burn, and I'm so distracted by the beast running alongside me that I don't spot the fallen tree in my path until it's too late.

My foot catches on one of the branches, and I cry out as I land on my injured arm.

I'm panicked, and I struggle to formulate complete thoughts as the beasts close in around me. They circle me, their jaws snapping as their red, beady eyes run over the length of my body.

Their gazes linger on my bloodied limbs.

A smaller one darts forward and bites my thigh before I have time to react, ripping off a chunk of my flesh and forcing another scream out of me. The pain is blinding, and my vision blurs as I grab at the skin in a sad attempt to stop the bleeding.

Another darts forward, taking another piece of my thigh, and I realize they aren't going to kill me as quickly as I hoped.

I press my back against the trunk of the fallen tree I tripped over, leaning against it as my attention flickers from beast to beast.

There are five of them, four adults and one smaller child, but I'm sure more are coming.

A loud, deep growl has the animals stepping back. They sit on their haunches, ogling my injured body with saliva dripping from their teeth.

Another beast emerges from the forest, this one larger than the others. I immediately know it's their leader.

He's the one who is going to kill me.

I expect him to lunge forward and attack me like the others, but he takes his time walking up to me.

I'm shaking, likely from both fear and adrenaline.

The beast's fur is dark brown and matted with blood, probably from some poor critter he killed earlier, and I hold my breath as he leans in and begins sniffing me.

Why is he doing this?

I wait for him to bite, but instead, he whines and begins to quiver. I've never seen anything like this before, and I'm pretty sure I'm hallucinating as the animal's limbs start to contort and break with painful, wet pops.

"I—" I say, at a loss for words as the beast transforms into a human man before my very eyes.

I blink several times to make sure I'm not imagining this. We've heard rumors that the beasts can take on human forms, but nobody's ever seen it happen.

I didn't think it was real.

The man is on his hands and knees, and his long limbs stretch as he rises.

His dark hair falls over his large brown eyes, and he frowns as he pushes the messy strands out of his face. He's naked, and every inch of his body seems to be covered in thick muscle.

He's terrifying, and everything grows quiet as he stares down at me.

He turns toward the beasts surrounding us.

"Go," he orders.

His deep voice brings goosebumps to my skin.

Most of the beasts leave at his command, loud yips pouring from their mouths as they take off in the direction I came from. My eyes roll back, but I shake the dimness away, desperate to remain awake.

I don't understand what's happening.

The man seems angry, his lips pursed as he grabs my good arm and yanks me to my feet.

My legs give out, my thighs too injured to hold my body weight, and the man smoothly turns and shoves me into the arms of another.

"Take her to the healer," he grunts.

I flinch as I'm handed off, my head lolling forward and smacking against a hard chest. There's a loud commotion as I'm pulled away, and my toes drag painfully against the ground as the world around me goes black.

Chapter 2

AINE

I'M NUMB.

It takes me a while to understand what's happening, the voices around me unfamiliar and confusing. They speak too fast for me to process, and I fight through my mind's fog to remember how to open my eyes.

By the time I manage to get them open, I'm even more confused. There's a woman hovering over me, one I haven't seen in years.

I thought she was dead.

"Jenna?" I ask.

My vision is fuzzy, but I'm pretty sure that's her. Her curly blonde hair and bright green eyes are identical to the woman I'm thinking of, and her crooked canine pushes against her lips the same way. Am I seeing things? I can tell I'm heavily drugged, my mind and body slower than they should be.

The woman shoots me a wide smile before turning and closing the curtain separating me from the rest of the room. She seems to be in a hurry, and I look down as she begins to adjust an IV sticking out of my arm.

My breath hitches, and I take a moment to process as I look over the state of my injuries. Thick, bloody gauze covers large parts of my body, and a needle sticks out of a still-open thigh wound.

I'm still wearing my black shorts and shirt, which is good.

"Where am I?" I ask. My tongue is heavy, making it hard to form words. "What happened?"

Jenna sucks on her teeth as she grabs the needle stuck in my thigh and pulls it through the wound.

I watch, intrigued, as the sharp object penetrates my skin. The string attached to the end pulls the wound shut and helps slow the bleeding. She moves quickly, sewing my cut with practiced ease until the skin on either side meet. Despite seeing it happen, I feel nothing as the needle repeatedly pierces my skin.

"Shouldn't that hurt?" I ask.

Jenna doesn't answer, choosing instead to shake her head with a low sigh. Grabbing the scissors, she cuts the needle loose and pats the outside of my leg.

"You're on a lot of drugs right now, and I don't understand what you're saying," she finally says. "Rest, and we'll talk later."

She moves to the other side of my body, and I frown as she lifts my arm and lays it so my wrist is facing upward. I can't tell what exactly I'm lying on, but given the room's sterility, I'd assume it's some sort of hospital bed.

"I thought you were dead," I say, my eyelids slipping shut in a slow blink.

Jenna glances at me and shrugs, a look of confusion settling on her face before she gets back to work. Her nimble fingers repeat the action she took on my thigh, and she carefully stitches my flesh until all that's left are thin wounds held together by black knots.

Why is she doing this? Why is she here?

She was one of the best elementary school teachers in our

village, but she was sent into the woods after being caught in a compromising position with another woman. It was years ago that they executed her, and up until me, hers was the last one we had.

I always thought her death was unnecessary, and I secretly assumed her rejection of our leader's advances was the real reason he sent her to the woods. He doesn't like being told *no*.

Shadows of people are visible just beyond the curtain that surrounds me, and I watch their silhouettes before turning back to Jenna.

How did I end up here? My memory of what happened in the forest is spotty, but I remember enough to know I should be dead.

"Who are these people?" I ask.

Jenna's fingers prod at the exposed bone in my arm as her eyes slide to meet mine.

"I still can't understand most of what you're saying," she mumbles before following my line of sight to the curtains. "We're in the beast pack, but I promise you're safe."

What? I stare at the curtains, my pulse racing as I watch the moving shadows. Are they beasts? My memory of a man shifting from animal to human plays in my mind, and I shake my head in the hopes of expelling the visual.

I don't want to believe it.

Jenna touches my shoulder, drawing my attention back to her.

"They brought you back here," she says, confirming my fears.

I open my mouth to ask why, but my body doesn't cooperate. Instead, only a loud exhale leaves my throat. Jenna pauses to watch me, her eyebrows pulled together as she tries to figure out what I'm saying, but she's distracted by the curtain opening.

My head lolls to the side to see who's entered. This woman is unfamiliar, but her long limbs and thick, dark hair have me wondering if she's a beast.

Her eyes roam my body before settling on my broken limb.

"How's her shoulder?" she asks Jenna, leaning closer to look at the bone protruding from my skin.

Jenna shakes her head. "Not great. It's going to hurt to re-align, and she's going to feel it despite the medicine I have her on."

The tall woman frowns, her lips pursing as she glances between my arm and Jenna. There's a tense silence as Jenna waits for guidance, and with a huff, the other woman turns and walks away.

She leaves the curtain open.

Curiosity gets the best of me as I peer into the large room, my eyes falling immediately to the bodies lying on similar beds to mine. Doctors hurry between the injured, all of them tall and imposing. Are they beasts, too?

Why did they bring me here? They were attacking me, fully intent on killing me, and they were only seconds away from finishing the job.

Did the bloodhounds come? I don't understand.

I try to see if I recognize any of the other doctors, but between the drugs and the speed at which they move, I can't tell.

"Why am I here?" I ask again.

Jenna continues to ignore me, her body stiff as she stares in the direction the woman walked. I turn back to the room outside the curtain, noting again how large all the doctors appear to be. They must have ample food here.

Jenna remains silent until the woman returns.

"Well?" she asks as the tall, definitely beast woman returns. Her hands are clenched into tight fists at her sides.

"He's still refusing to heal her, but we can't leave her arm like this," she says, reaching over me and grabbing my shoulder. "I'll hold her still."

Jenna groans, wiping at her brow with the back of her hand. It leaves a tiny smear of blood behind.

"Okay," she says. She sounds hesitant. "I'm sorry, Aine."

Her movements are quick, and before I can process them, she's grabbing my arm and forcing the bone back into place. My breath hitches as fire spreads up the limb and into my shoulder. I'm unable to force out more than a small groan due to the drugs, but if that weren't the case, I know I'd be screaming.

I breathe in shallow gasps as I struggle to think beyond the pain, my muscles seizing. The hands on my body are removed just as the pain stops, the fire simmering into a dull ache as both Jenna and the tall woman step away.

"That was the worst part, I promise." Jenna grabs a rag from behind me and dots it along my forehead to soak up my sweat.

I glance between the two women before turning to Jenna, my fear growing as some of the haziness of my mind disappears with the pain. The tall woman takes that as her cue to leave and disappears without another word.

"Where am I?" I ask again, praying Jenna can understand me now.

Jenna grimaces, shaking her head to convey that she still can't make out what I'm saying. The words feel clear as they slip from my lips, but it seems there's a disconnect between what I think I'm saying and what's being heard.

"I still can't understand you," Jenna says, sitting on the edge of my bed. "But I assume you're confused."

She takes a deep breath before continuing, her hands moving to the blanket that sits on my calves. She fiddles with the fabric for a moment, worrying it between her thumb and forefinger, before pulling it up to my belly.

"I don't know where to begin," she admits, offering a timid smile.

There's a pause as she adjusts once more, her cheeks

expanding as she fills them with air. Her hesitance to answer isn't comforting.

I'd like to believe her when she says I'm safe, but the beasts have only ever been a nightmare to us. The fact that she's alive and, seemingly, healthy after so long is a good sign, but my brain is swimming in questions she's clearly not in a hurry to answer.

I want to know why I'm alive and why they brought me here, and more importantly, I want to know what they want from me. I'm sure the beasts don't go around collecting humans for fun, and I'd be naive not to realize there's surely some reason they chose to spare me.

"Do you remember being attacked in the woods?" Jenna asks. She waits for me to nod before continuing. "The beasts usually kill the humans they come across, which you know, but not always. Sometimes they bring us in."

Jenna pauses, her fingers fiddling with one another.

I struggle to keep up, her explanations answering very little. Are they expecting me to work for them? I'm not particularly skilled in any fields, my role as a village cook not teaching me much beyond how to chop a carrot.

If they're planning to prostitute me, I'll kill myself.

"I know it's a lot to take in," Jenna continues. "The beasts believe in mates, which are like predestined soulmates. One of them has claimed you as theirs."

Her large eyes bore into mine as she tries to gauge my reaction, and I can tell my confusion is apparent as her face falls. She rubs at her cheeks with a quiet groan, her shoulders rolling forward in defeat.

"Our leader, Damien, says you're his mate." Jenna brushes my hair out of my face. "He's the man who saved you in the woods. The beasts are like us, and this place is similar to ours. They have two forms, but they're mostly human. They're not the savage animals we're raised to believe."

I disagree. I know the beasts are a mixture of animal and man, but they're not human. They may take our form, but we're nothing alike.

"I know they seem scary, but they're good to us," Jenna continues. "None of them are going to hurt you. You're safe here."

I shake my head, refusing to believe it.

I've been told a man wouldn't hurt me before, and it was a lie.

"Why me?" I ask, careful to enunciate.

Jenna leans in as I speak, her eyes focused on my lips. A look of understanding spreads over her features as I repeat myself for the second time.

"They believe fate determines who their mate is," she says. "They don't choose and don't know who their person will be until they meet them. I've heard them explain it as a soul-deep connection before, and it seems Damien felt that when he saw you."

I'm struggling to even wrap my head around the fact that I'm alive, let alone that a beast is crazy enough to think I'm some sort of soulmate to him.

The curtain around my bed slides open, and another face I'm unfamiliar with pops inside. This woman gives Jenna a wide smile, her straight teeth on full display as she steps entirely into the makeshift room. Is she a beast? She's got the same tall frame and brown hair as the other woman. I suppose it would make sense most of the people here are beasts. I'm in their pack, after all.

The woman is dressed in the same hospital apparel as the other doctors, and she takes a moment to scan my injuries before reaching for Jenna.

"It's getting late," she says.

Jenna takes her hand, and she holds the woman tightly as she hops off the side of my bed. Her feet thump against the hard floor as she lands, and she shuts the curtain before turning back to me.

She removes the IV from my arm and sets it somewhere behind my head.

"Your body will hurt as the medicine wears off, but we were able to convince Damien to give us some of his blood so you're going to be fine. Get some sleep, and I'll be back tomorrow morning to show you around."

His what?

She and the other woman are gone a second later, and I sag against the bed.

I was thoroughly prepared for my death, so convinced the beasts would be the end of me that I don't know how to feel about being spared. I'm happy to be alive, but I'm worried about the cost it's coming at.

I don't care to be the 'mate' of that man. I faintly remember him, and he didn't seem pleased to see me. Am I supposed to be his wife?

Jenna says he won't hurt me, but I know better than to believe that. We were never close, and while I don't think she'd lie to me, I don't trust the beasts.

They may have spared me, but they bit off pieces of my thigh beforehand.

One of them currently has chunks of me in their stomach.

The thought makes me nauseous.

People are moving beyond the curtain, but their footsteps are soft and I have to strain to hear them. There's less commotion now than when I first woke, and I wonder if the doctors are leaving for the night. I was sent into the woods at dusk when the beasts are most active, so it's got to be quite late by now.

Eventually, the entire building grows silent, the only noises I hear from the sheet I lie on.

The medicine begins to wear off shortly after the place goes empty, and I force myself to inhale slowly through my nose before releasing the air quickly through my lips. Jenna's promise that I should be fine is the only thought that runs through my head as I lie as stiff as a board, every movement sending fire through my body.

I'd kill to have that IV back.

Chapter 3

AINE

MY BODY SCREAMS for me to lie back down as I sit up and throw my legs over the side of the bed. Jenna said she'd return in the morning, but my anxiety's gotten the better of me. I need to look around.

I've spent all night worrying about the beasts, my mind replaying Jenna's words and wondering about the likelihood of me having completely imagined everything. I was pretty drugged up, so I wouldn't be too surprised to learn that I was hallucinating our conversation.

"Okay," I whisper to myself.

I curl my fingers around the thin mattress and rise off the bed.

The stitched wounds on my thighs sting as I put my weight on them, and I panic as my knees buckle underneath the pressure. I'm able to catch myself on the bed, and I take a moment to stabilize myself before releasing the mattress and making my way to the curtain separating me from the rest of the room.

My movements are slow as I fight through the pain, and I break out into a cold sweat, but I continue forward. I can't wait any longer for answers.

The curtain is made of a soft and thick fabric, and I fist the material before pulling it to the side. I'm met with an empty room, most of the injured from last night having gotten up and left long ago. There are a few people who remain, their bodies unnaturally large in the small hospital beds. I resist making any noises as I inch forward and evaluate the man closest to me.

He's tall, a good head above even the largest men from my old village, but that's not what stands out. It's his muscles that capture my attention, the thickness of them more than a little alarming. Our farmers and strongmen aren't nearly this big, and I stare at his biceps with horror.

Even in his sleep, he's terrifying.

My eyes trail down his bare chest, and I step back as I watch his ribs expand with breath. He's hairy, and his abdominals look like they're permanently flexed.

He's got to be a beast.

My mind is still a bit fuzzy—from the drugs or blood loss, I don't know—but I ignore it as I look for an exit. This room is bare, minus the hospital beds, with one hallway to my right and an unlabeled door directly to my left.

I think I saw one of the doctors earlier exit through this door, but I'm not positive. Still, I begin quietly shuffling in that direction.

I can't lift my legs high enough to disconnect my toes from the ground, but I manage to make good time by using the empty beds I pass for support. Footfalls echo as somebody begins walking down the hallway to the right, but I pray they don't notice me as I continue my escape.

"Can I help you?"

I flinch, slowing, but I don't turn around.

"I'm just looking for fresh air," I say.

The footfalls grow louder as the man approaches, and I resist the urge to cower as he rounds my body and steps between me and the door. The deep frown on his lips tells me he's unhappy, and I swallow past the lump in my throat as I face him.

He's as large as the man on the bed.

I scan his face for any animal features. I'm still not sure if I hallucinated everything Jenna said or not, but I'd rather be safe than sorry. I'll assume everybody's a beast until I'm told otherwise.

"You should be resting. Jenna will be here soon," he says, placing a hand on my shoulder and nudging me toward the bed I just escaped from.

His touch is soft as he turns me around, and I slump in defeat as I shuffle back to the bed. I need to know where I am, and I can't very well do that when I'm trapped inside this room.

A part of me wishes to argue with him and insist he let me leave, but I bite my tongue and refrain. I don't know this man, and the last thing I need is to make the wrong person mad and end up a chew toy.

Again.

"Jenna should be here any minute now," the man says.

He grabs my elbow when I stumble, my knees only moments away from giving out.

All this exertion isn't good for my injuries, and I wince as I sit on my bed and take the weight off my legs.

This escape attempt took a lot out of me.

Thankfully, the man doesn't stick around, and he leaves without another word the moment I'm settled. The curtains are left open, and I peer out and watch as he checks on the few patients here. He moves quickly, his hands efficient as he pokes and prods at the beings lying in the other hospital beds.

I'm so caught up in him that I almost don't notice the door opening, but the loud squeak of the metal rubbing together draws my attention. Jenna strolls in with a grin, her eyes crinkled as she greets the man and turns to me. That grin falls as she scans my body, her attention lingering on my legs.

"You've popped some of the stitches on your thigh," she says, frowning. Her lips purse as she grabs a suture kit from the small table next to my bed.

I glance at my thigh, grimacing as I take in the state of my leg. It doesn't look great. Most of the skin is still held together, but there's a visible gap where one of my sutures came out.

It must have happened during my escape attempt.

"Sorry," I murmur, poking at the inflamed skin.

Jenna lunges and grabs my wrist, stopping my movements. "Leave it alone."

I apologize again, and I suck in a deep breath as she prepares the needle. I'm no longer on pain medicine, and I have a feeling I'm going to feel the sutures this time.

It's going to hurt.

I hiss as Jenna slides the needle through my skin, the metal burning as it's pulled through my wound. That fucking hurts. Jenna mumbles quiet assurances as she ties the knot and trims the excess thread, her kind words doing nothing to help the pain.

The wound is red and inflamed around the edges, which is a telltale sign of infection. There seems to be advanced medical care here, at least more than there was back in my village, but these people aren't miracle workers. I'm willing to bet the mouths and claws of those beasts were far from clean, and infection almost always leads to death.

"Let me get you a wheelchair," Jenna says.

I cock my head to the side, confused. "A what?"

She laughs. "You'll see."

She disappears behind the curtain before I have the chance to inquire further, her speedy legs carrying her out of my line of sight. I pick at the skin on my fingers as I wait for her to return, flinching as I tear off a particularly large chunk of flesh. It's a nasty habit I picked up several years ago during a period of intense stress, and I haven't quite figured out how to stop.

Jenna returns with a giant smile, her hands holding the handles of a chair on wheels. It doesn't take an expert to realize this is the "wheelchair" she was referring to, and I hold in a frown as I look it over.

"I can walk," I argue, knowing that's far from the truth.

Jenna's quick to appease me. "Of course you can. But I want to show you around and that's going to be a lot more walking than your legs can handle right now."

She wheels the chair to the edge of the bed before grabbing my elbows and helping me stand. As much as I hate it, she ends up supporting most of my weight as I struggle to my feet. I wobble a bit, still exhausted from my earlier journey, before taking the two steps to the chair and plopping down.

It's surprisingly comfortable.

"This is a cool contraption," I admit, running my hands along the soft, wooden handles.

Jenna nods and walks behind me.

"It is," she agrees. "The beasts provide more care for their injured than Vik did. He kept us in the dark on a lot of healthcare and technology."

I cringe at the inappropriate use of our leader's given name, but I don't comment on it. I'm not necessarily eager to defend the honor of the man who sent me into the woods to die.

The chair beneath me begins to move forward, and I grab the handles and lift my feet in panic. I hold them for dear life before realizing it's just Jenna pushing me from behind.

"I'm excited to show you around," she says, walking around me and opening the door I failed to escape from. "We haven't had a human mate in years."

She pushes me through the door before it closes. I peer over my shoulder to look at her, noting the wide grin she wears.

"Until me, you were the last execution we had," I admit.

Anger flashes in Jenna's eyes, yet, in contradiction, she releases a laugh.

"I was the last *public* execution," she says. "There have been numerous others over the past few years."

I turn back around and prod at my thigh. I'm not entirely shocked to hear that. Our village is relatively small, so we notice when somebody goes missing. There have been several over the years, but we were told they were suicides. I've always wondered how many were actually executions.

The door slams shut behind us, and my eyes grow wide as I take in the land surrounding us. This place looks nothing like my home.

I'm able to catch glimpses of houses between the trees, but this place looks more like the forest than a pack.

"I was expecting a more cultivated land," I admit.

Jenna snorts. "The beasts like their privacy. It looks wild out here, but I promise it's an organized chaos."

She gives me a minute to look around before continuing forward. There's a small path she follows, a thin strip where the ground has been flattened from use.

"The most popular spots here are the training field and the dining hall," Jenna says after a moment of silence. "I don't want to overload you, so I'll just show you those two things before taking you home."

She grunts as she struggles to push my wheelchair over a rock.

Her words send a shiver down my spine, the uncertainty of this new life frightening. I don't want to think about the fact that some man has claimed me as his soulmate, and I avoid the topic like the plague.

It won't be the first time I've been forced into a partnership with a man I hardly know.

"How do they treat you?" I ask, turning again to look at Jenna.

She frowns, her lips flattening into a thin line. "The beasts don't love humans," she admits. "Sometimes I think they think of us as little pesky bugs, but since mates are so respected among their culture, they're generally pretty kind."

Her fingers instinctively move to her neck, and for the first time, I notice there's a large scar on the area where her neck meets her shoulder. I blink a few times to ensure I'm not imagining things, but the shape never changes. It's a bite mark?

Jenna notices my gaze and tilts her head so I can see it better. The scar stretches with the action, the teeth marks distorting.

"Instead of a marriage ceremony and rings, beasts like to bite to symbolize the bond between mated pairs," she says.

I blink, not following, and Jenna cracks a smile before continuing.

"I know it sounds crazy, but the mark creates a physical pathway between two souls. I can feel my mate's emotions through it, and she can feel mine. The bite is sacred to the beasts, and Damien won't do it without your permission." She tacks on the last bit when she sees my horror.

They bite one another? I'd much rather be forced to wear a ring than let a beast sink their teeth into my skin. Never again.

The mere thought has shivers running down my spine.

A tense silence stretches between Jenna and me, and after a second, I turn back around. I can tell she's passionate about her bite mark, and the last thing I want is to disrespect this culture she seems so entwined with.

I won't bite the hand that feeds me.

Literally.

The silence continues as Jenna resumes pushing my chair, and I take this time to peer around.

"Organized chaos" is a good term to describe this place, and the thin path we walk along weaves between hidden houses. Or, at least, what I assume to be houses. They're beautiful wooden buildings, well-maintained and big enough to hold large families.

"Where is everybody?" I ask.

Jenna pushes me over another large rock before answering.

"Most people are at the training fields right now," she says. "Everybody else is probably patrolling the woods or in the dining hall. Beasts don't usually stay inside their homes during the day."

"Oh," I say, unable to come up with a follow-up question.

We continue to move at a slow pace, and I lean forward as I begin to hear people moving about. There's shouting and the occasional cheer, and the commotion intensifies the closer we get.

Eventually we come up on a large clearing, and my jaw drops as Jenna pushes me past the final trees.

This must be the training field she mentioned. To the right of it is a large garden, but it's the field that captures my attention.

We had one back in my old village, but it was nothing compared to this. A giant plot of land has been completely cleared of foliage, leaving a large, open area full of people. There's a mixture of human-looking bodies and beasts mingling about.

I flinch as a man runs past, his muscular legs pushing at a speed I've never seen before. There are several beasts in their human form running laps around the perimeter of the cleared field.

My attention shifts to the beasts in their animal form. I faintly remember seeing these creatures during my execution, but their sheer size and power must have slipped my memory. Two particularly huge beasts ram into one another, their large teeth tearing into the skin as they take bites out of each other's flesh. Goosebumps rise to my skin at the memory of those teeth sinking into me, and I nervously reach down and prod at my stitches.

This is horrific.

Jenna ducks and brings her lips to my ear.

"There's your mate," she whispers, pointing to the right of the sparring beasts. "Over there."

I follow her finger, my heart pounding as I spot the man who saved me the night of my execution. He stands out among the others, and he stares at me with his hands clenched into tight fists. He holds my gaze for a second before looking away, pretending as if he hasn't seen me.

This is the man I'm expected to be with?

I can't make out too many of his features from this distance, but he doesn't look happy. For a man claiming I'm his life partner, he sure seems uninterested in me.

Jenna huffs. "He's being unreasonable."

I turn toward her, looking for clarification, but she doesn't provide any as she wheels me back into the forest.

I remain silent as the sounds of fighting disappear behind us.

"That's the man I'm to marry?" I ask, needing to know what, exactly, the expectations are of me.

Jenna laughs, a loud sound that feels unnatural among the quiet of the trees.

"In a way," she says. "I know this is a lot to take in, but I promise it's not as bad as it sounds. Damien's a bit standoffish, but he's not anything like Henry."

I recoil at the mention of my husband, painful memories moving to the forefront of my mind. My parents were forced to give me to Henry when I was still a teenager, his demands to wed me backed by our leader. It left little room for argument—not that my parents would've had much of one.

We were starving, and he promised to keep me fed.

Things got hard after Anthony died, my brother attacked and

murdered by the beasts after venturing too far into the forest. Hunger made him desperate, and he foolishly thought he'd catch an animal before being discovered.

I gesture toward the cluster of buildings up ahead to the right, not wanting to discuss Henry.

"What's that?" I ask.

Jenna looks where I'm pointing. "Apartments. Most unmated beasts choose to live there instead of by themselves in a big home." She clears her throat before continuing. "Do you want to check them out?"

I shake my head. That's the absolute last thing I want right now. Jenna chuckles at my quick response before veering to the left, putting even more space between us and the apartments.

"I was going to take you to the dining hall," she says, "but to be honest, my arms are growing sore and you'll see it later tonight with Damien."

With Damien?

"It's tradition that a beast introduces his mate at dinner," Jenna explains.

I try and fail to hide my panic. I suppose I knew Jenna wouldn't stick with me forever, but I was naively hoping I'd have more time alone with her. She's the only thing keeping me sane right now.

I'm not exactly excited to meet Damien, and I'm by no means extroverted enough to enjoy being introduced to a bunch of strangers. Especially considering those strangers tried to kill me less than twenty-four hours ago.

Jenna doesn't seem to sense my inner turmoil as she chatters about tonight's menu, her voice bubbly as she wheels me toward wherever it is I'll be staying.

How does she not see how weird this is?

"I'm taking you to Damien's home," she says, pivoting us

toward a large house on the right. It's constructed the same as the others I've seen, but there's a small white porch wrapped around the front. "He should be back soon, and he'll explain everything to you in more detail."

I tighten my grip on the chair handles, panicked as Jenna rolls me over a decomposing log.

"Are you sure that's a good idea?" I ask, cringing as my voice comes out in a high-pitched squeak.

I don't want to step on any toes, especially the ones that belong to the frightening man I saw back in the clearing.

"It'll be okay." Jenna's trying to be soothing, but I'm having trouble believing her. "Everything will be okay now, Aine."

Damien looked pissed to see me in the fields, and his clear indifference is making me wonder why he's claimed me as his mate in the first place. I don't trust it.

Jenna pushes me toward his house, and my nerves grow the closer we get.

"Don't worry," Jenna says. "He'll be home soon."

I nod, too overwhelmed to argue with her. This doesn't make any sense, but it's clear I don't have any other options.

My knuckles turn white as Jenna spins my chair so she can drag me backward up the front steps of his house, and I scan the forest for any sign of the beasts in the meantime.

Jenna grunts as she gets me on the porch, and I turn and look over my shoulder as she pushes open Damien's front door.

"I'm not allowed to go inside, so I'll just leave you here," she says, wheeling me over the threshold.

She's not allowed inside? Am *I* allowed inside? I panic, not wanting to be left alone, but Jenna shoots me a devilish smirk and slams the door shut before I get any words out.

"Jenna!" I shout, hoping she can hear me through the thick wood.

My hands grow clammy, my pulse racing when she doesn't come back. Is this some sort of sick joke?

Sucking in an uneven breath, I reach down and wipe my palms on my shorts. When my hands are dry enough to have some grip, I grab the wheels of my chair and try to roll out of Damien's house.

Jenna's refusal to enter, coupled with her sinister smile as she left, made it more than clear that I'm not welcome in this home. I don't know why she did this, but I don't have time to stew in my anger as I grip the wheels and try to push forward.

I'm able to stretch and pull open the door, but my wheel gets caught on the metal base of the doorframe when I try to leave. I hiss through my teeth as I try to force the chair over it, but my arms grow weak after only a few attempts.

They're too injured.

I release the wheel and roll back a few inches into the foyer. A stitch has popped in my bicep, and I watch the blood drip down and fall to the floor. It splatters as it hits the ground, and I tuck my arm into my body so it drips onto my chair instead.

Then I roll over the splatter, spreading the blood so it's harder to spot.

I don't want Damien to see it, but I realize I'm too late when I look up and see him. He's in the forest, his pace quick as he weaves between the trees. He's already spotted me, and he glances at the floor before looking up and meeting my gaze as he approaches.

To say he looks pissed would be an understatement, and my panic grows as I wait for him to reach the house.

"I'm so sorry!" I don't hesitate to launch into an apology the moment he's near. "Jenna left me here, and I can't get over the door frame by myself."

Damien doesn't respond, his body stiff as his eyes travel the length of my body. I watch as his attention settles on my bloody arm, lingering there before moving to the wound on my thigh. His close proximity has my heart racing, the size of him terrifying. He's much larger than Henry, and he seems even angrier.

If I'm to be with this beast as Jenna says, I don't have much hope for a happy future.

"You heal slow."

His words make me pause.

"Sorry? I—" I start, unsure how to respond to that.

"Sorry I'm late," a feminine voice rings out, interrupting me. My jaw shuts with a click as a small woman comes barreling in behind Damien. "I was held up talking to—"

She pauses as she catches sight of me inside the foyer, her body freezing mid-step. I tilt my head to the side as I look at her, trying to figure out if she's a human. She's got light blonde hair and bright blue eyes, so I assume she is. The beasts all seem to share the same dark hair and brown eye characteristics.

Is she one of Damien's mates? Does he have several? That would make things easier for me.

Damien turns his back to me.

"Take her to the cabin," he says. "Then meet me in my office."

He leaves no room for argument as he steps around me and disappears into his home.

The woman nods vigorously. I look between her and Damien's retreating figure, feeling both uncomfortable and embarrassed. She offers me a small smile, flinching slightly as the sound of a door slamming echoes throughout the house.

"Sorry about that," she says, walking around me. "I'm Olivia, Damien's assistant."

So, not another mate? I try to keep my disappointment hidden as she grabs the handles at the back of my chair and pushes me forward. I was hoping he would have several. It would keep his attention off me.

"Nice to meet you," I say, wincing as Olivia pushes my chair over the doorway. The movement bounces the wheels and jostles my body. It hurts.

"Oh, I'm sorry!" Olivia slows to soften the chair's movements. Small huffs fall from her lips as she struggles to ease me down the stairs. "You'll be staying in this cabin here."

She points to a small wooden cabin just opposite Damien's home. I didn't notice it when arriving with Jenna, the building hidden between the trees and hard to spot.

It doesn't look like much, and the wooden exterior is covered in dirt and grime. Is this where I'm to live?

Olivia pauses to catch her breath.

We rest in silence, and I listen to the birds chirping at one another from the treetops. The sound has me relaxing, but the peace doesn't last for long as Olivia releases a loud exhale and begins pushing me forward once more.

"Why were you executed?" she asks.

I freeze, panicked as I try to think of an excuse. "I, uh—" I stammer, my face heating up. "I was caught with a woman."

The lie doesn't roll off my tongue as smoothly as I'd like, and I sink my teeth into my lower lip as I wait for her response. It's why Jenna was executed, and it doesn't seem she's punished for it here. I saw her with that female doctor yesterday, and it didn't appear they were trying to be discreet.

Olivia snorts. "Don't let Damien hear you say that."

Her chuckle doesn't take long to turn into a full-blown laugh, and before I realize what's happened, she's hunched over, cackling, her hands resting on her knees to keep herself upright.

"I'm sorry!" She gasps.

A nervous laugh slips from my lips. Why does she find that so funny? After a couple of seconds, she straightens back up and wipes at her cheeks.

"I really needed that today." She grabs my chair and pushes me the last couple of feet to the cabin.

On either side of the door are overgrown rosebushes, and I try to make myself narrow so the prickers don't brush against me as Olivia wheels me inside.

I hold my breath as I look around.

This cabin is tiny, but I'm shocked to discover that only a bed and a small round table sit inside. I search for a bathroom or kitchen, but there doesn't seem to be one.

"Where will I go to the bathroom?" I ask.

Olivia gives me a pitiful look as she jerks her head toward Damien's house. "You'll have to go to the house for that."

Her eyes drift to the chair I sit in, her eyebrows furrowing as she takes in my current injured state.

"I'll remind Damien to come over every few hours to help you clean up and use the bathroom," she says. "You need a shower."

My jaw drops, indignation washing over me. While I may need some help getting to and from the house, I'm perfectly capable of using the bathroom and bathing myself.

"I don't need help using the bathroom," I hurry to say. "Or bathing. I just need help getting to the house."

Olivia looks me over once more before nodding, but it feels like she's doing it more for my benefit and not because she believes me. She glances around the small room, and she lets out a quiet sigh as her eyes land on the table. It's an odd reaction, but before I have the chance to ask about it, she straightens up and plasters a wide smile on her lips.

"I need to get going," she says.

Without waiting for my response, she spins on her heel and leaves, the flimsy door slamming shut behind her. I stare at the wood, my eyes tracing the gaps between the doorframe and the actual door. This place is poorly constructed, and I can already tell it will offer me little protection from the elements.

Nonetheless, I'm glad to have my own space, and I'll fix it up once I'm healed. I'm still wary of Damien, but I'm taking his disinterest in me as a positive. The fewer wifely duties I'm expected to provide, the better.

Objectively I know that just because he doesn't seem to care much for me doesn't mean he doesn't hold expectations, but I'll worry about that later.

Now that I'm alone, I take a better look around the room.

The bed that sits pushed up against the right wall is short and narrow, but it looks like it'll be able to hold my weight just fine. Thin, beige sheets sit on top of the mattress, looking clean despite the rattiness of the fabric. There's no comforter or heavy blanket to keep me warm, which isn't ideal, but I'll survive.

To the left, underneath a cracked window, is a small, two-person table. On it sits some scrap paper and a pen, and next to that is an empty cup.

Other than that, the room is entirely empty, and I hold back tears as I come to the realization that I have nothing. While I've never been a particularly materialistic person, I do enjoy my knickknacks and comfort items.

Particularly the ones that keep me warm at night.

What now? I debate trying to go outside and explore, but fear of getting lost or stuck keeps me still. Plus, there's a step to enter the cabin that I know I won't be able to get down.

Or back up.

I grab the wheels of my chair and roll myself toward the table so I can look out the window. It faces Damien's house.

The sky gradually grows dark as I wait for Damien to come and bring me to his house so I can use the bathroom. It grows cold, and I hug myself in a sad attempt to stay warm.

I want to grab the sheets off the bed and use them, but I'm still wearing the dirty clothes from when I was attacked. I'm not sure if I'll get the opportunity to wash my sheets often, and I want to keep them clean for as long as possible.

Lights occasionally turn on and off inside Damien's house, and I see his large shadow behind the thin curtains. The fabric is occasionally moved to the side so two dark eyes can peer in my direction, but that's the only attention I receive.

I squeeze my legs together as a painful pulse rushes through my body, my bladder screaming to be emptied. It's been hours, and nobody has come to take me to the bathroom.

Eventually the ache grows so intense I attempt to stand and walk outside, but I only make it a small handful of steps before growing too fatigued and needing to sit.

My body curls in on itself as I attempt to hold in my pee, small tears pooling in my eyes at the pain. The last light in the house turns off, and I crane my neck to watch it.

Is Damien coming to get me? I thought he was supposed to bring me to dinner. That's what Jenna said.

Nothing happens for a long minute, and my hope fades as a light on the top floor flickers on, exposing Damien in a bedroom. There are no curtains over these windows, leaving the view into the room completely open, and I watch as he strips to his underwear and shuts off the light.

The realization that he's going to bed feels like a stab to the gut.

My body shakes as I grip the arms of my chair and stand, my knees buckling before adjusting to the weight. I slide my feet along the floor as I head toward the door, painful gasps slipping from my throat as my wounds are stretched.

I just need to make it outside the front door so I can relieve myself. It's only a few steps.

I grunt as my foot catches on a floorboard and pivots me

forward, the near fall making me lose control of my bladder.

I hiss as I catch myself on the wall, humiliation washing over me. The hot liquid rushes down my legs and pools onto the floor. It stings as it enters my cuts, probably only further infecting them.

Shame warms my cheeks as I shuffle back to my chair, unsure what to do now. I can't make it to the house, I have no other clothing to change into, and it's far too cold to remove what I'm wearing.

My entire body aches as I sit back down, and I hug my torso as I turn and look back out my window. Maybe it wouldn't have been so bad if the beasts *had* killed me.

Chapter 4

DAMIEN

I FEEL HER watching me from the rickety cabin window, stalking my every move. It takes all the willpower I have not to look in her direction as I rise from my dining table and turn off the light.

I gave up trying to work hours ago.

The floor creaks as I walk across the hall and up the stairs.

Olivia moves around in her bedroom, humming quietly to herself as she unpacks her belongings. I don't like having her in my home, but I'd rather it be her than the woman my beast has infuriatingly claimed as his mate.

Drawers slam shut as I knock on Olivia's door, and there's a quiet smacking as she pats her cheeks to bring color to them. She's always been nervous around me, but I could care less about how she looks. My patience thins the longer she takes to pamper herself, and I raise my fist and pound at the door.

That seems to do the trick, and a second later, the door's ripped open.

"What'd she say?" I ask.

Olivia was alone with her, and as much as I tried not to care, my interest has turned into desperation. My beast is livid his injured mate is being taken care of by another, and it's messing with my head.

Olivia's face reddens as she meets my gaze. "Not much. She's quiet."

I frown. "What did *you* say?" I ask.

My people value the bond too much to let me send my mate away, their outward frustration with me for putting her in the cabin proving that point. Still, I don't know what to do with her.

"I asked why she was executed," Olivia admits, avoiding my gaze.

"Did she say why?" I need to know.

Olivia shrugs, staring at her feet. I can tell she doesn't want to answer me, the smell of her fear clouding the air. My beast pushes through, darkening my eyes as he senses her reluctance. The change only worsens the scent of fear.

"She wouldn't tell me," Olivia admits.

I suspect it's going to be a hassle to get that information from my mate. Humans are always reluctant to share their secrets, but it's only a matter of time before I get my answers. I already sent my beasts to kill the leader of her old village, and I bet they'll be able to find some documentation among his things.

I change the subject. "Did you say anything about me?"

Olivia shakes her head. "No. I only told her you'd help her to the bathroom while she's still healing."

I frown, annoyed she made such a promise on my behalf. I'd like to spend as little time as possible around my mate, even if it makes my people angry.

"Is there anything else I should know?" I ask.

"No. That's it."

Good. I nod and leave. I didn't get the information I wanted, but it's better than nothing.

Her eyes are back on me the second I enter my room, and I catch myself instinctively turning to look out the window.

She sits in her wheelchair peering over the window ledge, and I turn away before she realizes I'm aware of her gaze.

I'm glad Olivia and Jenna took care of her today, giving me space to clear my head. I'm on edge after seeing her so torn up in the woods, her body mangled and broken, and I probably wouldn't have had the strength to leave her in the cabin had I spent one more minute near her.

I don't want her, and it's only a matter of time before my beast realizes his mistake and agrees to take another.

Chapter 5

AINE

I'M PRACTICALLY HANGING out of my chair by the time the sun rises, my upper body slumped pathetically over the armrest.

My shorts stick to my legs in the places where the pee hasn't yet dried, and I feel unbearably itchy. The pungent smell of me vanished sometime during the night, although I'm certain it's just a result of my nose getting used to the scent.

I'm sure whoever comes to get me will be ambushed by the unpleasant air.

Unless I'm left in here to rot.

I glance at my hands, evaluating the blood surrounding my nail beds. I anxiously picked most of the skin off throughout the long night, and now my fingers look like shit.

Another shiver travels down my spine as a particularly large gust of wind rattles the cabin, shaking both the door and window as it seeps through the cracks into the small room. The cold air feels almost painful against the parts of my body that are still wet, and I rub my hands against them in a sad attempt to warm up.

It doesn't work, and I return my attention to Damien's house. He ended up being my entertainment for the night, the man seemingly having had as much trouble sleeping as I did. The lights were constantly flickering on and off as he moved around his home.

At some point in the early morning, he gave up on sleep and left his bedroom for a room on the first floor. The light has been on for several hours now, and occasionally I'll see his large frame move around behind the curtains. Other than that, though, the house is still.

Damien stands and walks past the window, his movements quick, before the light turns off altogether. Oh? Where's he going now? My guesses are almost always wrong, but it's an effective way to keep my mind occupied and away from my soiled clothing.

I purse my lips when I can't find him, and I lean forward to try and get a better view. There's still nothing, and in a fit of desperation, I place my hand against my seat and push up slightly. The movement burns, and I drop with a panicked squeak when the front door opens and Damien steps onto his porch.

My movements are frantic as I duck below the windowsill, my heart racing as his eyes lock with mine just moments before I disappear underneath the ledge. My hands shake as I roll myself away from the window, not wanting him to know I've been watching.

I don't want Damien thinking I'm interested.

Is he coming over? I do my best to mentally prepare as I fidget with the metal frame of the chair, running my fingers along the armrest in an attempt to calm my racing heart. The sound of snapping twigs and rustling leaves makes its way to my ears, and I ready myself for the interaction.

Damien rips open the cabin door and steps inside, his body taking up most of the doorway.

His nose crinkles as he turns to me, and a look of disgust spreads across his face as his gaze drops to my soiled pants.

Despite my attempts to keep them back, tears begin to spill down my cheeks. I'm humiliated.

"You pissed yourself?" Damien's voice is cold, and his question is more of a statement as he steps further into the room.

"I tried to go outside," I say, wiping at my face.

Damien only grunts in response, and he gives me another once-over before approaching and grabbing the handles of my chair. I spin to watch him over my shoulder, not trusting his motives.

"What're you doing?" I squeak as he begins wheeling me toward the door.

Damien stares past me. "I need to take you to breakfast. It's tradition," he says, wheeling me roughly over the doorway.

It hurts, and I wince as my body jostles in the seat.

"I thought the tradition was dinner?" I ask.

Damien doesn't acknowledge my question, and the silence between us quickly grows uncomfortable. I expected Jenna or Olivia to get me today, and I had mentally prepared for the shame of facing one of them.

I don't like that it's Damien.

"Tradition is that I accompany you to your first meal. It usually is dinner," he eventually says, pushing me in the direction of his home. "I thought we could do it early before the dining hall gets busy, but I didn't realize you were incontinent and would need to be bathed first."

Damien makes no attempts to hide his dislike for me, the negative emotion thick in all his words. A small part of me wants to argue that it's impossible to leave somebody without a bathroom for over twenty-four hours and not expect them to have an accident, but I keep my mouth shut. The last thing I need is to anger him any further.

Damien may have spared my life, but at the end of the day,

I'm sitting here bound to a wheelchair because of what his people did to me.

Despite Jenna's assurances that he isn't like Henry, his attitude and manner of speaking are exactly the same.

Everybody congratulated me for catching Henry's attention, impressed I was able to domesticate our village's notorious playboy. Still, I was covered head-to-toe in bruises and he was spotted at the brothels mere days into our marriage. Everybody knew, but it wasn't until the other women my age began to marry that I realized I'd gotten the short end of the stick.

I thought I was finally free of men like Henry, but now I'm stuck with a deadlier version of him.

Damien is silent as he brings me to his house, but I can practically feel waves of anger pouring off him. I bring my hands together and scratch at the cuticle on my thumb, my eyes darting around as he drags me up his porch steps and wheels me inside.

I didn't look around when Jenna brought me here, having been too occupied with trying to leave. The entryway is relatively tiny, but it almost immediately opens to a large room. A couch, table, and some bookshelves fill the space, but the walls and shelves are bare.

There's no personality in here, and I wonder if Damien's just moved in. It sure looks like it.

Past the large room is a dinner table. It's free of clutter—unsurprising—and looks brand new. The wall opens to the left of that, leading to another room I can't see from here. It's probably the kitchen.

Damien turns my chair toward the stairs.

"There's only a half-bath on the first floor," he grunts.

I eye the staircase, my heart racing as I contemplate just how I'm supposed to get up them. I'm going to rip open my stitches if I try to walk all the way up there, but knowing I have no other choice, I suck in a deep breath and push myself up.

A heavy hand drops onto my shoulder and forces me back into the seat before I make it far. I gasp as the fingers dig into one of my cuts, and I collapse onto my chair before wiggling out of Damien's hold.

Fuck, that hurt.

Damien releases me before lifting my entire wheelchair. My knuckles turn white with how hard I'm gripping the armrests, and I stare at my knees as he begins walking upstairs. I wasn't anticipating him carrying the entire thing.

Thankfully, Damien doesn't seem to struggle with my weight, and he smoothly walks to the second floor in one easy breath.

There's another large, open space at the top of the stairs, but surrounding it are closed doors. I assume they lead to bedrooms and bathrooms.

Damien doesn't give me any time to explore as he rolls me toward one of the doors on the right. He pauses just outside it before reaching over me and pushing it open.

The door swings to reveal a small bathroom, the room in no way large enough to comfortably fit my wheelchair. Damien seems to have the same thought as he turns and wheels me backward, pivoting toward the large double doors that sit to the left of the stairs.

He repeats the same process as before, but this time, the doors open to a bedroom. I immediately recognize it as his, identifying the curtainless windows I spent all night staring into.

Damien's room, like the rest of the house, is bare. A large, unmade bed sits in the center of the room, the wooden frame matching the dresser along the left wall. I crane my neck to get a better look, but I don't have a chance to see anything interesting before I'm taken into the ensuite bathroom.

The room is much larger, and Damien rolls me into the middle before finally letting my chair go. I freeze as he shuts the door behind us and Olivia's words from yesterday come to mind.

"I can clean myself," I say.

I know Henry isn't going to come for me, but the lingering fear of punishment for allowing another man to see me unclothed is enough to make my blood run cold.

Damien scoffs. "You can't even use the bathroom by yourself."

He ignores my clear panic as he once more scans my body and wet clothing. I bring my hands to my legs to hide my bottom half from him. I don't want his judgment.

Damien quirks a brow at my attempt for modesty before his expression darkens and he grabs my arms.

"Stop!" I gasp, fighting against him as he pulls my arms away from my torso.

My eyes fill with tears as he once again looks over my soiled clothing. Why is he doing this?

"Can you get Jenna?" I plead. I don't want his help.

Damien's pupils dilate as I speak, his fingers digging almost painfully into my skin.

"No."

Turning away, he reaches into the shower and turns on the water. I bring my lip between my teeth and bite at the skin, terrified of his clear plans to wash me.

"I can take it from here," I say.

I'm hoping he'll take pity on me and leave. It's wishful thinking, I know that, but I have to try.

Damien pretends he doesn't hear me, his focus never once leaving the shower knobs as he adjusts the temperature. To my shock, once he has it set, he steps back and begins removing his clothing.

His shirt is the first to go. I look around nervously, double-checking that nobody is present to witness the action. I want to be angry with him, but I'm all too aware that he's a beast. I don't know what he's capable of.

"What're you doing?" I ask.

His pants are next, and they fall to the floor with a quiet thud. I stare at the ceiling as I wait for him to finish, my face warm as I hear his last piece of clothing drop.

I'm sure my face is beet red.

"Can you take off your clothes? Or do you need my help with that, too?" Damien asks, his words mocking.

I'm careful to avoid looking at his lower half as I nod, and my hands shake as I grab the hem of my shirt and pull it over my head. The motion is nothing short of agonizing, but I push through the pain. I want to get this over with as soon as possible.

Damien taps his foot as he waits for me to undress, quiet sighs slipping from his mouth whenever I pause to rest. I wish he would get Jenna, and I wonder why he's even bothering to do this himself. He clearly has the means to get somebody else to deal with this.

Grabbing my armrest with one hand, I use my other to try and take off my shorts. I make little progress before I need to rest. The effort is killing me, but I force myself to lift again and push the fabric down another inch. I switch arms and repeat my actions on the other side, but Damien quickly stops me.

His impatience seems to have reached its peak as he wraps his arm around my torso and lifts me. Then he uses his free hand to swiftly rid me of my bottoms. I clench my jaw as his bare skin touches my clothing, knowing how aware we both are that he's feeling my cold pee. My underwear goes down with the shorts, leaving me uncomfortably exposed.

I kick the fabric off my feet as Damien lifts me entirely out of the chair, his arm supporting most of my weight. He remains silent as I tentatively shuffle toward the shower, my steps slow and careful.

The slick, wet floor offers little grip for my feet, and in a panic, I grab his bicep to steady myself.

Damien stiffens, and I let go.

"Sorry," I mutter.

My mind once more wanders to Henry as Damien helps me navigate to the in-shower bench. This interaction would've undoubtedly led to severe punishment.

I shiver at the thought, my body tensing in fear that his ghost will somehow find a way to do just that. His presence will always haunt me, a curse for killing him. It's the price for taking the life of another.

"Sit," Damien commands, his clipped voice leaving little room for argument.

I nod, lowering myself onto the bench. He doesn't have to tell me twice.

Damien steps into the shower once I'm settled. I was sentenced to death two days ago, and now the creature who was meant to kill me is naked in the shower with me, helping me clean myself.

It doesn't make any sense.

Damien openly looks over my bare skin, and I fight the urge to cover myself. I learned long ago it's better to let men have their fill. Instead, I focus on the wall to my left, watching the water droplets pour down the tile.

I make a pointed effort not to look at Damien, but it's hard not to. Human males are significantly smaller than beasts, both in height and strength. Damien looks unlike anybody I've ever seen before, and while I'd have to be crazy not to recognize he's attractive, I refuse to linger on that thought.

When he moves just right, I catch sight of a large scar on the inside of his thigh, the only marring visible on his skin. It's prominent, and it looks like a sizable chunk of his flesh was ripped off before awkwardly healing over. I turn away before I'm able to make out any more of it, though.

His thigh is too close to other parts of his body, and I don't want him to catch me looking.

Instead, I watch out of the corner of my eye as Damien grabs a loofah, the object looking comically small in his palms. He squirts liquid soap on it before building some suds, readying it for me. I hold out my hand, but he circumvents my outstretched limb and applies the soap to my body himself.

Every muscle in my body stiffens.

Damien washes me, the man efficient in scrubbing the grime and bodily fluids off my skin. He avoids cleaning my wounds, choosing to let the soapy water run over them instead. I flinch when he grabs my knee and spreads my legs, and I stare at his forehead as he runs the loofah up my thighs.

He frowns as he does so, his eyebrows furrowing together.

"Did Jenna take you to use the restroom yesterday?" he asks, breaking the silence.

I shake my head. "No."

Damien hums, the noise quiet as it emerges from his chest. Without warning, he wraps his arm around my waist and lifts me, forcing my wet, soapy body to press against his. I gasp, the sound ending in a choked cough as he pushes the loofah between my butt cheeks, cleaning me from the back.

"Done," he says, putting me directly under the shower spray.

I stare a hole into his chest as the suds fall from my body, refusing to look anywhere else in sheer embarrassment.

"Thanks," I mumble. I don't know what else to say.

I attempt to cover myself as Damien turns off the water and returns me to the bench. The quiet is deafening, and I can only imagine what he's thinking right now.

He steps out of the shower and tosses me a towel. His back remains turned as he grabs another for himself and wraps it around his waist.

"Dry yourself off," he orders, continuing to face away as he leaves the bathroom and heads into his bedroom.

Taking advantage of the privacy, I spread my thighs and dry all my important bits before moving to my arms and legs. Damien returns just as I get the towel wrapped around my body, the man already dressed in a t-shirt and shorts.

He's holding more clothing in his arms.

"These are Olivia's, so they might be a bit big on you," he says, handing me a dress and underwear.

He uses his wet towel to wipe off the wheelchair, cleaning the dried pee from the seat and metal before tossing the cloth into the trash can. I try not to be too humiliated over the fact that he's deemed it too dirty to even wash.

"I'll be back in five minutes," he says, leaving the room a second later.

I rush to throw the dress over my head, eager to be clothed by the time he returns. It's a plain beige and slightly loose, but I don't care. I'm just happy to have something to cover myself with.

The underwear is a bit of a struggle to get on, but I figure it out with only minor issue. I don't love wearing another woman's underwear, but I assume Damien doesn't have anything new for me to use.

I relax when I'm clothed, happy to have been able to get myself sorted before Damien returns. My muscles burn in response to my rushed actions, but I don't care. I'd rather be in pain than have him dress me himself.

I turn and peer at Damien's belongings. There are a few small personal items—shaving cream and a razor on the sink, a dirty sock behind the door, and a toothbrush next to me on the shower seat—but otherwise, the space is bare.

Damien storms into the room just as I grab and inspect his toothbrush, the object falling to the floor as I jump at the sudden intrusion. He looks between me and the toothbrush, frowning at its position by my feet.

"I needed to throw it out anyway. It's covered in your piss."

I work my jaw side to side, hating how he keeps bringing up the accident.

"It's time to go," Damien continues. He steps into the shower and helps me back into the wheelchair. "Try not to embarrass me."

I recoil. Embarrass him? It's not like I'm doing these things on purpose.

I don't respond, and a tense silence stretches between us as Damien brings me to the dining hall.

The terrain is rough, and I listen to his breathing as he pushes me forward. It remains steady, even when he wheels me over a rock or bump in the path. I suppose I shouldn't be surprised, though.

He did carry me and my chair up and down an entire flight of stairs with ease.

It's been almost two days since I last ate anything, and my stomach has been aching terribly in desperation for sustenance. Jenna seemed to think Damien was going to feed me, but that turned out to be untrue.

"What's your name?" Damien suddenly asks, his voice quiet among the trees.

He doesn't already know? Soulmate, my ass.

"Aine," I say.

Damien tests out my name for himself, the word falling quickly from his lips.

"You will call me 'Damien' when we're in public," he says.

His sentence is confusing, and I pause for a moment to think it over. What else would he expect me to call him if not his name? I know some people prefer to be referred to by their title, but that's usually more so in respect, not obligation.

"What do you want me to call you when we're in private?" I ask.

Damien grunts, a deep sound that brings goosebumps to my skin, before pausing outside a wooden building. It's larger than the others I've seen, and the walls are covered almost entirely in tinted windows. I suspect this is the dining hall.

"I don't plan for us to be together in private," he says, clearing his throat. "Don't tell anybody about your accident."

I nod. I wasn't planning to.

I don't understand what Damien wants or why he's claimed me as some sort of mate if he has no interest in me, but I'm not quite sure if I'm ready for the answer.

Not that I think he'd even give me one if I asked. Damien isn't exactly chatty, and whenever he does speak, it's only to be rude.

Damien reaches over my head and pushes open the door to the building, his force causing the heavy wood to slam against the wall.

I flinch, hoping that doesn't draw any attention, but I relax as I look around and realize there's almost nobody here. Most of the tables that fill the room are empty, and the few people inside pay Damien and me no attention.

A large, open kitchen is on my right, and in front of it is a long table filled with platters of food.

My mouth waters at the sight, and I can't look away as Damien leads me to a table in the back. Olivia catches my attention with a wave, the woman offering me a friendly smile as Damien rolls me in her direction.

I wave back, but I immediately drop my hand as I realize it

was Damien she was greeting. That's awkward. They make eye contact over my head, and after a second, she clears her throat and turns back to her plate.

Damien sticks me next to her before walking to the other side of the table. He's frowning, but I'm starting to think that's his usual expression.

"What do you want to eat?" he asks.

I shrug, my stomach rumbling loud enough that I know everybody at the table can hear it. "I'll eat anything."

Damien blinks, glancing at my stomach before turning and heading to the long table. I wait, trying not to get my hopes up as he grabs two plates.

Olivia's gaze burns into the side of my head, and after a second, I work up the courage to face her. She greets me with a soft smile, but it falls as she eyes my clothing.

"I'm glad to see you again!" I blurt out, all too aware I'm wearing her dress and underwear. "Damien gave me this, but I promise I'll give it back."

Her eye twitches, and her lips tilt momentarily downward before shifting into a smile.

"Damien gave it to me for my birthday," she says, reaching out to finger the fabric. "It's my favorite one."

I grimace. "I'm sorry."

Olivia laughs, the noise light and comforting. "It's okay." Despite her words, I can tell she's annoyed, and I feel my guilt grow as she turns back to her plate.

Is there something going on between her and Damien? It seems that way, and it would explain his coldness toward me.

Damien returns, and his arm brushes mine as he sits to my right and sets a plate in front of me. It's piled high with eggs and meats I don't recognize, and my mouth waters at the mere sight of it. It looks amazing and smells even better.

"Eat," he says, nudging the plate another inch in my direction.

I don't hesitate to dig in, my greedy hands grabbing as much food as I can and shoving it into my mouth. My eyes roll back as I mash the greasy breakfast between my teeth, swallowing it once it's broken into just enough pieces that I won't choke.

"I'm surprised Damien brought you here for breakfast," Olivia whispers, nudging my shoulder to capture my attention.

I turn toward her, watching as she glances between Damien and me.

"Nobody ever comes for breakfast," she continues.

"Oh," I say, unsure how I'm supposed to respond to that.

Olivia sighs, slumping forward and looking at me with pity.

"I don't understand why he's trying so hard to hide you." Her voice is so quiet, I can barely make out the words. "A human mate is nothing to be embarrassed about."

My spine straightens. I wasn't expecting her to say that.

"Olivia," Damien interjects, his body heat spreading across my back as he leans over me to look at her. "I left some papers on my desk for you to sort through."

Olivia's head lowers as he speaks, and her cheeks redden as she gives a curt nod. She's on her feet a second later, her food long forgotten as she tosses it in the trash and rushes out of the building.

I frown at her departure, upset to once more be alone with Damien. He continues to ignore my presence as he eats, his eyes locked on the back wall as he makes his way through his plate.

I'm relieved when a man approaches and begins to converse with him, distracting him enough for me to slip away in search of a napkin. Some of the hot grease from my food found its way into the cut on my knee, and the burn is intense.

I wheel myself backward and turn toward the kitchen. There's got to be some sort of rag in there I can use to clean myself with.

Damien doesn't seem to notice I've left, which I love. It's nice to have a moment to myself. I spot folded cloths sitting on the counter next to the sink, and I carefully run one under the water before bringing it to my leg. It stings, but it also brings almost immediate relief to my cut.

"What're you doing?"

My wheelchair spins, and I gasp as I look up and meet Damien's angry eyes. He's pissed.

I shrug, figuring what I'm doing is obvious. "I spilled grease on my leg," I explain. "I'm cleaning it."

Damien's mouth twitches, and his pupils expand as he stares at my wound. My fear skyrockets at the change, frightened it's a sign he's shifting into his beast.

I remain stiff as he circles me, his steps slow and cautious.

Damien pauses once he's behind me, and I have just enough time to gulp before he's wheeling me out of the room, his conversation with the other man long forgotten.

"Where are we going?" I ask, my fingers curling around the armrests of my chair.

Damien doesn't answer—unsurprising at this point—and remains quiet as he pushes me outside and into the forest. I try not to let my panic show, but I'm positive he can see it through my whitened knuckles and tense posture.

He continues to lead me through the woods, his pace unrelenting. I relax only slightly when I realize he's bringing me to the hospital.

At least he's not taking me to some undisclosed location to kill me.

I eye the hospital bed I woke up on as soon as we enter the building, but Damien wheels me down the hallway to the right. He pushes me into a private room and sets me in the center of it.

"Stay here," he orders before turning and leaving.

I nod, not that it's of any use. He's already gone. I trace my finger along the chair's armrest, tired of Damien's bad attitude and wanting nothing more than to be back in my shitty cabin. It's cold and smelly in there, but at least there's no Damien.

He storms back into the room, still frowning.

I attempt to roll away from him, and I squawk as he grabs my waist and pulls me from the seat. I'm both disorientated and annoyed by his actions, and another unattractive noise emerges from my lips as he not-so-gently drops me onto the hospital bed.

"So you can't escape again." He makes eye contact with me as he pushes my chair out of my reach. It rolls toward the back wall, coming to a halt just far enough away that I won't be able to shuffle over to it.

I scowl, filled with anger as I take in Damien's snarky smirk.

He turns and flees without another word, leaving while I try to think of something clever to say. He's gone before anything good comes to mind, and I glare at the hallway he disappeared into. I'm tired of his attitude.

He's the one who chose me as a mate. Not the other way around.

I glance at my chair, trying to calculate how hard it would be to walk to it. I could try to grab objects to steady myself along the way, but the last thing I need is to fall or get too tired to complete the journey and end up on the floor.

I've been shamed enough to last a lifetime.

I wait for what feels like forever for somebody to return, my anxiety only rising the longer I'm in here. Nobody comes, though, and after a while, I lie back on the bed. The ceiling is painted a crisp white, and in sheer boredom, I begin to count the tiles.

I'm almost at three hundred when I hear footfalls from the hallway outside. I sit up, quickly spotting Damien and Jenna walking toward me. The giant smile on Jenna's face is a drastic difference from Damien's scowl.

He refuses to look at me as he approaches, his long legs carrying him past my room and toward the exit. He doesn't even look back as he leaves, and he slams the door shut behind him.

I turn to Jenna.

"I'm glad to see you," I say, not bothering to hide the obvious excitement in my voice.

She laughs, shaking her head as she lifts her hand. My eyes follow the movement, and I pause when I realize she's holding a giant bag filled with what I'm pretty sure is blood.

I'm not sure I want to know why.

"Look what I've got!" she says, shaking the thing in my face.

I look wearily between her and the blood, unsure why she's so excited to be holding it.

I'm continually surprised by how different she's become since her execution. The Jenna I used to know would never be excited about holding a bag of blood. She'd be horrified and disgusted.

The beasts have changed her, and while I don't necessarily think it's a bad change, it's unsettling to see.

"Why?" I ask, gesturing to the bag.

"Damien gave it to me," she explains. She says it as if I should understand what that's supposed to mean, but I have no idea.

"He gave you a bag of blood?"

Jenna nods, the movement fast and full of enthusiasm. "Yes," she confirms. "For you!" She grabs a thin metal pole from behind me and hooks the bag to it. "This is a lot more than I needed, too. You're going to be as good as new, and then some."

I try not to look too confused, but I feel like she's speaking in riddles. She reaches into her pocket and pulls out a needle and tubing, and I internally panic as I realize she intends to put the blood inside me.

"I don't think that's a good idea." I hold up my hands to keep her away.

This is a form of medicine we've attempted several times in the human village, giving a wounded person the blood of another, and it almost always ends in the death of the receiver.

Jenna shakes her head, seemingly not understanding my concern. "Beast blood is full of collagen. It's how they heal so fast. When we put it in our human bloodstream, it helps us heal at their rate."

I don't know about all that.

"It's not going to hurt you," Jenna continues. "Trust me."

I scan her, looking over her face for any signs of a lie, and I give in when I don't find any. Not trusting the only person I know here isn't going to get me anywhere. Besides, the worst that can happen is I die, which at this point doesn't seem too awful.

Jenna moves quickly, wiping clean my inner arm before setting up the tubing and preparing the needle. I look away as she brings the sharp object to my arm, and I wince as it slides underneath my skin.

"There!" She tapes the needle to my arm and steps away with a clap. "That wasn't so bad, was it?"

Her smugness earns her a glare, but she ignores it.

"Watch your wounds," she orders, gesturing to my thigh.

I look at my leg. What exactly does she want me to watch? The wounds are unchanged, red and inflamed with black stitching holding the skin together.

I turn back to her. "Watch them for what?"

Jenna frowns, jerking her head in the direction of my leg. "Just watch."

My lips purse as I draw my gaze back down, and I hold in a sigh when nothing happens. I continue to watch, though, wanting to humor her. I'll admit the pain has diminished quite drastically, my achy muscles relaxing for the first time since my execution, but that's about it.

I poke at the corner of my most minor scrape, and I stiffen as the skin scabs over and heals before my very eyes. How is this possible? It leaves a tiny scar, but even that spot begins to lighten and disappear, continuing until the wound's entirely replaced by fresh skin.

I'm sure my shock isn't very well hidden as I look between my leg and Jenna, stunned as the larger cuts begin to copy the actions of the smaller one.

"What the fuck?" I gasp, reaching out to feel the hot skin heal beneath my fingertips.

A loud laugh bursts from Jenna's chest as she leans in to watch, the sight seemingly just as fascinating to her as it is to me.

"His blood will work its way through your system within a day or two," she explains.

I don't know what to say. I'm still in disbelief Damien's blood is healing my injuries, but I manage a small nod as I lie back on the bed. I think I'm going to faint.

There is no pain.

"Why didn't you give me some of this earlier?" I ask, turning to watch a gash on my arm scab over.

This is magic.

Jenna doesn't immediately respond, and when I look up, I realize she's grimacing. Her nose scrunches as she hesitates, and after a second, she huffs and runs a hand through her hair.

"Sharing blood is considered intimate among the beasts. Damien didn't want to give you any of his beyond what you needed to stay alive, but he also wouldn't allow anybody else to give you theirs," she says, examining my leg. "I don't know why he's fighting the bond so hard. He's treating you poorly."

I'm so happy to hear that she sees the way he's acting. It makes me feel less alone.

"He's our leader so there's not much we can do, but I want

you to know we're all on your side," Jenna continues. She pats my hand, trying and failing to comfort me. "Damien's usually a nice guy, and I truly believe he's going to come around."

I'm not so sure about that.

Damien doesn't seem at all inclined to change his feelings for me, nor does he seem like a particularly nice guy. After Henry, though, I'm not expecting much.

I gave up on men a long time ago.

Chapter 6

AINE

I LEAVE THE hospital with a noticeable pep in my step. Damien's blood healed me entirely, and never in my life has walking on my own two feet felt so good.

I raise my arms above my head and stretch as I begin heading in the direction Jenna told me I'd find Damien's house and my cabin. She said I'd pass a fallen log on the way, and I scan the ground for it as I walk.

After a good twenty minutes of this I begin to grow worried, and after forty I'm convinced I must be going in the wrong direction. How big is this place?

The paths veer off in thousands of directions, and I think I'm walking in circles.

"Are you lost?"

A woman steps out from between two trees, her sudden presence startling. She's the first person I've come across, and I take a step back to put some distance between us.

She's tall, and given her dark features, she's probably a beast. She could kill me in a heartbeat if she wanted. Even full of Damien's blood, I've never felt so small and weak before.

The woman watches me with a kind smile, and I awkwardly smile back before lowering my gaze. Between her legs is a small child, the girl's chubby hands tightly gripping the hem of her mother's dress.

Bears grow violent when you get too close to their young. Are beasts the same?

The woman grabs and lifts her daughter onto her hip. I take another step back.

"Yeah, I am actually," I say, my face flushed. "I'm staying in the small cabin next to Damien's house."

I'm secretly hoping using Damien's name will curb any thoughts she has about hurting me. It seems to work as the woman's eyes widen. She hides her shock behind another smile.

"You must be Aine, then!"

She steps forward, closing the space between us. How does she know who I am? There don't seem to be a lot of humans here, and I guess word has spread that one was saved from execution.

Or she was one of the ones who attacked me in the forest.

There was a small beast with them. It could've been this child. I eye the little girl, struggling to imagine her turning into a violent, deadly animal.

"It's nice to meet you. I'm Chloe, and this here," the woman pauses and gestures to the young girl on her hip, "is Nia. I believe you met my mate earlier today."

I blink, trying to remember. He must have been the man Damien was speaking to at breakfast. That's the only other beast I've met, but we didn't interact at all.

Chloe bounces Nia, trying and failing to keep the wiggly girl calm.

Nia lets out a bubbly squeal.

She looks young, maybe three years old, but it's hard to tell. The beasts are large, and I wouldn't be surprised to hear that she's only in her first or second year of life.

There's an awkward silence as Chloe and I wait for one another to speak, the sound only broken when Chloe clears her throat.

"Well, I'll show you to your cabin," she says, turning slightly and gesturing to the left.

I was heading in the opposite direction.

"Thanks," I mumble.

Chloe walks through the woods with unwavering confidence, and I can't help but be impressed she's able to navigate them so easily. I'm sure I'll figure it out eventually, but it's still so new to me right now.

"What do you think of Damien?" she asks.

I struggle to find the words I want to say. In all honesty, I don't know what I think of him. He's an asshole, but I'm choosing to take it as a good sign that he hasn't hurt me.

"I don't have a strong opinion yet," I say, not wanting word to get out that I'm talking poorly about him. I don't think he'd take to that very well.

Chloe hums, the sound barely heard over the noise of the cracking twigs beneath her feet.

"Well, if it makes you feel any better, everybody is angry with him for moving Olivia out of that cabin and putting you in there." She scoffs and shakes her head in disbelief. "I heard he didn't even provide you new furniture when she took hers with her."

I shrug, not answering.

"Where'd he put Olivia?" I ask, guilty for having unintentionally forced her out of her home.

I have a feeling she doesn't like me too much, which makes perfect sense now. I'd be pissed, too, if my life were uprooted to make room for some random woman my boss was seeing. I fiddle with the fabric of my dress and make a mental note to apologize again when I give it back.

Chloe pauses to peer at me.

"You don't know?" she asks.

I shake my head.

"She moved into Damien's guest bedroom," Chloe says. "It's only temporary, but we don't approve."

"Oh," I say, unfazed either way.

Honestly, I'm glad he put me in the cabin. It's nice having my own space, and I imagine he's not exactly a fun person to live with.

I speed up as I spot the roof of Damien's house. The cabin is too small to be seen from this distance, but after a few more seconds of walking, I see the wooden frame through the trees.

"Thank you so much!" I say as we approach.

I'm grateful for the help, even if it came from a beast.

Chloe waves away my thanks, her movements limited as she tries to settle a very fussy child. Nia wiggles in her arms, and Chloe groans before giving in and setting her down. The second Nia's feet hit the floor, she's gone, running into the woods as fast as her chubby, little legs will take her. Chloe rolls her eyes and shoots me an apologetic smile.

"I'm happy to help. Don't hesitate to reach out if you ever need something." She laughs as her daughter disappears between the trees. "I should go find her."

Without another word, she turns and runs off, her movements unnaturally lithe. It makes me uneasy, and I can't stop staring until she's out of sight.

She was friendlier than I thought she would be.

It's been a long day, and I need time to decompress before figuring out what, precisely, my next steps look like. I run my fingers through my hair and let out a low sigh as I walk the rest of the way to my cabin.

Olivia is standing in front of the rickety door, her arm only inches away from the thorny rosebush.

She's fingering through a stack of papers, and she looks up as I approach.

"You look a lot better," she compliments. "I heard Damien gave you two pints of blood."

My cheeks warm, surprised she knows that. It truly doesn't take long for news to spread here. That's something this place has in common with my old village.

"Yeah, it was nice of him," I say dryly.

Olivia's lips purse as she looks me over. "It was."

I rock back on my heels as I wait for her to tell me why she's here, my hands clamming up the longer she takes to answer.

"Yes, well," she starts. "Damien sent me to give you the rundown on your new job."

A job? I expected to have one, but I assumed they'd give me more time to adjust before putting me to work. Just this morning I was in a wheelchair covered in my own body fluids.

That's probably the real reason Damien gave me his blood. He wants to put me to work.

Olivia's eyes dart along the paperwork she holds, a low hum falling from her lips as she finds what she's looking for.

"It seems you'll be working with Alex in the gardens." She points in the direction of the training fields Jenna showed me yesterday. "You'll like Alex. He's kind, and you'll find the gardens next to the training field. They're hard to miss."

I nod, feeling more than a little overwhelmed. This is all so much at once, and I'm still struggling to digest the fact that I'm even still alive. I didn't think I'd get to live to see today, and now I'm living in a dingy cabin and am full of the blood of some strange man who's claimed me as his mate.

Maybe I'm dreaming. That would make much more sense

than this.

At least I'm assigned to the gardens. I worked in the kitchens back in my old village, and when I fell out of favor, I was forced to do the breakfast, lunch, and dinner shifts. I hated it, and I rarely saw the sunshine.

Olivia doesn't stick around for long. She mumbles something about running late before spinning and scurrying in the direction of Damien's house.

The door to my cabin is open, and as I enter, I notice some things have been left on the table and bed. I don't love that somebody came in here while I was gone, but I suppose privacy isn't a luxury I'm afforded here.

An oversized comforter has been placed on top of the thin mattress, and I smile as I feel the thick fabric. It'll keep me warm.

On the table is food and clothing. I rush to the food first, so happy I could cry as I sift through the protein bars and fruit that's been left for me. There's also a bowl of nuts, and I grab a handful and shove them in my mouth.

I've been dreading the thought of having to go to the dining hall again, and this is enough to hold me over a few days.

Smiling, I shift my attention to the clothes.

I've been given two pairs of bottoms, and I scan them before changing into the short, black linen ones. The material is lightweight and comfortable, and I hope it'll hold up while outside all day in the sun. I do wish they were a bit longer, the seams ending just an inch or two below my butt, but it's better than nothing.

Looking through the tops, I grab and put on a tight red shirt.

There are a few items remaining, underwear and socks along with two other outfits.

One is a lightweight dress I doubt I'll ever have a reason to wear, and the other is a simple shirt and pair of shorts. I wish I'd been given pajamas, but beggars can't be choosers.

It's better than nothing.

I set my clothing on the window ledge and put Olivia's dress near the door so I don't forget to return it to her. I still feel guilty for wearing her favorite dress.

A few minutes pass in boredom as I pace around my cabin. Should I go to the gardens now? I'm not quite sure what expectations are of me, and Olivia didn't clarify. I glance around the small cabin, taking in the cramped space before figuring I might as well head out and meet this Alex I'm to be working with.

Pretty much everybody, minus Damien, has been kind to me so far, and I hope Alex will be the same.

The rosebushes outside my cabin door brush against my arm, and I curl up so I don't cut myself. I've just healed, and I'd like to remain uninjured for a while.

"I think this way," I mumble to myself, turning to the right and heading into the woods.

The training field and gardens were huge, so I imagine they'll be hard to miss. I just need to go straight and eventually, I'll run into them.

My steps feel loud as I walk through the woods, small twigs and leaves cracking beneath me. A walk this long would usually leave me winded, but I feel great.

It must be because of Damien's blood.

Jenna said its effects will last a couple of days, and I wonder if I'll be able to convince him to give me more when it wears off. I haven't felt this good in years, my nerve endings thrumming.

I keep my eyes peeled as I march through the trees, hoping to spot somebody for directions, but either they're not out or they're hiding from me. If it weren't for the occasional houses I pass, I wouldn't be able to tell I'm walking through the middle of a pack. Everything blends in so well with the natural landscape.

I get confirmation I'm heading in the right direction as the sound of snapping jaws makes its way to my ears. The noise amplifies the closer I get, reaching its peak as I push my way through the final tree line.

Massive beasts sprint around the open field, their heavy paws crashing into the ground as they slam their bodies into one another with painful-sounding thuds. It looks incredibly violent, and it sends shivers down my spine.

Damien is near the far edge of the field, and the sight of him stops me in my tracks. He's in his human form, and he and another man circle one another.

The other man looks fresh and clean, a drastic difference from Damien's sweat-soaked skin. It's clear Damien's been fighting for a while, and I wonder how well he'll hold up against the other man.

Damien's larger than his opponent in both height and width, but the other man is faster and smoothly dodges his attacks. They dance around one another before the smaller one jumps forward, his fist flying toward Damien's face faster than my eyes can follow.

The man lands a sickening punch to Damien's jaw, the impact forcing his head to swivel to the side. I expect Damien to fall to the ground, or at least stumble, but instead, he laughs and straightens right back up.

His gaze lands on me as he raises his fists once more, and I watch his smile vanish just as quickly as it appeared. He lets his eyes trail the length of my body, his face impossible to read.

I wish again that my shorts were longer.

The other man takes Damien's distraction as an opportunity to strike again, and I try not to be impressed with the way Damien easily dodges the blow. He refuses to look away from me as he fights, not once wavering even as the man attempts another hit.

My mouth gapes as the smaller man suddenly falls to the floor, his body going limp before I have time to process Damien's fist connecting with his temple. A few beasts run into the area to check on him, but Damien doesn't so much as spare his opponent a glance as he stalks toward me.

The chatter among the field quiets as he approaches, and the beasts don't bother pretending they aren't paying attention to us. I step back as Damien nears, and I nervously pick at the skin around my cuticles.

I stop when Damien's attention briefly flashes to my hands.

"What are you doing here?"

His voice sends shivers down my spine. The cold, calculated tone reminds me I'm not a welcome guest of his.

"Olivia said I'm to be helping Alex in the gardens," I say.

Damien clears his throat. "I didn't anticipate you starting today."

I shrug. Olivia didn't clarify.

"There's nothing else for me to do," I admit, turning toward the garden.

The garden area is almost the same size as the training field, and there are several rows of large plants that look about ready to harvest.

There are only a few people working in it, and I'm surprised to see they don't have the long limbs and fluid movements I'm learning to associate with the beasts. Are they humans? I wouldn't be shocked to learn we're all given similar jobs.

"Does the clothing fit?" Damien asks, changing the subject. "I see you're wearing them."

I glance at myself before giving a curt nod.

Silence falls between us, and Damien eventually grunts before returning to the training field. I watch him leave, exhaling in relief as he meets once more with his fellow beasts. Being around him is confusing, and I still can't tell whether he hates me.

Squaring my shoulders, I turn to the gardens with a fake smile plastered on my lips.

Finding Alex should be easy enough to do.

There's only one man in the garden, and he's also coincidentally the only beast. He's tall and muscular, and he's got the signature dark hair and eyes of the beasts. He looks like he'd be a good fighter, and I'm surprised he's not with the others in the training field.

I'm not entirely surprised to see a beast is in charge, but a small part of me hoped I'd be working for a human. He's facing away from me, but I'm sure he's aware of my presence as I approach.

"Are you Alex?" I ask.

The man spins to face me.

"I am." He bends slightly to set a basket he's holding on the ground. "You must be Aine!"

He juts out his hand, and I hesitate for only a second before reaching out to shake it. His grip is tight and sweaty, and I hope I do a good job pretending not to notice. I'm sure my palm isn't any better, both the heat and nerves leaving my hands embarrassingly clammy.

"I didn't expect to see you today, but I'm glad you're here. We've doubled the size of the garden this year, and we need all the extra hands we can get." He wipes at the moisture on his forehead with a laugh. "Have you worked in a garden before?"

I shake my head, noting the slight downturn of his lips.

"Well, okay. Let's start you off with something easy, then." Alex grabs his basket and points toward the large shed near the back of the garden. "Follow me," he orders, leading the way.

I'm careful not to step on any plants as I maneuver through the garden, and I'm sure I look silly with my long, uneven steps.

Alex's back stiffens as a crunch sounds out from underneath my foot, but much to my relief, he says nothing.

We manage to reach the shed without harming another vegetable, and my chest deflates as I release the breath I'd been holding. I can't help but glance at Damien, but I quickly look away when I realize he's already watching me.

I don't understand him, and I ignore my warm cheeks as I follow Alex inside the shed.

It's suffocatingly hot inside, and sweat immediately begins to trickle down my temples and underarms. Alex leads me to a small bin in the far-left corner of the room.

"Find a pair that fits and meet me outside," he says.

I look inside, noting the numerous pairs of thick gloves scattered about. Do I really need these? My hands are rough from my time in the kitchens.

I'm not going to argue, though, and I grab and try on a pair as Alex leaves. It takes a few tries before I find a clean-enough pair that fits, and I hurry to leave the shed once I do.

It's overwhelmingly hot inside.

Alex is leaning against the wall next to the door, waiting for me with a bottle of water. He tosses it over as I approach, and he mumbles something about humans having slow reflexes when I miss the catch.

"There are two others that work in the gardens. Mia and Abby," he says, gesturing toward the two woman I noticed earlier.

They look up as he says their names, their expression guarded as they each lift an arm and wave. They're clearly twins, both identical from the curl of their long black hair to the thickness of their upper lip.

"They're pretty quiet, so don't take offense if they don't speak to you much," Alex continues.

He leads me to the far corner of the garden.

"You'll be pulling weeds until you get the hang of things," he explains, crouching. I copy his movements, but I hurry to inch away when my bare arm brushes his.

He hardly seems to notice as he grabs a small, grassy tuft of weeds. He pinches the base and rips it out of the ground.

"Pull anything that looks like this," he orders. "If it doesn't look like this, don't pull it. Call me over if you have questions."

He's back on his feet before I have time to process what he's just said.

"Feel free to get up and move around if your back hurts or you need to stretch your legs. Beasts have good hearing, so just speak normally if you need to call me over. Otherwise, you'll distract everybody training." He points to the large field of fighting animals.

I nod, glad for the tip. "Noted."

Alex lingers for another moment before seemingly deciding I've got this handled and returning to his own work.

Of all the jobs I could've been given, this is arguably one of the better ones. Working in the heat all day isn't ideal, but it's loads better than my old assignment.

Being stuck inside a small kitchen with ten other women could get overwhelming at times. Especially after I put in the request to leave my husband. Our leader laughed me out of his office and immediately put out word that I was an unworthy wife.

It left me ostracized by the community, and it ultimately made the work unbearable. My husband was furious when he found out what I did, and he ensured I received adequate punishment for embarrassing him.

Sighing, I push those memories down. I don't want to think about that.

The area Alex has me working in is covered in weeds, and I tentatively reach out to pull one. It's hard to feel my grip through the thick gloves, but I manage to wrap my fingers firmly around the base before yanking as hard as I can.

The plant dislodges easily, and I choke on my spit as my body flies backward.

I don't know why I anticipated it would be hard to pull, and a shocked laugh slips from my lips as I land in the dirt. I'm sure my cheeks are beet-red, and I spin around to ensure nobody saw.

My eyes widen as I realize the entire training field is looking at me, and the realization that they all heard and watched me fall makes me want to crawl into a hole and die. Alex wasn't kidding when he said beasts have good hearing.

I can't help but search the field for Damien, and I feel nothing short of relief when I realize he's not here. As foolish as it is, I find myself wanting his approval.

He's the one who saved my life, and he can take it back at any moment.

Unwanted tears fill my eyes as I turn back around, and I discretely reach up to wipe them away before they're noticed. I resist the urge to look and see if the beasts have lost interest and returned to their fighting as I get back to work.

Time passes rather quickly, and before I know it, I've finished an entire row. My back screams for me to stand, a request I've been ignoring, but I find myself unable to resist any longer as I pull off my gloves and rise.

My knees crack, and I wince as I twist to stretch my back. It pops several times, which feels amazing, and I sigh in relief before straightening back up.

It seems while Damien's blood healed my cuts, it doesn't help much with the sore muscles caused by my bad posture.

Alex is lingering near the shed, his shirt now removed and tied around his head. His body shines from sweat, but I'm sure mine looks no better. The heat is punishing today.

Alex waves me over. "You made good progress." He cranes his neck to look at the weed pile I spent all afternoon building.

I smile, happy to hear I didn't make a complete fool of myself today. Despite the odd situation with Damien, this place doesn't seem as bad as I originally thought. Everybody's been friendly, and my job is easy.

"Thank you," I say.

Alex nods, his eyebrow raising as he glances at my exposed skin. I already know what he's seeing, and I grimace as I look down at my sweaty, red arms. I look like a roasted pig.

"You smell like Damien," he says.

I'm not sure how to respond to that.

Alex doesn't seem to mind, though, as he wordlessly grabs another bottle of water from the small cooler at his feet. "Go on and head home. You've done enough for today." He tosses the bottle in my direction.

I successfully catch it this time.

Alex resumes working, and I head back to my cabin. I've only been working for a few hours, but the time in the heat has me exhausted. Damien's blood is not nearly as helpful as I initially thought.

All I want is to take a shower and crawl into my sad excuse of a bed. Olivia said I'm expected to shower and use the bathroom in Damien's house, though, which I'm not sure is worth the risk.

The beast isn't fond of me, and I'm hesitant to do something that's going to make him angry.

Maybe I can sneak in and out without him noticing.

There's the small bathroom right at the main entrance that will be convenient to use when I need to pee, but the only guest shower available is upstairs past his bedroom door. I'll need to be extra stealthy.

My cabin appears untouched when I enter it, which is a relief.

Damien's made it clear he feels comfortable entering, or having people do it for him, when I'm not home, and I'm nervous he's going to do it again.

I grab a change of clothing and Olivia's dress, wishing once more that I had pajamas to change into. My old village was entirely self-sufficient, mainly because the beasts made the forest so dangerous to enter. I doubt that's the situation here, though.

I'll have to ask around and see where everybody gets their goods and clothing. I don't have any money, but maybe I can trade things or do favors for pajamas.

I peek at Damien's house through the cabin window, checking for lights or movement behind the curtains. There isn't any, and figuring now's as good a time as any, I clutch my clothing to my chest and hurry toward his house.

It feels wrong to enter unannounced, but I'd rather sneak in and get caught than ask permission and be told *no*. Damien clearly isn't a fan of me, and I don't want to risk him denying my request.

The front door creaks as I push it open, and I wince as I stick my head inside and listen. The house is silent, which is good, and I hold my breath as I step inside. As tempted as I am to look around, I run immediately upstairs.

I remember where the guest bathroom is from when Damien brought me here, and I head straight for it.

Nobody spots me as I slink into the room and shut the door, and I continue to rush as I turn on the shower and strip. Removing my clothing takes a bit longer than I'd like, the fabric sticking to my sweaty skin, but I manage to rid myself of it in record time.

Thankfully, the shower is fully stocked, and I make quick work washing my hair and body. I suspect these are Olivia's products, and I hope I'm not using a soap I shouldn't.

They're all so nicely scented, and they clean me better than anything I've ever used before. I wonder where she got them from.

Shutting off the water, I rip back the curtain and search for a towel. There are none visible from where I stand, but I eventually find one in the small closet to the left of the shower. There are several inside, and I pull the top on out.

Like everything in this house, the towel is high quality. If I weren't so afraid of losing shower privileges, I'd take it with me to my cabin. It's soft against my skin, and it feels like a crime to part with it.

Once I'm dressed, I bundle up my dirty clothes and crack open the bathroom door.

My eyes lock with Damien's, and I let out a shocked gasp before stumbling back into the bathroom and slamming the door. I've been caught.

I press my forehead against the wood as I reevaluate my reaction, knowing it made me look foolish, before plastering a smile on my face and pushing open the bathroom door again.

Damien stands outside his bedroom waiting for me, his eyebrow raised as I step into the hallway.

"You can leave your dirty clothes in the hamper." He gestures to the small basket behind me, and he watches as I throw my items inside. "Come to my office tomorrow after work. We have much to discuss."

Why? I can't think of one good reason why Damien wants to meet with me, especially in such a formal setting. I hope it's because he's finally going to tell me about the mate bond and why he's chosen me, but I doubt I would be so lucky.

What if he's changed his mind and wants to see through my execution? For all I know, I could be walking into an ambush. He might just want to get me alone so he can kill me without any witnesses.

I wouldn't put it past him.

I don't have much of a choice, though. It's not like I have

anywhere to run to, and even if I tried, his beasts would hunt me down in minutes.

My pulse races, and I clear my throat before giving a jerky nod.

"Okay," I say.

Damien turns and enters his bedroom, leaving the door open behind him. I can't resist peeking in as I walk past.

His back is to me, and his front faces a woman lying on his bed. She's disheveled, her clothing half off and her hair sticking up at odd angles. I haven't seen her before, but she's as tall and beautiful as all the other beast women I've met.

She and Damien are having a heated conversation, but I don't risk eavesdropping. What Damien does is none of my business, and with quiet footfalls, I leave his house and return to my cabin.

Chapter 7

AINE

JENNA LETS THE door swing shut behind her.

"I'm both a doctor and happily mated, Aine. I don't care about your tits," she says.

I shake my head in a sad attempt to clear the grogginess clouding my brain. What's she going on about? My fingers dig into the soft fabric of my comforter as I tighten my grip on it, the material conforming to my hand as I hold it protectively below my chin.

The lack of pajamas provided by Damien led to me sleeping naked last night, which I was fine with until Jenna came bursting into my cabin with no warning.

She continues to laugh as I struggle to catch my breath. I thought she was a murderer.

"You could've knocked!" I snap, watching through narrowed eyes as she moves farther into my cabin and makes herself comfortable at my table.

She looks around the place with interest, her eyes darting everywhere before she runs her finger along the windowsill. The action kicks up some of the dust coating the surface, the particles highlighted by the sunlight filtering in. They float through the air before sinking to the ground.

I should probably clean that.

"This is where he's got you staying?" she asks.

Assuming she's talking about Damien, I nod.

A displeased hum emerges from her chest as she continues to look around, her disapproval of my cabin painfully evident. "I heard he has you working in the gardens?"

"You heard correct," I say. "I'm working with Alex."

Jenna hums. "Alex is nice. You'll like him. How's Damien been treating you?"

Her question makes me pause. Where's she going with this? How a man treats a woman is not typically discussed in my old village, and when it is brought up, we're expected to lie.

"We haven't spoken much," I admit. I figure that's a good way to share the truth without expressing any outward dislike for him. "He wants me to meet with him after work."

I don't know why, and I'd be lying if I said it doesn't stress me out. Is he going to ask about my execution? Or maybe he plans to punish me for something I've done.

Jenna clicks her tongue against the roof of her mouth before glancing out my window. I'm not sure if the noise means she's displeased, but if I had to guess, I'd say it does.

Taking advantage of her back being turned to me, I pick up the clothing I left on the floor last night. She remains where she is as I slip them on and join her at the table.

Her attention is elsewhere as I approach, and I follow her gaze toward Damien's house. He stands on his front porch, and he looks furious as he stares at Jenna through the window. His eyes briefly flash to me as I come to stand next to her, his frown deepening.

We only lock eyes for a second before he turns and walks back inside.

"If he remains cold, let me know," Jenna murmurs, slowly turning to face me.

I nod. "I will." It's odd talking with somebody who outwardly shows so much concern for me. Even my parents didn't dare do so, fearful of what our leader would do should somebody overhear.

Jenna doesn't stick around for long, and she excuses herself and disappears just as quickly as she arrived.

I suppose I'm up for the day, and I put my hair in a loose braid before heading to the dining hall. I still worry about getting lost, so I make sure to stick to the thin trails.

The dining hall is just as empty as it was yesterday, and I'm grateful nobody tries to make conversation as I sneak to the back and fill up my plate. There are more beasts in this pack than I originally thought there were, but thankfully, none seem particularly excited to meet me. They're polite, but slightly standoffish.

I find an empty table in the back and shovel down my food before heading to work. I'm not quite as lucky finding the gardens as I was yesterday, and by the time I arrive, I'm covered in sweat.

At least Damien isn't here today. It's easy to work when I don't constantly have to worry about him watching from the training field.

Why does he want to meet with me this afternoon?

Alex is standing next to the shed speaking to Abby, and he waves me over as I begin to maneuver through the crowded rows.

His smile quickly transforms into a frown, and I pause and look down to ensure I'm not stepping on another plant.

I'm not, my feet planted securely in the empty dirt.

Alex is already walking toward me when I look back up, and I hurry to meet him halfway.

"You're wearing jean shorts to garden?" he asks, his tone

indicating how crazy he thinks me to be.

I don't blame him.

"I wore the only linen clothing I have yesterday," I admit.

The corners of his lips turn down, and he gives me another once-over before sighing and gesturing for me to follow. He doesn't wait for my response before heading in the direction of the woods. I watch him for a moment, shocked, before obeying and scurrying behind.

Nobody seems to care about our departure, and the few beasts we do come across offer polite smiles before continuing with their day.

"Where are we going?" I ask.

Alex points to a house up ahead. It's hard to see from here, but I'm able to spot what looks like a chimney and front porch.

"My mate had a lot of good gardening clothes," he says. "You can have them."

Had. It doesn't go unnoticed that he used the past tense when speaking about his mate, but I don't comment on it.

"Thank you," I say instead. "That's very kind." I whisper the words, but I know he hears them by the way his head dips.

The remainder of the walk is quiet, and I patiently wait on his porch while he runs in and grabs the clothes. I'm shocked when he comes out with a giant bag of items, my eyes widening at the sheer amount.

"Come on," he says, throwing the bag over his shoulder without breaking pace.

My cheeks warm as I follow him. To say I'm flustered would be an understatement. I hadn't expected anybody here to be so generous with me, especially a beast I just met.

"I appreciate you giving me these." I jog slightly to keep up with his fast pace.

Alex shrugs, but I notice him holding back a smile.

"They've been sitting in my closet collecting dust for years now," he says. "Honestly, it feels good to get rid of them."

A comfortable silence stretches between us as we walk to my cabin, and I try to memorize the path. It'll do me good to pay attention and learn the lay of the land, especially if I'm to stay here long term.

"How do you like it here so far?" Alex eventually asks. My cabin is just visible up ahead.

I shrug. "I've got no complaints."

Alex's eyes grow wide as he walks up the steps to my home, his eyebrows raising as he pushes open the door and welcomes himself inside. I resist the urge to roll my eyes. Clearly, the people here feel more than comfortable entering each other's personal spaces.

"This is where he's got you living?" Alex mumbles to himself. "I thought he would've had it made nice."

I don't respond, and Alex seems to take the hint that I don't want to talk about it as he sets the clothing on the table. He opens his mouth a few times, looking like he wants to say something, before shaking his head and leaving.

"I'll wait outside while you get changed," he says.

The door closes quietly behind him, and I rush to inspect the clothes. All the items he left are high quality and, conveniently, my size. I grab the first long sleeve I find, happy to have something that'll protect my skin from the sun.

Alex waits just outside the cabin door while I change. He eyes me up and down as I exit, nodding to himself in approval before leading us back to the garden. We cross paths with two beasts along the way, but once again, they don't pay us any mind.

"Are you okay picking weeds again today?" Alex asks.

"I'm happy to," I say.

Picking weeds is easy, and it makes the time go by quickly.

Honestly, I wouldn't mind if I were tasked with that job every day.

I'm sure Damien will find another job for me once the garden dies in the winter, but I'll worry about that when the weather begins to grow cold.

"Great," Alex says. We enter the garden, and he points to a new area. "Can you focus over here?"

I stretch my limbs before getting to work. The weeds were relatively soft and painless yesterday, so I skip wearing my gloves. All they did was make my hands sweat.

I stress about my future meeting with Damien while I work, and I think it's to reprimand me. He's made it clear he's not interested in engaging with me in any way that isn't necessary, so a lecture seems the most likely outcome.

I've followed all the directions that've been given to me since arriving, so I can't imagine I've done anything too upsetting.

Despite Jenna's insistence that mates are an important thing in the beast culture, Damien hasn't done anything to prove that's true. He doesn't seem to have any interest in me, sexual or otherwise, and he acts like I'm a nuisance to him more often than not.

"What're you thinking about?"

The voice is startling, and I lift my chin to look at Alex.

"About how hot it is today," I lie, wiping the sweat that's accumulated on my face.

Alex's lip twitches as he extends his arm and offers me a half-empty water bottle. I take it without complaint, eagerly gulping the contents. I'm sure it makes me look desperate, but I'm too thirsty to care.

"You're free to head out for the day," he says.

I'm relieved. I'm not sure if it's because he's a beast, but his ability to spend all day in the sun without getting physically exhausted is impressive. After only a few hours, I feel about ready to pass out.

It seems Damien's blood is all out of my system because the slight soreness I felt yesterday is nothing compared to how I'm feeling now.

With a muffled groan, I stand and stretch my back, satisfied as my spine pops. Alex visibly recoils, his nose scrunching in disgust.

"Do you know where Damien's office is?" I ask.

Despite my effort to sound confident, my voice quivers. I can tell Alex hears it by how his face screws up. I'm terrified of Damien, and I'm not doing a great job hiding it.

"He works out of a small cabin behind his house," Alex says, running a hand through his hair. "Why?"

I gulp. "He told me to meet him there once I finished working."

I closely watch Alex's reaction, relieved when he doesn't look too concerned. I'm going to take that as a good sign. Alex seems like a nice guy, and I'd like to think he wouldn't lead me straight to a slaughter.

"His office is behind his house?" I clarify.

Alex nods, and I linger and kick at the dirt before working up the courage to leave. I want to get my conversation with Damien over with quickly.

This must be a busy time of the day, as I cross paths with several beasts as I make my way to Damien's house. Despite my fear of these people, I give them small waves. This is an opportunity to start over, and I don't want to be an outsider forever. I should at least try to acclimate.

Most of the beasts smile back, and one even goes as far as to wave. The children are almost always excited, their chubby hands lifting as high in the air as they can manage to get them.

I spot two humans on the path, and I'm surprised to see how

happy they look. They're hanging off the beasts they walk with, and one is even being carried.

It's odd, and I can't lie and say I don't feel a bit annoyed they got loving mates while I got stuck with Damien.

I debate running inside to change into clean clothes as I near my cabin, but I decide against it. The sooner I meet with Damien, the sooner I can take a shower, shove some fruit and nuts into my mouth, and crawl into bed.

My heart begins to race as I walk around Damien's house. It's hard to miss the office in the back. It's easily twice the size of my cabin, and the entire wall is covered in large, tinted windows.

It's sleek.

I will myself to remain calm as I push open the door and step inside. It's bright in here, sunlight streaming in through the windows. I expected Damien's office to be dark and gloomy, but this is the opposite.

Olivia sits behind a small desk along the left wall, and I force myself to smile as I approach her. She's hidden partially behind a large bouquet of flowers, and I lean around them until I can see her face.

"Damien told me to come here after work." I shift nervously as I glance at the large double doors behind her. He must be behind them.

Olivia nods. "He told me. You can go right in," she chirps.

I wipe my sweaty palms on my shorts before walking through the doors.

Damien sits behind a large wooden desk situated in the center of the room, his eyes cast downward at some papers. The room is also bathed with light, and I note that while the window tint prevents me from seeing in, it doesn't hinder his view of the outside.

He must have seen me walking here.

"Close the doors behind you," Damien orders.

I do as he says, promptly pushing them shut. He watches, his face void of any emotion as he gestures for me to sit. I wipe my hands on my shorts again, annoyed by their sweating.

I haven't done anything wrong.

I hold my breath as I lower myself into one of the leather chairs in front of Damien's desk.

"There are a couple of reasons why I asked you to come here today," he starts, scooping up several papers and placing them in the small wooden basket on the corner of his desk. "We'll start with why you're here in this pack."

I nod, relaxing into my seat. I've been eager to hear why he's chosen me as his mate and what that's supposed to mean. Jenna explained it as a soulmate, but Damien's shown little interest in being with me.

Not that I'm complaining.

"So?" Damien asks.

I cock my head to the side, confused with what he's looking for me to say.

"Why were you executed?" he clarifies.

I stiffen as my brain processes his question, my mouth going dry. Damien continues to stare as he waits for my reply, his lips pursing when I hesitate.

"I don't have all day, Aine." He leans back in his chair. I watch the motion, my jaw clenched as I try to conjure up a response.

"I, uh—" I stammer, before deciding to continue with the lie I told Olivia previously. "I was caught with a woman."

Damien quirks an eyebrow and drops his hands to his desk with a loud bang. The sound makes me jump, my heart hammering inside my chest. I should've prepared better for this conversation. I knew it was inevitable, even if I'd hoped otherwise.

"I'm not playing around," Damien says. "I need to know what you did."

I lick my lips. "Why?"

Damien seems to grow larger when he gets angry. "I'm not putting my people's lives at risk because my beast decided to choose a criminal."

There's no way to sugarcoat the fact that I killed my husband, and given Damien's concern for his people, I already know nothing good will come from telling him the truth.

"So, you'll… what?" I ask. "Kill me if you don't like my crime? You beasts are bigger and stronger than me on my best day. I'm not a danger."

I have no doubt that his people, whether in their beast or human forms, could easily overpower me if needed.

Damien hums.

A small bead of sweat drips down my inner arm as I wait for his response. I foolishly hope he'll give up and drop the subject, but I'd never be so lucky. I wrack my brain for any crimes I can claim that'll be accepted positively, but panic renders my mind blank.

"There are children and humans here," he points out.

My eyes begin to water, and I stare at the ceiling to keep the tears from spilling. The fact that he ignored the first part of my question doesn't go unnoticed. He'll kill me if he doesn't like my crime, and I can't think of anything worse than murder. If I tell him, I'll be executed.

There's a creaking as Damien shifts in his chair, his lips downturned as he waits for me to compose myself.

"I'm not going to hurt anybody," I say.

Damien doesn't look like he cares. "That's not what I asked, is it? What did you do?"

I remain quiet, desperate for a lie to come to mind.

"It was an accident," I eventually blurt out.

Damien stands, his seat flying back and smashing into the wall behind him. I jump to my feet, my fight-or-flight instinct preparing me to run from the room.

I keep a close eye on Damien as he stands behind his desk, his chest heaving.

"Fuck, Aine," he snaps. "Just tell me what you did!"

My chin wobbles as I shake my head, refusing. He'll kill me if I tell him. I know he will.

His face turns red as I suck in a sharp breath and wipe at my cheeks. Damien runs a hand down his face before pinching the bridge of his nose and sitting back down.

"Stop crying," he grunts.

I can't.

I continue wiping at my cheeks, and Damien's anger visibly grows as he watches my panicky movements. After a long silence, he gestures toward the door.

"Go," he says.

I blink, shocked, before rushing out of the room. A part of me knows he's not going to let this go, but I push that thought aside as I hurry past Olivia and scamper across the lawn toward my cabin.

Chapter 8

AINE

ALEX APPROACHES ON my right, his tall frame casting a shadow over the section of garden I'm working on. I'm not ready to be excused, so I pretend not to notice him. I've been trying to kill as much time as possible in the garden since my conversation with Damien, hoping to avoid him and his questions.

Fortunately, he's returned to basically pretending I don't exist, which has given me enough time to come up with a lie. It'll be hard to convince him since I messed up so badly when he asked why I was executed, but I think I can accurately play the scared, confused card. I'll pretend I was too overwhelmed to think properly in his office.

It's my best bet.

"Today's your lucky day," Alex says, prodding my calf with his toe.

Lucky me. Alex lingers as I set a clump of dirt on the ground. He's smirking, and there's a dangerous glint in his eye I don't entirely trust. I like Alex, the beast friendly and easy to talk to, but it's obvious he's a troublemaker.

He spends all day joking with Mia and Abby, and only once

in the past week have I seen him actually work.

Sometimes I catch him staring at the beasts in the training field, and he once walked over to participate, but Damien sent him back to the gardens with a shake of his head.

"My lucky day?" I ask. "Why's that?"

Alex gestures for me to stand, and with a groan, I push up off the ground. I hold back a smile as I crack my back, enjoying Alex's disgusted shiver at the noise. He does it every time I pop my bones, the man quite vocal in his hatred of it.

"You're going to learn how to stock the veggies in the kitchen." Alex claps his hands together before pointing to the wheelbarrow we put all the picked, ripe vegetables in.

I nod, bouncing slightly on my heels. As much as I loved picking weeds and thought it was the best job ever, it's become tedious these past few days. Plus, my back is in a permanent state of soreness from hunching forward for such long periods of time.

Alex gestures for me to follow him, and I do my best not to look at the training field as I do.

Most of the beasts are already gone for the day, but Damien is still here. The beasts usually leave around this time, I assume to go home and freshen up before dinner. Both Jenna and Alex have been nagging me about joining them in the dining hall, but I've managed to successfully dodge their friendly concern.

I'm trying hard to restart my life here, but I'm still overwhelmed by the thought of eating with the beasts who tried to murder me only a week ago. I've made it a personal goal of mine to avoid it for as long as possible.

Damien stands in the center of the training field, and I can practically feel him staring at the side of my head as I trail behind Alex. His constant staring makes me uncomfortable, but I've gotten pretty good at pretending I don't notice.

It helps that he spends mornings in his office and doesn't

come to the field until after lunch. I get to work early to avoid him, and Alex typically lets me go shortly after Damien arrives.

"I'm glad I'm advancing past picking weeds," I say.

Alex snorts. "Me too," he admits. "I'm worried you're going to become a permanent hunchback if you do it much longer."

I gasp, offended by the truth in his words. Still, I like that he's joking with me. Alex has been kind, and I wouldn't mind being his friend. I should try to befriend more than just Jenna.

Stepping forward, I reach out and lightly push Alex's arm. It's meant to be a friendly gesture, but Alex's laughing comes to an abrupt halt the moment my skin meets his.

He hisses. "Don't touch me."

I rip my hand back to my chest, and my face warms as I direct my gaze toward the ground. Well, that was humiliating. I want nothing more than to run back to my cabin and hide beneath my sheets forever.

I try not to let myself be upset by Alex's rejection, but I'm hurt he's so uneasy being seen joking around with me. While I'm aware we aren't best buddies or anything, I thought he was open to a friendship.

Kicking out my foot, I slide it along the soft dirt as I wait for direction on what to do next.

"So," Alex starts, readjusting his grip on the wheelbarrow handles. "Whenever this gets full, we'll bring it to the kitchen stockroom. There's a small path from the garden that leads there."

I purse my lips. "Good to know."

Alex points out the path, and we walk the remainder of the way to the dining hall in tense silence. This feels awkward.

I can tell Alex is trying to move past it as he makes joking complaints about the wheelbarrow and shares several tips on how to manage it. I only nod in agreement, occasionally letting out a quiet hum.

We walk inside the dining hall and through a small doorway along the back wall. It opens to a giant walk-in pantry, and Alex leads me to a large shelf on the left.

"Most everything will be eaten tonight, and leftovers will be canned and saved for winter," he pauses and points to another large shelf full of canned goods. "The cooks should be here any minute now to begin dinner, so we should hurry to get this stocked."

I nod and begin placing today's harvest on the shelf.

Alex stares at the side of my head.

"You should join us for dinner tonight," he eventually says.

I avoid eye contact and continue piling the food. It's a conversation he's tried to start several times now, and one I fully intend to ignore.

I'm just not ready.

Alex's hand on my wrist makes me pause. His grip is loose, but it's most definitely there. I eye his fingers, confused. Just ten minutes ago, he was yelling at me for nudging his arm.

"I thought we weren't supposed to touch?" I ask, pulling away.

Alex shrugs. "Not when Damien is watching," he says, tutting quietly to himself. "It's like you're trying to get me killed."

I purse my lips, eventually deciding to drop the subject. Damien doesn't seem to care about who or what I do, but I'm not going to argue with Alex about that.

We continue stocking in silence.

"You can head home," Alex says as we finish.

"Thanks."

I turn and begin to walk away, but I'm stopped by Alex's hand wrapping around my wrist once again. Unlike last time, the action isn't so shocking, and I sigh before spinning around. What does he want?

"Please consider coming to dinner tonight," he says. "Everybody wants to meet you, and your poor mate is being hammered every night with questions about you he's unable to answer. It's sad to watch."

What kind of questions are they asking Damien? I hope nothing about my execution.

I open my mouth to say *no*, but as I take in his pleading eyes, I find myself nodding instead. Both he and Jenna have been nothing but nice to me since I arrived, and I can't hide forever. Besides, I doubt Damien will try anything with so many people around.

"Fine." I huff. "I'll come."

Alex smiles wildly at my words, his fists raising into the air in mock triumph. I roll my eyes, trying to hide how endearing I find the action, and I wait until he leaves before letting my smile fall.

The thought of sitting through a meal surrounded by beasts makes me sweat, and as I walk back to my cabin, I try not to think about all the ways I'll likely embarrass myself tonight.

I crunch my arms to my sides as I squeeze past the thorny rosebushes crowding my cabin door.

"Fucking—" I freeze as I step inside and spot Damien sitting on my bed.

He looks almost comical on the small object, his large body causing the frame to visibly dip underneath him. My muscles are tense as I close the door behind me and move to sit at the table, careful not to take my eyes off him.

"Yes?" My voice cracks.

Damien's eyebrows raise, but he doesn't comment on my visible nervousness as he looks at the folded clothing sitting on the windowsill. He doesn't seem pleased, but he never does.

"He gave you clothing?" he asks.

I nod, assuming he's referring to the items Alex gave me. "That was nice of him."

Again, I nod.

Damien's eyes darken, and I slyly plan my escape. I'd have to get past the bed he sits on to reach the door, and even if I were to somehow get past him, I doubt I'd make it far before he catches me.

"What other nice things has he done for you?" Damien asks, his tone condescending.

I shake my head.

"Nothing," I quickly say. Is this a trick question? "Sometimes he brings me water, but he does that for Abby and Mia, too."

Damien smiles. I'm not dumb enough to think his reaction is genuine, but my inability to pinpoint what exactly he's feeling has my anxiety at an all-time high. I should've remained by the door to have this conversation, and I was stupid to trap myself in here with him.

"Everybody saw you touching him today," Damien continues, slowly rising from the bed.

The floorboards creak underneath his weight, and I gulp as he steps toward me. Our proximity makes me panicky, and I grip the seat of my chair in an attempt to still my shaking hands. Jenna's assured me multiple times that Damien has no desire to hurt me, but I'm not sure if I believe that.

My shaking grows as he rounds my body and comes to a halt behind my chair.

I feel like a lamb being led to the slaughter, and my breath hitches as Damien's fingers graze against my skin. His fingertips run along the column of my throat before sinking into my hair and pushing it to the side.

"I heard you promise him you'd go to dinner," Damien whispers.

I flinch, but the hand on my neck stiffens to keep me in place. Damien's touch causes goosebumps to pebble up along my skin, and as much as I'd like to believe it's a result of fear, I know that deep down, his touch excites me.

I'm desperate for affection, and after seeing how all the other mates here treat one another, I'm desperate for Damien to want me. I want him to fawn over me as all the other beasts do to their mates. I'm jealous and angry that he doesn't, even when I tell myself it's for the best.

"I don't need people thinking I don't please my mate." Damien's lips are directly next to my ear as he speaks, and moments later, those lips are on my skin.

My muscles tense beneath him, my body stiffening and lungs ceasing to work. I open my mouth to gasp—or scream—but nothing comes out as he places soft kisses from my shoulder to my ear.

I don't trust this.

Damien wraps his arm around the chair I sit on and settles his hand on my thigh, his fingers curling around the muscle. I drop my chin and stare at it, but Damien weaves his other hand into my hair and yanks my head back.

I hiss, trying to dislodge myself from his hold, but he refuses to let go. Why is he doing this? Is he jealous of Alex? The thought is laughable.

Damien licks my neck one last time before pulling away. *Finally*. My relief at his retreat is cut short when he strikes forward and sinks his teeth into the side of my throat. There's an immediate burn where he bites me, and I choke out a scream as I try to move away.

There's a tugging in my chest followed immediately by an intense wave of anger I don't recognize, but the emotion is gone in a heartbeat. Are those Damien's feelings? Jenna mentioned she could feel her mate's emotions through the bond, but clearly Damien can hide his. Good.

Even with the anger gone, the odd sensation in my chest remains. It's uncomfortable, but it's nothing compared to the pain of his teeth sinking into my neck.

Jenna said this action was special, and that it created a soul pathway or something equally as horrifying sounding. She also said Damien wouldn't do it without my permission.

I need to learn to stop trusting her.

I grab Damien's hand and try to yank it off my thigh as I struggle to rip my neck out from between his teeth. He refuses to move, his grip on my leg tightening before he calmly pulls his teeth from my neck and steps away.

I scramble to the door the second I'm released, my hands frantically covering the wound on my neck. I try not to let my horrorstruck tears fall as Damien moves toward the window and smiles.

What the fuck was that?

"That should do it." He straightens out his clothing.

"Why?" I choke out.

"I'll answer the questions we receive tonight about our marking. I don't want you speaking about it." Damien sighs, glancing at my covered neck before meeting my gaze. "Go take a shower. We'll walk to dinner together."

I want to scream. I want to hit him and demand he tell me why he's claimed me as his mate and why the hell he just bit me, but none of that happens. Instead, I stand on shaky legs and watch silently as he saunters out of my cabin.

I learned long ago it's better just to do what I'm told.

Damien's nowhere to be seen when I eventually work up the strength to enter his house, and I carefully slip upstairs and into the guest bathroom. I look like shit, and I stare at myself in the mirror before rubbing my puffy eyes and evaluating the bite.

It's red and inflamed, but as I reach out and poke it, I'm shocked to discover it doesn't hurt. If anything, it's soothing, leaving a satisfaction similar to the one felt when scratching a mosquito bite. I poke it again, but I rip my hand away as the sensation changes to one more pleasurable.

I don't understand why Damien did this, and despite knowing I should be happy he isn't beating me or demanding I tell him of my crimes, my anger remains. Jenna said marking was sacred and Damien wouldn't do it without my permission, and I suppose I was dumb for trusting that.

I sure as fuck know Damien doesn't care for me, and I don't understand why he felt the need to put such an intimate claim on me. It almost seemed like he was jealous of Alex, but I don't want to jump to conclusions.

He'd have to care about me first to get jealous.

I reevaluate the mark before stepping in the shower. I've already wasted too much time.

Damien is standing at the bottom of his porch steps when I finally work up the courage to drag myself out of his bathroom. He wears a bored expression, and I expect some sort of rude remark about how long it took me to get ready, but to my surprise, he remains silent.

"You'll be asked a lot of questions tonight," he says, leading the way to the dining hall.

I figured as much.

"I'll try to answer most of them, but you can handle specific ones about your hobbies and interests."

Easy enough.

Damien sighs, clearly exasperated with my silence. "I'm going to lie about our relationship." He turns to face me. "Try not to look too surprised or confused by the things I say."

I cock my head to the side. We don't care for one another, and I don't see the point in lying about it. It's painfully obvious.

"Why?" I ask, breaking my silence.

"Mates are important to beasts. My people will want to hear that I'm," Damien pauses, clicking his tongue as he searches for the right words, "cherishing mine."

I can't hold back the snort that bursts from my throat, and I quickly reach up to cover my mouth and hide it. Is he serious? I can't imagine him "cherishing" me if his life depended on it, and given his inability to even be kind when others are around, I doubt he'll be able to put on a convincing performance.

Damien frowns at my reaction.

Maybe if tonight goes well, though, I can convince him I'm not a danger to his people. He hasn't pushed the topic of my execution since my refusal to share, but I doubt he's forgotten about it.

Composing myself, I lower my hand from my mouth and gesture for Damien to lead the way. He remains still, looking me over, before rolling his eyes and resuming walking. This reaction alone proves my point that he'll be unable to genuinely convince anybody he's "cherishing" me, but I say nothing and follow behind him.

"Can you feel my emotions now?" I ask.

I hope not.

Damien shakes his head. "No. You haven't marked me."

And I never will. I'm glad the bond is one sided, and I hope Damien keeps his emotions locked up tight. I don't care to feel his feelings.

I hear the rumblings of everybody inside the dining hall before we even reach the doors, and Damien stops seconds before we enter so he can place his hand on the small of my back. I jolt at his touch, detesting it after the forced marking, but I don't push him away.

Even if I want to.

This act feels eerily identical to what I had to do with Henry, and I straighten my shoulders as I wait for Damien to lead us inside. Plastering a smile on my face while standing next to the man who terrifies me is nothing new, and I'm confident I'll be able to play the part of doting mate successfully.

Damien's lips transform from his typical scowl into a wide smile, his expression matching mine.

I hold my breath as he pushes open the door, fearful all the attention will shift to us, but thankfully, the conversation only dwindles a tiny bit. It's evident by the occasional glances that the entire room is aware of our presence, but the beasts are polite and pretend not to notice us.

I suppose that's really all I can ask for.

The room is jampacked, and if I had to guess, I'd say there are at least three or four hundred beasts present. I didn't realize there were this many in the pack, and my hands begin to sweat as I look over all of them. I don't spot Jenna or Alex, but I figure they're here hidden at one of the tables.

Damien leads us to one in the back and pulls out a chair for me. My hands shake as I sit, and I hide them under the table as Damien takes the seat to my right.

The woman and child who once helped me find my way back to my cabin are across from me, and next to her is the man I assume to be her husband. All three of them grin as I push in my chair.

"Aine!" Chloe shouts. "I'm so glad Damien was able to convince you to eat with us."

I'm not sure "convince" would be the accurate word. "Force" is more like it, but I have a feeling Damien wouldn't be pleased if I corrected her.

Damien plucks a clear decanter off the table and pours me a glass of wine.

Another woman I faintly remember seeing before comes rushing toward us with two plates in hand. She's the woman who worked on me in the hospital with Jenna. It's odd seeing her without her stern, serious expression.

Her eyes scan the areas where I was injured before she sets the plates in front of Damien and me and clasps her hands behind her back.

"Aine," she greets me. "I'm Avia, Jenna's mate. It's nice to formally meet you." Her eyes dart between Damien and me. "I was beginning to fear you'd never join us for dinner."

I open my mouth to respond, but Damien beats me to it. He grabs my hand below the table, his grip tight.

"It took a lot of convincing," he admits, squeezing my knuckles. I assume it's to keep me silent.

Avia's eyes follow his movements, her smile transforming into a smirk. She raises her eyebrows suggestively at me, clearly falling for Damien's gesture, before excusing herself. I expect Damien to remove his hand as she walks away, but he keeps it in place, politely ignoring the sweat that seeps from my palms.

A few others stand and approach us, their excitement visible as they introduce themselves. Nobody asks anything too personal, and they keep their visits short. I appreciate it, and I feel hopeful this dinner will go by quicker than expected.

My eyes follow the line that forms as everybody grabs plates and serves themselves. I spot Avia in it, and I flush as I realize she probably gave us the plates she filled for herself and Jenna.

Alex wasn't kidding when he said most of the veggies in the pantry would be eaten today, though. My plate is full of today's picks, and it's topped off with a large chunk of meat.

I wonder what kind of meat it is I've been served, but I refrain from asking in fear of sounding dumb. We didn't eat a lot of meat in my old village, and I'm not familiar with it. Occasionally, a deer or larger mammal would wander too close to the village and get caught, but it was a rarity and the meat was almost always reserved for our leader and his close friends.

"So," Chloe starts as she cuts up her daughter's food. "How are you liking it here?"

Everybody within hearing distance perks up at her question, and I feel Damien's hand tighten around mine. It's a silent reminder that I'm supposed to lie.

"I like it," I say, setting my fork on my plate. "Everybody's been kind to me."

There are a few chuckles at my response, and I instinctively turn to Damien in panic. My stress has me overanalyzing everybody's reaction, constantly worried I'll say the wrong thing and anger him. He gives my hand a gentle squeeze, and I take that as a sign I haven't said anything wrong.

"And I see it didn't take long for Damien to mark you," a woman farther down the table points out, causing all the ladies to start giggling while the men shake their heads.

She's clearly a beast, but the large yellow hat she wears makes her look much less intimidating.

I hesitantly smile before reaching up to touch the bite mark. Damien's grip on my hand tightens as my fingers meet my wound, and before I can register what's happening, he's ripping me out of my chair and pulling me into his lap.

An unattractive shriek falls from my lips as my body's thrown around, and I flail to stabilize myself. The entire table howls in laughter, causing those at the other tables to stop what they're doing and look over.

Damien wraps his arms around my midsection and holds me firmly against him.

"Stop touching it," he whispers into my hair before pulling away and dropping his head on my shoulder.

"What can I say? I couldn't resist." He presses a sloppy kiss to my cheek for good measure.

I try not to look too stiff, but I'm sure my tense muscles are incredibly transparent to anybody who looks hard enough. I drink my wine in a sad attempt to settle my racing heart.

Damien's breath brushes against his bite as he chats, the sensation more arousing than I want it to be. My shame is only amplified by the fact that Damien is the one causing it. He's made it clear this is all an act, but my attention-starved body has not gotten the memo.

The beasts sitting at the table continue to hammer us with questions, but Damien handles most of them. His acting is better than I anticipated, and at some point, I find myself leaning into his chest.

He doesn't seem to mind, tightening his arms around my waist in response.

"Did you like the food?" he eventually asks, nodding toward my empty plate.

I'm surprised I managed to eat everything I was given. My plate was full, but once I started eating, I couldn't bring myself to stop. It's been so long since I had a warm, full meal.

"It was delicious," I admit. "It's fun eating the food I harvested."

Damien chuckles and kisses my exposed shoulder. It admittedly feels good to have somebody caring for me, and I do my best to remember this is all just an act. I repeat this to myself as Damien's fingers trail underneath my dress and trace along the lace of my underwear.

I push his hand away, blushing at the laughs from around the table. My rejection wasn't as subtle as I thought it was.

"Can we expect to see you here more often?" the man sitting across from the woman in the yellow hat asks. He points his fork at me.

I don't immediately respond, taking a second to think over my answer. While I expected this meal to be painful, everybody's been surprisingly nice. Plus, it's refreshing getting to eat a full dinner and have conversation that isn't with Alex or Jenna.

I have to put up with Damien, but if he's going to be on his best behavior during meals, I think it's doable.

"I should hope so!" Damien chimes in when I take too long to respond. He lightly pinches the sensitive skin on the inside of my thigh to bring me back to the present.

I brush him away again.

There's idle chitchat as everybody begins to finish up their food, and the beasts gradually begin to leave once they're done. They give me polite waves as they exit, and I wait patiently until Damien nudges my thigh and urges me to stand.

He places a hand on the small of my back. "We should get going," he says, speaking to the few who remain.

The people at our table pause and wish us a good night before returning to their conversations. There's a soft smile on my face when we leave the building, my excitement at how well the dinner went filling me with hope.

Damien was kind to me tonight. Not once did a snarky remark leave his lips, and it makes me wonder if there's any truth to the things Jenna says about the mate bond. I'm not looking to be in a relationship, but I'd appreciate some kindness from Damien.

He drops his hand from my back the second we're out of eyesight, an audible sigh leaving his lips.

"That wasn't too bad," I say.

Damien glances at me with a frown before nodding once. I hurry to follow behind him, not confident about navigating the woods at night. It's too dark to see the path.

"Is it like that every night?" I ask, jogging slightly to keep up. He has a fast pace, and I blame his long legs.

Damien nods once more, but he remains silent. I can tell he isn't in the mood to talk, but the two glasses of wine I drank are making me chatty.

"Everybody seems to really like you," I continue.

Damien stops walking before looking over his shoulder to shoot me a sharp glare. I take a step back, unsure what I've done to make him so mad.

"Have you always been this desperate?" he asks.

My cheeks warm. "Excuse me?"

While I'm aware Damien's not my biggest fan, I didn't realize my presence was so upsetting to him. He forcibly marked me tonight, which I know is a huge thing to the beasts, and I lied about it for him.

I'm not saying he owes me, but I've done nothing to deserve this level of hostility.

"I'm nice to you for one hour and you think we're best friends. I sit you on my lap for thirty seconds and you're scenting up the whole room with your arousal." Damien pushes back my hair to expose my mark. "It's pathetic."

I jerk away from his touch, offended and humiliated by his words. I'm not proud of my body's reactions to him, and if I could turn off my misguided attraction, I would in a heartbeat.

Damien isn't worth my time, and I regret having been fooled into thinking his friendly attitude during dinner would continue once we left.

He's not my friend.

Damien turns away as my eyes fill with tears. I make sure to keep my distance as I follow him, silently wiping at my face as I will myself to stop crying. I feel pathetic.

Olivia is waiting for Damien on the front porch, and I resist the urge to scoff. Jealousy isn't going to get me anywhere. She's already wearing her pajamas, and she gives Damien a small wave as I break away from him and head to my cabin.

Chapter 9

AINE

I PAUSE WITH my fist in the air, debating turning around and going home, before giving in and knocking on the door. There's a clatter heard from behind the wood, and seconds later, Jenna's pulling it open with a wide smile.

"Aine!" she shouts, pulling me into a hug. "What brings you by?"

I huff, holding out my arms to show her my red, peeling skin. I've gotten a nasty sunburn these past few days, and I only managed to get an hour of work in this morning before Alex was shooing me away. According to him, I've grown too gross to look at and I'm not welcome in the garden until my body's back to its regular color.

Jenna's face scrunches as she eyes my burn. "Oh."

Her quiet tone worries me, and I watch through narrowed eyes as she gingerly grabs my arm. Her fingers hurt where they dig into my skin, but I say nothing about it as she turns my arm over and inspects it. Her gaze follows the redness to my bicep, up my shoulder, and into my sleeve.

Before I know it, she's pulling me inside and demanding I

remove my clothing.

"Come on," she says, turning and searching through the cabinet next to her small desk. "Take everything off."

I hiss as I wiggle out of my clothing, my skin burning where the fabric rubs against it. I remove everything but my underwear, and I stand in front of Jenna with my arms held out to my sides.

"It looks painful." She winces. "Have you been wearing sunscreen?"

I shrug. "I don't have any."

"Well, that, I can fix," she says, grabbing a glass jar from the cabinet. "Take this."

She places the jar on her desk before opening another and scooping a handful of clear gel onto her palm. It's thick and chunky, and I resist the urge to shiver as she begins spreading it on my skin.

It brings immediate relief, and I relax as she rubs it into my arms and chest. This is amazing.

"Damien needs to give you more blood." Jenna grabs another glob from the jar and orders me to spin.

I snort, shaking my head at the mere thought. "I doubt he'd be willing to do that."

Jenna takes a moment to collect her thoughts before responding. "I thought you two were beginning to get along?"

Should I lie? I still can't tell what's expected of me here, but it seems like she's genuinely curious about how things are going with Damien.

"Not really," I admit. "He's a dick, and I'm pretty sure he hates me."

My legs have taken the most damage, and my knees buckle as Jenna applies her gel to them. Simply existing has been causing me pain, and for a moment, I'd forgotten how it felt to live without it. Jenna returns to her shelves and scoops a hefty amount of gel into a jar for me to take home.

"Put this on before bed," she orders, setting it next to the sunscreen. "And Damien doesn't hate you. You're his mate."

Her tone implies that being his mate is supposed to mean something, but I'm more than positive it doesn't. I don't have the energy to argue, though, and I'm afraid of offending her by bashing the mate bond the beasts claim to treasure so much.

Still, Jenna seems to recognize my hesitation as her shoulders drop and she gestures for me to redress.

"You're the only woman his beast will ever be interested in," she insists, her words earning a surprised laugh from me.

Olivia is living with him and there was a half-naked woman in his bed just the other week. Damien holds no affection for me, and the fact that people think he's pining after me is laughable.

Jenna's eyes narrow. "What is it?"

"Damien and his beast are very much not holding out for me," I say, shaking my head at the mere notion.

Jenna's lips purse, the woman clearly upset with my lack of belief in her words. It's been made abundantly clear how much most of the beasts worship this bond, but that doesn't mean Damien feels the same way about it.

"Look," I start, ignoring my flushed cheeks. "I thought maybe he'd come around at some point, but he's made it crystal clear he has no interest in me. Besides, I'm pretty sure he's already seeing a couple of women right now."

Jenna shakes her head, disagreeing with me. "I simply don't believe that." She tosses the gel and sunscreen into a paper bag.

"I saw a half-naked woman in his bed the other day," I deadpan.

Jenna groans, throwing her hands in the air. "Beasts aren't unfaithful. Damien isn't cheating on you. He wouldn't do that." Her voice rises in pitch as she speaks, slowly transforming from friendly banter to full-on scolding. "Sure, Damien isn't perfect, but he's been through a lot. Have you tried talking to him?"

I stiffen, shocked she'd ask this. I thought she was on my side.

"He's the one who claimed me as a mate," I argue. "You can't honestly expect me to beg for his attention after he's treated me so poorly. I don't have the luxury of safety. Nothing's stopping him from beating or killing me, and it's foolish to believe something as silly as a mate bond would prevent him from doing so."

Jenna dips her chin and adjusts her stance before looking back up at me. She seems embarrassed, but the expression is quickly replaced by determination.

"You're not understanding, Aine. When I tell you their mate bond is sacred, I truly mean it." Jenna's clearly desperate for me to understand the deep meaning of this stupid bond, but I don't. "Will you at least give him a try? He just needs a bit of encouragement."

I shake my head. "I don't think so."

My body is slimy from the gel, and Jenna tosses me a rag to wipe the excess off. There's a mysterious glint in her eye, and her lips are turning up in the corners. I don't trust it.

"I'll make a deal with you," she says, handing me the bag of creams.

I frown. "Let's hear it," I say.

Jenna claps her hands together, clearly excited. "Damien's blood will help with your burn. Ask him for some. If he ignores your pain, I'll drop the subject and never bring it up again. But, if he makes efforts to soothe you, which he will, you have to admit that maybe he cares more than he's letting on."

I roll my eyes. This is the dumbest thing I've ever heard, yet despite the childishness of her idea, I find myself agreeing. Either he ignores me and Jenna will leave me alone, or he'll give me his blood and my sunburn will heal.

I get what I want either way.

I don't love the thought of being alone with Damien, still worried he's going to pry into my execution. He hasn't tried to discuss it again since our conversation in his office, but I doubt he's forgotten about it.

I hope he has, but I can't be sure.

It's not as if I'm a physical threat to his beasts, and I believe I've more than proven I'm not going to spring some sort of random attack on any of the humans or children here.

Jenna shoos me out of her office with a wide grin, and I begin my slow journey back home. I can't believe I agreed to this stupid plan, and by the time I make it to Damien's office, I already regret it. He isn't going to care about my issues. If anything, he'll probably get a kick out of seeing my burn.

If that's what it takes to get Jenna off my back, though, I'll do it.

Olivia isn't at her desk, and with a shaky inhale, I approach the double doors that lead to Damien's office. It's too early for him to be at the training field with the other beasts, so I know he's here.

I worry I'm making an awful mistake as I push open the doors and welcome myself inside. Damien is sitting at his desk, and Olivia is standing to his right.

Both snap their heads in my direction. Olivia seems shocked by my entrance, but Damien just looks annoyed. The beasts have good senses, so he either heard me coming or he spotted me walking here through the windows.

Olivia inches away from Damien as I step into the room, her cheeks reddening.

I can tell by their positioning that nothing was happening between them, but it seems Olivia is nervous about how I'll perceive their proximity.

Damien doesn't seem to have the same concern.

He leans back in his chair and brings his hands behind his head, his eyes narrowing. He doesn't look happy, he never does, but he doesn't seem angry by my intrusion.

I'm taking that as a good sign, and I clear my throat as I lower myself into the chair on the opposite side of his desk.

"Have you ever heard of knocking?" he asks.

I shrug, shoving my trembling hands underneath my thighs. I don't want him to see how nervous I am. He might try to take advantage of it.

"There's something I'd like to discuss with you." I lift my chin with false confidence.

Damien ignores my words. "You don't want to walk in on something you don't want to see," he continues.

I hold back a sigh. I'm not sure what's going on between Damien and Olivia, but I know nothing was happening when I entered. Damien looked too frustrated.

"Between you and Olivia?" I ask. "I don't mind." Olivia's eyes widen, and Damien sucks his cheeks into his mouth. I gesture toward them. "You don't have to stop on my account."

I want to call Damien on his bluff. I want him to be the one to grow uncomfortable and change the subject for once. A smirk threatens to spread across my face as Damien drops his hands from his head, his palms landing on his desk with a loud thud.

"What?" he barks.

I grin, feigning indifference as I gesture to Olivia. "Don't let me ruin your fun."

Damien rises slowly, and I tense as I wait to see his response.

I expect him to yell at me or kick Olivia out of his office, maybe even do both, but instead he grabs Olivia's waist and lifts her onto his desk. She gasps, her skirt riding up her legs.

I refuse to back down, and I hold Damien's gaze as he sweeps his paperwork to the far side of his desk.

"You don't want to play this game with me, Aine," Damien threatens. "You won't like the way it ends."

His pupils dilate as he speaks, his voice deepening as he sets his hand on Olivia's exposed thigh. Her eyes dart rapidly between Damien and me.

I work my jaw side to side. "As I said, don't let me stop you," I repeat.

If looks could kill, I'd be long dead with the way Damien's glaring. I'm sure he's hoping for me to give in and drop the whole thing, but I hold my ground. I refuse to give him the upper hand.

Damien doesn't move for a long minute, and the silence is only broken by Olivia's loud breathing. There's a ghost of a smile on her lips, but I only look at Damien. He's frowning, his body stiff as he waits to see what I'm going to do.

He looks so angry, and uncomfortable. He doesn't want to touch her.

Good.

Eventually Damien turns back to Olivia, and he curls his hand into a fist before relaxing and pushing her knee to the side. Then he turns back to me, watching my every reaction as he trails his fingertips up her inner thigh.

I refuse to ask him to stop.

"Damien," Olivia says, her voice hushed. "Are you sure you want to do this?"

Damien scoffs. "Yes."

I wonder if they've done this before. Olivia looks mighty comfortable on top of Damien's desk, and she's sure not doing anything to stop him.

I shift in my seat, capturing Damien's attention.

"Are you sure you don't want me to stop?" he asks.

I shake my head. "No."

If Damien wants to go around acting like a whore, he can do so in front of me. I'm tired of giving him the upper hand.

Damien stares at me as he touches Olivia, his lips twitching every time I re-adjust or tense. He seems to be fighting with himself, and he adjusts his stance as he drags his hand up her chest. He lingers below her breast before clenching his jaw and cupping it.

Olivia spreads her thighs. I raise a brow. Fuck them both.

"I'll keep going," Damien threatens me.

I shrug. "I'm sure you will."

He releases Olivia's chest and returns his hand to her thigh, his movements robotic and awkward. For a man as confident as he usually is, I'm surprised to see him looking so tense.

"Does this not upset you?" he eventually asks me.

I shake my head, lying. A small part of me hoped Jenna was right and he secretly cares, but this is the nail in the coffin. I'm almost relieved he's doing this. Now I don't have to sit around hoping he'll change his mind about me.

This proves he doesn't care.

Damien continue sliding his hand up Olivia's thigh, continuing until he reaches her underwear. I'd pay to know what's going on in his head right now.

Without warning, Olivia reaches out and grabs Damien, her fingers digging into his bicep. I frown, my eyes narrowing in on her hands, and Damien jerks away.

"Don't touch me," he orders.

He turns to me with wide eyes.

"She won't touch me."

His words sound like a promise, and I can't help but wonder why he'd even bother to make such assurances to me. I've already told him I don't care, and I mean it.

I resist the urge to get up and leave. What the fuck is happening right now? I just wanted some blood to stop my burning, and now I've gotten myself into a dick measuring contest with the man I hate.

"Touch yourself," Damien orders, drawing my attention.

He lowers his gaze to my thighs, and I immediately shake my head *no*. That's the absolute last thing I want right now. This isn't doing anything for me.

"What the fuck do you want from me, then?" Damien snaps. "You've got me touching my assistant while you sit two feet away watching."

He releases Olivia and steps around his desk. I stiffen, my pulse racing as he places himself between her and me.

"I'm not *making* you do anything," I argue.

Damien scoffs and runs a hand through his hair. He opens his mouth to say something, but he seems to think better of it and snaps his jaw shut with a quiet click. I try not to be scared by his changing eyes, the pupils expanding and contracting.

"This isn't your fucking office!" he finally shouts, returning to his original complaint. "You can't just march in here like you own the place."

I concede with a nod of my head.

Olivia slips off Damien's desk and fixes her clothes. She eyes the two of us, her lips twitching as she holds back a smile. It pisses me off, and I bite my tongue as she steps forward and places a hand on Damien's arm.

"Damien?" she asks.

He spins, and I take advantage of the distraction and wipe my sweaty palms on my shorts. Coming here was a mistake and making that deal with Jenna was childish.

"Fuck off, Olivia," Damien hisses.

She recoils, her cocky smile falling before she rushes out of the room. The door slams shut behind her, trapping me alone with Damien.

"I shouldn't have come here," I say, not wanting to get caught in the crosshairs of Damien's temper. This was a stupid idea.

"Sit," Damien orders, pointing to the chair I just stood from.

I shake my head, refusing.

"Aine!" he snaps, stepping forward and grabbing my arm.

I stiffen, pain shooting through me as Damien touches my burned skin. He forces me back into my seat, but he releases me like he's the one being hurt when I yelp.

His eyes dart between his hand and my arm, his frown growing as he lifts my sleeve.

"Why are you so red?" he asks.

He releases the fabric before bending and inspecting my legs.

I don't respond as he leans in and pokes my thigh, his actions surprisingly gentle. Despite my better thoughts to pull away, I remain still as he crouches by my feet and cups my thigh, his palm covering practically the entire surface of it.

Then he lifts my leg and inspects the back of my thigh.

"Does this hurt?" he asks, backing up his words with a firm poke.

I grunt and yank my leg out of his grasp. "Yes!"

Damien returns to his desk and begins fixing the papers he pushed to the side for Olivia. The memory of them leaves a sour taste in my mouth, and I suck in my cheeks to prevent myself from making any visible facial expressions.

I can't tell who won that stand-off, but I'd like to think it was me. I never asked him to stop touching Olivia. He did that all on his own.

"I need more of your blood," I say, fumbling over the words before I lose my confidence.

Damien doesn't immediately respond, but his back muscles

flex through his thin shirt. He continues to fix his desk before turning to me. His eyes are black, the pupils fully expanded. I look away, afraid to make eye contact with his beast, but I watch out of the corner of my eye as he approaches.

What's he doing?

Damien drops to his knees, and he spreads my thighs before shuffling between them. He's never acted this way before, and I don't know how to react as he leans in and licks my thigh.

Is this another way beasts can heal their mates?

There's so much I don't know, and I curl my fingers around the armrests of my chair as Damien licks me again.

Heat coils in my lower abdomen as his soft tongue grazes my sensitive skin. It's confusing, and Damien wraps his arm around my leg to hold me still as he runs his tongue from the side of my knee to my inner thigh.

I attempt to squeeze my legs together to stop him, but his body's too much in the way. Damien continues to trail his tongue upward until he reaches my shorts.

He's definitely not doing this to heal me.

"Damien, I say, palming his forehead and pushing his head back.

He grumbles, his pupils still dilated. He holds my gaze as he leans in and bites my skin. His teeth aren't nearly as painful as they were when he forced his mark on me, but they still sting against the sunburn.

"I'm not attracted to you," I say.

Damien's a good-looking man, but I refuse to give him the satisfaction. Besides, his shitty attitude outweighs any sort of attraction I may have for him.

His grip on my leg tightens.

"So?" he asks, his tone mocking. "I'm attracted to you, and I'm offering to make you feel good."

He's attracted to me? I highly doubt that. Given his humiliating comments about my arousal the one time we went to dinner together, he probably thinks I'm desperate for him. This is all just a game to him.

He wants me to be some obsessed puppet, but I don't think he realizes just how little he affects me.

Refusing to let him win, I grab the fabric of my shorts and tug them down my legs. Damien frowns as he takes in the full view of my reddened skin, but he doesn't comment on it as I grab his hand and bring it between my thighs.

He smiles, his pupils still expanded as he pushes my underwear partway down. He can touch me all he wants, but he won't get the satisfaction of hearing or seeing my enjoyment.

And when he wants me to return the favor afterward, as all men do, I'm going to take great pleasure in denying him.

Damien grazes his fingertips over my clit. It admittedly feels good, and he does it again before slipping a finger into me.

"Fuck," he gasps.

He continues rubbing my clit as he rocks his finger back and forth, and I remind myself this means nothing as he slides in another.

"Did you like winning against me?" he asks. "Calling my bluff?"

I'm not going to answer that.

I clench my hands into fists before moving them to Damien's shoulders, gripping the muscle as he begins to properly fuck me with his fingers. He licks his lips and leans in as I wiggle against him, but he doesn't put his mouth on me.

I wonder what he'd do if I were to grab his head and pull it forward, but I resist the temptation. This is good enough to get the job done, and I bite back a moan as Damien kisses my knee.

He mumbles something into my skin, but I can't make it out

as he crooks his fingers upward and quickens his motions with his thumb. He knows exactly where to touch me, but I remain strong and refuse to let him see my pleasure.

Still, my hips begin to move on their own accord, and Damien hides a smile in the bend of my knee. I hate him, and I sink my teeth into my bottom lip when I finally cum. I grab Damien's wrist in the process, holding it tight as I ride my high.

He moans into my thigh, and he continues to finger me until I grow too sensitive and pull away. Even still, he remains between my thighs, his fingers trailing the line of my burn. I push his hand away and snap my legs shut.

"I thought you'd be more of a prude," he admits, finally rising.

The outline of Damien's erection is visible through the material of his pants, and he shamelessly pulls it into his waistband.

Then he turns away, not trying for more.

My smirk falls. I thought he'd ask me to return the favor and I could reject him. Why is he not doing that?

I want to reject him. I need him to see that I don't want him.

I scramble to get my clothes back on. My thighs burn as I slide my shorts up them, but I don't care. I deserve a bit of hurt after being so stupid.

I wipe at my cheeks, angry with myself.

"Why are you crying?" Damien asks.

He bends, trying to see my face, but I turn away so he can't see. I won't give him the satisfaction, and I refuse to humiliate myself further by explaining my thoughts and feelings.

"Can I have your blood?" I ask, avoiding his question.

I can't see Damien's reaction, but I imagine he doesn't look happy. The room is silent and tense before he lets out a sigh.

"Fine."

Despite the win, my eyes continue to water as I leave his

office, shutting the door behind me. Olivia's sitting at her desk, and when she turns to face me, I can't help but laugh.

"This must be quite the view," I joke, wiping at my cheeks. "Two human women crying outside Damien's door after being rejected."

Her eyes widen before she shakes her head in a panic.

"He can hear," she whispers.

Of course he can. I glance at his office door, wishing I knew what he was thinking. Olivia watches as I linger in the doorway, and I force myself to turn and leave before I begin to look desperate.

As much as I'd like to blame Jenna for getting my hopes up, I know what happened today is my fault. Damien has made his views of me quite clear, and it would do me well to stop searching for something that doesn't exist. I shouldn't have made myself so available for him.

I head straight to Damien's house, eager to shower and clean myself off. I don't want his saliva on me, even if it has long since dried.

I've taken to hiding a spare change of clothing in one of the guest bathroom cabinets, which comes in handy when I don't want to walk to my cabin first.

When I reach the upstairs landing, though, I freeze, my eyes landing on the woman I saw in Damien's bedroom the other day. She stands in the bathroom doorway with a small, white towel wrapped around her body.

"Oh," she gasps.

She looks shocked to see me, but I know it's not genuine. She's a beast, and she most definitely heard me walking up the stairs.

Her nostrils flare as she looks me over, her attention lingering on my exposed thighs.

I shift uncomfortably. Can she smell him on me? I know the beasts have good senses, but I like to think they aren't that strong. I'm ashamed of what I let Damien do to me, and I don't want anybody to know.

The woman smiles, but it still doesn't look genuine. Who is she to Damien. I'm desperate to know.

"Naughty, naughty," she says, chuckling. Then she disappears into Damien's bedroom.

Chapter 10

AINE

JENNA ONCE AGAIN attempts to rip my bedsheets off me, and I groan and kick with my foot to keep her away.

"This is sad," Alex mutters. "Come to dinner with us. Everybody wants to see you again."

I don't know why they thought it'd be a good idea to ambush me like this, but I'm not in the mood.

"Just tell us what happened," Alex continues.

I shake my head, too embarrassed to speak about it. Jenna's constant talk about mates had a small part of me fooled into believing I meant something to Damien, and now I feel dumb.

Knowing he was with that woman just hours or even minutes before being intimate with me has me feeling horrible, and any sort of wayward hope I may have had for him disappeared the moment I saw her. I was annoyed when he touched Olivia, but knowing I instigated and he didn't want to be doing it helped soothe my irrational jealousy.

I'm done with Damien, and no amount of begging from Jenna is going to change my mind.

My embarrassment has led to me hiding away in my cabin,

not wanting to risk running into Damien and his women. Other than my early morning breakfast runs to the dining hall and my sneaky entries into Damien's downstairs bathroom, I've successfully managed to avoid everybody and everything for the past three days.

Until now.

"At least let me give you his blood." Jenna paces my cabin. "He's been coming in every morning to see if you've taken it," she continues.

I shrug, indifferent.

"I don't need his blood," I argue, ripping my blanket off so she can see my tanned skin. "I'm already looking better."

The last thing I want is for Damien to turn around and use my need for his blood against me. Knowing him, he'll probably claim that I'm indebted to him or something because of it.

"Until you go outside and get burnt again," Alex says, ignoring the glare Jenna shoots in his direction.

Jenna sighs. "Honestly, I don't understand what he could've done to make you so upset." She sits at the foot of my bed. Then she turns toward Alex. "Maybe we should talk to him."

I sit up in a panic, unable to tell whether she's joking. The absolute last thing I want is either of them asking Damien why I'm upset. I wouldn't put it past him to happily share what happened between us in his office, making me look like some desperate human. He claims he wants to keep up appearances and pretend he's being an honorable mate, but he's not very good at it.

Alex nods. "I think that's a great idea."

"Please don't," I beg, angrily throwing my feet over the bed in a gesture of defeat. "I'm getting up."

Alex smirks as he props his legs up on my bed, his long limbs easily crossing the entirety of the room. I don't love the proximity of his feet to my pillow, and I glare at them until he moves.

"Some fresh air will be good for you," he says, far too chipper for my tastes. "Besides, taking Damien's blood and coming to dinner will only show that whatever he's done doesn't affect you."

I'm not so sure about that, but I can't sulk forever. Even if I really want to. What's done is done.

I step around Alex and grab a fresh outfit off my windowsill. Both he and Jenna turn away, and I change into something more appropriate for dinner.

"You aren't going to shower?" Jenna asks.

Showering means going into Damien's house and risking running into either him or his girlfriend. Neither of which I'm particularly excited for.

"Not today," I say.

Jenna frowns, but she doesn't push the subject. Alex doesn't seem to care at all as he stands and rubs his hands together. He's still dirty from work, his hair greasy and his clothing covered in mud.

We step outside, and I pull in my shoulders as I squeeze past the overgrown rosebushes. They're growing quickly.

"Can you take these down for me?" I ask Alex.

He peers at me over his shoulder. "Why me?" he asks. "They have thorns."

I raise a brow. That's exactly why I want him to do it. If he pricks himself, he'll heal within seconds. I'll be stuck with puncture wounds for days.

Alex frowns. "Our palms don't heal as quickly as the other parts of our bodies. I'll give you shears to trim them back."

I suppose that's better than nothing.

It takes everything in me not to peek at Damien's house as we walk past it, the wooden building taunting me with every step. I haven't seen Damien since the incident, and I don't want to start today.

He's probably going to be in the dining hall, though. I'm pretty sure he goes almost every evening.

I wonder if his girlfriend accompanies him when I don't. Or Olivia. It wouldn't surprise me.

"I heard the hospital is still waiting for the new blankets to come in," Alex says, striking up conversation with Jenna.

She huffs, and I kick at a rock as I listen in. I've learned that the beasts have supplies brought in from a nearby human village, but Damien handles all the shipments so there's no hope of me getting pajamas.

"They were supposed to be here two weeks ago," Jenna pouts. "Damien said they're delayed because he put in a furniture order last minute," she continues, scoffing.

I raise a brow, pleased she's angry with Damien. I'm glad I'm not the only one he pisses off. I want everybody to hate him as much as I do.

Alex and Jenna continue to chat as we walk along the path leading to the dining hall, their easy conversation bringing to attention just how close they are. I didn't realize, and I laugh along as Alex cracks a joke about Jenna's mate.

I don't want them to see how much I'm freaking out right now. I don't want to see Damien.

My palms grow sweaty as we near the dining hall, and I wipe them on my shorts. We're arriving late, so hopefully the place has already cleared out.

Alex pushes open the door, and I hold my breath as I step inside. The tables are still full, but thankfully nobody pays us much attention. A few beasts sitting near the doors look up and nod in our direction, but most don't seem to notice our tardy entrance.

Damien sits at the table in the back, and he turns his head and body entirely in my direction as he notices my arrival. He looks a bit shocked by my presence, but I refuse to give him the satisfaction of my attention and casually look away.

Alex leads us to an open spot in the center of the room, his steps long and confident as he maneuvers around the beasts. I sit in the seat facing away from Damien.

I know myself, and if I'm facing him, I'll look. I won't be able to help it.

Jenna sits opposite me.

"Where's Avia?" she mumbles, looking around. I enjoy seeing how her face lights up when she spots her mate a few tables over.

Avia stands and hurries over, and she plants a small kiss on Jenna's cheek as she sets a full bowl on the table.

"It might be cold by now," she says.

Jenna flushes and grabs a fork, and Avia squeezes into the seat beside her.

I can't help but feel jealous as I look at them, their happy relationship making me realize just how much I want somebody to look at me that way. Henry and I were never in love, oftentimes unable to even be in the same room as one another.

When we first wed, I tried to make him love me. I'd fulfill his every request and try to serve his needs before he even knew he had them, but all that did was drive him further away. Eventually I gave up, my childish infatuation turning into a painful mixture of fear and hatred the longer we were together.

By the end, I was only expected to spend time with him when he wanted sex. My only saving grace was that he was always so preoccupied with other women, he rarely demanded such intimacy.

Here, though, everybody seems to be so happy with one another, constantly spending time with their mates and appearing genuinely in love. I suppose they could be pretending, as Damien does with me, but that seems doubtful.

Damien is terrible at pretending he cares about me, even with witnesses, and I like to think I'd be able to tell if everybody around me was acting.

My stomach twists. I didn't realize how hungry I was until entering the dining hall and smelling food. Today's main dish looks to be some sort of grain bowl, and just seeing it has my mouth watering.

"Come on," Alex says, already eyeing Jenna's bowl. "Let's get something to eat."

He places his hands on the table and pushes himself to his feet, but he freezes when his attention is grabbed by something behind me. I turn to see what it is, but I'm stopped by a large hand dropping onto my shoulder. I tense, immediately knowing it's Damien behind me.

He brushes his fingers over the mark on my neck, and I stiffen as unwanted pleasure courses down my spine. He's doing this on purpose.

I jerk away, trying to keep my anger toward him concealed.

His breath hits my ear as he crouches to my level, his body pressing against my back in the process.

"I'm happy to see my little mate has come out of hiding," he whispers, setting a full bowl of food on the table in front of me. "Eat up."

I'm sure the beasts in our proximity heard him, which is probably his intention. There's no way they're falling for his act. It must be incredibly apparent at this point that we don't get along.

Alex visibly cringes, the corners of his lips twitching. I scowl, already regretting agreeing to come here. This was a mistake, and I should've stayed in bed. My bed is cold and uncomfortable, but it's safe.

"I'm going to get some food," Alex mutters.

He disappears, the traitor, and Damien slides his hand over my shoulder. I roll them, wishing he would release me, before leaning forward and grabbing a fork.

Damien's warm chest presses into my back, making him impossible to ignore, but I do my best.

"Damien!" Jenna pipes up, smiling in his direction. "Are you sitting with us tonight?"

I glare at her, but she doesn't seem to notice. It's frustrating how she's so friendly with him. I want her to hate him as much as I do.

Damien chuckles and slips into the seat on my left. Then he reaches beneath the table and grabs my hand like he did the last time we ate together. I try to pull away as his fingers wrap around mine, but he tightens his grip before I have the opportunity.

"Of course," he says, nudging his thigh against mine. "Would you like me to sit with you, Aine?"

I clench my jaw, trying to rein in my anger before saying or doing something I regret. Damien squeezes my hand when I don't immediately respond, his grip crushing my knuckles. It hurts, but when I wince, Damien immediately loosens up.

Still, the silent warning is heard loud and clear.

"Yes, Damien," I say. I hope he can tell I'm being sarcastic. "I'd *love* for you to sit with us."

Damien smiles, giving my hand another squeeze before turning to Jenna and starting a conversation. I ignore them both, opting instead to shovel down the food Damien brought over. The sooner I finish eating, the sooner I can leave.

I try removing my hand from Damien's every few seconds, but he refuses to let me go. Eventually I give up, and I try to distract myself by observing the others in the room.

Almost everybody here is a beast, but there are a few humans lingering about.

My village was secluded, and I never had the pleasure of leaving it. Travel is too dangerous, and our leader only allowed it in dire situations. He also only gave permission to the men.

I've always wondered what the other human villages are like, though. There are rumors that they're larger and more advanced, and I've even heard that some have friendly relationships with beasts.

Alex drops his bowl on the table, the ceramic clattering. The abrupt action is unlike him, and I cock my head to the side as I notice the glare he's shooting at Damien.

Damien visibly tenses at the outward display of aggression, but he doesn't comment on it.

"Guess who I ran into?" Alex asks, sweeping his arm in the direction of the kitchen.

I immediately look to see who he's talking about, and I'm surprised when I spot Damien's girlfriend watching us. She waves when she notices I'm looking, and she grins wildly as she locks eyes with me.

Damien finally releases my hand and stands, his quick movement drawing the room's attention. His girlfriend's smile falls as he stomps toward her, and she stumbles over her feet as he grabs her arm and begins pulling her toward the exit.

I can see her mouth moving as she speaks, but I can't make out the words being shared. The entire room is silent as he drags her out of the building, and seconds later, Alex is running after them.

My palms grow clammy as I realize all the eyes in the room have turned to me. The beasts look away as I catch their eye, seemingly uncomfortable with my presence. My appetite disappears, and I tighten my grip on my fork before setting it down.

"It's okay," Jenna whispers, leaning in so nobody hears. "Do you want to leave? I can come with you."

I shake my head, rejecting her offer.

"I'm going to go," I say, pushing back my chair. "You can stay."

I told Jenna that Damien was seeing other women, and I hope this proves it. I don't know what else I can do to prove to her that he doesn't care about me.

I rush outside, relieved that both Alex and Damien are long gone. I'm not sure why Alex ran after Damien and his girlfriend, but I don't bother searching for them as I hurry back to my cabin.

The sun began to set during our brief time inside the dining hall, and I'd like to make it back before it gets too dark and I inevitably get lost.

I struggle to navigate the woods, but as I pass the fallen tree that sits halfway between my cabin and the dining hall, I'm assured I'm heading in the right direction. I only make it a few more steps before I hear snarling up ahead. My pace slows, and my heart pounds as I crouch and weave through the trees, fearful of what I'm going to see.

After listening to the beasts fighting all day in the training field, I'm able to recognize the noises: loud growls accompanied by pounding footsteps and clashing jaws. I make myself as small as possible as I peer through the foliage.

Two giant beasts are fighting just outside Damien's house, their bodies striking at a speed I struggle to follow. They look nearly identical, both covered in black fur with white specks throughout. It's hard to get a good look, but I assume I'm witnessing Damien and Alex fighting one another.

I'm not sure who else it would be.

The woman Damien dragged out of the dining hall is standing on the front porch, her arms wrapped tightly around her waist in a self-hug. She wipes at her cheeks every few seconds, but I find it hard to feel pity for her.

Olivia is behind her, but her expression is one of fear and is directed exclusively at Damien's girlfriend. Why is Olivia scared of her?

I take another step forward to get a better look, but I freeze as a twig snaps underneath my foot. The noise is quiet, but it's enough to capture the beasts' attention. All three of them turn toward me, and the two in their animal forms back away from one another.

Damien's girlfriend stands up straighter. "Go home, Aine," she's quick to sneer. "These family matters don't involve you."

Family matters?

"What's going on?" I ask, looking between the two beasts.

The woman sighs, clearly annoyed by my presence. I don't understand her relationship with Damien or why Alex feels the need to fight about it, but considering Damien's supposedly my mate and Alex is my friend, I don't feel it's too out of line to inquire.

"It's none of your concern," the woman answers for them.

I ignore her, choosing instead to scan both Damien and Alex. Neither appears to be injured, which is good, but it's hard to tell what's going on underneath all the fur.

"Alex?" I ask, trying to figure out who's who.

I've seen Damien's animal form a few times in the training field, but up until now, I've never seen somebody who compares to him in size. Why does Alex work in the garden if he's this large? I imagine he'd be a great fighter.

The beast on the right steps forward.

Damien's girlfriend takes a threatening step off the porch. "My mate is of no interest to you," she says, her voice rising in pitch.

Her mate? She's Alex's mate? He's mentioned his mate

before, but I was under the impression she was dead. That's how it sounded when he gave me her clothing.

Both Alex and Damien begin to convulse, their bodies twisting painfully as they shift into their human forms. It's a quick transition, but I still turn away in disgust. When the noises stop, I return my gaze to them, my cheeks warming as I take in their naked states.

"You are *not* my mate. My beast no longer recognizes you," Alex shouts before shifting his attention to Damien. "And you're a fucking idiot."

Damien ignores him, turning toward me.

"Go home, Aine," he orders.

I look back and forth as I try to make sense of the scene in front of me. If this woman is Alex's mate, what's she doing with Damien?

Alex scoffs. "You don't get to tell Aine what to do when you're living with Freya." He stomps in my direction, and I pointedly avoid looking below his waist.

Damien's body twitches with each step Alex takes, his hands clenching into fists by his sides. "I'm not *living with Freya*," he argues, also stomping in my direction. "Not in the way you think. She had no place to go."

Alex lets out a dry laugh. "I don't give a fuck." His body quivers as he speaks, and I wonder if he's holding back another shift. "How are you giving her a place to live after everything she did to us? You're my brother, yet you choose her over both me and your mate."

They're brothers? Why did nobody ever tell me that?

I take a step back as Damien approaches Alex, and I scramble to take another when I realize it's me he's heading to. He quickly closes the gap and grabs my upper arm.

"Come on." He drags me toward my cabin.

Alex and the woman continue to argue as we walk away, both taking turns screaming harsh words at one another. As much as I try to piece together what the argument is about, there are too many missing elements for me to get a clear understanding.

Damien and Alex are brothers, but I'm still unclear on if that woman is Alex's mate and, if so, why she's sleeping with Damien.

Sleeping with your brother's wife was frowned upon in my village, and given the apparent importance of mates here, I'm willing to bet that sentiment is shared among the beasts as well.

"Is that Alex's mate?" I ask as Damien drags me through the woods.

We reach my cabin, and he pushes me inside. The rosebush thorns cut my arms, and Damien grunts as he bends and rips the plants out at the base. Blood drips down his palm, but he hardly seems to notice as he tosses them aside and begins walking away.

I follow.

"Wait!" I shout, running back outside. I spot him near the tree line, his body almost entirely hidden by the foliage. He turns at the sound of my voice and stomps back over.

"What?" he asks.

I gesture toward his house. "Who is she?"

Although I know I have no claim to Damien, I can't help but want to know who the woman living in his house is. It's morbid curiosity.

Damien sighs, running a hand through his hair.

"Freya is Alex's mate. She left years ago and came back last week," he says, his answers only creating more questions.

"You're sleeping with your brother's mate?" I ask. I'm judging him, and it's clear in my tone. I don't think I could hide it if I wanted.

"No." Damien shakes his head, his throat bobbing. It seems I've struck a nerve.

I want to pry further, but Damien's leaving before I get anything out.

"Damien!" I shout.

He refuses to acknowledge me as I call out to him, his strides long as he marches into the woods. I consider following him to see what else I can learn, but I doubt I'd get far before being caught.

The shouting between Alex and Freya comes to an abrupt halt, but given the sound of hatred in their voices, I doubt they're anywhere near finished. I hesitate as I stare at the tree line, hoping to catch a glimpse of one of them, but it's too dark to make out much of anything.

What the fuck is going on?

Chapter 11

AINE

THE BEASTS REFUSE to look me in the eye as I march through the woods, their attention shifting to the ground the moment they notice my presence. The incident at dinner last night has made them uncomfortable around me, and I wish I knew what I could do to ease some of that tension.

I'm scouring the garden for Alex the second I push through the tree line into the training field, more than a little eager to see a friendly face. Mia and Abby look up as I storm through the garden, and I give them a curt wave before locking eyes with Alex.

He's standing in his usual spot near the tool shed, his expression unreadable as he watches a pair of beasts sparring in the far corner of the fighting field.

My heart thumps as I head toward him, acutely aware of Damien's gaze on me. He's always staring, and I'm slowly losing hope that he'll grow bored and leave me alone. I don't understand him, and I'm tired of trying to.

Alex dips his head in a silent greeting as I approach.

"Are you okay?" I blurt out.

He ignores my question and gestures to a wheelbarrow

already stacked to the brim with veggies.

"You're late. I was worried I'd have to take this all by myself," he says. I think he's trying to joke, but it falls flat.

I hesitate, wanting to know what happened after Damien brought me to my cabin last night, but I don't want to make him uncomfortable.

It's clear Freya's a sensitive topic.

"Well, I'm here now," I say, forcing myself to sound chipper.

Alex is quiet as I grab the wheelbarrow handles and begin pushing, but his toe clips my ankle every few steps. I ignore it the first two times, but when my shoe is shoved below my heel, I turn and glare.

"Stop that!" I order.

Alex apologizes, his lips twitching, and he does it again the second I resume walking.

"You can't come if you're going to be annoying," I threaten.

Alex snorts, seemingly unconcerned as he nudges me out of the way and grabs the wheelbarrow handles himself.

"*I* push the produce," he says.

Since when? Still, I allow him to take the lead. Despite his happy demeanor, I can tell by his slumped shoulders and dark eyes that last night took a bigger toll on him than he's letting on.

Alex is amazing, and I can't imagine why Freya would choose Damien over him. I sure know if *I* had a choice, I would choose Alex. It wouldn't be a hard decision at all.

The dining hall is empty, and we begin stocking the pantry shelves in comfortable silence.

Alex is the first to speak. "I didn't think she'd ever come back."

I hum, remaining quiet to give him the opportunity to share without interruption. There's a tense moment before Alex sighs and continues.

"Damien and I are twins, and tradition states we fight for the alpha title. Freya was mad at me for refusing to fight Damien for his position, but I never wanted it. Even if I did, I never would've won. Fighting has always been Damien's thing."

"Is that why you work in the gardens?" I ask.

Alex shakes his head. "No." He frowns as he recalls the memory. "I was banned shortly after Freya left. I was angry, and I was getting too violent during the fights. Damien banished me to the gardens after I accidentally hurt one of the teens."

Oh. I'm surprised to hear that. Alex doesn't seem the violent type, and Damien doesn't seem the type to care about somebody getting hurt. He hasn't pried into my execution despite his apparent concerns, which tells me they were never genuine to begin with.

"Anyway," Alex continues. "Damien got drunk one night and—" he pauses, clearing his throat. "Freya found her way into his bed."

He turns and leans against the shelves, his weight causing them to whine and bend. "Damien wasn't in a good state of mind. She left after he rejected her, and she hasn't been back. Last night was the first I've seen her in years."

Alex lets out a choked snort, his voice cracking as he pushes off the shelving. He moves for the wheelbarrow, but I throw my arms around his midsection before he reaches it.

He freezes, but after a second, he relaxes and returns the hug. I can't imagine how hard this must be for him. Damien's a real piece of work for treating Alex like this, his behavior cruel and spiteful. I don't understand what the beasts even see in him.

"I'm so sorry," I whisper. "You deserve better than that."

Alex's arms tighten around my waist. I continue holding him as his body curls around mine, pretending not to notice the shaking of his shoulders as he cries silently above my head. We stand like this for a while, and I gently rub his back until he sniffles and pulls away.

His eyes are red and wet as he looks down at me.

"Do you feel better?" I ask, hoping talking has helped.

I was never allowed to talk about Henry, but I think it would've made me feel better.

Alex nods, his teeth sinking into his bottom lip. There's an odd glint in his eye as he evaluates me, and his lips are on mine before I have time to decipher it.

I freeze underneath his touch, my muscles tense, but I find myself relaxing after a second. I know this isn't a kiss of lust or desire. I'm familiar with the need to feel wanted after such a painful experience. It was one I searched for myself after finding my husband with another woman for the first time.

Alex's lips are soft and still against my own, and no attempts are made to deepen our kiss beyond a peck. I slide my hand up his bicep and squeeze, trying to show my support and care.

"I shouldn't have done that," Alex murmurs, straightening back up.

"Probably not," a deep voice rings out behind me.

My blood runs cold as I spin to face Damien. He stands in the doorway, his expression murderous as the wooden door frame cracks under his hard grip.

Alex doesn't seem at all surprised by Damien's presence, and he steps away to put space between us. I gulp, watching with wide eyes as he runs a hand through his hair. He refuses to look at me. Did he know Damien was here?

Damien steps to the side, opening the doorway so Alex can pass. I'm shocked by how calm he is, and maybe even a little impressed, but as his hand curls around Alex's throat, I realize I assumed too quickly.

Alex chokes as Damien cuts off his oxygen supply, his

movements frantic as he tries to pry his brother off. Seeing them fight is unnerving. I adored my brother, and I'd give anything to have him back.

These two shouldn't be acting like this.

"It wasn't his fault," I say, moving forward to try to help Alex.

Damien's pupils dilate as his head snaps toward me, his lips curled. He looks me head to toe in disgust, and I pause. These beasts are strong and dangerous, and there's nothing stopping Damien from killing me if I make him too angry.

Getting involved will only get me killed, and I'd do well not to forget that.

"This makes us even," Damien says to Alex, his grip tightening with each word. "Next time, I'll rip out your teeth."

Alex stumbles as Damien finally releases him, the man audibly panting as he tries to get oxygen back into his body.

"Even?" Alex gasps. "I don't think so."

"You don't?" Damien asks. "What is it you want, then?" His gaze slides to me. "Do you want to fuck Aine?"

I gulp, looking between the two in horror. This wouldn't be the first time I was offered up to settle a bet, but never has actual sex been on the table. The possibility of pregnancy is too great.

Alex scoffs, and my supposed mate pulls me against his chest. I try to push away from Damien, shrieking as he wraps his arm around my waist and forces me to face Alex.

"I can hold her still if you'd like?" Damien offers, grabbing my elbows and pulling them behind my back.

I hiss at the sudden stretch in my shoulders, my eyes filling with tears as I try to rip free. Alex looks sad, but the expression is short-lived as all emotion disappears from his face.

The room is silent as both Damien and I wait for Alex's response, and I struggle to hold back a sob as Alex looks me over. He wouldn't do that, would he? There's no way. Alex isn't that type of person.

Damien, maybe, but not Alex.

"Yes, Damien," Alex eventually says, deadpan. He meets Damien's eye in a silent challenge. "That's exactly what I want. To rape your mate."

Damien's grip tightens. It's obvious Alex is being sarcastic, but the words are still jarring to hear. A tense moment stretches between the two.

"Leave," Damien eventually orders.

I try to meet Alex's eye in a silent plea for help. I don't want to be left alone with Damien. Not when he's this angry. Alex doesn't look in my direction, though, and my heart drops as he pivots and leaves the room.

I fight to free myself from Damien, terrified of what he's going to do when we're alone. His hands slide from my elbows to my waist.

"Let me go," I cry.

"Aine." Damien grunts as I jab my elbow into his ribcage, so I do it again. "Stop fighting me!"

I ignore him. I'll be damned if I go down without a fight, and I try again to shove my elbow into his side. Damien catches the limb before I connect, and he spins me toward him.

He backs me up against the wall, his body towering over mine. My chest heaves as I continue to fight, my hands and legs kicking with every opportunity.

Fuck him.

Damien doesn't hit me back, but he does shove my limbs away when they get too close. He's toying with me. Eventually, I have no other choice but to stop, my lungs and heart unable to keep going. I sag against the wall and glare at his smug expression.

"Are you finished?" he asks.

I nod, remaining still as he finally releases me.

"I knew Alex was going to say *no*," he says, bending until he's eye level with me. I resist the urge to spit in his face. "I'd never let somebody rape you."

I look away, refusing to believe a word he says.

Damien scoffs, daring to act like I'm the one in the wrong. "I walk in on my mate kissing my brother, yet somehow, she has the audacity to be mad at *me*." He laughs to himself, concerningly unable to understand how offering me up to his brother is worse than anything I may have done.

"It's unbelievable," he continues. "You're to move into my home so Freya can take up residence in the cabin. My brother was correct in saying it's inappropriate for her to be living with me. I came here to offer my assistance in helping you move."

I shake my head, refusing his help.

The thought of moving into his home fills me with dread, and if it weren't so pointless, I'd argue to remain in the cabin. I doubt I'll ever get any sleep knowing Damien's just a few rooms away.

Admittedly, I know he could easily enter my cabin whenever he pleases, but the distance between us brings me comfort at night.

"I would *like* to assist you," Damien insists.

Assist me with what? I own next to nothing.

Again, I shake my head, not understanding why he'd even want to help. There's probably some ulterior motive I'm not getting, and I'm not in the mood to be made the butt of his joke today.

Damien backs away at my rejection, his pupils dilating once more. "Fine, but don't come to me when you get tired."

He says this as if he isn't the absolute last person I'd ever go to for help. I remain silent as he finally turns and exits, his movements stiff. The pantry door slams shut behind him, and a couple of seconds later, I hear the front door slam shut as well.

I don't move.

My head aches as I struggle to make sense of what just happened. I've been working hard to build a new life here, and while it wasn't much, I felt I had a solid friendship with Alex.

Now that's broken.

My legs shake when I finally step away from the wall, my body exhausted after exerting so much energy trying to fight Damien. While I've always thought him to be a bit of a dick, today was a real eye-opener into just how awful of a person he is.

He'd give Henry a run for his money.

The walk to my cabin is bleak, my body numb as I grab my few belongings and make my way to Damien's house. It's empty, but one of the bedroom doors has been left open. Is this where Freya was staying, or was she sleeping in bed with Damien? He says he wasn't intimate with her, but I don't believe him.

Either way, the bedroom is empty, and I drop my things on the mattress before heading back to grab the last of my clothes.

Freya walks out of the cabin as I approach, her lips downturned and arms crossed over her chest.

"You've taken enough of my things already," she says. "I'll be keeping the rest."

"Alex gave them—" I start, stopping as I realize it doesn't matter.

There wasn't much left in there, anyway.

I return to Damien's house. As ashamed as I am to admit it, a small part of me is excited to not have to brave the cold or listen to the window rattling every time so much as a breeze brushes against it at night.

Olivia rushes to stand outside my bedroom door as I walk up the stairs, her cheeks red as she waits for me to reach the top.

"Hey?" I say, confused by her presence.

We haven't spoken since the incident in Damien's office, and if I'm honest, I was planning on avoiding her for the rest of my life. She dips her head in greeting, the blush on her cheeks deepening.

"I just wanted to say I'm glad you're moving in here," she says, shuffling awkwardly. "And I wanted to know if you need any assistance?"

The fact that she uses the exact same phrasing as Damien doesn't go unnoticed. I'm sure he told her to come offer, probably just so he can bring it up later in an attempt to prove how generous of a man he is.

"I'm okay. Thanks, though," I say.

Olivia frowns, her hands moving to grip the hem of her dress. It's the one Damien once gave me to wear, and I resist the urge to shiver at the memories that surround it.

"Look," she says, stepping back with a quiet sigh. "I know you and Damien haven't gotten off to a good start, but he does care."

I blink, unsure how I'm supposed to react to that information.

Olivia doesn't seem to mind my lack of response, a quiet laugh erupting from her as she continues. "He purchased three bedroom sets before settling on one he thought you'd like. He was going to furnish the cabin for you, but he had everything set up in here, instead."

I shrug, indifferent. It doesn't matter how many bedroom sets Damien purchases if he's going to follow it up by offering his brother the opportunity to rape me. Olivia looks confused about my lack of care, clearly having expected me to swoon.

"Thanks for telling me." I scratch the back of my neck as I peer into my new bedroom.

She seems to take the hint and backs off, her shoulders slumping. I stare at her retreating figure before entering my room.

I didn't pay any attention to the furniture before, but now I can't resist taking a closer look. Both the bed frame and corresponding nightstands are made of dark cherrywood, and it seems Damien even purchased complementing creme sheets. Is this the furniture Jenna mentioned was holding up the hospital's blanket delivery?

The closet is empty, but it's large. I hold back a smile as I begin hanging my few pieces of clothing. I've never had a closet before.

Sweat pebbles up along my hairline as I get my room sorted, and I collapse on the bed once I finish. Damien's house is stifling today, the sun shining through the open windows and heating it to an unbearable level.

"This was my bedroom when I was a kid."

I turn to find Alex in the doorway, and I quirk a brow at his unexpected arrival.

"I'm really sorry." He scratches the back of his neck. "I shouldn't have kissed you or provoked Damien like that."

He looks uncomfortable as he stands in the doorway, his hands twitching at his sides and his feet shuffling slightly along the floor. I nod, agreeing that he shouldn't have done either of those things.

"Is Damien going to be mad you're here?" I ask, not wanting to anger him any further today.

Alex shakes his head. "He saw me walking in, and he would've stopped me if he'd had an issue with it." He sticks his head into the room and looks around. "I don't like the way Damien's decorated."

I snort, unable to hold the loud noise back. Honestly, I think it looks nice in here. If Damien weren't such an asshole, I'd probably defend his work, but since he is, I remain silent.

Alex cocks his head to the side before stepping back to put some additional space between us. His actions are surprising, but I realize why when I hear the heavy footfalls a second later.

Damien takes his sweet time walking up the stairs, letting his feet slam into each step to alert the house of his presence. Olivia's door creaks open, and seconds later, she's rushing to wait at the top landing. She looks nervous.

"What're you doing?" Alex asks, also distracted by her sudden panic.

Damien answers for her. "She's supposed to be helping Aine."

Olivia wilts, her actions only serving as a reminder that Damien's a cruel man who thrives off the fear he invokes.

"She said she doesn't need my help," Olivia says.

Alex inserts himself between Olivia and Damien. He places a hand on her back, and he trails it from the top of her neck to the base of her spine. It's an intimate action, and I cock my head to the side when he lingers. Odd.

"Come on," Alex mutters, nudging Olivia toward the stairs.

His apologetic eyes meet mine before he disappears downstairs with Olivia, leaving me alone with Damien. He's making a habit of doing that, and I'm not a fan.

"Is the room to your satisfaction?" Damien asks.

I nod, sliding off the bed. If I need to escape, it will be easier to do if I'm already on my feet.

He scans me head to toe, his lip curling and pupils dilating. My palms grow sweaty under his gaze, and I calmly search for the best escape route.

Damien clears his throat. "What will it take to get you to stop whoring around with my brother?"

I gasp, my body stiffening. "Excuse me? I'm not *whoring around* with anybody." Heat rushes to my face and chest at his accusation.

"It's clear you're starving for affection." Damien tilts his head to the side. "I will agree to pleasure you daily and accompany you to every dinner."

Is he dumb? In what world does this man think those are things I want? While I'm by no means an expert on all the cultural ins and outs of the beasts, I've seen enough to know this is not typical behavior for them.

"Is that not enough?" Damien asks, seemingly misreading my silence. "I know you're attracted to me."

I shake my head. "I don't know how you'd like me to respond to that."

He really is dumb.

Damien grunts. "Then tell me what you want."

I stare blankly, my mind racing through scenarios on how to handle this situation. I'm scared to anger him, but I also don't want to agree to spend time with him. Damien waits impatiently for my response, his foot tapping against the ground in a quick rhythm.

"I don't *want* anything," I say, wincing at the shake in my voice. "And I'm not attracted to you."

Damien throws his head back with a laugh, his disbelief at my words frustrating. This man is delusional, and if I could trade him in for another mate, I would in a heartbeat.

"Aine," he coos, crossing the threshold of my door and stalking up to me. "I'm not saying you love me." He grazes his fingers over my mark. "But you can't deny that you want me."

I shiver as his fingertips push into the sensitive scar on my neck, and I jerk away as the interaction makes my knees buckle. Damien laughs, his body crowding over mine for the second time today.

"Want to see something fun?" he teases, pressing his free hand against my stomach to trap me against the wall.

He then jabs his thumb into my mark, and I slump against the wall with a choked moan. It feels good, and I hate myself for it.

"Please," I beg, wanting him to stop.

Damien smirks. "You want more?" he whispers, shoving a

knee between my legs.

"Stop!" I choke out.

Damien's grin falls, his thumb stilling where it presses against my mark. His throat bobs as he gulps, and his nostrils flare as he smells the air.

Almost immediately he stumbles back, his eyes wide as a feeling of sheer panic floods through our infuriating bond. The emotion is gone a moment later, Damien once more blocking the foreign connection.

"You're afraid," he says, running a hand down the front of his face. "There are so many scents up here, I didn't—" The floor groans as he takes another step back and gestures around the room. "I thought you wanted this."

I remain still as Damien continues to try to explain himself. His body shakes as he fights the urge to shift into his beast form, his pupils dilating and constricting as he struggles to calm himself. I'm confused about what's gotten him so upset, and his intense emotions are only stressing me out further.

After another minute of flustering, Damien turns and retreats downstairs. The back door slams a second later, signaling his exit. I remain frozen in my spot, unable to move as I wait for my heart to return to a normal speed.

The moment it does, I sneak downstairs and out the front door.

There's only one place I can go, and I hope nobody sees me as I sprint through the woods toward the hospital. Jenna's safe, and I highly doubt Damien would do anything harmful to me in her presence.

She's sitting behind her desk fiddling with some plants when I arrive, but she jumps up with a smile when I step inside her office.

"Aine!" she shouts, pulling me into a hug. "Where have you been? I went to the gardens to find you, but you and Alex weren't there."

Jenna pulls away to look me over, her face hardening as she takes in my red eyes and splotchy cheeks.

"What'd he do?" she asks, her voice low as she pulls me to the small couch in the corner of the room.

I shrug, not wanting to talk about it. There's no pleasant way to say that my mate caught me kissing another man, then offered my body to said man, and then followed that up by demanding I move into his house. If that isn't bad enough, he then shoved his grubby fingers in my mark.

It's a bit of a mouthful, and if I'm honest, it feels shameful to admit. It's nothing compared to what Henry would do to me, and I know Jenna hasn't exactly had an easy life, either. I don't want to sound whiny.

Thankfully, she doesn't push, but her eyes show just how badly she wants to. If I'm honest with myself, I'm surprised by the resistance she's showing.

"I heard you moved into Damien's home." She's clearly fishing for information, but she feigns disinterest as she fiddles with some papers on her desk. Jenna's a terrible actress, but I don't blame her. I'd be curious too if I were in her position, and I'm sure women showing up to her office crying isn't a common occurrence.

"He did," I admit. "Freya's in the cabin now."

I'm still upset about it, too. I liked the privacy that came with living in the cabin, and Damien's already shown me just how little he respects my personal space. A small part of me wants to ask for the cabin back, but after today, I'm hesitant to ask Damien for anything.

Jenna frowns, shaking her head at the mention of Freya. "The nerve of that woman," she says. "I bet she thinks Damien will reject you because you're human."

She snorts and sorts the papers on her desk. Underneath them are leaves. There's a mixture of fresh and browned ones, and I watch as she sets them in a bowl with a few other plant-looking items. I've never seen most of these herbs before, but Jenna seems comfortable as she crushes them into a powder and pours them into large capsules.

"What's that?" I ask.

Jenna smirks, turning to me with a dangerous glint in her eye. It's quite fearful.

"I was making some calming medicine when you came in, but after seeing you, I've changed the recipe," she says.

I step behind her chair to get a better look.

"Changed it to what?" I ask.

Jenna smirks. "Nothing too crazy," she answers vaguely.

"That only brings about more questions."

She laughs. "It's still a calming medicine, but I made it strong. If you mix this in with Damien's drink or food, he should fall asleep within a few minutes." She sounds proud of her cocktail. "It'll knock him out for hours, so you can sleep without worrying."

Jenna shoves the capsules into a paper bag and hands it over, and I hold back a smile as I accept it. I'm grateful to have an ally who knows her way around medicines.

I'm not sure how I'll manage to slip Damien something without him noticing, but I hope I'll find an opportunity. I can use these capsules to knock him out should I need to escape.

"Keep me company," Jenna says, pointing to the small couch in the corner of the room. "I spend all day by myself, and it gets lonely."

I take a seat. "I'd be happy to."

It doesn't seem like the beasts rarely, if ever, need medical attention, and Jenna complains loudly about it while she continues fixing up her medicines.

Eventually, Avia joins us. She looks at me as if she can read my mind, and I force myself to smile and speak in my cheeriest voice so she doesn't feel bad for me.

I think it works.

Jenna's in the middle of telling a story about her first time giving stitches when Avia lifts her hand and turns her head to the side. The room goes silent as she listens to something my human ears can't detect.

"Damien's coming," she says.

I clutch the bag of capsules to my chest and try to act normal. If Damien notices the medicine, I'll lie and say it's for me, but I'd rather he not know I have them.

He enters the room a second later, and Jenna rises. She looks him in the eye and crosses her arms over her chest, not at all pretending to be happy with him. I appreciate it, my friend loyal even if I haven't told her the details of what happened between us.

Damien gives both Jenna and Avia a slight nod before turning toward me.

It seems he's come to collect.

I fight the urge to run away as I walk over to him. He says nothing as he places a hand on my back, the tension between us thick as he leads me out of the room. I crane my head to look at Jenna and Avia, beyond panicked. Jenna only gives me a thumbs-up, which isn't particularly encouraging.

Everybody's trust in Damien is worrying. Back in my old village, we openly feared our leader behind closed doors. Here, though, everybody seems to genuinely like Damien. Even when they know he's being cruel towards me.

Damien must truly have everybody brainwashed.

My movements are stiff as I follow him outside. He drops his hand from my back the moment we exit the building, but he continues walking by my side.

I prefer when he walks ahead.

He breaks the silence first. "I wanted to apologize for my actions earlier today," he starts. "Beasts rely on scent to detect emotion. There were too many upstairs, and I couldn't accurately pinpoint yours."

I gulp, surprised he's taken it upon himself to apologize. I didn't think he knew how.

Damien clears his throat before continuing. "It wasn't until you asked me to stop that I realized I was smelling Olivia's arousal, not yours. It won't happen again."

Why was Olivia aroused? Despite what happened in Damien's office, I doubt it was because of him. She looked nervous when he came upstairs, not excited.

Maybe it was because of the way Alex was touching her back. I suppose that would make sense.

Damien stares at the side of my head, waiting for me to acknowledge his apology.

I don't want to.

The remainder of the walk to Damien's house is spent in uncomfortable silence. Freya sits in a chair outside the cabin watching us, her gaze making me tense. Damien doesn't look at her, but he does adjust to put his body between ours.

Is he afraid she's going to attack me? Wonderful.

Olivia is just beginning to walk up the stairs as we step into the foyer.

She pauses to greet us. "Perfect timing," she says. "I left dinner on the counter for you, Aine."

She gestures toward the kitchen, and I mumble a quiet thanks and step away. Damien's footsteps are loud as he follows me, and I try not to look too nervous as he eyes the bag Jenna gave me. Can he smell what's in there? I hope not.

Jenna would've warned me if he could.

Damien watches through narrowed eyes as I grab the dinner plate off the counter and begin shoveling the stewed meat into my mouth. The sooner I finish eating, the sooner I can go upstairs and hide in my room.

"Will you pour me a glass of water?" Damien doesn't wait for my response as he turns and walks into the entryway bathroom.

This is peculiar.

Still, I hold my breath as I spin around in search of a cup. My hands shake as I pull one from the cupboard and fill it with tap water. Now is the perfect opportunity to give him the sleeping medicine, even if I'm mildly convinced it's a trap.

I waste no time reaching into the bag and ripping open the capsule, internally panicking as some of the powder spills on the counter. What's left gets poured into his cup, and I scoop up the bit that was spilled and dump that in as well. I debate putting in two vials, but the sound of the toilet flushing foils those plans.

I use the handle of my fork to stir the mixture until it's disintegrated and impossible to detect.

Damien returns with his ever-present frown and grabs the cup. I hide my shaking hands beneath the counter as he brings the glass to his mouth, his nose wrinkling. Can he smell what I've done?

His eyes meet mine as he downs the liquid in two gulps.

"I'm going to bed," he grunts, slamming the empty cup on the counter. "Goodnight, Aine."

Chapter 12

AINE

MY HEART POUNDS as I peek into Damien's bedroom, nervous about the way he's sprawled on the bed. I didn't think to check on him last night, but I wish I had.

He probably wouldn't be dead, then.

The floorboards creak as I tiptoe toward him, my panic rising the closer I get. His face is smooshed into a pillow, and I wait anxiously to see if his back moves with breath. He didn't even change out of his clothing or take off his shoes before falling face-first into the sheets.

I don't think he's breathing. I touch his shoulder, gently prodding at the muscle. The beasts will kill me when they discover what I've done.

I could've gotten a head start on running if I'd realized last night.

Damien's body is warm, the sign of life filling me with hope. I give him a gentle shake, but he doesn't react. I try again, spreading my fingers and rocking his shoulder into the mattress.

"Are you okay?" Olivia asks.

I jump, trying not to look too guilty when I spot her standing in the doorway. She's still in her pajamas, and if her messy hair is anything to go by, I'd say she just crawled out of bed.

"I'm trying to wake him up," I admit.

Olivia hums, her lips twitching as she glances at Damien and steps into the room. She seems a bit nervous as she approaches, her movements slow and timid.

"That's maybe not a good idea," she says. "Damien's quite grumpy in the mornings."

"Fuck off, Olivia."

I sag at the sound of Damien's voice, relief flooding my system as he wraps his arms around his pillow and hugs it to his chest. He groans before turning to look at us, his eyes hazy and unfocused.

Olivia rushes out of the room. I should probably do the same.

"Will you take off my shoes?" Damien asks, his voice slurred from sleep.

He blinks slowly as he waits for my response, his body gradually curling in on itself. I don't regret giving him the sleeping medicine, but I worry I may have given him too much.

Damien kicks his leg out when I don't move, his desire for me to remove his shoes quite evident. The action's childish, but effective. I step closer and grab his leg.

I'm nervous he's going to attack me, but he remains still as I untie the laces and slip his shoe off his foot. His breathing grows deeper as I do the same with his other leg, and he eventually buries his face back into his pillow.

It feels like a weight's been lifted off my shoulders. I was entirely convinced I'd killed him and would have to run away before anybody found out. Still on edge, I check one last time that he's breathing before leaving.

It's still early, and I want to get breakfast from the dining hall before heading to the gardens. Olivia and I work around one another, polite but distanced as we take turns using the bathroom.

Freya stares from the cabin when I finally step outside. I look straight ahead, refusing to meet her gaze for fear of provoking her. I'm surprised Damien's letting her stay after all the pain she's caused Alex, but I guess I shouldn't be too shocked. He's never claimed to be a good man, nor have his actions ever suggested so.

He doesn't care about Alex as a brother should.

There's only a small handful of people in the dining hall, and they shoot me friendly smiles as I fix myself a plate. The cooks made pancakes today, one of my favorites.

People are still tense around me after Alex and Damien's fight, so I eat quietly by myself in the corner. I don't enjoy drama, but somehow, it always seems to find its way to me.

I force down my food, my eyes continually darting to the large clock hanging from the wall. I'm running late today, and Alex is going to kill me.

He's big on punctuality.

Damien's already in the training field chatting with a group of teenage beasts when I arrive. He's teaching them some defensive maneuver, and we make brief eye contact before I clear my throat and turn away.

I'm beyond relieved he's alive and in good health, and it's hard to believe that just an hour ago he was begging me to take off his shoes.

Alex greets me with a wide smile, faking happiness despite the dark bags under his eyes. He looks like shit.

"Good morning!" He stares at my clothing. "Jenna has ordered me to confirm you're wearing sunscreen before allowing you to work."

I grimace. Jenna's adamant I wear the sunscreen, but it completely slipped my mind this morning. I was too busy stressing about having murdered Damien, then rushing to get ready once I realized he was still alive.

"I forgot it," I admit.

Alex plants his hands on his hips as he evaluates my exposed arms. My long sleeve tops are dirty, and this t-shirt is the only garden appropriate thing I have left to wear. Damien has his laundry washed once a week, but I don't have enough clothes to comfortably make it through. Especially since Freya took some of her things back during the move.

"I'm not excusing you if you get burnt again," he warns.

I shrug, having figured as much.

Alex leads me to one of the back rows and directs me to pick the ripe eggplants. It's easy enough to do, but I'm continually distracted by the fighting beasts. Damien keeps shouting adjustments, and I look up every time.

He takes his training quite seriously, always correcting when the beasts do something wrong. Honestly, I think it's a bit of an overkill. The beasts are already strong, and they could probably take down an entire human army without even breaking a sweat.

Are there other beast packs? That would explain all the training.

I wipe my forehead and neck with a quiet sigh. The sun is punishing today. I can already see redness spreading across my arms, and I have no doubt that by the end of the day, they're going to be quite painful.

There aren't many people tasked with working in the gardens, though, and I don't want to be the one person who doesn't pull their weight. I'll suffer through.

"Aine."

I freeze, already annoyed as I look up at Damien.

He grins, and in his hand is my jar of sunscreen. I stare at the container, not understanding why he's here or what he's doing with it.

"I went back to the house and got this for you," he says. He holds out the jar. "You told Alex you forgot to put it on."

I don't trust this, and I stare blankly between him and the sunscreen. Damien isn't kind.

He hums as he realizes I'm not going to take the sunscreen from him, and with a snort, he tosses the container toward me. It lands on the ground in front of my knees.

"I'll wait here until you've put it on," he says.

I frown, glancing nervously around. Has he done something to it? Poisoned it, maybe? I screw open the cap and sniff the contents, but it smells normal and looks unchanged.

Damien cocks a brow.

"Would you like me to put some on my skin to prove it isn't poisoned?" he asks. "I believe we both know I'm not the one in this relationship who does that."

My cheeks warm at the accusation, and I shake my head as I scoop out a handful of product. He knows what I did last night. I knew he would.

He's going to punish me for it.

I'm tense as I spread the sunscreen on my arms and face. Each second feels like a year as I wait for it to react negatively with my skin, but nothing happens. I don't trust Damien as far as I can throw him, and I wouldn't be surprised if he mixed something painful in with the sunscreen.

After a minute or two, I begin to relax.

Damien seems to sense it, too, as he chuckles and walks a circle around me. It feels threatening, but I'm pretty sure he won't do anything with so many people around. He's too desperate for the beasts to perceive him as a good mate.

"Let me put some on your back," Damien offers.

He crouches behind me, his body so close his breath moves strands of my hair. His arm grazes mine as he plucks the bottle out of my hand, and I hate myself for the way my body enjoys it.

No matter what I do, I can't seem to find it within myself to hate his touch. Even when he's treating me like shit, a small part of me still enjoys the attention. It reminds me of how I felt when I first married Henry, of how weak and naive I was.

Damien plants his hands on my shoulders, and I suck in a sharp breath as he smears the cool cream on the exposed skin of my back. He's efficient, not lingering in any one spot for too long, but I can just tell he's finding enjoyment out of this. If not by touching me, then by watching me squirm.

"We're going to have a private dinner together tonight," he whispers in my ear. "My request is that you shower and be ready by seven."

He dips his fingers into the back of my shirt, and I swallow past the lump in my throat as he begins to massage me. Hunching over the plants all day gives me the worst back pain, and I'd be lying if I said his hands rubbing my achy muscles doesn't feel amazing.

"Can you do that?" Damien asks when I don't respond.

It's not like I have a choice. I sink my teeth into my bottom lip before nodding in agreement.

"Good."

Damien's gone without another word, his long legs carrying him to his beasts. They wait patiently for his direction, their trust in him seemingly unwavering. I can't imagine how he ever managed to earn it.

Although, to be fair, it seems I'm the only one he treats like shit.

The sunscreen helps prevent any further burn to my skin, but my achy back still hurts. I ignore it for as long as possible, but after only a few hours, I seek out Alex.

He gives me a brief once-over before waving me away. I head

home and hide in my bedroom until the time comes for dinner.

I wonder what Damien would do if I refused to clean up. He'd probably take it upon himself to wash me like he did after my accident. The memory makes me shiver, and fear of him doing just that is the driving force behind me dragging my sorry, sore butt into the bathroom.

Olivia keeps the shower well-stocked, and I clean myself before throwing on a fresh outfit and tackling the situation with my hair. Calling it a rat's nest is generous, and I curse Damien for not owning conditioner as I angrily run a brush through it.

I don't know why I'm bothering to make it look nice, but my anxiety for this evening has me doing it anyway.

It takes several minutes to get all the knots out of my hair, and I stare at myself in the mirror as I fiddle with the neckline of my shirt. I worry Damien's going to touch my mark if it's exposed, so I'm wearing a turtleneck.

It's not the most convenient, given the hot weather, but if it'll keep me safe from Damien's wandering hands, that's what I'll do.

I flinch when somebody knocks on the bathroom door.

"Are you almost done?" Damien shouts, his voice muffled as it travels through the wood.

I don't understand why he wants to have a private dinner, and I don't like the idea of being left alone with him.

He's still standing outside the door by the time I work up the courage to leave the bathroom, and he raises an eyebrow as he looks over my outfit. I wait for his inevitable comment, but he says nothing as he turns and gestures for me to join him downstairs. I'm careful to keep my distance as I follow, and my movements halt when we reach the first floor.

Damien steps to the side so I can see what he's done.

"I thought it'd be nice for us to get to know one another without hundreds of beasts around," he says.

The dining room has been cleaned, and the table is set for what can only be described as a date. Candles and wine are visible from where I stand, making me worry about Damien's intentions. Husbands and wives don't typically enjoy romantic meals where I'm from, and when one's presented, there's usually an ulterior motive.

Henry loved to make me dinner, then demand I give him children.

"Olivia helped set it up, but she's staying the night at Alex's," Damien says when I don't respond.

He looks awkward as he pulls out a chair for me, his eyes darting all around the room. I move slowly toward the table, still suspicious. I don't love that he sent Olivia away for the night. What does he have planned that she can't be here for?

"Thank you," I say, clearing my throat and sitting on the very edge of the chair.

Damien sits opposite me. He's wearing nice clothing, black pants with a tucked-in button-up shirt. The sleeves are rolled up his forearms, exposing his muscles.

"Do you want wine?"

He doesn't wait for my response before pouring two glasses.

"Why are you doing this?" I ask, unable to hold back any longer.

Damien hesitates, his mouth flattening into a straight line. I remain silent, eager to hear the reasoning behind this silly idea.

"Is it so wrong to want a nice evening with my mate?"

The sarcasm is loud and clear in his tone, and I roll my shoulders before taking a sip of wine. His abrupt switch from hating me to setting up a date is suspicious, and I won't be led to believe otherwise.

If I had to guess, I'd assume his people are angry with him for allowing Freya to stay in his house, and this is an attempt to prove he and I are in a good place.

"I've been watching you," Damien finally admits. "It's become clear my beast isn't going to choose another mate, and I don't enjoy feeling like an outsider. You're warm with everybody else, and I've decided it's time for you to be warm with me, too."

He's such a fucking asshole. And creepy. He had the opportunity to get to know me, but he was too busy avoiding, insulting, and ignoring me. I no longer have any interest.

"So," Damien pauses to clear his throat, "how was your day?"

I shrug, biting back a snarky remark. "It was fine."

It would've been better if he wasn't staring at me the entire afternoon.

"Mine could've been better," Damien admits. "I had a hard time waking up this morning, and when I did, it was only to discover that my mate left me all alone, unprotected."

I snort. Like this man needs any sort of protection. I'm sure even in his drugged state, he could have fought off an attacker. Damien smirks at my visible disbelief, and my face warms as I realize this was the reaction he wanted from me.

"I don't know why you're laughing," Damien jokes. "I could have been hurt."

I clear my throat to hold back a chuckle. I refuse to be tricked by his fake affection. He called me pathetic the last time I tried to be friendly and open with him, and I'll be damned if I make that mistake again.

"I'm sure you were fine," I say, taking another sip of wine.

Although it's clear Damien wants to chat before eating, I reach forward and lift the domed metal lid keeping our food warm. Damien frowns, but he doesn't try to stop me as I begin serving myself. The sooner this pseudo-date ends, the sooner I can leave.

"I didn't realize you were so hungry," he says.

I don't respond, and the silence between us stretches as he

grabs his plate and serves himself once I'm finished. I'm unsure what kind of meat I'm eating, but I recognize the carrots and rice mixed within. We don't harvest rice here, and it's rare for Damien to order a shipment of it to be delivered. I'm pleased, and I quickly begin shoveling the food into my mouth.

Damien watches, his throat bobbing, before he grabs my hand resting on the table. I freeze, staring down at where we connect. After several seconds, Damien retreats.

"Aine, I'm really trying here," he says.

I want to snap back and remind him that *he's* the one who called me pathetic for wanting to have a relationship with him in the first place. It's unfair of him to treat me like shit and then expect me to turn around and plead for his attention the second he decides he's willing to give me a chance.

Damien clears his throat. "Do you miss your husband?"

My blood runs cold as he brings up Henry, fear permeating every inch of my body. Has he found out what I did? I haven't told anybody about Henry's death, but that doesn't mean anything.

I briefly remember Damien's beasts running toward my village after my execution. I don't know what came of that, but I haven't asked for fear of finding out that everybody I've ever known and loved is dead.

I'm not ready to hear the answer.

"My husband?" I ask, trying and failing to sound calm. "Why do you care?"

Damien shrugs and takes a bite of food. He's watching me too closely, his eyes zeroed in on my every reaction.

"Jenna told me you were married," he says. "I imagine it must've been hard to leave your husband after your execution."

The wording he uses makes it sound like he doesn't know about my crime, and it fills me with the hope that my secret remains unknown. I'm willing to bet the beasts don't take kindly to murderers here.

Damien cocks his head to the side as he waits for my answer, and I fumble to come up with something truthful and non-concerning.

"Not really," I say. "We didn't have the best relationship."

"Why?"

I shrug before mindlessly repeating the words I've heard thousands of times before. "I was an unworthy wife."

Damien seems shocked by my answer, his body jolting and hand tightening around his wine glass. He throws back the rest of his drink and pours himself another before responding.

"How so?"

I debate on whether to tell him the truth. Maybe if I do, he'll better understand why I had to kill Henry. I have zero intentions of telling Damien about the murder, but if he finds out, he might be lenient if he knows how awful Henry was to me.

While most couples in my village didn't have loving relationships, Henry's and mine was especially bad.

"I was unable to produce male children," I admit.

Damien's pupils dilate, and a look of complete horror washes over his face. "You have children?"

I shake my head. "No. Henry would take me to the prediction healer to determine the sex whenever I fell pregnant. It was always a female, so he had it removed before I got too far along."

Despite my best attempts to remain calm, I choke up as I think back to those days. I'd get so excited whenever I was late to bleed. It was silly, but I was always hopeful it'd be a boy and Henry would finally be happy.

"How?" Damien asks, pulling me from my thoughts.

"How what?"

Damien looks annoyed by my lack of attention to our conversation, but he explains, nonetheless. "How were they *removed?*"

I fidget with the stem of my wineglass as I try to think of a way to share that information delicately. It's not a happy explanation, and I don't enjoy speaking about it.

"He'd beat me until I miscarried." I spit the words out before I begin to cry. "It's not a common practice back in my village, but it does happen occasionally."

Damien's glass shatters. His hand is bleeding, and it takes everything in me not to get up and run as he stands and moves away from the table. His body shakes as he walks, and I watch with wide eyes as his back muscles flex.

Is he trying to fight off a shift?

Shit. I shouldn't have said anything. A small part of me is flattered he seems so angry about my prior treatment, but a larger portion of me is concerned he's mad about my inability to produce males.

"Are you okay?" I ask.

Damien doesn't respond, choosing instead to move toward the back door and stare out it. He sucks in a deep breath, and I try not to look too afraid as he turns toward me. His face appears relaxed, but I can tell how riled up he is by his dilated pupils.

"How many times?"

"Only once," I lie.

Damien's footfalls are loud as he moves toward me, his steps fast and hard. I gulp as he crouches by my knees and grabs my sweaty hands. I wish to have back the rude, callous beast I've grown accustomed to.

I knew what to expect from that man.

"How many times, Aine?"

"Three times," I admit, not wanting to speak about this any longer.

Damien attempts to meet my gaze, but I refuse to look him in the eye. He runs his thumbs over the back of my hands, which I think is an attempt to comfort me.

At least he's not angry.

"Aine—" he starts.

I interrupt. "I'm finished eating."

I don't care to talk about this any further, and I especially don't care to see the pity I know resides on Damien's face. It's the same look I always get, and I'm tired of it.

If he ever discovers what I did to Henry, I hope this will be enough to excuse my actions. I didn't murder a good man.

Damien tightens his grip on my hands before releasing me.

"Very well," he says. "You may go."

I jump to my feet and rush out of the room before he changes his mind. I don't understand what his game is, and I don't care to play.

Chapter 13

AINE

ALEX CURSES AS he scrambles to pick up the tomatoes he's dropped.

"Have you spoken to Freya?" I ask.

He looks up as her name falls from my lips, his chest sinking as he lets out a deep sigh. The tomatoes mush between his fingers as he struggles to hold them in one hand, and after a moment of watching, I take pity and help pick them up.

Freya's grown cocky recently, proudly marching into the training fields every morning and showing up to the dining hall every night. Everybody ignores her, but she doesn't seem to care.

At one point she even tried to help us garden, but Damien came around and shooed her away. He seems to be the only one she listens to, which aggravates me more than I care to admit. I want to know what's going on between them.

I'm pretty sure I'm not the only one.

Her presence has more than thrown Alex for a loop, the man constantly pulling me into the kitchen pantry to hide. He refuses to talk about her, and it doesn't help that Damien refuses to discuss why he's allowing her to stay, either.

"She's been coming to my house at night wanting to speak with me, but I haven't let her in," Alex admits.

My lips purse, but I keep my less-than-kind thoughts to myself. At the end of the day, she's still his mate, and I don't want to offend him by talking badly about her.

Alex takes the vegetables from my hand and sets them in the small bucket on the shelf. Today was a big day for tomatoes, and I'm excited to see what the cooks do with them.

"How was your date with Damien?" Alex asks, changing the subject.

I shrug, a light blush tinting my cheeks. I've told Alex a thousand times already that it wasn't a date, but he insists on calling it that.

Besides, Damien hasn't spoken to me since that evening. I'm still embarrassed I told him about my abortions. I hoped speaking about the abuse would lay the framework as to why I had to kill Henry, but all I ended up doing was admitting my inability to produce a male.

I should've used a different example.

"It was uncomfortable," I admit.

Alex shakes his head before letting out an unattractive snort.

"I heard you rushed to eat, then ran to your room."

I huff, annoyed with how much he knows. Did Damien tell Alex the secrets of my children, too? I was under the impression the two men were fighting.

Alex leans against the shelf as he waits for my reply, his face impossible to read.

"Damien told you that?" I ask, neither confirming nor denying the statement.

"Olivia did," he says. "Why didn't you enjoy your meal? She said Damien worked hard trying to make it nice for you."

I shrug, not quite believing that. I don't think Damien's

worked hard on anything a day in his life.

"I don't trust his motives," I say. "He hasn't been nice to me."

Alex rolls his eyes. It's frustrating how nobody seems to understand my hesitance toward Damien, dismissing my concerns the second I voice them. Even when they do seem surprised by what I report, they're quick to come up with an excuse for his behavior.

"At least he's trying now?" Alex crosses his arms over his chest. "It's better late than never."

I frown. Damien's attitude will change when he inevitably discovers the reason for my execution.

Alex and I loiter in the pantry, neither of us in a hurry to leave. We don't acknowledge that we're lingering as we rearrange the shelves and fidget with the already stocked vegetables.

We only stop when Olivia enters the pantry. She looks uncomfortable as she peeks inside, her eyes darting around the room before landing on me.

"Damien wants to see you," she says. "He's in his office."

She glances nervously in Alex's direction, her face turning red as she murmurs a quiet greeting.

"Do you know what he wants?" I ask Olivia.

She shakes her head.

I bet she does. She's probably keeping it from me, though. She and Damien work close enough together that I'm sure she's heard something.

My palms are soaked with sweat as I walk to Damien's office, and I hope he can't smell my nerves as I step inside. He barely looks up before gesturing to the chairs in front of his desk.

I remain standing.

"Yes?" I cut to the chase.

Damien's still sweaty from the training fields this morning, and I watch as he swipes a hand over his temple and gestures again for me to sit. I gulp, stepping forward and lowering myself into the seat. He waits for me to get adjusted, the silence almost as unnerving as his furrowed brows and thinned lips.

Something's wrong.

"I sent men to your village," he says, reaching underneath his desk. "They brought back something interesting."

He sent men to my village? Vik doesn't welcome beasts, and I can't imagine he'd take kindly to their intrusion. What has Damien done?

He straightens up and drops a large book on his desk. It lands with a loud *thump*, the bolded words printed on the top making my mouth run dry. I'd recognize the black snakeskin cover anywhere.

This is Vik's book, the thick item full of documentation on everybody who lives in my village.

My fingers curl around the armrest of the chair.

Everything we did was recorded to our file, and at the end of every year, we had to stand in front of a committee and defend any actions they found questionable. If there were too many, we faced punishment.

My execution is most definitely outlined in there.

Damien closely watches my reaction.

"Is there anything you want to tell me before I look in it?" he asks.

I glance between him and the book. It was dumb to think he wouldn't find a way to discover the information he wanted. I open my mouth to respond, but I clamp it shut just as quickly.

Anything in the binder there will contradict my truth. Vik didn't see Henry's treatment of me as wrong, and he'll call him out to be a wonderful husband and me an unfit wife.

Damien isn't going to believe a word I say.

He's going to kill me.

That's the only thought in my head as I spring from the chair and run to the door. Alex or Jenna will defend me. I just need to make it to one of them.

Damien curses just moments before the sound of his chair hitting the wall reverberates throughout the room.

"Aine!"

I ignore his shout as I rip open the door and run toward the exit. Olivia jolts out of her chair at my sudden intrusion, her eyes wide as I fly past her in a sad attempt to flee. I make it less than five steps before Damien catches me.

He wraps an arm around my middle and holds me against his chest. Then he lifts me off the ground and marches me back into his office.

I push at his arms and kick my legs in an attempt to break free, but it's all in vain as I hear the door slam shut behind him.

"No!" I cry, unable to see beyond my blinding fear. "I'll leave. I'll leave and I won't bother you again."

Damien refuses to release me.

"Calm down," he orders.

He sets me on my feet, and I push against him and jerk to the right. He grunts as I smash my skull into his side, and the arm not wrapped around me is moved to hold my head in place.

As his forearm grazes my lips, I instinctively open my mouth and sink my teeth into his skin. I'd never consider doing this if I were in a calmer state of mind, but my fight-or-flight response has been forced into *fight*.

Damien tenses as my teeth bury into his arm, his chest heaving against my back.

"Aine, Aine, listen to me," he whispers, his lips grazing my ear. "If you break my skin, you're going to mark me as I did to you. I can assure you my arm is the absolute last place I want such a sensitive scar."

I struggle to form coherent thoughts. I doubt Damien's going to believe that I killed Henry in self-defense, and having a large chunk of his arm between my teeth isn't helping my case.

I could mark him. He'll be pissed, but he'd be even further tethered to me.

Damien continues speaking.

"Calm down, Aine. Why don't you take the book off my desk?" He inches us forward a few steps. "You can take it with you. I won't look."

Damien scoots us closer to his desk, his movements slow and cautious.

He's going to snatch the binder out of my hand the second I release him. My peaceful argument is no longer valid after having just attempted to attack him, and my backup plan of running to Alex won't work when I'm unable to leave Damien's office.

I begin to panic as the knowledge that I'm stuck between only shitty outcomes cements itself inside of me. It's that thought alone that drives me to jerk and bite down.

The metallic taste of blood fills my mouth, signaling I've broken the skin. I relax my jaw and release Damien at the exact moment his knees buckle.

I plant my hands on his desk as his weight drops on my back, and his hand lands painfully on top of mine as he does the same. The room is dead silent as Damien unwraps his arm from my belly and steps away.

"You fucking…fuck!" he shouts.

I spin and jerk away just as he moves to grab me once more. His face is red and full of anger as he snatches my wrist and yanks me into his chest. I cry out as I stumble and smack my face into his hard body.

"What the fuck, Aine?"

The tears in my eyes make everything blurry as I try to push away from Damien. He releases me just as quickly as he grabbed me, his actions sporadic as he struggles to settle on an emotion.

I back up against his desk as he lifts his arm and begins inspecting the mark.

He wipes away the saliva and blood, revealing an already healed scar. Every tooth, from my molars to my canines, punctured the skin, but there's a clear gap where my front teeth couldn't.

"You didn't even do a good job," Damien grumbles, tilting his arm in different directions so he can see the mark from every angle. "It looks like you've mauled me."

I can't help but feel a bit embarrassed by my inability to leave an adequate mark, but I don't dwell on that as I eye the door. Is he distracted enough that I can slip away?

Taking a slow inhale, I tentatively step around Damien. He doesn't seem to notice, his attention still on the mark I gave him. Despite his complaints, the bond between us says something different. Damien's excited—elated, even—the emotion leaking through before he realizes what he's doing and cuts off the connection.

He continues to insult my work as I inch closer to the door. Vik's book still sits on the desk, ready to be viewed at any moment, but it's too risky to grab it.

I reach for the door handle.

Damien huffs. "I know you killed your husband."

My hand freezes midair. Damien's still examining his mark, his arm inches from his face as he pokes at the scar. I stiffen, feeling pleasure every time he touches it. Can he feel whenever I touch mine?

"I've known for days," he continues, finally looking at me. He gestures for me to sit. "I was hoping you'd admit to it, though."

Damien lowers himself into the chair I was in earlier, a quiet sigh slipping from his lips as he grabs the book. I glance at the door one last time, my chest deflating as I realize he locked it. It would take a few seconds to unlock, and he'd no doubt catch me before I'm able to get it open.

"Sit, Aine," Damien orders, his voice firm.

I clench my hands into fists and make my way to the empty chair next to him. My mark stands out on his arm, and the scarred skin catches the sunlight as he flips through the book pages.

I'll admit the placement is less than ideal. It's right in the crook of his elbow, and it will probably press against his bicep whenever he folds his arm. It'll be an adjustment for him to learn how to move without triggering it.

He watches as I evaluate the scar.

"Do you want to see it?" he asks.

I shake my head, uninterested in getting an up-close look at the mark further tying us together. I already regret doing it, but maybe now his beast will push him to be lenient with me.

"It was an accident," I say, pointing to Vik's book. "I didn't mean to kill Henry."

Damien hums as he mulls over my words. Then he opens the book to a marked page. I assume he's reading what's written about me, and I watch intently for any sort of reaction.

"Care to elaborate?" he eventually asks.

"Henry came home drunk. He was trying to hold me down so he could try for another child." My voice trickles out as I crane my neck in an attempt to read what's written on the page Damien's fact-checking my story with. He's quick to notice and adjust his hold so I can no longer see the words.

"I kicked at his stomach to get him off," I continue. "He lost his balance and fell into the fireplace."

My jaw clenches as I think back to that night.

Henry screamed in agony as the fire burned through his

clothing and skin, his cries drawing the attention of our neighbors. I tried to get him out, but he was too drunk to think coherently and kept pushing me away. By the time the other villagers broke into our home and got him out, he was long gone.

They took one look at my ripped clothing and battered face and determined I must've pushed him in a fit of rage.

I begged and pleaded for them to understand it had been an accident, but they refused to believe me. They were already upset with me for requesting a divorce months prior. Nothing I said made a difference.

Damien remains silent as he continues reading my file, his jaw clenching every few seconds.

"Why do you have so many marks for 'insufficient performance leading to husband's dissatisfaction'?" he asks. "What does that mean?"

I'm surprised he's asking about marks unrelated to the murder. I assumed my execution was all he cared about, but apparently, he intends to judge my performance as a whole before settling on a punishment.

"It can mean a couple of things, but I assume those marks were added whenever Henry was spotted with another woman."

My cheeks are hot, and Damien looks surprised.

His pupils dilate slightly. "*You'd* get in trouble when Henry was unfaithful?"

I nod. "If I were a better performer, he wouldn't have had to seek satisfaction outside of the marriage." I repeat the words that have been spoken to me hundreds of times.

Damien rolls his eyes, but he remains quiet. The room is tense as he continues to read over the papers. I wish he'd say what he's thinking, the unknown making me anxious.

"Are you going to have me executed?" My voice is noticeably shaky, my fear more apparent than I'd like it to be.

Damien lets out a long exhale before meeting my gaze.

"You're my mate, Aine." He looks mildly amused by my fear, and his anger at my forceful bond seems to be dissipating. "I'm not going to have you killed."

My chest deflates, relief softening my muscles. While I'm sure the punishment I receive will be painful, I'm ecstatic it won't be death.

"What *are* you going to do?" I ask.

Damien sets Vik's book on his desk. His movements are slow and calculated, which I hate.

"Absolutely nothing, my little mate."

I blink, disbelieving. "Why?"

Damien's face softens, the pity I hate to see thick in his expression. I glance at the floor, watching as his brown shoes appear in my peripheral vision. They stop directly in front of me, and his knees are quick to join as he crouches and puts his face in my direct line of sight.

"Why would I punish you for defending yourself?" he asks. "I'm not nearly as heartless as you think me to be."

He stands and knocks my knee with his fist. "Jenna has my blood. Go take some. You've marked me, and I don't want to feel your sunburn all day long."

Chapter 14

DAMIEN

I FOCUS ON the work laid out on my desk, uninterested in listening to Freya's angry ramblings.

"You let her mark you," she snaps. "We had a deal."

I can visualize Freya's exact position without even looking. She's standing with her right hip cocked, both hands resting on her waist. Her hair is probably also tucked behind both her ears, and in a few seconds, she'll start tapping her left foot against the ground.

Freya frowns as I look up at her, wanting to confirm.

I was right.

"What do you want?" I ask.

She gestures to my marked arm, and I hold back a smile as I glance at the new scar. Aine's got a bit of a fiery streak within her.

I quite like it.

I just wish I could've waited until she felt comfortable enough to tell me about her husband. All humans saved from execution are expected to confess to the crimes that led them there. Beasts may be strong, but there are humans and children here that need to be protected. I can't make exceptions just because Aine's my mate. Even if I want to.

Freya clears her throat when she realizes I'm not listening.

"We agreed I'd stay silent as long as you kept her from marking you," she repeats.

I tap my fingers against my desk, struggling to juggle the feelings of excitement from my beast and panic from my brain. Alex will never talk to me again if he knows what I let Freya do to me.

"What do you want?" I relent, desperate to know what else I can offer to keep her silent.

Freya's sudden return couldn't have come at a worse time, although I'm sure it wasn't a coincidence. She would've felt when my beast recognized his mate.

She hums as she mulls over my question. I drop my arms as I wait for her response, twitching as my mark brushes against my abdomen. Pleasure shoots down my spine at the contact, and I internally curse Aine for her positioning of it.

I'm going to have to wear really long gloves in battle.

"I want you to find me an alpha," Freya finally decides.

I shut my eyes, more than a little annoyed. "Alex is your mate. I won't do that to him."

Freya scoffs. "You will."

Given her track record, it'll be hard to find even a common beast to accept her, let alone anybody of high status. She's of low quality.

"It will be hard to find one who wants you," I admit.

Freya shrugs. "Okay. I'm more than happy to tell Alex that the mark he cried and begged me to give him was given to his brother instead." She glances at her nails in mock disinterest. "I wonder how Aine would feel to discover her mate was already taken by another."

Chapter 15

AINE

A QUIET GRUNT erupts from my throat as Damien takes another jab to the abdomen. I don't know if it's because I marked him, but I can feel every time he's hit. It's not ideal, and even though the pain is muted, I'm very quickly growing sick of it.

Damien's movements are quick and smooth, yet he visibly holds back and allows his men to strike him. That's not unusual, but he doesn't typically take as many hits as he is today.

I bet he's doing it to punish me.

My fingers tighten around a clump of weeds before I rip them out with a quick tug. I went to the hospital and had Jenna give me his blood as ordered, and it's got me feeling on top of the world.

Or, at least, it did until Damien decided to ruin my day.

The man he spars with falls with a dramatic shout, drawing my attention. Damien follows, and the pair roll on the ground before the man accepts defeat. Damien stands with a triumphant smirk, his eyes briefly flashing to me before he squares up with another beast.

I force myself to look away as Damien spins and provides me a clear view of his muscular back. Alex is standing near the garden shed chatting with Olivia, and I watch them instead. They seem to be having a heated conversation, and Alex's body is rigid as he listens to whatever she's saying.

Olivia moves to place a hand on his arm, but he jerks away before any contact is made. Her shoulders curl in at his rejection, making me wonder if something's going on between them that I don't know about.

They continue to argue before Olivia shakes her head and storms off. She doesn't look in my direction as she passes, but her downturned lips and teary eyes are obvious from the side.

My attention gradually shifts back to Damien.

He's still fighting, but he's moving too fast for me to get a clear picture. When he first joined the beasts in the training field, I was scared I'd feel the effects of his mark every time somebody brushed against it, but it hasn't been an issue.

Even when he's grabbed directly on top of it, there's nothing.

It must only be triggered when him or I touch it.

The man he's fighting dodges a series of punches before striking forward with a few of his own. Damien locks eyes with me as he sidesteps them, a smirk spreading across his face as he catches me watching him. The smile remains as he connects his fist with the man's jaw.

The beast stumbles, his hands moving to cover his face as Damien continues to hit him. I flinch, turned off by the amount of violence encouraged in this pack. It doesn't take long for the man to fall to the ground in a heap of uncoordinated limbs.

Damien turns away from his men and begins walking in my direction. Panic rushes through me, and I begin picking at the weeds to discourage him from coming over. My attempts appear to be in vain, though, as moments later, his shoes enter my line of sight.

"You're staring at me," Damien says. "It's quite distracting."

I pretend I can't hear him.

"My men are teasing me about your visual molestation," he continues.

Excuse me? My neck cracks as I snap my head up to glare at Damien. What the fuck is that supposed to mean? I was casually watching him, sure, but I was by no means 'visually molesting' anybody.

"I was not," I argue. "You were looking at me, too."

Damien's lip twitches as I straighten my back and narrow my eyes in an uncomfortable mixture of anger and embarrassment. My muscles are tight as I glance toward the training fields. A handful of beasts are outwardly staring, some even laughing.

"Of course I was." Damien crouches, his knees grazing the plants as he brings himself eye level with me. "Why wouldn't I stare at my mate?"

I purse my lips as I struggle to think of an intelligent response. I don't like how Damien always leaves our conversations with the upper hand, and if I weren't so afraid of him, I imagine he'd be fun to joke with.

He doesn't wait for a response as he grabs a handful of cherry tomatoes from my bucket. I scowl, my fingers twitching as I resist the urge to move it out of his arm's reach.

"We aren't supposed to eat directly from the garden," I say.

Damien tosses the tomatoes into his mouth and grabs two more. He looks almost proud of himself as he holds one out for me. I shake my head. Alex made it quite clear that all the food we collect is to be taken directly to the pantry for the cooks.

"Open your mouth, Aine," he teases.

I shake my head, rejecting his offer.

While I'm willing to admit Damien's being kinder, I'm not going to fall for it. Even attempting a friendship seems risky, and I worry he'll turn around and use it against me the moment it becomes convenient for him.

The sound of feet clomping into the ground draws my attention. A beast I haven't met approaches us with a red face, and he frantically whispers in Damien's ear. I try to eavesdrop, but he speaks too quietly for me to pick up on what he's saying.

Moments later, a dissociated panic courses through me. I've noticed Damien's emotions have been coming through more since I marked him, and I hope it's not a permanent change.

My bite must have strengthened our bond or something, making it harder for him to hide them from me.

Damien tilts his face so I can't read his lips as he whispers something back to the beast. The man nods before standing and turning to me.

"Good afternoon, Aine," he rushes to say. "I'm happy to see you have accepted Damien, and I hope to see you at dinner soon."

He disappears, and I turn to Damien.

"What did he say to you?" I ask. It seemed serious.

Damien licks his lips as he mulls over my question. It seems like he's considering telling me, but my budding excitement vanishes when he shrugs.

"Stand up," he orders, rising.

I do so with only minor hesitation.

Damien steps over the row of plants separating us, making me nervous. What's he doing?

He brings his face close to mine, his intentions to kiss me clear. I consider backing away or turning my head, but I remain stiffly in place as he cups my cheeks and presses his lips against mine.

I like it more than I should.

He moves his lips slightly to deepen our kiss, but I refuse to let it go any further than a peck. A part of me expects Damien to force it, but to my surprise, he takes the hint and pulls away.

"Why?" I ask.

Damien gulps, the feeling of panic reemerging. It's intense, and I fight the urge to plant a hand over my chest. What's he so afraid of?

"Why? Because this might be the only chance I ever have to kiss you," he admits.

What's that supposed to mean? Damien's warm breath fans across my cheek as he brings his mouth to my ear.

"Freya and Alex are causing a scene at the dining hall," he whispers. "I need to separate them."

I struggle to hold back a grin. If I'd known that allowing Damien to kiss me was all it took for him to talk, I would've done that ages ago.

Well, I probably wouldn't have, but it's nice to know now.

Damien runs into the woods, following the path leading to the dining hall. I'm hyper-aware that he's able to feel my emotions now, and I struggle to taper them down. I don't want him to think I'm excited because he kissed me.

I'm indifferent to Damien's sexual desires. At least, that's what I tell myself whenever he looks at me for too long.

Damien disappears into the forest. I can only imagine what Freya and Alex are arguing about, and I hope nothing too bad has been said. Alex has been trying so hard to avoid her recently, and I'm sure if they ran into one another, it was her purposeful doing.

I follow Damien. I'm sure he'll arrive long before me, but given his history of choosing Freya over his brother, I'd like to make sure somebody there has Alex's back.

A crowd is forming by the time I arrive, several beasts huddled together as they watch Freya and Alex argue. Their oversized bodies push against one another and create an impenetrable wall, but some take pity and step aside so I can wiggle my way to the front.

I do a double take when I get there.

Alex stands shirtless in front of a terrified-looking Olivia, his face red as he screams indistinguishable words at Freya.

Olivia stands directly behind him, her hands gripping his belt loop as she hides from the female beast. She appears to be wearing Alex's shirt, the long fabric falling to her knees and covering her frame like a sack. I look around for her clothing, quickly spotting them in the hand of a very angry Freya.

She waves the items as she screams, her fury only rising as Alex puts himself in front of the shaking human and yells back. They shout at the same time, making understanding their words impossible.

I try to make sense of what they're saying, and I raise a brow when Freya accuses Alex of cheating.

Alex laughs. "Would you rather I fuck your sister?"

My attention slides to Damien, and I feel only slightly satisfied as he clenches his jaw and glares at the sky. He looks about ready to melt as he shifts his weight from foot to foot.

I wonder what the point of him rushing over here was if he's just going to be a bystander and watch them argue.

"She's a whore!" Freya shouts, pointing to Olivia.

Alex lunges and grabs Freya by the throat.

The beasts surrounding me go silent at his violent outburst, their shock mirroring my own. These are actions I'd expect to see from Damien, but never in a thousand years did I think I'd see them come from Alex.

"Watch your fucking mouth," he threatens.

Alex's eyes darken as he grips Freya's throat and walks her backward until she bumps into Damien's chest.

Damien remains still as he's used as a wall, his hands clasped behind his back and head tilted toward the sky. Freya gasps and tries to pry Alex's hands off, her face going red as she scratches at his arms.

"You don't get to make demands of me after all you've done," Alex says, his body twitching as he fights back a shift. "I owe you nothing."

Olivia is shaking, and large tears drip down her cheeks as she turns toward the crowd. The beasts give her disgusted looks.

It's identical to the way people would look at me whenever Henry would have a public outburst. Despite my personal feelings for Olivia, my heart aches for her in this moment.

I push the rest of the way through the crowd. She may be mildly cold to me, but she doesn't deserve this harsh treatment.

Her body crumbles as I wrap my arms around her, and I grab the back of her head and tuck it into my neck to hide her from the prying eyes of the beasts. It's what my mother would do for me when things got especially bad, and it always made me feel safe.

I instinctively look toward Damien as all the attention falls on me. He seems surprised, undoubtedly having expected me to stay in the gardens after he left.

His lips purse before he shifts his body to the side and wraps his arms around both Freya and Alex. They hunch forward as he holds them in identical headlocks, their faces cast downward as they continue to scream at one another.

"We'll finish this in my office," he says before turning to me. "Will you take Olivia home?"

I nod. I was already planning to do so.

Damien begins forcing Freya and Alex toward his house. They both fight against his hold, but he doesn't let up.

"Let's go," I mumble, rubbing Olivia's back.

She flinches, her red-rimmed eyes meeting mine before she begins to move. I want to ask what happened, but I figure I already know. It doesn't take a genius to realize Freya must have walked in on an intimate moment between Olivia and Alex.

Despite Freya's reputation, the beasts glared at Olivia like she was in the wrong, which is surprising. It's ridiculous to expect Alex to remain abstinent after his mate cheated on and abandoned him.

Damien and the arguing pair are nowhere to be seen when we near the house, and I let out a sigh of relief as I lead Olivia inside. I was worried we'd run into them.

It's nice to know his long legs are good for something.

Olivia unsuccessfully tries to hold back her tears as I guide her upstairs and push open her bedroom door. I pause in the doorway, taken aback by the clutter, before lingering as she sits on her bed and drops her head into her hands.

"Are you okay?" I ask. It's a stupid question, but I'm not sure what else to say.

Olivia's chest expands as she sucks in a deep breath, and I fiddle with the ends of my hair as she clears her throat and shrugs.

"I'm fine. I brought it upon myself."

I shake my head, disagreeing completely. "I don't think there's anything wrong with you and Alex being together."

The fact that she and Damien had their moment in his office only a few weeks ago is a bit uncomfortable, but that's an issue for her and Alex to sort out themselves. I kicked my husband into a fire, so I'm not exactly in a place to judge.

"It doesn't matter, anyway." Olivia lets out a hollow laugh. "I'll be dead by the end of the month."

She lies back on her bed and stares at the ceiling like what she said wasn't a complete shock. What's that supposed to mean? I clear my throat, running her words through my mind. I must have heard her wrong.

"Why do you say that?" I ask, looking for clarification. Is she sick? She looks healthy.

Olivia turns in my direction, her eyes wet. "Damien's going

to a human village in a few days, and I know he's looking to replace me. You don't like me, and I haven't been performing as well as I should be." She pauses to peer out her bedroom window. "I'm not a mate, so if I'm no use to the beasts, there's no reason to keep me here. They'll make me leave, but no human village will accept me after spending so much time with the beasts. Either I become a prostitute, or I kill myself. It's an easy decision for me."

My brain struggles to process all that she's saying.

"You've been working for Damien for years." I'm pretty sure I heard Alex mention that once. "I've never spoken ill of you, and I doubt he'd replace you because of a few weeks of poor performance."

Olivia shakes her head and lets out a dry laugh. "He's taken all my work, and he hasn't given me a thing to do in days. I knew what I was getting myself into when I agreed to work for the beasts, but I did it anyway. I was stupid, and I dreamed I'd be a mate."

My throat is dry. While Olivia and I aren't exactly friends, the thought of her dying makes my blood run cold and my head throb. She doesn't deserve that.

"I'm sorry for what I did that day," Olivia whispers. I know she's talking about letting Damien touch her in front of me. "I was jealous when you came into the picture, and I took advantage of your poor relationship with Damien. We'd never been intimate before that day, and he's not shown interest in me since."

I don't know what to say. I appreciate the apology.

"If it counts for anything, I think Damien really does care about you. He's a lot less..." She cracks a smile before continuing. "*finicky* when you're around."

I snort. Finicky is a kind word to use to describe Damien.

"Is there anything I can do to help?" I ask.

Damien doesn't care much for my opinion, but I want Olivia to keep her job. She may not be my favorite person, but I can understand why she did what she did, and it means a lot to me that she apologized.

Olivia shakes her head and runs a hand through her hair.

"I think I'd like to be left alone, if you don't mind."

"Of course," I say.

I return to my room, and several minutes later I hear Damien walking up the stairs. I wait, struggling to build up some confidence, before approaching his bedroom door. I hesitate for a moment, debating whether this is a stupid idea, before tapping my knuckles against the wood.

It's pulled open immediately, and I gulp at the sight of Damien's shirtless chest only inches from my face. I hope he can't feel or sense my anxiety as I peer up at him.

There's a small smattering of blood along his jaw and ear, but I refuse to let myself be distracted by it.

"I heard you're going to a human village," I say.

Damien glances at Olivia's door, and I hope he isn't angry she told me. That's the literal opposite of what I want.

"Can I come?" I ask.

He can't find a replacement if I'm there to steer him away from every human woman he encounters. Plus, I'd genuinely like to visit another human village.

Damien's abs flex as he takes in my request, the muscles rippling underneath his skin. I force myself to focus on his face, knowing nothing good will come out of lusting for this man.

"Under normal circumstances, yes," Damien says. "But I have important business I need to attend to, so no."

I frown, shifting my weight from foot to foot. "Please?"

Damien's pupils expand as I beg. I'd be lying if I said the sight of his beast doesn't frighten me, but I refuse to back down even as he reaches out and cups my cheeks.

His hands are rough with callouses, but his touch is gentle enough that they don't irritate my skin. The pads of his thumbs rest on my cheekbones while his other fingers splay out across my temples and bury into the hair behind my head.

I resist the urge to pull away.

Damien seemed more inclined to do what I wanted after kissing me in the garden earlier today, and I hope he'll agree to bring me with him if I let him touch me now.

"I'll take you next time," he promises.

I shake my head, immediately refusing his offer. Olivia might already be gone by then.

"I'd really like to go this time," I say.

My face warms as I grab Damien's biceps. This used to work on Henry, and I hope it also works on Damien as I step back and drop to my knees.

Damien catches me before I touch the ground, his arms wrapping around my waist as he yanks me back to my feet.

"What the fuck are you doing?" he asks.

Despite the anger in his voice, I feel his arousal seeping into me through the bond. He wants me, and if giving myself to him is what's going to save Olivia's job, then that's what I'm going to do.

I press my hands against his chest. The muscles are hard underneath my palms, and I slide my fingers to the trail of hair leading into his pants.

"I want to go," I repeat. "Please, Damien."

Damien grabs my wrists and pulls my hands away. I gulp, unsure what else to do. I thought this would work. It always has before.

"I don't know what the fuck you're doing," Damien scoffs and steps back into his room, "but I'm not a fan."

He shuts the door in my face, thoroughly surprising me. I stare at the wood, my heart racing. Of all the ways I anticipated this going, Damien rejecting me was far down on the list.

Olivia's door creaks open, and her red and puffy eyes meet mine through the crack. I open my mouth to apologize, but she shakes her head to stop me. Then she disappears behind her door just as Damien did.

My heart constricts, and I can't help but think about all the times I was absolutely convinced Henry was going to take another wife and be rid of me.

I can't just stand by and let Damien do the same to Olivia.

I should be walking to the garden, but I find myself heading toward Damien's office instead.

He's been ignoring me for two whole days now, and I've made no progress on convincing him to bring me to the human village. I'm losing sleep over the issue, and it's only a matter of days before he leaves.

I'm running out of time.

My heart pounds as I push open the door to his office and sneak inside. Olivia's desk is empty, and I clench my hands into tight fists as I walk toward Damien's shut doors.

A small part of me hopes he's not here, but I'm pretty sure he is. If he's not at the training field, he's almost always here.

Ignoring the slight tremor of my hands, I knock on the door. I can barely hear my knuckles tapping against the surface, but I'm sure Damien can. He's got good hearing.

All the beasts do.

"Come in!" Damien's deep voice rings out.

I straighten my spine and square my shoulders as I push open the door. Whenever I've come here in the past, Damien barely pays me any attention, but this time, he watches my every movement. If I didn't know any better, I'd say he looks concerned, but I brush that thought away.

I take a seat in the chair opposite his desk and shove my hands under my thighs.

"Where's Olivia?" I ask, clearing my throat when my voice cracks. I hope he hasn't already fired her.

Damien leans back in his chair and crosses his arms over his chest, the relaxed, confident pose making me feel small.

"I'm not sure," he says. "I told her I don't need her coming in today."

"Why?"

"Because I don't need her today."

I tug at the hem of my shirt as I search for the right words. I doubt coming right out and asking Damien if he plans to fire Olivia is the best course of action, but I'm not smooth enough to get the answers I want without making my intentions known.

"Why are you here, Aine?" Damien asks, resting his elbows on his desk.

The action brings his body closer to mine.

"I don't want you to get rid of Olivia," I blurt out.

Damien blinks. "Okay?"

His answer isn't what I expect, and I'm opening my mouth and speaking before I can stop myself.

"I heard you're going to the human village to find a replacement, but I like Olivia and I don't want her to leave. Humans are good at a lot of things, and even if she isn't your assistant, I think you should let her stay," I say, rapid-fire. Damien says my name, but I can't seem to shut my mouth. "We're good at gardening and cooking and organizing and—"

Damien stands in the midst of my rambling and walks around

his desk. The action has my heart racing and words spewing out even faster than before.

"Aine!" His shout is startling enough that I snap my jaw shut. "I have no intentions of replacing Olivia."

Damien looks almost stressed as he runs a hand through his hair. "I'm setting Freya up with another alpha. We're meeting in the village."

I freeze as I process that information.

"Why?" My eyes narrow. "Does Alex know?"

Alex is annoyed Damien's even letting Freya stay here, and I doubt he'd be happy to discover they're traveling together to the human village so she can meet a new man.

Is that why he doesn't want to bring me? He doesn't want me around when he's spending time with Freya. My lips purse at the thought, and I force the irrational feelings of jealousy aside so he doesn't feel them. I don't care what Damien does.

Damien cocks his head to the side as he tries to read my sudden anger, but I don't offer any explanation. It's none of his business how I feel.

"No, Alex doesn't know," Damien admits. "I'd appreciate it if you didn't say anything to him, either."

He wants me to lie to Alex? I won't.

"Why are you going with her?" I ask. "Freya's capable. I'm sure she can meet the alpha by herself."

This is suspicious, especially considering he's going behind his brother's back to do so. I bet there's more to their relationship than they let on, and I wouldn't be entirely surprised to learn Freya and Damien have some secret affair they're trying to cover up.

I know she was with Damien at least once, and I bet there are more instances they're trying to keep hidden. Maybe they're still together.

I stand and step away as Damien closes the distance between

us, but he ignores my rejection and wraps his arm around my waist. I hate when he touches me, and I shriek and shove at his chest as he picks me up and sits me on his desk.

He doesn't hesitate to slot himself between my legs, his torso wide enough my inner thighs stretch to accommodate him.

"I was unaware how sensitive you are about our relationship," Damien says, clearly finding enjoyment in the minor jealousy I feel. "I'm faithful to you," he continues.

It's bold of him to think I care about what he does and with whom. I'm only upset because I think he's doing a shitty thing to Alex.

Damien tries to run his hands up my thighs, and I don't hesitate to push them away. He frowns but doesn't try to touch me again.

"I'd still like to go with you to the village," I say.

Damien wastes no time rejecting me. "No."

He refuses to look me in the eye, which only confirms my suspicions that he's doing something he knows he shouldn't. He's feeling guilty for a reason. Or maybe he just doesn't want anybody to know he has a human mate. Is he embarrassed of me?

Henry may have treated me like shit, but he was never shy to show me off.

"Why not?" I push.

Damien remains silent. He sinks his teeth into his bottom lip before dropping his hands on my knees, probably trying to distract me. It isn't going to work.

I wrap my hands around his forearms, intending to push him back, but I freeze when my palm lands on his mark.

I'm pressed firmly against the small scar, and the contact sends a wave of pleasure through us both. I make a pointed effort never to touch mine, and I forgot how good it feels.

Damien flexes his arm up against me, further pressing the

mark against my palm.

"Fuck," he moans, dropping his chin to his chest.

I suck in a shaky breath before deciding to take a risk and wrapping my fingers the rest of the way around his forearm.

It takes me a second to find my voice. "I want to go with you," I say.

Damien groans. "No."

I twist my palm over his mark, my thighs clenching around his waist.

"I want to go with you," I repeat, watching with wide eyes as his roll back. "Or I'll touch my mark every hour on the hour from the moment you leave until the moment you're back."

Damien's lips part, but he makes no sound as he drops his forehead against mine. I rub my palm roughly over his mark, desperately hoping it makes him as needy as it makes me.

It feels like every one of my nerve endings are firing off at once, and I fight the urge to roll my hips as I pull back and dig my fingernails into the scar.

"Aine," Damien pants, covering my hand to stop me. "I know you're bluffing."

His eyes are unfocused, and I take advantage of the distraction and press my fingers into my own mark. I immediately gasp, unable to remain silent as I arch into his chest. That feels better than I thought it would.

Damien moans as I give in and roll my hips, desperately seeking contact with his. He's quick to provide it, and he grabs my waist and pulls me forward so I'm pressed against his erection.

"Do you want to take that risk?" I ask, letting him replace my hand with his mouth.

I cry out as he licks my mark, and he grinds against me before pushing me flat against his desk. My mind flashes to the memory of Olivia and him together, but I force the thought away before I get upset.

Damien follows me down, his face buried in my neck as he continues licking my mark. He flattens his tongue over the sensitive spot, licking softly before stiffening the muscle and tracing the imprints his teeth left in me.

It feels so fucking good, and I wrap my arms around his waist so he can't pull away.

I know I'll regret my brazen actions later, but I can't bring myself to care as I slide my hands up his shirt. I've never touched the muscles in his back before, but I've always wanted to.

Damien looks me in the eye. His pupils are completely blown out, and it's satisfying. I bet Freya never made him feel this way.

"I'll do it," I insist. "Every hour on the hour. You won't be able to get a thing done."

Damien licks his bottom lip, his attention lingering on my panting chest before shifting to my flushed face.

"I suppose it's a risk I don't want to take," he admits.

His face is back in my neck before I have time to celebrate my victory, his teeth digging into my mark before he soothes it over with his tongue.

My thighs shake, and I wrap my legs around Damien's waist for a better angle. He seems to enjoy it as he begins to grind against me, his hard cock pressing perfectly against the seam of my pants.

I want to feel his bare flesh on mine, but as he sinks his teeth into my skin, I realize there's no time.

"Damien, I—" I choke out, my fingers digging into his sides as I both push and pull him away. His muscles flex as I tense underneath him, my body seizing as I come undone.

Damien continues rubbing against me, his movements frantic before he lets out a loud moan and stiffens. His teeth feel uncomfortable as he slides them out of my skin, my body sensitive to the pleasure that still erupts from my mark. Thankfully, it dissipates as he buries his face into a different part of my neck.

I worry he's going to make a snide remark like last time, but to my surprise, he kisses my sweaty skin and holds me silently.

"I can't believe I just came in my pants," he eventually whispers.

I ignore his statement. "So, I can come?" I ask instead.

He nods. "You humans are a sneaky breed."

Chapter 16

AINE

DAMIEN'S LOUD VOICE echoes up the stairwell and into my room, and I scramble to finish packing.

"Hurry up, Aine!" he shouts. "I'm leaving in five minutes, with or without you."

I groan. "I'm coming!"

As angry as I am that he's taking this trip with Freya, a small part of me is excited that I'm getting to visit a human village. Damien's angry about it, that's evident by how he's been ignoring me since I forced his hand, but I don't care.

He can be mad all he wants. His ego can stand a bit of bruising.

I don't regret what I did, and I find it comforting to know I can force things out of him with little to no repercussions. Henry would've beaten me bloody if I ever tried to manipulate him like I did with Damien. Or he would've chained me to our bed without food or water until he returned.

If he were in an especially bad mood, he would've done both.

Olivia shoves several of my belongings into the small travel bag Damien gave me to use, her smile growing as she watches my visible excitement. I asked her for advice on what to bring, but I didn't anticipate her getting so excited that she'd force her way into my room and pack the entirety of my bag herself.

She's been in a good mood since learning that Damien isn't trying to fire her, even if she's annoyed I won't tell her the true reason for the visit.

"Do you want me to pack you anything sexy?" she asks, peeking into my underwear drawer.

I choke on my spit. "No!" My eyes dart to the door, and I hope Damien isn't listening to our conversation.

Despite the attraction we both seem to feel for one another, I'll be damned if I start acting like a desperate female after our intimate moment. Everybody's been hushed about it, but I've heard the whispers. Damien's had more than his fair share of women in his bed.

I refuse to be another notch in his bedpost, even if I'm technically his mate. I expect several apologies and explanations before I'm even willing to consider it.

Olivia gives me a sideways glance, but she doesn't push the underwear issue. She grabs a few last items from my drawers and shoves them in my bag.

"All done!" she says, tossing it in my direction.

I fumble to catch it before giving a rushed thanks and running downstairs. Damien's threatening to leave without me, and I don't want to miss my opportunity.

I fear I've done just that when I head outside and realize he's nowhere to be found. My chin dimples, and my bottom lip wobbles as I scan the area.

He's already left.

I should've known this was too good to be true. My disappointment grows, and I deflate before spotting him walking out of the woods.

I hope he can't feel my relief.

I greet him with a smile, but he chooses to glower as I set my bag at his feet and wait for further direction. I know he doesn't want to bring me, and I'm pleased he hasn't gone back on his word.

He begins removing his clothing, and I feel my pulse quickening as his shirt is pulled over his head and shoved into his bag. I refrain from looking anywhere other than his face as he begins to repeat the action with his bottoms.

"What are you doing?" I ask.

Damien unzips his pants and lets them slide down his legs.

"How do you think we're getting there, Aine?" he asks. "I'm going to shift, and you're going to ride on my back like I'm a fucking horse."

Despite the angry words, he laughs as he says them.

I purse my lips, not having realized that was how we were going to travel. I've never ridden an animal before, let alone a beast, and I already know I'm going to embarrass myself.

There appears to be no riding contraption, and I spin in a circle, hoping I've overlooked it somewhere.

Damien sighs as he drops his underwear. "Why are you frightened?" he asks, acting as if his nudity is entirely normal. "You've seen me naked before."

It was only once, and I was too busy agonizing about the fact that I was covered in my own pee to pay much attention to him. I suppose I also saw him that night he and Alex fought about Freya, but I didn't look.

I shake my head and stare at the sky. If I look at him, I won't be able to stop my eyes from wandering, so I'm going to play it safe and stare upward until he shifts into his animal form.

"Where's your saddle?" I ask instead.

The sounds of his footfalls halt. "*What?*"

I clench my jaw. "Your saddle. So I can ride you?"

Damien grabs my chin and forces me to look at him. His nostrils flare as he glares down at me, and I rack my brain trying to understand what I've done to make him so angry. Is he upset I don't want to look at his naked body?

"It'll be a cold day in hell before I ever let you put a saddle on me," he says, his pupils expanding as his beast makes its anger known. "It's humiliating enough having to show up with a human riding my back."

His grip softens as my fear hits him through the bond.

"You'll lie on your belly and wrap your arms around my neck," he finally explains. "I'll do my best to remain steady as I run."

I nod, the movement stunted by his grip on my face.

Damien shuts his eyes and sucks in a deep breath. His anxiety is hitting me through the bond, the emotion muted but still there. I can't tell what's making him so nervous, and I wonder if it's because I'm joining him. He was adamant about not bringing me.

It's probably because he's afraid I'm going to tell Alex everything upon our return, which I fully intend to do. I wanted to tell him everything last night after Damien told me, but he was impossible to find. He's been keeping a low profile since the public run-in with Freya.

I asked the two women who help manage the garden if they've seen him, but they haven't. I even tried going to his home, but he didn't answer.

Damien finally releases me and steps back.

"Let me know if you grow tired and need to rest," he says.

I nod, averting my gaze as he begins to shift. It sounds unpleasant, and I wince every time a pop or crack makes its way to my ears.

The way the beasts shift is gruesome and, I assume, painful.

If I were a beast, I doubt I could ever bring myself to do it.

Soft fur brushes against my chest as Damien's beast rubs against me, and I take that as a sign he's finished. I haven't been this close to a beast since they attacked me in the woods, and my heart pounds as I eye the giant animal standing before me.

Damien easily reaches my chest on all fours, and he would tower over me if he stood on his hind legs. It's terrifying, and I tell myself he's not going to hurt me as I reach out and place a hand on his shoulder.

His coat is dark and long, and the fur shifts as the beast circles and sits at my feet. I assume that's his way of telling me to get on, and I suck in a shaky breath before attempting to slide my leg over his body.

The beast steps away with a whine before I get settled, its oversized head jerking to the left. I follow his gaze with flushed cheeks, slightly embarrassed as I spot all our bags still lying on the ground. I completely forgot about them.

I jog over and slip both over my shoulders.

"Shit!" I curse, jolting as I turn and realize Damien's directly behind me.

Despite his size, he moves quietly. His stealth makes me worry, but I try not to think about it as I climb on his back. As directed, I wrap both of my arms around his neck and clasp them together in the front.

His fur is surprisingly soft, and I bury my face in it to keep the wind away as he starts trotting through the forest. Damien gives me time to adjust before speeding up to a slow jog, and he eventually breaks into a full run once I get settled. He moves faster than I could ever imagine, his paws smacking against the ground at a rate I can't even follow with my eyes.

As promised, he keeps his movements steady, running in a mostly straight line and taking wide turns so I don't fly off the sides. I still squeeze his waist with my thighs, holding on for dear life.

After several minutes, I work up the courage to look up.

"Woah," I whisper. The trees are flying by. "This is so cool."

Damien grumbles and picks up the pace.

We run for what feels like hours, and I'm surprised by how much stamina Damien has. There's no way I could run this distance myself, let alone with an entire person on my back. My thighs gradually grow sore and my arms stiff, but I force myself to endure the pain.

I'm excited to get to the human village, and I inch up further when I spot smoke rising above trees.

Damien continues to run at his quick speed, only slowing when we're nearly to the smoke. He comes to a gradual stop before snorting and plopping onto his belly so I can get off. It takes me a few seconds to remember how to use my legs, and I tangle my fingers in his fur as I shake the jelly feeling out of them.

Damien remains deathly still as I use him for balance, not even moving with breath. I stumble while trying to get used to the feeling of walking, and I avoid looking in his direction as he shifts back into his human form.

The loud cracks and pops echo throughout the small field he's brought us to, and I stare in awe at the slivers of buildings visible through the trees. We're so close.

Damien speaks up. "I need my bag."

I turn without thinking, and I cough as I catch sight of his naked frame. Despite my best attempts to avert my gaze, my eyes immediately slide down his torso. He's so fucking muscular, and his cock hangs heavy between his thighs.

He's larger than Henry, even while soft.

Damien laughs when I aggressively look away and toss his bag in his general direction, the sound surprisingly quite pleasant.

He takes his sweet time getting dressed, and I bounce on my heels as I wait as patiently as I possibly can.

"Stop rushing me," he huffs.

I frown, debating arguing before deciding not to. That will only slow him down.

Despite being on the very outskirts of the village, I can already hear the bustling of life just beyond the trees. It reminds me of my old village, which is a painful realization.

I haven't been able to work up the courage to ask Damien what happened to it after my execution, but I know I need to.

Damien grabs my hand. His grip is tight, likely to prevent me from pulling away, and I hold back a snarky remark as he leads me in the direction of the smoke and buildings.

His skin is warm as his fingers entwine and wrap around mine, and I swallow past the lump in my throat as I realize I like it. I'm desperate for affection, but I know I'm going to regret this. It's only a matter of time before Damien lets his true colors show.

"This is a big village, and I don't want you getting lost," he says. "I feel I should warn you that the clothing style here is different, so try not to stare. If you see Freya, ignore her."

I'm not planning on engaging in conversation with Freya, so that will be easy to do. Everything about her makes me uncomfortable, and I personally think she's a horrible person.

I nod and walk ahead of Damien, hoping he'll pick up the hint and hurry his pace.

Damien snorts. "You're an impatient little human."

Nonetheless, he speeds up. It's hard to see through the trees, and as we pass the last one, I'm met with the back of a large, brick building. I assume there's a formal entrance that leads into the town, but I'm not too surprised Damien's taking us through the back.

It supports my theory that Damien is embarrassed of me. The

big bad beast is unable to come to terms with the fact he's mated to a human. If anything, it's *me* who should be embarrassed by *him*.

The beasts have hunted and murdered my people for centuries, yet here I am living with one who's claimed me as a mate.

Damien leads us around the side of the building and onto the main street, his grip on my hand tightening as we join the humans. It takes everything in me not to let my jaw drop as I look around. This place is enormous.

There are buildings as far as I can see, and hundreds of people bustle around with arms full of groceries and other random items. Several of them gawk at Damien as they pass, but none say anything or try to approach him.

Damien wasn't joking when he said the people here wore different clothing. While nobody's entirely naked, most of the men are wearing only thin bottoms and the women are in sheer dresses. I try not to stare, but it's hard.

Damien hardly seems to notice as he looks idly at the buildings that line either side of the road we walk down. We pass dozens of large shops with open doors, and I peer in each one to see what's inside. Most seem standard: grocers, dressmakers, and small specialty shops.

What's uncommon, though, is the building with naked women inside. All of them are in some sort of provocative pose, their legs and bodies spread in a way that leaves nothing to the imagination.

They giggle as we walk past, their eyes lingering on Damien.

I've never seen anything like it before, but I have suspicions.

"What's that?" I ask, tugging lightly on Damien's hand.

I don't want anybody to overhear and think I'm rude, but my curiosity overrides my need to be liked.

Damien turns to see what I'm referring to, his lips pursing as he catches sight of the unique shop. He looks annoyed, and instead of answering, he pulls me further down the street. It's frustrating.

"Well?" I pry.

Damien sighs, his shoulders slumping forward in the gesture I've come to learn means I won.

"That was a brothel," he says. I've never heard that term before. "Men can pay to have sex with those women."

Oh. My face warms, and I clear my throat as I turn to peer into the shop once more. I'm surprised it's so publicly located. Anybody can see who is entering and exiting.

Henry would've loved this place. He enjoyed humiliating me, and he especially enjoyed sleeping with other women.

"We don't have anything like that where I'm from," I admit.

Damien doesn't respond, his desire to change the subject quite clear. I'm surprised by how uncomfortable he looks with the topic, the beast usually more than happy to talk about sex.

I squeeze his hand as the pieces click together.

"How often do you frequent that place?" I ask.

Damien sucks on his teeth, pretending he didn't hear me as he continues dragging me down the street. I try to stop walking, but he pulls until I have no choice but to stumble behind him.

He guides us around the first corner and leads me up another identical street. There's a woman up ahead who wears the same attire as the ones in the brothel: nothing. She looks like me, shorter in stature with wide hazel eyes and brown hair. Her lips are pursed, and I can't help but notice how toned her muscles are.

Her eyes widen momentarily as she catches sight of Damien.

She glances at our joined hands before sliding her gaze up his body, a knowing smirk toying at the corners of her lips. Her dark hair sways around her waist as she glides past us, her body unnecessarily close to Damien's.

He stares ahead and pretends he doesn't see her, but I feel his hand stiffen around my own. Feelings of jealousy and annoyance flash through me at the sight of her, but I remind myself I don't care about who or what Damien does.

I'm indifferent. What he does doesn't concern me. If he wants to visit brothels to waste his time, money, energy, and dignity, that's his problem. He can be as dirty as he wants. I don't care.

I repeat that to myself.

Damien breaks the silence. "I'm not proud of my past."

I ignore him, happy with myself for how good I've gotten at doing that, but I can't seem to keep my face from warming as he ducks and presses his lips to my cheek.

"Where are we staying?" I ask, changing the subject to something that makes my heart pound less painfully in my chest.

Despite my anger, I'm still excited to explore and learn as much about these humans as I possibly can. This place is at least triple the size of the village I grew up in.

Damien lifts our conjoined hands and points to a large brownstone up ahead. It blends in with the other shops and honestly doesn't look like much, which I find surprising. I anticipated Damien would want to stay at the nicest place here.

"The walls are thick, and they do a good job blocking out the street noise," he says, answering my unspoken question. "Most beasts stay here when they visit."

I nod.

It must be hard to stay in such a crowded village when you can hear everything happening within a five-block radius. Despite how cool it would be to have some of the strength and senses the beasts possess, superior hearing is one thing I'm grateful to be lacking. I'm a notoriously light sleeper, and if I could hear even half as well as Damien, I doubt I'd ever get good rest.

"Is Freya staying here, too?" I ask.

Damien frowns, and as if fate herself has decided to intervene, Freya steps out of the building. She smirks when she spots us, and

I instinctively tense as she approaches.

"Damien," she says, shooting us a wide smile. "You brought your human!"

I'm not *his* human, but I keep my mouth shut.

Freya leans in to hug me, and I squish myself into Damien's side to keep her away. Damien smoothly wraps an arm around my waist and pivots to put himself between her and me.

I'm relieved.

He's the lesser of two evils here.

Freya steps back and examines us both from head to toe.

"It took you two long enough to get here. I've been waiting for hours." She looks around the street. "Who's the alpha you've arranged for me to meet?"

Damien's fingers slip under the hem of my shirt and rest against my side. I tense, but I don't want to push him away in front of Freya. The petty side of me wants her to see him so willingly touching me.

"His name's Owen," Damien says. "He's staying at the inn on the other side of the village. I figured you wouldn't want him seeing your…" Damien pauses as he searches for the right words, "extracurricular activities."

Freya seems pleased with that, if her wide smile is anything to go by. I take the opportunity to get a good look at her. She's wearing a modest dress that falls to her mid-calves, and despite it covering most of her body, it's impossible not to see her curves underneath. She's beautiful, the thought sending a shiver of jealousy down my spine.

I can see why Damien would be interested in her.

"Are you going to rid yourself of the human's scent before dinner?" Freya asks, turning to me.

The human has a name.

I imagine Damien must smell heavily of me after I spent all

morning riding on his back, and I stare at the side of his head as I wait to hear his response.

"I have no intentions of doing that," Damien says, thoroughly surprising me.

Freya snorts out a laugh, acting as if that's the most humorous thing she's ever heard. Do I really smell that bad? I've never been told I have an unpleasant odor before, but nobody's also ever gone out of their way to tell me I smell pleasant.

"I'm glad to see you two are getting along," Freya says, pushing away a strand of hair that falls over her eye. "I hope nothing comes in the way of that."

Damien grunts, not answering, before slipping his hand back into mine and leading me past Freya into the inn. His anger hits me through the bond in a sharp wave before disappearing altogether. Why has what she said made him so angry?

I'm desperate to know what's going on between them.

Damien's grip is firm as he leads me through the front doors. The lobby is small, but it's cozy with wooden furniture and lit candles. There's a front desk straight ahead, and a man stands behind it with a pen in hand.

He perks up when he notices us, his neck elongating and spine straightening.

"Alpha Damien!" he says, ignoring my presence. "It's been so long. I'll get you and your companion into the usual suite."

He bends to pull out a large book from underneath the desk, and I suck my cheeks into my mouth as I realize he's just mistaken me for a prostitute.

How often does Damien stay here with women? The mere thought makes my stomach churn.

Neither Damien nor I correct the man's incorrect assumption as he sets a heavy book on his desk and flips through the pages in search of an empty section to fill with Damien's information. Even if I wanted to correct him, I don't know what I'd say. How would I describe my relationship with Damien? The beasts call me his mate, but that term feels unnatural, and partner or husband feels wrong.

It's not as if Damien and I are in a romantic relationship, and the only time he seems to enjoy my company is when sexual touching is involved. My heart falls as I realize that, to some extent, I am nothing more than one of Damien's whores.

"And how long will you be staying for?" the innkeeper asks, peering up at Damien.

Damien clears his throat. "My mate and I will be here for three days," he says, giving my hand a squeeze. "And we'd like separate beds."

The man stills as Damien says the word "mate," and his face begins to redden a second later. He stares at me with a slack jaw, and I hope my discomfort isn't too evident as I give him a closed-mouth smile.

He continues to gawk at me, but he looks away when a quiet rumble begins to emerge from Damien's chest. I've never heard the sound before, but it seems to shock both the innkeeper and me.

The man drops his head and updates his book with the new information, his hand visibly shaking as he rushes to finish and hand Damien a key.

Damien's movements are too fast for me to follow as he snatches it up, and he places a hand on my waist once more before guiding me to the stairwell.

"We're on the fifth floor." He bends and wraps his arm around the back of my thigh, and I gasp as he lifts me off the ground. "I'll carry you."

I'm eye level with Damien for the first time, but I refuse to look at his face as he begins carrying me up the stairs. This is the most humiliating thing I've ever lived through, and I'm already beginning to regret coming here. It's been less than an hour and I've already encountered a prostitute Damien favors and have been mistaken of being one myself.

Damien is trying to get me to look at him, but I won't give him the satisfaction of seeing the tears building in my eyes.

I'm embarrassed of them, and it's none of his business.

"The beasts know you're my mate. It's only the humans who will be confused," Damien says.

I shrug, not wanting him to think I care.

Damien reaches the fifth floor and sets me on my feet. "I'll correct them whenever a mistake is made," he promises. "Word will spread, and everybody will soon know how to address you. You're my mate, and I won't let people think you're anything less than that."

I cross my arms over my chest. "It doesn't matter to me either way."

Damien unlocks the door to our room, and I step inside.

The room is small, but I don't mind. I make my way to the bed farthest from the door and set down my bag. Damien watches from the entrance, thankfully taking the hint that I want him to stop speaking.

After several seconds he steps inside the room and sets his bag on the other bed.

"Will you accompany me to dinner tonight?" he asks after a moment of tense silence. "Freya and Owen will be there, and I'd like to formally introduce you as my mate."

I already assumed I'd be joining him, but I guess I appreciate the invitation. Still, I'm too annoyed to let that show.

"I don't enjoy your formal introductions," I say. I'll never forget the way he treated me during my first few days in his pack. I was abandoned in that damned cabin, and Damien made me out to be a giant inconvenience.

When he finally brought me to the dining hall, he did so when he knew his people wouldn't be present. He was embarrassed of me, and it was degrading.

Damien runs a hand down the front of his face, but to my surprise, he doesn't argue back.

"I'm sorry," he says. "It won't be like that tonight."

There's a long moment of silence, and only when I can't take it any longer do I speak.

"I'll join you," I say.

Damien smiles, and I turn away before I do the same.

We have some time to kill before dinner, and I rip open my bag in search of feminine products. The cramps began on the way here, and I'd like to get my menstrual cup in before Damien smells my monthly bleed.

The object is nowhere to be seen, though, and I try not to appear too frantic as I mentally curse myself for letting Olivia pack my bag. I can't be mad at her for not thinking of packing my cup, and it was foolish not to double-check before leaving.

I knew my bleed was going to be starting soon.

Damien stares at me, his eyes boring holes into the sides of my head.

"What's wrong?" he finally asks. "I can feel your panic, and it's making me anxious. Is this about dinner? I promise it's not going to be like before."

I don't respond. I'd rather seem rude than tell Damien I don't have my menstrual cup. I shove aside a handful of clothing and scan the black fabric on the bottom of my bag. It's definitely not in here.

I shut my eyes and count to ten before turning toward Damien.

"I need money," I say.

Damien blinks. "Why?"

I glance between him and my bag, not sure what to say. My

monthly bleeding is something I've been raised to believe should be handled in private, and I'd rather not see the disgust I know will cross Damien's face when I tell him what's happening.

"Did Olivia forget to pack you something?" Damien glances at the bag I've spent the past five minutes frantically searching through. "I'm happy to buy you anything you need."

He's not going to give me money without an explanation. I'd rather die than provide one, but I have no choice. He'll smell my bleed soon enough.

"I need to purchase feminine products," I admit.

Damien, like the absolute monster he is, sniffs the air. Why the fuck does he have to be like that? Can't I just live in peaceful shame?

"You're not bleeding," he says.

He sounds genuinely confused, and I pinch the bridge of my nose to keep from lashing out. He doesn't have experience with this.

"It's going to begin soon, and I forgot to pack my cup," I quietly admit.

Damien frowns. "I'll purchase one for you, then." He stands and moves toward the door. "Stay here."

My jaw falls open in horror, but Damien's gone before I can insist he let me go alone. I stare at the door for a second before lunging forward and sprinting into the hallway, but it's already empty.

This is arguably one of the most embarrassing things to ever happen to me, and I sulk back inside the room and lock myself in the bathroom, fully intending to hide until Damien returns.

It's all I can think to do.

I sit on the toilet seat and drop my head into my hands. Damien probably doesn't even know what to buy, and I'm not confident he's going to get the right items. I stare at my reflection in the mirror as I wait, my feet tapping anxiously against the floor.

After what feels like forever, the bedroom door creaks open. I remain where I am, stiff as a board as knuckles tap against the bathroom door.

"Aine?" Damien calls out. "I have your cup."

I wish the beasts had killed me all those weeks ago. That would've been significantly less painful than this.

I drag my feet along the floor and crack open the door. Damien holds the cup in the air, and I hide behind the wood as I snatch it from his hand. Then I slam the door shut in his face for good measure.

"There were two sizes, and I purchased the smaller one," Damien says through the door. "I'm unsure if the size correlates to vagina or blood, but your hole is small and you have light bleeds, so I figured this was the better option."

I lean against the closed door and stare in horror at the cup Damien bought me. Men aren't supposed to know, let alone talk about, these private issues. It's like Damien's trying to humiliate me.

My stomach cramps as I give the cup a quick clean, and I curl in on myself until the cramp settles into a tolerable pressure.

I'm scared Damien's listening to what I'm doing in here, so I leave the water running as I fold the cup in half and stick it inside myself. It's stiff, but after some careful maneuvering, the cup suctions in place.

Damien is sitting on his bed when I finally work up the courage to leave the bathroom, an almost-wary look on his face as he watches my every movement.

"Thank you for going to the store for me," I whisper.

It's uncommon for him to go out of his way to help me, and I'm grateful he hasn't shamed me for my bleed. I anticipated Damien to be the type of man to express extreme disgust and disregard for female issues.

He nods as I sit on the edge of my mattress. I'm glad he got us a room with two beds, even if they're only inches apart. I could probably reach out and touch him from the center of mine.

The mental image of Damien trying to fit on such a small mattress brings a tiny smile to my face, but I'm quick to replace the expression with a neutral one. His body's going to be hanging off every edge of the bed, and I can't wait to see it.

"There's something I'd like to speak with you about," Damien says.

That's suspicious.

"Yes?"

Damien sighs before continuing. "Alpha Owen is rumored to be a particular man, and I think it would be best if we remained silent about Freya's history. I'd like for us to paint her in a good light tonight."

I resist the urge to roll my eyes. I'm angry with Damien's desperation to help Freya, and I begin to lash out before I can stop myself.

"So, no telling Alpha Owen that she fucked you while mated to your twin brother?" I ask.

Damien recoils. "It wasn't like that."

He sounds angry, but I'm not dumb. I know what Alex meant when he said she warmed his bed.

"Oh, so your dick hasn't been inside her?" I ask.

Damien's quick to his feet, and I match the action and stand just the same. I can tell his beast is pushing to be released, his pupils dilating and claws extending. The visible outrage is terrifying, and I immediately wish to take the words back. I don't know what Damien's capable of, and I'm not sure I want to find out.

"I was drunk," Damien says. "Too drunk to understand what

Freya was doing and stop her. Family is everything to me, and I would never willingly have sex with her."

Oh.

Damien stalks toward me, backing me up against my bed.

I sit.

"She raped you?" I whisper.

My question only seems to further enrage Damien. "I'm an alpha," he spits out. "I was not *raped*, and you should refrain from saying such stupid things."

His face is flushed, and I feel guilty for pushing. It took me years to come to terms with and accept that what Henry was doing to me was wrong, and I'm sure it's even harder for Damien.

A renewed hatred for Freya fills me with the knowledge of what she did to Damien. If I were a beast, I'd rip her head clean off her body.

"I don't think it's right to lie to that man about Freya," I say. "He deserves to know the truth."

Damien continues to glare at me as he runs a hand through his hair. He takes a step back and collapses on his bed, the frame creaking underneath his weight. I'm afraid it's going to break.

Damien doesn't appear to share the same fear, though, as he lies back on the mattress and throws an arm over his face.

"I'm aware it's not ideal," he says, "but it needs to be done."

"Why?" I ask. "I don't understand why you're helping her."

If it weren't for Damien's chest moving with each breath, I'd worry I'm looking at a corpse.

He clears his throat. "I'm not going to discuss that with you."

Chapter 17

AINE

I HOPE I don't look too stiff as I walk between Damien and Freya, and I press my side firmly against Damien's in a sad attempt to keep distance between me and the beast woman.

Freya was on us the second we left the inn, and I'm half convinced she was lingering outside waiting for us. Damien didn't so much as look at her when she approached, but he did slip his hand in mine.

I'm not sure how I feel about it.

Freya chats animatedly to Damien over my head, her tone chipper. I don't know what to make of the information he shared, and my hatred toward her only grows now that I know she took advantage of Damien.

He may be a dick, but nobody deserves what she did to him. Even if he doesn't want to call it rape, that's exactly what it was. Drunk people can't consent.

Damien squeezes my hand as we approach the restaurant doors, and I find myself holding my breath as he pushes them open and leads us inside.

The place is already quiet when we enter, but the slight chatter diminishes even further as the humans take notice of the two giant beasts present. My palms grow sweaty as Damien leads us to the back, and I can't help but notice the way the human women are looking at me with upturned noses and pursed lips.

It's clear they don't like me, but I can't tell if it's because they don't like the beasts or if it's because they're jealous of me. Given the fact Damien's already slept with several of the human females here, I doubt it's because they don't like the beasts.

A man sitting at a table along the back wall stands as we approach, his tall frame and confident posture immediately giving him away to be a beast. He's handsome, they always are, and he wears a well fitted suit. People in my old village never dressed so formally, and neither do the people in Damien's.

"Good evening, Owen," Damien says, guiding me to stand in front of him. "This is my mate, Aine." He slides his hands over my shoulders and down my arms, his touch lingering. I resist the urge to shiver. "And this is Freya," Damien continues, gesturing toward Freya.

Owen licks his lips, his eyes lingering on me before he shifts his attention to Freya. He looks excited to see her, which I think is annoying. Freya doesn't deserve a kind man.

She deserves to be kicked in the throat.

She giggles as Owen takes her hand, and she absolutely beams as he kisses the back of her palm and pulls out the seat next to his.

"Sit," he says.

I watch their every interaction through narrowed eyes, and I only turn away when Damien pulls out a chair for me. I'm annoyed, and I ignore Damien's warning look as I sit with a loud *thump*.

"We appreciate you traveling all this way to meet with us," Damien says, sitting and placing a hand on my knee.

The sudden contact makes me jolt, but it's subtle enough not to draw attention. I'll never forget the time Damien called me desperate for getting aroused when he sat me on his lap during dinner, and I suck my cheeks into my mouth to stop something similar from happening now.

Damien slides his hand up my thigh, and I reach down and push him away. He relents, dropping his hand to my knee. I'd appreciate him releasing me altogether, but I doubt that'll happen.

Alpha Owen shrugs. "You know I couldn't turn down such an enticing invitation."

He scans the perimeter of the room. The chatter amongst the humans resumes as we settle at our table, but it never reaches the volume it was at before we arrived.

I wonder what it must feel like to be the strongest person in the room. To know your safety is an absolute guarantee.

"I didn't know you had a mate," Alpha Owen says, turning his attention to me. "When did Damien find you?"

I don't love his word choice, but I plaster a smile on my face anyway. I'm not trying to get on the bad side of another beast. I'd like to think Damien would protect me if I was in trouble, but I can't rely on that.

"A few months ago," I say.

Damien chimes in when it becomes apparent I have nothing further to add. "It was a large adjustment on both our ends, but we've settled into it nicely."

He tightens his grip on my knee. I'm scared he's going to squeeze the bone in punishment for not being friendly enough, but I relax when I realize he's simply adjusting.

My cheeks redden as Damien turns to me with a frown, probably wondering where my sudden fear is stemming from. I ignore him.

"Interesting." Alpha Owen chuckles to himself. "I'm both surprised and relieved to see you settling down, Damien."

I would by no means refer to Damien as "settled down," and I'm surprised that's the vibe Owen's getting from him. It makes me wonder what the old Damien was like. I haven't seen much, if any, of a change in him, but I admittedly haven't been paying attention.

I've spent the past several weeks avoiding Damien as much as I possibly can.

Damien clears his throat, looking mildly uncomfortable with the topic. I'm sure he doesn't want me hearing about his long history with the village sex workers.

Alpha Owen turns toward Freya. "How do you and Damien know one another?"

Freya smiles, but it's sad. "Damien *was* my mate's cousin. We've remained close since my mate passed away several years ago."

The lie rolls smoothly off her tongue, and I resist the urge to scream when Alpha Owen places his hand on hers. I don't approve of the way Damien and Freya are tricking this man. It's not right.

"My mate has passed as well, and I find a lot of peace in remaining close to her family," Alpha Owen says.

I turn to Damien, silently begging him to call this whole charade off. Alpha Owen is a lovely man who's clearly been through a lot. He doesn't deserve this.

Damien pretends not to notice me as he calls a waiter over, and he continues ignoring my angry stare as he orders food for the table.

I don't know how our marks convey emotions, but I try to force all my negative ones into Damien's head. I want him to feel how pissed and disappointed I am in him.

Freya and Owen happily fill the silence until our waiter returns with a bottle of white wine for the table.

Damien immediately plucks the bottle and pours me a large

glass. He smiles as he hands it over, his fingers grazing mine. He's probably hoping the wine will keep me docile.

He's stupid.

He returns his hand to my upper thigh, and I hate the way my pulse races at the touch.

I know he's playing me, but no amount of reminding myself of that is helping to stop the shameful desire I hold for him. Henry always said all he needed to do was fuck a woman to lose interest, and maybe if I have sex with Damien, these childish feelings will disappear.

I doubt it, though. I know myself, and if I give myself to Damien, I'll only be further ensnared in his trap. Henry was exceptionally skilled at holding back emotions, and I don't have it within me to treat sex the same way he did.

Still, I wonder what sex with Damien would be like. He's quite large, and it would probably be painful if he wasn't gentle. Henry was half the size of him, and even he hurt to take when he was too rough.

I slide my gaze to Damien's hand, recalling how good it felt when he used his fingers. He was gentle then, giving me time to adjust as he sunk them into me.

If he could do the same with his cock, I bet it'd feel amazing.

Damien tightens his grip on my thigh, his fingers sliding upward, and I snatch my glass of the table and gulp down the contents.

I can see out of the corner of my eye that Damien's staring at me, and I bet he can either feel or smell the unwanted arousal that's spreading through me like fire. I hope Freya and Alpha Owen can't sense it.

My pulse races as I finish my wine, and Damien makes polite conversation with Alpha Owen as he refills my glass. I'm surprised he's able to keep tabs on me while actively engaging in a completely different task.

The three beasts continue to chat and laugh amongst themselves while I sit silently and observe. Damien and Alpha Owen will occasionally go out of their way to include me, but the conversation naturally drifts back to the three of them rather quickly.

I'd usually take offense to being excluded, but I'm glad not to partake during this particular meal. I don't agree with what we're doing to Alpha Owen, and Damien's fingers sliding up and down my inner thigh are painfully distracting.

I should push him away, I know I should, but I can't bring myself to do it.

Damien doesn't refill my drink once I finish my third one, and when I reach for the bottle myself, he slyly moves it out of my reach. I'm offended, but I realize it was probably the right call.

Damien doesn't know this, but I'm known to have loose lips after a couple of drinks.

"Excuse me," I say, brushing Damien's hand off my thigh so I can stand.

His head snaps in my direction, but his pinched expression softens as I gesture toward the bathroom. Damien nods and returns to the conversation.

My steps are a bit unsteady as I escape to the toilets, but I make it there without embarrassing myself. Other than the occasional glass here and there, I haven't had any alcohol since arriving at Damien's pack.

My tolerance has taken a hit in that time.

I drop my head into my hands as I use the bathroom, sighing as I let myself truly relax for the first time since getting to this village. That relaxation is short-lived as the sound of Freya's laughter echoes throughout the room.

I peer through the crack of the stall to see Freya lingering near the sink. Did she follow me in here?

Her gaze locks with mine as I finish peeing and push open the stall door. She seems calm as she leans against the sink, her face and posture relaxed.

"What do you think of Owen?" she asks.

I shrug, already knowing this is some sort of trap. "He seems nice."

Freya nods, seemingly happy with my answer. "I agree, and cute too." Her voice rises as a look of excitement spreads across her face. "Would you fuck him?"

I blink, taken aback by her bold question. "What?" I ask, hoping I misheard.

Freya spins to look at herself in the mirror. "If you weren't mated to Damien, would you want to fuck Owen?"

I remain silent, unsure what she's looking for me to say. Alpha Owen's handsome, all the beasts are, but I don't want to fuck him. My interest in beasts is little to none.

"Don't be so shy, Aine," Freya says. "Men never listen to bathroom noises. It's taboo in our culture." She stares at me through the mirror's reflection. "Besides, I'm sure you've heard by now how much Damien loves to share his women. I bet he'd be happy to pass you around with Owen. I'd be willing to share if you are."

I most certainly am not. Is she looking for me to offer up Damien on a silver platter or something?

"I see," I say, hoping she'll lose interest in speaking to me if I keep my answers short.

Unfortunately, Freya doesn't seem to mind at all, and she continues talking before she's even had the chance to take a breath. She must have lungs of steel to talk for so long without pause. She doesn't even seem winded. I'd be impressed if I didn't hate her so much.

"Although Damien did stop sleeping around after I marked him," Freya says, capturing my attention. "The poor guy was so scared of it."

Freya *marked* Damien? I'm sure I would've heard of that by now if it were true.

"He didn't tell you?" Freya asks, wiping away the smudges of her makeup. "It was my mark he wore up until you overrode it with your own." She meets my gaze through the mirror's reflection. "He pretends to hate that I put it on him, but I could feel every time he rubbed it to get off."

Freya pushes off the sink with a laugh before turning and leaving the bathroom in a flurry. I remain where I am, struggling to process all that information. I'm not dumb, and I know her telling me this was intentional. I just don't understand what she hopes to get out of it.

Damien's reluctance to call what she did rape makes me wonder how the other beasts see it. It might be a cultural thing to believe an alpha male can't be taken advantage of, and maybe she's hoping I'll get angry and fight with Damien about it.

It wouldn't surprise me. Freya clearly loves stirring up trouble.

My hands shake as I push my hair out of my flushed face. Freya's probably hoping I come bursting out of the bathroom and make a scene, but she won't get that satisfaction tonight.

Damien is watching the bathroom door when I finally work up the courage to leave, and his eyebrows pull together when I give him a tense smile and slide into my chair. He returns his hand to my thigh, and I meet Freya's waiting gaze.

Her excitement visibly drops as she realizes I'm not going to be saying anything, but she's quick to plaster a smile on her face and strike up another conversation with Alpha Owen. The rest of the meal is awkward, at least on my end.

Did Damien hear what Freya told me? She said beasts don't eavesdrop on bathrooms, but Damien seems especially nosy.

When the server finally comes with the check, I'm beyond relieved. Freya and Owen make plans for her to stay the night with him, their hands touching as she eagerly shares that she'll run back to pack a bag before meeting him.

The second the meal is paid for, I grab Damien and pull him to his feet. He gives me a sideways glance, but he doesn't make a fuss as I tug him toward the exit.

My heart is pounding, and I keep a quick pace as I drag Damien down the street. He wraps an arm around my waist, easily matching my speed.

If anything, he's probably happy with the faster movements. When beasts aren't walking alongside humans, they walk fast. Humans slow them down.

"Did you enjoy your food?" Damien asks.

We reach the inn, and he pushes open the doors for me.

Freya runs ahead to pack her bag. She's sure eager to share a bed with Alpha Owen tonight, and I glare at her retreating form before turning toward Damien.

"Dinner was good," I say.

I think the food back at his pack is better, but I'm not going to admit to that. It's a compliment, and I don't want to compliment Damien. He doesn't deserve it.

He leads me inside, his hand resting on the small of my waist.

It's obvious he can sense something's on my mind, but he doesn't ask what it is. I'm relieved. I don't feel comfortable telling him that Freya shared his private information with me.

A small, petty part of me wants to bring it up so he feels the way I did when he sent his men to collect Vik's book and learn my secrets, but I don't. That would be too cruel, and I don't have it in me.

"Did your cup hold up all right?" Damien asks.

We reach the stairs, and I choke as he picks me up. My hands instinctively rest against his chest as he carries me up the five flights.

"Did it?" Damien repeats when I don't answer.

I'm going to kill him. Why does he even care?

He grins when I grudgingly nod, seeming almost proud at the knowledge that my cup has worked. That haughty expression doesn't lessen as he reaches the fifth floor and sets me on the ground, and I cross my arms over my chest as he unlocks the door to our room.

"Then why are you so upset?" he asks. "What did Freya say to you?"

So, he didn't eavesdrop? My brain short-circuits as I try to think of an excuse. I suppose I appreciate Damien waiting until we're alone before asking, and I mentally curse myself for not taking that time to come up with a good lie.

Damien sighs and brushes past me. "I'm trying to be a good mate and make up for the mistakes I made when we first met, but it's hard when you refuse to open up."

It's clear he's upset by my silence, and he shakes his head as he begins to search through his bag.

"Would you like to shower first?" he asks.

I nod. "Yes."

Damien might be a little upset about me not sharing my secrets, but I know he'd be even angrier if I told him what Freya said to me. If he wants me to know, he'll tell me himself.

I grab the pajamas Olivia lent me and hurry into the bathroom. The clothing is lightweight, but I'll survive being cold for a night or two. If it gets too unbearable, I think I could get Damien to loan me one of his shirts.

The shower's tiny, and I can't help but wonder how Damien

is going to fit in here. He'll physically be able to enter, but there's absolutely no way the water will be able to reach anywhere above his chest.

Goosebumps spread along my arms as I slip out of my clothes, and I let out a relieved sigh as I drop my pants and remove the pressure from my waist. My pants usually fit comfortably, but my bloating has them digging painfully into my skin.

I take my time showering before returning to the bedroom.

Damien's lying on his bed when I finally emerge, the clothing he plans to change into resting on his chest. His head lolls to the side as I climb in my bed and slip underneath the sheets. My cramps, which I was able to ignore at dinner, are slowly making a vengeful comeback, and I curl into a ball as Damien leaves for the bathroom.

I struggle to keep my breaths steady as he turns on the shower. He's shown an odd interest in my reproductive system today, so I do my best to avoid showing any physical signs of pain. I don't need him asking dozens of personal questions about how my body works.

Damien showers in under five minutes, and I listen to the quiet sounds of him shuffling as I try to fall asleep. He's visibly damp when he finally comes strolling out of the bathroom, and I gulp as I realize he's only wearing underwear.

His muscles flex with every movement, and I stare until he turns off the room's light. I don't like not being able to see what he's doing, and I roll onto my stomach as I listen to him walking around the room.

There's a quiet rustling as he messes with his bag, and it's not until I feel my own bed dip that I realize something is amiss.

I flail my arms and attempt to roll over, but Damien places his palms on my back and pins me to the mattress.

"It's okay, Aine," he says. "I'm going to relieve some of the pressure in your hips. I could feel your pain while I was showering."

He runs his hand down my spine before taking a seat on my butt. I grunt, shocked by his weight, and Damien lifts slightly so I'm not being crushed.

"I've got you," he whispers, pressing his palms into my lower back and digging his thumbs into the tight muscle.

I relax as I realize what he's doing actually feels good, and he continues to massage my muscles until I fall limp. My lower back *does* ache, and this feels amazing.

"Can I lift your shirt?" he asks.

I hum, debating, before giving a jerky nod. I'd let him do anything if it meant he keeps massaging me.

Damien lifts my shirt, making room for him to lay his bare palms flat against my back.

"My dad used to do this for my mom when I was a child," he says, digging his thumbs into the tail end of my spine. "It always made her feel better."

I gulp, not wanting Damien to know how interested I am in hearing about his family. Neither Damien nor Alex have ever mentioned their parents, and I'm honestly surprised he's bringing it up. Given Damien's bad attitude, I assumed his parents were cruel and unloving people. His statement makes me think otherwise, though.

The bedsheets shift as Damien readjusts himself and lifts my shirt higher up my back. I remain relaxed.

My mind races as I try to make sense of his actions, unsure how I feel about Damien's new attitude toward me. One minute I look at him and see the man who forcibly marked me, and other times, I see the man who let me drug him simply so I could have a good night's rest.

"What happened to your parents?" I eventually give in and

ask. I hope he's in a talkative mood.

Damien tucks his fingers into the waistband of my shorts and pulls them down, giving him better access to my lower spine.

"They're dead," he says. "My sister, Jess, fell into a river when she was a toddler. My mom jumped in to get her out, but the current was strong and killed them both. My dad died shortly after I was titled alpha." Damien clears his throat before continuing. "It's not uncommon for a beast to die after their mate passes."

I press my palms into the mattress and try to sit up, but Damien pushes me back down.

"I'm not done," he pouts.

I huff, but I don't try to sit up again.

"I'm sorry to hear that," I say. I can't imagine how hard that must've been. "How old were you?"

Damien trails his fingers up my spine, borderline playing with the notches. "My mom and sister died when I was ten, and I became alpha at sixteen. Children normally wait until they're in their twenties to take over, but my dad was struggling without my mom, so I agreed to step in earlier," he says. "He died a few months later."

He begins massaging to the center of my back. My eyelids flutter shut as I allow myself to enjoy the sensations. Nobody's ever done this for me before.

Damien shifts again before pressing a light kiss to my cheek. His affection is unusual, and I turn to look at him. It's hard to make out his face in the dark, but we both know I'm able to see as he leans in again and presses his lips to mine.

I know I shouldn't, but I crane my neck so more of our mouths touch. Damien keeps the kiss short before sitting back up and returning to his massage.

"Go to sleep, Aine. I'll be here."

I wish him saying that wasn't as comforting as it is.

Chapter 18

DAMIEN

OWEN LOOKS ANGRY as I approach, his fingers tapping impatiently against the table.

"You lied to me," he snaps.

I raise an eyebrow, surprised by his lousy attitude. He seemed quite happy last night when he invited Freya to stay in his room. I sit across from him, glancing around the small restaurant. It smells good, and I'll bring Aine here for breakfast before taking her to the park.

"What'd she do?" I ask.

When we set this meeting up last night, I assumed the topic of conversation would be much cheerier. I should've figured Freya's self-sabotage would ruin this, but I wanted to remain optimistic.

Owen snorts. "What *didn't* she do? You promised me a respectable young woman with good virtues. This one dropped to her knees before I'd even closed the door to my room."

I can tell he feels passionate about Freya's promiscuity, but I'm unable to hold back the laugh that erupts from me. Is he genuinely upset she wanted to suck his cock? Before I met Aine, I was delighted when women were so eager for me.

My chest aches at the thought, and my beast fights to push free until I assure him that Aine's the only woman whose mouth I want.

He already knows this, though. He can feel how much I want my short, angry human, but he's gotten into the habit of forcing me to actively think it. I don't mind it as much as I once did.

"And you stopped her?" I tease Owen, knowing damn well he allowed Freya to please him before expressing dislike toward her actions.

Owen's pupils dilate at my laughter, his beast emerging in response to my disrespect. I pay it no mind. He may be an alpha, but he's no match against me.

We both know this, and I find satisfaction in watching him force his beast to calm.

I sigh, tapping my fingers against the table. I was hoping to keep this friendly, but I can already tell Owen's not going to make this easy for me.

"You'll take her, and you won't complain about it," I order.

It's clear Owen's not going to willingly change his mind, and I promised Aine I wouldn't be gone for long this morning.

I smile at the memory of her relaxing beneath me last night. She fell asleep so quickly, and as I ran my hands over her warm skin, I decided this situation with Freya ends here. She will not be returning to my lands, and that means either Owen takes her or she gets left in a ditch.

Aine's finally starting to trust me, and I'll be damned if I let my brother's shitty mate ruin that.

Owen stands, his chair flying behind him and clattering against the far wall. His reaction's a bit dramatic for me, and I ignore it as I examine the food the humans are making. *Fuck.* It smells so damn good.

"You're not invincible anymore, Damien," Owen spits. "You

have a vulnerable human as a mate, and you'd do well to remember that—"

My hands are around his neck before the words are entirely out of his mouth. Owen laughs and tries to pull away, but he freezes as he realizes my claws are fully extended. One wrong move and his body and throat will be on opposite sides of the room.

"What do you mean by that?" I ask.

I tighten my grip, only slightly satisfied as Owen audibly struggles to breathe. He tries to pry my hand away, but no amount of pulling is going to make me let go.

The humans scatter as they take notice of us, their fear intoxicating as it fills the small space. Even the workers run to the back to hide, their pounding heartbeats loud as they shove their bodies underneath shelves and cabinets.

"Tell me what you mean," I repeat.

Owen tries to claw at my face, but I use my free hand to snap his wrist. It breaks with a wet pop.

"Let me make this clear," I say. "You're going to take Freya as your mate, and you'll bring her back to your dirty little pack to rule as female alpha. You'll give her babies and whatever the fuck else she wants, and you'll do it with a smile. I don't want her, and if she tries running back to me, I'll snap her neck before finding you and doing the same."

I tighten my grip to accentuate my point.

Owen gasps when I finally ease up.

"And if you so much as *think* about Aine again, I'll hunt you down, and I'll make you watch as I slaughter your entire pack. Women. Children. All of them."

Chapter 19

AINE

TIME SEEMS TO pass at a snail's pace as I wait for Damien to return. When he and Owen planned this early morning meeting, I didn't realize I'd be stuck in the room the entire time.

I thought I'd be let out to explore.

I contemplate sneaking out, but then I recall Damien's threats before he left. If I try to leave this room, he's going to have us moved into a room with one bed.

He seemed quite excited by the thought, especially after last night.

My cheeks warm as I recall his sweet actions, and they redden even further at the faint memory of him crawling under the covers with me afterward. I think he initially went to his own bed, but he silently moved to mine when he heard my chattering teeth.

I cup my face to physically hold back a smile as I think about how he rounded his body around mine and grunted when I shoved my ice toes against his skin. He was like a furnace, and I slept soundly after he joined me.

Groaning, I flop on my bed and stare up at the ceiling. I need to stop letting him get to me. It's dangerous.

The door flies open and smacks against the wall, and I turn just in time to watch Damien come strolling in with a wide grin.

"I could hear you groaning from the hallway," he says, gesturing for me to get up. "Come on now."

I hum, trying to hide my excitement as I jump out of bed and follow him out of the room.

"What's got you in such a good mood?" I ask, frantically grabbing his shoulders as he begins carrying me down the stairs. "You don't have to keep doing this. I can walk."

Damien smiles. "I like to," he admits, throwing me halfway over his shoulder. "You hate it, which pleases my beast."

I shriek as my face is slammed into his back, and I reach around to grab the bottom of my dress so my butt doesn't show. Damien helps hold the fabric against my thighs, but he refuses to put me down until we're on the first floor.

My cheeks puff up as I straighten out my clothing and glare, wanting him to know I'm annoyed. Damien's cocky smile only grows, and he takes my hand in his before leading me outside.

The fresh air feels good.

People on the street stop and gawk at us, but I pointedly avoid meeting any of their stares. A group of young kids cluster together to gossip, and one of the older girls screams as a boy pushes her in Damien's direction.

Damien looks over, and the girl's cheeks turn beet red as she realizes she's captured his attention. Her wide eyes slide to mine moments later, and I offer her a small smile in an attempt to seem friendly.

She turns back to her group and hides behind them. Damien lets out a quiet laugh at the interaction, clearly amused, but otherwise remains silent.

"Why do the beasts visit and enjoy this village but kill the people in mine?" I ask.

I face Damien as I wait for his response, watching his lips turn down at the corners. He's avoiding looking at me. It's obvious he doesn't want to answer, but I'm not going to drop the subject. I want to know what made my people not good enough to deserve the gift of life.

Damien's chest falls as he lets out a deep sigh. "This city is bigger and offers us entertainment. Yours was small, and the humans generally unfriendly." He pauses before continuing. "Beasts enjoy a good hunt and, unfortunately, your village got the short end of the stick."

My shoulders slouch. I figured he'd say something like this, but it's still disheartening to hear.

"Do the humans here actually like beasts, or are they just too scared of you to do anything?" I ask.

Damien releases an abrupt laugh, apparently finding my desire to learn funny. I'm offended, and I work my jaw side to side as he squeezes my hand and guides me around a street corner.

"Both, I suppose," he says. "Humans find us attractive, which leads to them desiring our approval, but they're also pretty terrified of us."

I hum. "How often do you come here?"

Damien's pace slows as he guides me toward a small pastry shop. He pulls open the door, all with a frown.

"Is this your way of asking how often I visit the brothels?" he asks.

I wince. I wasn't thinking at all about the brothels when I asked, but now that it's been brought up, I *am* a bit curious.

"No," I respond honestly. "But how often did you go?"

Damien sucks in a slow breath. I wait silently for his answer, and I'm surprised when he chooses instead to kiss me. His movements are quick, and before I can react, he's pulling away and taking his place at the back of the line.

I glare at him before looking around the shop. It's designed to be a grab-and-go type of establishment, but there are a few two-person tables for those who want to linger. It's cute, and if Damien weren't annoying me so much, I'd ask to sit inside and eat with him.

Why won't he tell me how often he went to the brothels? My anger grows the more I think about it, and I tense up as I stand beside him. It's probably because he was there all the time.

Damien tries to grab my hand, but I move it out of his reach. He doesn't get to hold my hand.

"Aine," he says, his voice low. "I visited them frequently, but I'm not proud of it and I don't like talking about it. I don't ask about *your* sexual past."

I gulp, unhappy that he's made a good point. There isn't much in my past that Damien doesn't already know, but he doesn't know that.

"I haven't gone there since we met, I promise." Damien snatches my hand before I can reject him again. "You're the only woman I want to be with."

The bell above the door dings, and a small group of friends step inside. They seem confused as they spot Damien at the counter, and they linger by the door before getting in line behind him.

It's cramped in this shop, and I capture Damien's attention before jerking my head toward the door. He doesn't look pleased, but he doesn't try stopping me as I step outside. I'm sure he'll have no issues sniffing me out after getting his food.

I feel like I blend in more without Damien by my side, and I take advantage of being invisible as I wander aimlessly down the street. The humans no longer give me sideways glances as they pass, and some even bump my shoulder when I get in their way.

A soft smile spreads over my lips as I wander around,

overjoyed with the comfort and familiarity being here brings. I miss being around other humans. There are a few back at Damien's pack, but Jenna's the only one I've really spoken to.

The others seem so busy with their lives and mates, and they haven't made any effort to approach me. I suppose I haven't either, though.

Would Damien let me stay here? I doubt it, especially now that he's making his odd efforts to get close to me.

A large shop across the street catches my attention, and I stroll over and peer in the windows. Dozens of tiny animals sit and play in a large container just on the other side of the window, their bodies slamming into one another before falling and rolling over on the ground.

Some are so small I could hold them in the palm of my hand.

I'm in love, and I'm entirely entranced by their fluffy bodies and fumbling movements. Tiny pointed ears sit on top of their heads, occasionally twitching as they try to take stock of their surroundings. They look like miniature beasts.

I glance at the pastry shop, making sure Damien isn't looking for me, before stepping inside.

"Morning!" a deep voice yells as the door closes behind me.

I turn toward the sound, quickly spotting an older man standing in a front of a small, open cage. He looks friendly, and he shoots me a toothy grin as I walk over.

Spanning the entire wall are cages filled with the tiny beasts. Some are sleeping, but most are wandering around making quiet cooing noises.

"Let me know if you want me to take any out for you," the man says, flinching as one of the beings lunges and playfully attacks his arm.

I chuckle and walk up to one of the cages. Inside is an orange animal, and I tentatively stick my finger through the metal grate.

"What are they?" I ask.

The miniature beast sniffs my fingers before rubbing its face against them, and I smile before hissing and yanking my arm away when it abruptly sinks its sharp teeth into my palm. Fuck.

A small bead of blood pools where I was bitten, but thankfully the injury is small. I don't want to think about what Damien would do if he found out I ventured off and got myself injured.

The man snorts as he watches my awkward interaction with his pets. "These little guys," he says, walking over and picking up the one that bit me, "are called cats."

Cats? I feel as if I've heard the word before, but we didn't have anything like this back in my own village. Vik would have never approved it.

The man holds the orange cat out, and I hesitate before taking it. Thankfully it doesn't try to bite me again, choosing instead to latch on to my shirt with its sharp nails and climb up me. I stiffen, praying it doesn't attack as I run my hand over its soft fur.

The cat's chest eventually begins to vibrate, and I smile at the soft noises it lets out.

"He's purring," the man explains. "That means he likes you."

"He's cute," I say as it nips my finger. *Little bastard.* "Do you—"

My voice trails out as a young boy, no older than eight, comes barreling in with a red face and wide eyes. I look at the man expectantly, assuming he knows the boy who's just appeared like a bat out of hell, but the man looks just as startled and confused as me. The boy must be here for me, then.

"Are you Aine?" he asks, confirming my suspicions.

I nod.

"The beast out there wants you." His hand shakes as he points out the large storefront window.

I turn to look, not at all surprised to see Damien standing

outside. He looks pissed as he stares in at me, his chest heaving.

I don't trust Damien when he gets angry, and I nervously clutch the small animal to my chest. The shop owner gently pries the pet from my hands, his friendly attitude disappearing as he realizes I'm here with a beast. I thought it would take Damien longer to order and receive his food.

"It was nice meeting you, but you need to leave before that beast comes inside," the man says, gently nudging me toward the door.

My feelings are hurt at the dismissal, but I understand where he's coming from. I wouldn't want Damien in my shop, either.

I square my shoulders and step outside, prepared to face Damien's wrath. He's scolding me the second my foot crosses the threshold, his voice embarrassingly loud.

"What the fuck, Aine?" he shouts. "You can't just run off."

A few humans stop to stare, no doubt enjoying the show. I shrivel underneath Damien's harsh glare, unhappy and frustrated by his lecturing.

"You saw me leave," I point out, glancing nervously at the nosy humans.

Several snicker to one another as they watch the interaction, probably happy to witness the human who's been parading around with the beast get publicly reprimanded. Damien's eyes darken as he glares at me, and his body shakes as he struggles to fight off a shift. I bet those people wouldn't be laughing so brazenly if they knew how close they were to witnessing a beast in his animal form.

Damien pauses to breathe and, hopefully, calm himself down.

"I thought you were going to wait nearby," he says.

I look toward the pastry shop. It's admittedly far down the street, and I frown as I realize I wandered farther than I intended. I understand why Damien's upset, but that doesn't give him the right to yell at me like this.

"I'm not a child," I say, my words surprisingly firm. "I just wanted to look at the cats. They're cute and fluffy."

Damien huffs and peers behind me into the shop. "*I'm* cute and fluffy."

I pause, and a loud laugh bubbles up out of my throat before I can stop it. Damien looks toward the sky and sighs, his face red as he runs a hand through his hair.

"That didn't come out the way I intended it to," he says, trying to backtrack.

I raise an eyebrow. "How *did* you intend for it to come out?"

Damien huffs, and I let out a triumphant smile when he grabs my bicep instead of answering. I love that he's embarrassed himself, and my cackling continues as he drags me down the street. It's about time the roles were reversed.

The red tinge on Damien's cheeks darkens as he leads me to a large, grassy field filled with humans. It's surprising to see such a human emotion on him, and I find this Damien a welcome change from the cruel and emotionless one I've grown accustomed to.

"Can I have one?" I ask, referring to the tiny beasts inside the store. "I've never seen a cat before, and I liked the orange one."

Damien grimaces, looking almost apologetic as he shakes his head.

"They see beasts as predators," he admits, "and they panic when we're nearby. That's why I didn't go inside the shop. A cat wouldn't be happy in our home."

I open my mouth, ready to make a snide comment about his home not being mine, but I shut my mouth at the last second. Damien's in a good mood today, and I don't want to ruin that.

He maneuvers us around the humans until he finds an empty spot in the field and sits. He pats the area next to him, clearly wanting me to join, and his face falls when I hesitate.

"Is it wet?" I ask, bending to touch the grass. I don't enjoy having damp clothing.

Damien shakes his head, and I decide the grass is dry enough to sit on. I try my best to ignore the way Damien's staring at me as I take a seat.

"Are you hungry?" he asks.

He pulls out one of the cheesy breakfast sandwiches he purchased from the bakery. It's easily the size of my head, and I'm shocked as I watch him pull out two more. One is slid in my direction, the other two meant for Damien.

The beasts have hearty appetites, but this is extreme.

"Thanks," I mumble, looking around as I pick up the sandwich.

There's a group of teens playing on our left. They run around laughing as they kick a ball between them, their bodies sweaty from exercise.

The sight brings back memories of being with my friends when I was a child. They abandoned me after word spread about me asking for a divorce, but I can't help but long for those days again. Before Henry, I loved to spend time outdoors, and I had a competitive spirit that made me relatively good at those silly games.

The human teens look in our direction every few seconds, their sly glances not nearly as hidden as I assume they think them to be.

"Are you ever bothered by the staring?" I ask, bringing my sandwich to my lips.

I gasp and cough as the cheese burns my mouth. Damien sets down his food to try and help, but I wave off his attempts to pat my back.

Damien shoots me a concerned look before responding. "Not

really. You get used to it after a while."

I hum, unsure how much I believe that. I don't know if I could ever get used to drawing this much attention in public.

"You can smell strong emotions, right?" I ask, changing the subject.

Damien's nose scrunches. "I can smell the product of heightened emotions, but not necessarily the emotion itself. If a person is scared, I can smell the sweat they emit, or if a woman is aroused, I can smell her wetness." He takes the last bite of his first sandwich and grabs the second. "Over time, we learn how to connect the dots on scent and emotion pretty well."

I nod as I absorb that information, fascinated with the beasts' abilities. I don't know how much I love that when he said he could smell my arousal, he literally meant he could smell my vagina, but I suppose it makes sense. I'm not sure what else he'd be smelling. Maybe pheromones or something.

Damien splits his sandwich and tries to hand me half as I finish mine. I shake my head, unable to imagine eating any more than I already have. I had to force the last few bites down.

"I'm stuffed." I laugh as he continues to try to push the sandwich toward me. "Thank you, though."

Damien looks annoyed as I refuse his offer, but after some light arguing, he finally retreats. Or at least, that's what I thought.

"I'll leave it here in case you change your mind." He sets the sandwich half in the space between our bodies.

My lips twitch, but I don't let him see how much his kind actions affect me. Damien's been going out of his way to be accommodating, and I still don't trust it.

"Why have you been so nice to me?" I can't help but ask. Not knowing is going to drive me insane.

Damien shrugs. "You're my mate."

"I've been your mate this entire time, but you weren't kind

when we first met," I argue. "In fact, you were downright cruel."

Damien's shoulders slump as I speak. I try to make eye contact, wanting to see his reaction, but he refuses to look in my direction. He stares at the grass by his knees, instead.

My eyes grow wet at his callous response, and the tears I've been holding in for weeks finally begin to seep out. The muscle in Damien's jaw twitches as I reach up and wipe away the wetness on my cheeks. It's clear he's uncomfortable talking about this, but if I'm ever going to forgive him, I need to air my grievances.

"You made me sit in my pee for hours." My voice is shaky as I bring up the painful memories, but I force myself to speak about them anyway. "Then you called me incontinent and forced me to shower with you."

Damien pulls me into his lap and tucks my head under his chin as I start to cry in earnest. I know I should fight it, but I don't.

His body's warm and unmoving as I leak snot all over him, but I'm grateful to be hidden from the prying eyes of the nearby humans.

I'm sure they'll be able to tell I'm crying by the shaking of my shoulders and cooing of the giant man who surrounds me, but at least they can't see my face.

"I'm so sorry, Aine," Damien whispers into my hair. "Olivia said you needed me to take you to the bathroom, but I assumed Jenna or Avia had already helped you that evening and I'd begin in the morning. I would never have left you in that state if I knew." He runs his hands down the back of my head. "And I know I shouldn't have washed you like that. I was angry with myself, and I took it out on you."

While I appreciate his apologies, they do little to make me feel better. They don't remove the painful memories.

I sniffle loudly before continuing. "Freya was in your bed the first week I arrived."

Damien's chest expands as he sucks in a deep breath. "She snuck in and unclothed while I was in the shower. You happened to walk past while I was in the midst of kicking her out."

"And Olivia?" I challenge.

I lean back to watch Damien's reaction. While he may have a semi-decent explanation for everything else, I can't imagine what he could possibly have for moving her into his home instead of me, and then touching her in front of me.

"I was being a dick when I moved her into my house, but nothing has ever happened between us." He grimaces. "Other than the incident in my office, which I deeply regret."

Damien continues speaking.

"You don't have to worry about other women, Aine," he promises. "I know I was cruel when we first met. I thought it would prevent me from feeling anything, but the more I got to know you, the more I realized I *wanted* to feel something. You're my mate, Aine, and that may not mean a lot to humans, but it's everything to us."

I purse my lips, unsure if I want to bring up what he did to me that day I moved into his home. He seemed genuinely apologetic when he realized I wasn't enjoying his touch, and he went as far as to let me drug him as punishment.

After a moment's hesitation, I decide to let it go. It's the only time he's ever forced himself on me in that manner, and I know it was a misunderstanding.

I'd rather focus on the things that weren't accidental.

There are a thousand other painful memories swarming around in my head, all of them caused by Damien, and I pick the one most pressing to discuss next. It's been haunting me since it happened.

"You offered for Alex to rape me," I say.

Damien stiffens. "I should never have done that, and I don't have an excuse. I'm sorry."

He sounds genuine, and I can't help but think about what Freya said to me in the bathroom yesterday. She forced Damien, and I'm hurt he'd turn around and offer for somebody to do the same to me.

Even if he didn't intend to go through with it.

Is offering his women to Alex something he's done before?

"Freya told me you like to share your women," I say.

Damien grabs my chin and forces me to look into the darkened eyes of his beast before the words are fully out of my mouth.

Despite his assurances that he won't hurt me, I feel nothing short of terror at the sight of his beast. He could snap my neck with a flick of his wrist, and I flinch as he forces my head and jaw into whatever direction he pleases.

"No." Damien's words are spoken lowly. "I'd sooner kill my entire pack than willingly share you with another."

My jaw aches under his tight grip, but he loosens when I let out a quiet whimper. His face softens as he takes in my terrified one, and after a second, he releases me entirely. I slide off his lap, no longer comfortable with our proximity.

"What else did she tell you?" Damien asks.

I can tell he's trying to be sweet as he rubs his thumb across my cheekbone, but it means little to me after his painful, scary actions.

I smack his hand away. "She also told me she marked you."

Chapter 20

DAMIEN

ALEX IS TOO big for this hospital bed, his long limbs looking dumb as they dangle off the sides of the mattress. I hardly remember carrying him here, this entire night a blur I wish to forget.

My eyes slam shut, and I throw my head against the wall as I recall Freya taking off my clothing just a few hours ago. I like to sleep naked, and I thought she was helping so I'd be comfortable. She's helped me change thousands of times before, my limbs uncoordinated after a night of too much drinking, but she's always stopped at my underwear.

I didn't think anything when she began to take off her clothing, either. I assumed she was going to throw on something of mine before going back home. She probably just got sick or spilled a drink on herself.

She's done it before, and nudity is normal among the beasts. We see one another naked all the time when we shift, and I've caught glimpses of her bare skin hundreds of times over the years.

Still, I made sure to look away as she stripped and moved around my room. I shut my eyes and relaxed into my mattress as she sorted herself out. I thought she was going to leave.

Why linger when your mate is waiting for you back at home?

It wasn't until she was climbing on top of me that I realized something was wrong. I remember trying to speak to her, to ask what she was doing, but I couldn't get the words to form in my mouth. She looked me in the eye as she grabbed me, her mouth moving to form words I didn't listen to and can't remember.

I think it was at that moment I realized I'd been drugged.

I shook my head. I tried to tell her *no*. I tried to yell and kick her away as she stroked me until I was hard enough to be shoved inside her. Things went hazy after that, her movements rhythmic and blurry as she forced me into a place I didn't want to be.

I don't know how long she was on top of me, but then she was shouting, her face contorted into an angry scowl as my body refused to stay hard. My beast was screaming at me to get up, to fight back as she crawled between my legs.

My cheeks grew wet as her mouth caused my body to betray me for the second time. I closed my eyes and willed for it to be over as she began to kiss my thighs, her teeth scraping against the skin. I was only able to knock my knee into her face.

She held her nose and cried as it bled, but she was back a second later. I was able to get up on my elbows, and I was so proud of myself for being able to move. Freya shoved me back down, though, the action disorienting as I struggled to find the strength to get up again.

Her teeth on my thigh had me fighting even harder to get away, my mind panicked and frightened. Touching teeth to my skin is sin, an even worse one than had already been committed. What if she accidentally marked me? What if she stole from me the one thing I had to give my mate? She was robbing Alex and me of our dignity.

She laughed as I tried to fight back, claiming the fates made a mistake pairing her with Alex. She smiled and told me I was hers, that I'd give her a child tonight and we'd be mates. I've never seen her so crazed before.

Her hands were on my hips before I could register what was happening, her mouth on my thigh and her teeth in my skin. I thought I was dying as they sank inside, marking me as hers.

My beast screamed for me to let him take over my body, to let him move me and kill her. I tried to drop down the barrier in my mind, but I couldn't focus enough to see it through. Freya was everywhere at once, and it was overwhelming.

I couldn't get her off me. I cried and begged and pushed at her thighs as she forced me back inside her. She tried so desperately to make me hard, rocking and whispering dirty words I refused to listen to.

Before I could register what I was doing, I sunk my claws into her abdomen. I didn't care if I killed her. The only thing on my mind was ripping out her uterus. I'd die before I allowed her to carry my child.

Freya froze as my fist closed around whatever part of her innards I could grab, and she screamed as I tore them from her body. It wasn't enough to kill her, but it was enough for her to back off.

Losing the ability to ever conceive a child must have been a shock.

She was long gone by the time I managed to stumble my way downstairs, the woman not even bothering to help me find Alex and bring him to the hospital.

Mates can feel whenever the other is disloyal, and he would have felt Freya and me together.

Tears trickle down my cheeks at the memory of him on the ground halfway between our houses. He'd been coming to us, and he must've collapsed when she'd marked me.

I can't imagine the pain. I don't want to.

Avia pulls me from my self-loathing as she drops a pair of shorts on my lap, her demeanor cold as she tends to Alex. I'd be cold, too, if I were her. For all she knows, I just happily fucked my own brother's mate.

Alex is never going to forgive me.

I'm never going to forgive me.

Chapter 21

AINE

THE SILENCE BETWEEN Damien and I is long and tense as he absorbs what I've just said. His mouth opens a couple of times as he prepares to speak, but he snaps it shut before anything comes out.

I already regret my words, and I grimace as I watch him search for a response. It isn't my place to force him to confide in me and, despite my anger, I should've waited until he brought it up himself.

I can practically see the cogs turning in Damien's head as he tries to make sense of the fact that I know Freya marked him. I'm about to speak up and change the subject when he lets out a loud sigh and drops his hands to his lap.

"What, specifically, did she say?" he asks.

I shrug, hesitant to give more information than I already have.

"Just that it was her mark you wore until I forced mine on you," I eventually admit, feeling ashamed for my actions.

Two wrongs don't make a right, and despite Damien forcing his mark on me, I wish I would've waited until I had permission to do the same to him. The bonds are everything to the beasts, and

I can't even begin to imagine how upsetting it must've been to have a mark forced on him twice.

To me, it was nothing more than a crazy man putting a pleasurable scar on me, but I know it was more meaningful to him.

"I didn't want her to do it," Damien says. "I was drunk, and she marked the inside of my thigh before I realized." He sounds frantic as he grabs my face and urges me to look into his eyes. "I swear I've been careful about my drinking since then, and I no longer put myself in positions to—"

"Damien!" I shout, cutting off his rambling. His jaw snaps shut with an audible click. "You don't have to explain yourself to me."

I hope he can't feel my pity as I reach up and cup his hands, which still rest on my cheeks. He's clearly distraught over this, and I have no intentions of making him feel worse.

Damien's eyes are wide as he searches my face, and I offer him a small smile to show I'm not angry. His throat bobs as he gulps, and I'm not sure what I expect, but it isn't for him to drop his hands and scoot away.

"I don't understand," he says. What doesn't he understand?

"Why would I be upset with you for something another person forced on you?" I ask.

Damien scoffs, and he looks disgusted as he shakes his head and pushes himself up off the ground. I can't tell if it's directed at me or himself.

"I'm your mate," he says. "You're supposed to be upset somebody else marked me."

I blink, struggling to keep up with his thought process.

"Are you seriously mad that I'm not mad at you?" I ask.

I understand this is hard to talk about, but Damien needs to do a better job of communicating his feelings if this is ever going to work between us.

He ignores my question as he bends and begins to shove our sandwich wrappers back into the paper bag they came in. I watch him in angry silence, not appreciating his confusing reactions. It's times like these I wish he couldn't hide his emotions from the bond. It'd be a huge help right now.

"I obviously don't want you to be angry, but I want you to care enough to be angry," he eventually says, crumbling the sandwich bags. "I'd be furious if you let another mark you."

Damien shakes his head before turning and walking to the nearby trash can. I rub at my temples and take a deep breath to calm myself down. Getting frustrated isn't going to get us anywhere.

Damien walks slowly to the trash can, his feet dragging behind him in a clear attempt to waste time. I tap my foot against the ground, impatiently waiting for him to return.

When it's clear he has no intentions to do so, I take the initiative and meet him by the trash. I feel like this argument isn't one that should be shouted across a large field, and if that means I need to be the one to crowd him for once, then that's what I'll do.

"I'll admit I'm a sad somebody marked you before me, but that doesn't mean I'm mad at you," I try to explain. "What Freya did was wrong, and I don't think you should blame yourself for being taken advantage of."

I reach out and grab Damien's forearm, but he's quick to pull away. I gulp as his pupils dilate and his body begins to shake. He isn't trying to scare me, I know that, but it's still the reaction his angry beast invokes.

"Stop pitying me," he snaps. "I'm an alpha. It's my responsibility not to let these things happen."

Damien's voice is thick, and he refuses to meet my eye as I stare up at him. I shouldn't have told him I know what Freya did, and I should've waited until he brought it up himself. I'm sure this conversation would've gone much differently if I hadn't pushed.

"I'm not going to tell anybody," I promise.

The muscle in Damien's jaw twitches as he turns away. "I don't care."

I think he does.

I'm undecided on whether it's a good idea to take his hand, but after a slight hesitation, I lace our fingers together.

He's held my hand before, but I've never initiated it. Damien doesn't wrap his fingers around mine as he usually does, but he doesn't try to pull away, which I consider a good sign.

He's clearly embarrassed about this, and if he's not ready to talk about it, I'll drop the subject. The silence feels awkward as we both stare at our interlocked hands.

"Are you ready to head back to the inn?" I ask.

I was looking forward to exploring the village, but after this conversation, I don't know how much fun that'll be. It's put a damper on our day.

Damien sighs, his fingers finally curling around mine.

I'm relieved, and I let out an unattractive snort when he abruptly pulls me against his chest. I wasn't expecting it, and I press my free hand to his abdomen to stabilize myself.

"I'm so sorry, Aine," Damien whispers, kissing the top of my head. "I've made so many mistakes since I found you, and if I could take them all back, I would."

I'm starting to believe that.

Damien was horrible to me at first, but he really seems to be trying to make up for it. He's been kind to me recently, and he's given many apologies.

I slide my hand around Damien's torso and pull him in for a hug. My ear presses against his chest, and I listen to his pounding heart as he squeezes me.

Damien is the first to pull away, and he kisses my forehead as he does.

Then he lifts me.

"Damien!" I scream. He grabs my thighs and wraps them around his waist. "What are you doing?"

He laughs before placing his hand underneath my butt to hold down my dress. The humans in the field stare open-mouthed as Damien begins to walk, and after a moment of trying to fight with him, I give in and hide my flushed face against his chest.

"We're returning to the inn to start this day over," he says, carrying me out of the park and onto the main street. "You'll put on your pajamas and get into bed, and I'll wake you the way I should have this morning."

There's a dangerous glint in his eye as he mentions waking me up, and despite my better judgment, I find myself excited. I'm tired of fighting with him, and he seems genuine in his apologies. I might regret this, but I want to give him a chance.

I want to feel the love all the mated pairs in his pack share.

Even while carrying me, Damien keeps a brisk pace as he walks toward the inn. He's doing a poor job concealing his smile, and I find myself quite pleased this day isn't going to be completely ruined.

The front door to the inn smacks against the wall as Damien pushes his way inside. The shopkeeper is standing behind the counter, and he looks borderline horrified as he watches Damien storm toward the stairs.

"You've scarred him," I tease.

Damien shrugs, carrying me up the stairs.

"Good."

He unlocks our room door and sets me down next to my discarded pajamas.

"Get dressed," he orders.

I thought he was joking about me putting them on and

returning to bed.

Damien stares impatiently before bending and grabbing the items off the floor. His face gives nothing away as he holds the clothing out for me. Is he serious? When he waves the fabric in my face, I laugh and take them.

My laughter grows when he pats my butt and ushers me off to the bathroom to get changed. I can't quite wrap my head around his sudden shift in emotion, but I'm enjoying it too much to question it.

He's fun to be around when he's in a good mood.

Damien doesn't try to hide his appreciation when I finally leave the bathroom in my pajamas. He took it upon himself to change as well, and my throat runs dry as I realize he's in nothing more than his underwear.

I've seen him in less, but I still take a second to stare. The beasts are painfully attractive, Damien included. I've always found Damien beautiful, but I've refused to let myself enjoy it until now.

Damien sits back on his bed, his muscles flexing with each movement. Would Damien let me touch them? I'm pretty sure he would.

I fight the urge to do so as I slip back my bedcovers and slide underneath. Damien shuts the curtains, blocking the morning sun from seeping into the room.

My heart pounds as I roll onto my side, and I hold my breath as Damien climbs into bed behind me.

Arms wrap around my waist and pull me into a chest, and I tense only slightly as I'm pressed entirely against Damien.

He's aroused, but I politely ignore it as I wait to see what he's going to do. I'm not sure what to expect, but given that I'm on my monthly bleed, I assume Damien plans to kiss me and provide some minor over-the-clothing groping before nudging me out of bed.

I wiggle my toes while I wait, the suspense building.

After several painfully long seconds, Damien begins trailing his fingertips over my hips. The touch is gentle, and he dips underneath the fabric of my shirt before moving toward my waist. I instinctively arch my back, pressing further into him.

"Aine," Damien says, his voice barely audible as he adjusts and places his lips against my neck.

He's only inches from my mark, and I tilt my head to give him more access. I like his mouth on me more than I'd care to admit, and I pant as he moves closer to the teeth imprints permanently scarred into my neck.

When his lips finally find it, I gasp into the sheets, wishing for nothing more than to kiss him properly. Before I can spin and do just that, he's shoving his hand down my pajama shorts.

I panic, grabbing his wrist to stop him. Damien shouldn't be touching me when I'm bleeding.

"Damien!" I grunt, aching for precisely what he's offering.

He kisses my mark, his fingers finding my clit. It feels good, and he gives it a slow rub as I tighten my grip on his wrist and try to pull him away.

"You can't do that," I say, digging my nails into his skin.

Damien chuckles. I don't understand what's so funny, but I lose my train of thought as he presses his fingers more firmly against me.

"My little human," Damien coos.

I'd be lying if I said this wasn't pleasurable, but it can't happen when I'm bleeding. I pull on his arm again.

Damien pauses, sensing my request for him to stop is genuine, and pulls his fingers away.

"Do you not want this?" he asks.

He sounds confused, and my face warms as I realize he must

have forgotten about my condition.

It takes me a second to work up the courage to speak. "I'm bleeding," I admit.

Of all the reactions I anticipated, a loud booming laugh was not one of them.

"That's all?" Damien asks. "Thank you for the unnecessary reminder." He nips at the skin above my mark. "Now, will you stop trying to push me away and let me pleasure my mate? I have a lot of lost time to make up for."

I loosen my grip on his wrist before changing my mind and tightening it again. "You can't go any lower," I say, scared he's going to mess with my cup and create an unwanted leakage.

Damien hums, the low noise vibrating down my spine. I instinctively arch against him, and I clamp my thighs around his arm as he massages my clit in a slow, torturous circle.

"I don't care if you're bleeding," he says. "I fully intend for my cock to slip into you after I've made you cum by my hand."

He backs up his words with a roll of his hips, his hard length prominent as it digs into my butt.

I gasp, cursing my body for its poor timing.

As much as I'd like that, I can't take the risk. Damien will be disgusted by the blood, and I don't want him to think I'm dirty for it. I shake my head *no*.

There's absolute stillness from Damien, the unknown making me nervous, before he presses a small kiss to my shoulder.

"Okay," he relents. "I'll go no lower than your pretty clit." He pulls his hips away, disconnecting himself from my back. "It's already so swollen for me."

I bury my face into my pillow to silence my cries as Damien works me, and for a slight moment, I'm grateful he's had enough experience to know what to do.

Henry never did.

A muffled moan slips from my lips as I rock my hips, and I press against Damien. He groans as I rub myself against his hard cock, his hips twitching occasionally, but he continues to focus only on my pleasure.

He touches me at just the right tempo with just the right amount of pressure, and I know it won't take me long to finish. It's better than anything I've ever experienced before, and I pant as my orgasm builds.

"I want you to scream my name when you cum," Damien says, his breath tickling my ear. "I want every beast in this building to know you're mine."

He slides his fingers through my hair and pulls my head back with a painful tug. I moan, and he thrusts against my ass as he rubs me faster.

"D-Damien, I—" I stutter, trying to warn that I'm close.

His teeth dig painfully into my skin. "Louder."

I try to fight it, I really do, but I can't help but shout his name as I cum. I can tell it's not as loud as he'd like, but it's damn well loud enough that any beasts in nearby rooms will have heard.

Damien plays with my clit until I'm too sensitive and push him away. He's still thrusting against me, but he pulls his hips back as he removes his hand from my shorts.

I relax into the mattress before spinning in his arms, eager to face him. He's already looking at me, and his eyes convey a soft emotion I'm unfamiliar with seeing on him.

"Good morning!" He smiles and pulls back the covers.

He moves so fast, and in fear that he's going to climb out of bed before I can express my desire to touch him, I skip the pleasantries and grab his cock.

Damien grows entirely still as my fingers curl around his length, the skin warm even through the fabric of his underwear.

"It's my turn," I say.

Damien's pupils dilate as I slide my hand underneath his underwear. He's so hard, and I like how his hips twitch when I pull him out of the restricting fabric.

I've always assumed Damien would be large, but as I hold him in my hand, I realize just how much I underestimated his size. My fingers barely touch one another, my thumb and middle finger just slightly grazing.

I like it.

Damien gasps and jerks when I stroke him from base to tip, my grip light.

"Aine," he warns.

He grabs the bed sheets, straining the fabric as he tries to hold himself back. The sight of his struggle provokes a surge of confidence within me, and I tighten my grip before stroking him again.

"It feels so good," Damien moans, dropping his forehead against mine. "My mate touching me is better than I could have ever imagined."

Quiet gasps slip from my throat every time Damien makes a noise or movement. He's truly enjoying what I'm doing, and my inner thighs grow wet as I listen to him.

I wish I weren't bleeding so I could feel him inside me.

I already know he'd stretch me wide, filling me entirely as he fucks me into the mattress.

"Can I try something?" I beg, looking to Damien for permission.

I'm nervous to act on my idea, but knowing how enjoyable our marks are, I think he'll like what I have planned.

Damien nods with a grunt. I curl my fist around his cockhead before using my other hand to grab his marked arm. I note how uneven and ugly the scar I left on him is, but I don't dwell on it as I adjust his arm to comfortably face me.

I stare into Damien's curious eyes as I lean forward and lick the scar. It feels good for me, too, but Damien seems to get the brunt of it as he throws his head back and moans loudly in my face.

"Fuck—" He gasps as I repeat the action with more pressure. His hips jerk forward again, and he begins fucking himself into my fist as I focus on his arm.

I suck harshly on his tender skin before sinking my teeth into the mark. Damien turns his face into the pillow to bite at it, his eyes screwed shut as he frantically rocks into my hand.

"I want you to say my name." I repeat the words he said to me earlier.

Damien cries, and his tip disappears into my fist as he grinds against me.

"Aine!" he moans, his voice loud.

Damien shoves his forearm against my face in a not-so-subtle hint for me to put my mouth on it again, and I chuckle before latching back on. Unsure how best to pleasure him with it, I suck and bite as I would to give a hickey.

"Aine, I'm—" He moves until he's practically lying on top of me. "Don't stop."

I bite him harder, continuing until I feel the skin break beneath my teeth. It seems to be enough to push him over the edge, and Damien buries his face into my pillow to muffle his shout. It's louder than mine was despite being dimmed by the fabric, and I feel good knowing I've brought this reaction out of him.

I also like that the other beasts will know it's me he's with.

Damien continues grinding against me as he cums into my hand, and I continue stroking him until he pulls away. My hand is sticky and warm where it lies between our bodies, but I hardly notice as Damien turns to look me in the eye.

There's a calmness I haven't seen in him before, and I crane my neck as he leans in and kisses my lips.

He pulls away with a smile. "This is going to have my beast in an excellent mood for the upcoming hunt."

I use my clean hand to smooth his hair out of his face, not sure what he's talking about.

"The what?"

Chapter 22

AINE

I'VE NEVER BEEN so angry.

"I'm ready to leave," I snap.

Damien begs me to slow down as I shove my dirty clothes into my bag. I can't bring myself to look at him, and I ignore his very existence until he hurries forward and picks my bag up off the bed.

"Give it back," I order.

Damien hesitates, and I snatch it out of his hand and continue packing.

"Will you talk to me?" he asks, quiet and tense.

I shake my head, refusing. I have absolutely nothing to say to him. And to think I'd almost convinced myself he was a good man who genuinely wanted to be with me. Somebody who truly wanted to be with me wouldn't lead an annual slaughter of innocent humans.

Damien hunts my people for sport, and I'm beyond disgusted. I know the beasts kill the humans who venture too far into the forest, but I saw it as them protecting their land. I had no idea the beasts go out in search of humans, actively hunting them down.

"Please, Aine," Damien begs.

I refuse to give him the time of day. I'm ashamed of myself for falling into his trap in the first place. He showed me who he was when I first arrived in his village, and I shouldn't have let myself believe otherwise.

Foolish.

My anger spikes as I turn around and get an eyeful of Damien's soft cock.

"Will you put on some fucking pants?"

I search for his discarded clothing, quickly spotting them on the floor next to the bed. Damien nervously covers himself with his hands as I scoop up his clothes and throw them at his face.

"Get dressed," I order.

For the first time ever, Damien listens, and he rushes to slide his pants up his legs in a sad attempt to curb my anger.

"I'm sorry, Aine," he says as I zip up my bag. "I thought you knew."

I scoff. "You thought I knew you lead a yearly slaughter of innocent humans and didn't care enough to bring it up?"

My voice is loud, but I don't care if the beast in the neighboring rooms can hear. I'm sure they're having a field day with the sounds coming from us. We're pleasuring one another one second, and I'm hurling insults the next.

Damien watches from the corner of the room as I begin packing his bag.

"Let me explain," he begs.

"What could you possibly have to say?" I ask. "There's no justifying the hunt, and I don't care to hear you try."

Damien takes a tentative step forward, but he pauses as I move back. I don't want him anywhere near me. Never again.

"We don't hurt women or children," he says. "Only the men who have wandered into the forest."

I laugh, the sound dry and unamused. "When my brother

traveled into the woods to find and bring home meat for our starving family, was it you who tore him apart and left him for dead?"

My voice cracks as I recall the memories, but I remain facing Damien. I want him to see my pain, and I want him to know that he's the one who caused it. Him and his people.

"Or did you just watch and laugh as he screamed and begged for mercy?" I continue.

Damien swallows, his throat bobbing, but he remains silent. I take a step toward him.

"Did you *enjoy* watching as your beasts tore apart my flesh after my execution? Did you find pleasure in listening to me scream and sob in agony?" I ask. Damien's eyes flash as I bring up that day, but I ignore it and take another step forward. "Imagine if you hadn't come and saved me when you did. Do you think your beast would've enjoyed the sight of my mangled, dead body decomposing on the forest floor?"

I open my mouth to continue, but I freeze as Damien suddenly stalks forward. I trip over my feet as I back away, continuing until my back meets the wall.

Damien's toes touch mine.

It takes all my courage to look up and meet his eye. His pupils are fully extended, showing me just how close he is to losing control.

Damien places his hands on my neck and presses his forehead against mine. His palm lands directly on my mark, but both of us ignore the pleasure. Damien shuts his eyes and inhales.

"My mate," he whispers. "That day haunts me."

Despite my anger, I remain still as he rubs his head against mine. I close my eyes as I wait for his beast to calm. We both know my momentary softening is only that—momentary. Rage and disgust still roll through me in suffocating waves.

"Call it off," I order.

Damien sighs, the noise quiet and sad, before shaking his head and backing away. "I will not. It's tradition, and I can't abandon it."

I turn away. Murder isn't a tradition, and it shouldn't be treated as some fun sport.

"You're disgusting," I say.

Damien's eyes widen, and I can't believe he even has the audacity to looked shocked by what I've just said.

"We don't harm women or children," he repeats.

Like that makes it any better.

"I'm ready to return to your pack."

"*Our* pack."

I scoff. "*Your* pack."

The room is plunged into a tense silence, and when it gets unbearable, Damien grabs his bag and finishes the rest of his packing.

I wait by the door.

"Aine," Damien says as he finishes.

I ignore him, something I'm growing quite skilled at doing. He grabs both our bags and throws them over his shoulder, and I step to the side and gesture for him to lead the way.

We leave the room, but Damien pauses as we reach the stairwell. I know he's debating whether to try and carry me as he's done since we arrived, and I make the decision easy as I shove past him and walk down the stairs myself.

I can tackle stairs perfectly fine on my own. I don't need him.

Damien follows me, but once we reach the main floor, he moves to the front and continues leading the way. I'm not entirely surprised when he ignores the man at the front desk, and I stop walking.

Damien notices almost immediately.

"You need to pay," I say, my voice loud.

The beasts inside the lobby watch us with raised eyebrows and poorly concealed smirks, but I hold my ground. Damien's eyes narrow, his spine straightening as he turns to the man behind the desk.

I can practically see the anger seeping from him as he reaches into his pocket and pulls out a few coins. They clink loudly against the counter as he tosses them down, and the innkeeper scrambles to grab them as they bounce around.

The outward disrespect has me wondering just how often the beasts stay here without paying.

I turn toward the innkeeper. "How many times has Damien paid after staying here with his prostitutes?"

The man pales as he glances between Damien and me. I don't have to look at Damien to know he's absolutely seething, and when the innkeeper doesn't answer, I shift my question to Damien.

"Well?" I ask. "Do you pay after staying here with your prostitutes? I'm sure you leave a nasty mess in the sheets."

If looks could kill, I'd be long dead. Damien's lip curls as he reaches into his pocket and pulls out a large handful of coins.

The muscle in his jaw twitches as he sets them on the desk.

"Satisfied?" he asks.

Not even close.

Damien storms out of the inn, and I follow. Despite the loud noises and distractions the village offers, I'm unable to stop thinking about Damien as he leads us into the woods and shifts into his animal form.

He yips and nips at my ankles, his beast acting like the cats I saw in the store, and I resist the urge to scream as I throw our bags over my shoulders and climb onto his back.

I hope the bond lets him feel my anger and disgust as he begins the journey back to his pack, and I bury my face in his fur and count down the hours until we arrive.

My legs burn when Damien finally slows to a stop in his backyard, and I waste no time clambering off his back. I throw his bag to the ground and march inside the house.

Alex is in the kitchen in only his underwear, and he looks shocked as he glances between me and the angry Damien on my heels.

"Aine," Damien yells. "Wait!"

"Everything okay?" Alex asks.

I ignore both men and continue to my room. Well, I continue to the room I've been forced to live in.

I overhear Damien mumble something to Alex about opening the windows and airing out the house, but I could care less about the smells only the beasts can sense. If Alex and Olivia want to have dirty sex all over this place, all the power to them.

Hopefully Alex doesn't get bored and kill Olivia as Damien so loves to do to my kind.

Damien follows me upstairs.

"Please stop and talk to me," he pleads.

"I have nothing to say to you."

"It's too late to change the plans," Damien says, "but we can come up with an agreement for next year."

My heart pounds as I turn to face Damien. I shouldn't let him keep distracting me.

"Like what?" I ask. "That you only kill *ten* innocent people? Or that you target only the old ones who have little time left anyway?" I scoff and spin back around. "I'm not interested in speaking to you."

Damien continues to plead with me as I enter my room and slam the door shut. Then a painful thought hits me, and I rip open the door once more.

I'm met with the chest of my mate, and I take a step back so I can look into Damien's eyes. I want to see his face when I make my demand.

"I want to see my parents."

His expression alone gives the answer to my unspoken question. They're dead. He's killed them all. Everyone in my village. That's how he got Vik's book.

My heart pounds. "Go fuck yourself."

Damien's eyes widen, and my knees waver as I slam the door in his face.

Sleep doesn't come to me that night, or the following.

I lie in bed staring at the ceiling, listening to Damien stomp around hour after hour. He can be angry all he wants, but I'm not leaving this room until he's called off the hunt. I don't want to see him.

It's happening tonight, and he should be leaving in a few hours.

I sit up and look out my window, watching Damien walk from his office to the house. He looks up at the last second, and we make brief eye contact before I pull away and rip the curtains shut.

He looks just as pitiful as he did when I caught him sneaking into my room this morning. I was prepared to scream, but he set a plate of food on my desk and left before I could get anything out.

I considered leaving the food untouched to punish him, but my hunger won out and I ended up eating everything. I'm not proud of it.

The back door slams as Damien enters the house, and I sit silently as I wait for him to leave. After several minutes, there's a light tapping on my door. I pretend not to hear it.

"I'm leaving soon," Damien yells through the wood. "I'd love to see you before I go."

Does he really think I would ever wish him goodbye before

he leaves to slaughter my kind? He's a larger fool than I initially took him for.

"Call it off," I beg.

My voice is barely above a whisper, but I know he can hear it.

My request is met with silence, the noise broken only by a quiet thud. I assume it's Damien dropping his head against the door, but even the image of him slumped over, defeated, isn't enough to pull me from my rage.

"Aine, please," he says.

Silent tears stream down my cheeks as I return to bed and slip underneath the covers. Damien killed my family. He slaughtered everybody I've ever known and loved, and now he's going to do it to some other poor woman.

I let out a cry as I recall how my father begged Vik to pardon me. He loved me, and now he's dead. Damien's pleading ceases at my escaped noise, and I know he's listening to me mourn the loss of my family.

"I didn't kill them," Damien says. There's another thump against the door, this one harder than the last.

I'm not stupid. I saw his expression when I asked to see my parents, the way his lips pursed and his eyebrows furrowed. He killed them.

"They, well..." Damien starts. He pauses before continuing. "Please open the door, Aine. I want to speak to you face to face."

It'll be a cold day in hell before I open this door.

"Tell me," I demand.

There's another thud. I pick at the skin of my fingers, anxiously waiting to hear what he has to say. Are they alive? I feel foolish for having hope, but I can't stop it.

"Vik had them killed after your execution." The knob jiggles as Damien tries to open the door. "My men tried to save them, but we didn't get there on time. They were hung."

I slide off the bed and onto the floor. No. There's no way.

"I'm so sorry, Aine," Damien continues.

I clear my throat. "What happened to Vik?"

My voice is hoarse, but I'm hardly in a state of mind to care. Vik killed my parents. Why? Why didn't Damien tell me this sooner? It's been months. He's had months to tell me.

"He's dead," Damien says. "My men made sure it was long and painful."

Good.

I struggle to breathe, and I tug at the neckline of my shirt as I hold back a sob. It's too hot in here. My family is dead, and my mate is about to slaughter my kind for sport. This can't be real.

"Call the hunt off," I beg, desperate for Damien to listen to me just this once.

"I can't. It's too late."

It's not too late. Damien's the alpha, the leader of this entire fucking pack. He can order it to be called off. If the beasts need to hunt something so bad, they can take down the large animals that live in the forest.

There are plenty of bears and elk, and they'll be more of a challenge than some starved, scared human.

"I'll never forgive you for this," I say.

There's a long stretch of silence before Damien responds.

"We're mates. You'll forgive me with time."

If I weren't so empty, I'd laugh at the thought. Damien fails to realize that I don't feel the mate bond as he does. There's a bit of an unnatural pull, but it's nothing compared to what I assume he feels on his end.

"If you go, you're as good as dead to me," I threaten.

I'm met with silence, and a few minutes later, I hear the back door slam shut. I look out the window to see Damien storm into his office. I guess that's his answer.

He doesn't try to speak to me again, allowing me to mourn in peace. Hours pass before somebody knocks on my door, but I ignore it. I don't want to speak to anybody, and I wish people would leave me alone.

"Aine?" It's Alex's voice that travels through my bedroom door. "Are you in there?"

He knows I am. "Go away."

"Will you let me in if I tell you I don't agree with the hunt and I'm not going?"

Does he mean that? Would he lie about that? Probably not. I roll out of bed and crack open my bedroom door.

Alex barges inside the moment he sees my red-rimmed eyes.

"About time." He walks toward my window and rips open the curtains. I wince at the sudden brightness. "I understand your pain, but it's my job as your friend to make sure you're eating and getting fresh air."

Alex nods to himself when he notices the empty plate on my floor. "Damien will be pleased you've eaten."

I shrug, not caring what Damien finds pleasing.

Alex makes my bed and tidies up my room to his liking, and I stand tensely by the door and wait for him to finish. It's not until he grabs a tissue and begins wiping my face that I lose my composure.

My cries come fast and hard, and Alex tries to keep up before giving up and pulling me in for a tight hug. I sob into his shoulder, not caring if I ruin his shirt.

"It's okay," Alex whispers, running a hand down the back of my head. "You're okay. Damien is a fool for continuing the hunt. He thinks he'll lose the pack's respect if he ends it."

I roll my eyes. "I don't care why he's doing it. It's cruel and needless."

Alex pushes my messy hair out of my face. I wince as his

finger snags a knot, the action encouraging him to grab a brush off my dresser and spin me around.

"I agree," he admits.

We fall silent as he works the brush through my hair, smoothing out the strands. He's surprisingly good at this, knowing to start at the ends and work his way to the roots. I assume it's something he learned from Freya. She has long hair, and I'm willing to bet he was all too happy to help care for it.

"The beasts are leaving soon," Alex says. "Many choose to stay behind, and the humans get together and drink in the dining hall the first night the hunters leave."

I understand why.

"Jenna and Olivia are already there," Alex continues. "I think we should go."

It *would* be nice not to be alone right now.

"I don't want to see Damien," I say.

Alex tosses my brush onto my bed and opens the door. I jump as he shouts downstairs.

"Make yourself scarce!"

He places a hand on my back and leads me out of my bedroom. The back door slams shut just as we reach the bottom of the stairs, and Alex leads me out the front.

He talks nonstop in a clear attempt to distract me, and he rubs soft circles into my shoulder as he leads me to the dining hall. I pause just before we enter, and I turn to pull him into another tight hug.

"Thank you," I say. I don't think he knows just how much his kindness and friendship means to me.

Alex gives me a tight squeeze.

"I missed having a sister," he admits.

We pull away from one another, and I wipe at my cheeks as he pulls open the doors to the dining hall. I'm almost immediately bombarded with loud laughter and slurred words, and I take a moment to collect myself before stepping inside. The place is packed, and I search for a familiar face.

Jenna and Avia stand in the center of the room, and I wave to them both. Despite the loud volume in the room, I hear Jenna squeal just seconds before she grabs Avia's hand and rips her away from the beasts they're chatting with. She stumbles as she runs toward us, but every time I think she's going to fall, Avia hoists her back up.

"Aine!" Jenna shouts as she barrels into me.

I'm caught off guard by her body slamming into mine, but Alex catches us mid-tumble. Avia laughs as she gently pulls Jenna away.

"She forgets after one too many drinks that she can't launch herself at other humans the way she can to the beasts," Avia explains, wrapping her arms around Jenna's midsection to hold her steady.

Jenna presses a sloppy kiss to Avia's lips, and Alex mumbles something about getting us a drink before disappearing into the crowd. I feel uncomfortable as I look at all the unfamiliar faces surrounding me, and Avia wordlessly leads Jenna and me to a quieter corner of the room.

"I know it's a lot," she says. "The humans have a tough time with the hunts, and they tend to go overboard with the drinking. Jenna especially."

How can Damien continue supporting the hunt when he sees how it affects so many of us? Clearly the hunt creates a large divide within the pack, so why not pick the option that doesn't cause mental anguish.

Alex returns with two drinks in hand, and I don't hesitate to snatch one and down it. His eyes grow comically wide, but he quickly hides the reaction and hands me the one meant for him. I throw that one back too.

"I'll get more," he says, returning to the bar.

I force thoughts of my parents aside as I turn and chat with Avia and Jenna.

Alex doesn't police my intake like Damien does, and before I know it, both Olivia and Jenna are grabbing my hands and pulling me into the food pantry. I stumble behind them, laughing as Olivia slams her hip into a counter on the way there.

Chapter 23

AINE

JENNA SNORTS AS she chucks the large onion at my head. I scramble to catch it, but my hands refuse to move fast enough and the vegetable hits me in the center of my forehead before falling to the floor.

I choke on my laughter and drop down to grab it, my knees smacking painfully against the cement as I land with little to no grace. Olivia follows suit, plopping to the ground with a huff.

"Bite it!" Jenna orders. "You absolutely have to."

Olivia giggles, eager to chime in with her own peer pressure.

"Jenna made me eat one during my first hunt," she says. "Don't make me be the only sad onion eater."

I tip onto Olivia's lap as I bring the onion to my lips. It's covered in dirt, but I've got nothing better to do. I shrug and open my mouth.

Alex swipes the food out of my hand just moments before I bite down. Avia stands by the door looking exhausted, but it's hard to tell when there are two of her overlapping one another.

Olivia's thighs are soft underneath my head, and I close my eyes to relax before realizing it makes the room spin. A loud groan slips from my lips as that feeling travels to my stomach and throat. That's not good.

Alex seems to be expecting this as he lifts me from Olivia's lap and sticks my face into the nearest trash can.

I heave, and Jenna immediately turns and begs Avia to let her stay. The deal is we can stay out and drink as long as we want, but we agreed to go home without complaint the second one of us starts to get sick. It seems I'm the one ruining the fun.

Alex rubs my back as I press my face into the side of the trash and cry.

"Are you okay?" he asks.

I nod, and he momentarily leaves to help Olivia to her feet. She whines, but she still accepts his help before reaching for my sweaty face and pulling my hair back.

"Damien is stupid," she whispers as I struggle to catch my breath. "We'll find you a better mate. I promise."

Her voice is quiet, but Alex hears her anyway and scolds her for putting such thoughts in my head. He can suck my nuts.

Jenna and Avia are long gone by the time I find the strength to pull my face out of the trash, and Olivia's lost interest in me and directed her efforts into climbing Alex. He smiles and shakes his head, the action flirty, before leaning back so she can straddle his lap.

I clear my throat, not sure I'm supposed to be seeing this. They break apart, and Alex rises to help steady me.

"Let's go home," he says, guiding us both out of the pantry.

A few beasts notice and laugh at Alex as he visibly struggles to wrangle both Olivia and me in, and I stumble around and say my goodbyes to everybody I've befriended tonight. It takes Alex at least thirty minutes to get us outside, and by the time he does, it's clear his patience has expired.

The sky's black when we finally begin our journey home, and

after Olivia falls and bursts into tears over a scraped knee and I trip over Alex's foot, he lifts us both underneath his arms. Our feet drag against the floor as he carries us.

Olivia and I make brief eye contact before bursting into a fit of giggles.

"I think he's mad," I mock whisper.

Olivia nods. "He's not mad at me because he loves me," she announces after a moment. "But he might be mad at you."

I crane my neck to look at Alex. He refuses to acknowledge my stare, and I struggle to free my arms so I can poke him. When I finally do, I accidently aim for the wrong cheek and end up sticking my finger in his mouth.

Alex gags before snapping his teeth around my finger. I hiss and rip my hand back to my chest. Damien wouldn't be happy to hear that Alex put his teeth on me.

I don't care what Damien thinks, though.

"Is that true?" I tease, remembering Olivia's words. "Do you love Olivia?"

Alex remains silent, but I don't think anything of it. He stopped being fun hours ago. Olivia seems to take offense at his refusal to answer, though, and bursts into tears.

I reach across Alex's torso to wipe at her wet cheeks.

"It's okay," I promise her. "*I* love you."

Alex's chest expands before he hikes Olivia up higher and plants a kiss on her cheek. I can't make out what he's whispering to her, but her crying stops before she buries her face in his chest.

I can't help but feel jealous at their not-so-hidden, secret relationship, and I fall silent as I stare at the ground in front of me. We're almost back, and I count the seconds until Damien's home comes into view.

Alex places us on the front steps.

"Don't move," he orders.

"I'm sorry," Olivia says as Alex hurries to open the front door. "Alex told me not to say anything about us because he doesn't want you to be sad that you and Damien aren't—"

"That's enough," Alex interrupts.

He pulls Olivia to her feet, and she groans as he wraps his arm too tightly around her stomach.

"I'll be right back," he promises me.

I lean against the railing and stare into the woods, contemplating the absolute mayhem my life's turned into these past few months. A small part of me wishes I could reverse time and go back to how it was before I killed Henry.

He may have been a dick, but at least I knew what to expect and how to react. Life was predictable, and I miss that.

Being with Damien is admittedly exciting at times, but the unknown and constant back and forth terrifies me. What happens when he wakes up one day and realizes he's changed his mind about having a human as a mate? Will he kill me in my sleep and take another?

Despite his words, his actions tell me that's precisely what he'd do. Men who value human lives don't go out and hunt them for sport.

After getting Olivia situated, Alex returns and helps me inside. He politely ignores my wet cheeks as he leads me upstairs.

I turn to enter my bedroom, but Alex tuts and forces me to enter Damien's room instead. My tears start up again as I'm shoved into my mate's private space.

"I don't want to be in here," I say.

The bed's unmade, and there are a few articles of clothing strewn about. Other than that, the place is immaculate. Alex brings me to Damien's ensuite bathroom.

"We both know you're going to do more puking tonight, and Olivia's already taken up residence in the hallway bathroom," he says, putting me in front of Damien's toilet.

I'm glad to see it's been cleaned, the chemical bottle still sitting on the floor. Did Damien expect me to be in his bathroom tonight? Did he tell Alex to bring me here?

I try to stand, wanting to leave, but Alex places his hands on my shoulder and forces me to remain seated. I struggle against him, but Alex refuses to relent. When I finally give in, he drags all of Damien's bedsheets inside and makes a pile in the bathroom corner.

"You will sleep here," he says, pointing to the makeshift bed. Then he points to the toilet, "and puke in there."

I nod.

"I hate him," I say.

Alex frowns, looking conflicted, before crouching beside me.

"I assume you know what happened between Damien and Freya?" he asks. "I don't imagine you could've gone on that trip with them and not figured it out."

I blink, struggling to wrap my mind around Alex's question. He knows? I was under the impression nobody knew. Damien made it seem that way.

"You know?" I ask.

Alex laughs, but the sound lacks joy.

"Damien can't keep things from me, despite how hard he may try." Alex pauses to clear his throat. "My father abolished the hunt when he first became alpha. Many of the elders were angry, but there wasn't much they could do."

I sit up, eager to hear more. I don't know anything about Damien's past.

"The pack hated Damien after everything with Freya," Alex continues. "They thought he was unworthy to lead after sleeping with his brother's mate. He didn't want to tell them the truth, so he reinstated the hunt to keep them happy."

Alex clears his throat and begins braiding my hair.

"I don't agree with the hunt—many don't—but enough do. Damien thinks it's the only way to keep their respect, which isn't true, but I won't hate him for it."

I remain silent as Alex steals an elastic from my wrist and ties the end of my hair.

"I understand why you're furious—I really do—but I hope you'll give Damien a chance to earn your forgiveness."

Alex stands and fills the cup on the sink with water.

I accept it, but I don't know what to say. This isn't something I have the mental capability of processing right now. I'm so fucking angry, but a small part of me does understand that Damien is stuck between a rock and a hard place.

Alex nods, jerking his head toward the door. "I'm going to check on Olivia before heading to the dining hall to help clean up. Try to get some sleep. I'll be back in a few hours."

My thoughts race as I crawl to the makeshift bed and sink into Damien's sheets. They smell like him, and I breathe it in before I can stop myself.

It takes a while until I can close my eyes without the room spinning, and just when I fall asleep, I wake up to a loud commotion downstairs. I lift myself with a groan, searching through the sheets for my pants. I must have gotten hot and kicked them off, and I fumble to pull them up before crawling out of the room.

As much as I didn't want it at first, I'm glad Alex put me in Damien's bathroom. Despite my anger, I must admit his sheets are softer than mine and being close to the toilet is coming in handy.

I cry out as my shoulder slams into the doorframe. I can't see anything in the darkness of the room, and I grow frustrated as my toe slams into a dresser.

Something shatters downstairs seconds before Olivia screams, the noise prompting me to ignore my injuries and move faster. My shoulder continues to hit just about every fucking wall, but I find the stairs and make my way down them in record time.

"What's going on?" I ask as I reach the bottom. "Did you drop something?"

All the lights are off, and I hold out my arms as I navigate to the kitchen. Damien usually leaves nightlights plugged in so we can see, but Alex must've forgotten to turn them on.

Olivia doesn't respond, and I groan as a wave of nausea washes over me. I'm never drinking again. My foot slams into something soft and warm, and I crouch to feel it.

"Olivia?" I whisper, frantic as I grab her unmoving frame and try to shake her awake.

My hands are wet when I pull them back to my body, and I hurriedly stand and search for a light switch. I know it's on the wall to my left.

I freeze when my hands meet a rigid torso instead of plaster.

"Damien? Alex?" I ask, already knowing it's neither. They wouldn't find enjoyment in scaring me like this.

The person doesn't respond, choosing instead to grab my elbow and yank me toward the back door. Given the size and strength, I know it's a beast.

I can't tell who, though.

My clothing does little to protect my skin from the frigid air, and a hand clamps over my mouth when I try to scream. I try to bite their fingers, but the person quickly pulls back and smacks my face.

Almost immediately I feel blood begin to trickle out of my nose and spread along the lower half of my jaw.

"Shut the fuck up," the man orders, his voice hushed.

I'll be damned if I go out without a fight, and I open my mouth to scream into the forest as loud as possible. My body's bent forward and my head slammed into a knee before I can get anything out, though, the sudden impact bringing on an immediate headache.

The shock of it has me going quiet, and I groan as I try to think past the pain. Calloused hands wrap around my biceps and push. I fall onto my knees, but the person picks me up and forces me to continue walking.

Tears stream down my face as I struggle to remain focused, the effects of alcohol and shock making it hard to stay alert.

Where's Damien?

The man forces me into the woods and throws me over the back of a large animal. A horse? I attempt to slide off, kicking out my feet, but the man pins me down and ties my wrists and ankles together. My bloody face smashes into the side of the animal's ribcage as I'm then tied to it.

The man shifts into his beast form. I can barely make out the silhouette of him transforming, and I curse myself for having so much to drink as his image blurs.

I try to scream again, but the animal I'm tied to lets out a loud whine and begins sprinting through the woods alongside the beast. They remain close, and I frantically try and fail to loosen the ties on my wrists.

The jerky movements of the animal have my stomach twisting, and with a loud groan, I crane my neck away from its body and heave.

I don't understand where this beast is taking me or what I've done to make him so angry, but I hope Alex or Damien notice I'm gone sooner rather than later. Preferably before I'm dead.

The skin on my wrists and ankles splits open as it rubs along the rope, the blood pooling and falling from the tips of my fingers and toes. It continues to pour from my nose as well, a sign that the bone is probably broken. I let out a pained yelp every time my face is smashed into the animal's side, my blood coating its skin and spreading all along my face and neck.

The beast and animal continue running long after I give up trying to escape, my brain too fuzzy to get anything productive done.

My consciousness fades in and out as we travel. Each time I wake and realize what's happening, I panic and plead into the darkness for the man to bring me home, but my requests are always ignored.

When the sun begins to rise over the trees, I take the opportunity to look for clues as to where I am and who has taken me. I know we're heading east, given the direction of the sunrise, but beyond that, I know nothing.

My breath hitches when I look at the beast running alongside us, but he doesn't return my gaze. If anything, he seems to be actively avoiding it. I silently cry until my consciousness fades again.

I jerk awake to the sound of a loud howl, the noise followed by the horse I'm on coming to an abrupt stop. My head still spins as the beast shifts into his human form, and my eyes spring open as I realize it's the alpha we met in the human village.

"Alpha Owen?" I ask.

He smiles, his teeth on full display as he stalks forward and begins to untie my limbs. His fingers turn red as they touch my torn skin, and I can't refrain from hissing as the rope is pulled out of my wounds.

I fall to the ground as I come loose, my legs unable to support my weight. Owen looks down and sighs before pulling me to my feet. I stumble as my vision tunnels and knees buckle beneath me. What's he doing?

"Where's Damien?" I ask.

Owen only laughs.

He drags me through his pack, leading me past houses and beasts. There aren't many around, but the ones we do encounter look at me with disgust.

"Damien?" I call out.

I already know he's not here, though.

Owen grabs the back of my neck, and I barely have time to react before he raises his arm and backhands me. My head snaps to the side. Fuck, that hurt.

"You're not to speak his name," Owen spits.

He leads me into the pack's center and presses me against a large, wooden pole. What the fuck is this? I try to push against Owen, but he doesn't budge as he grabs my shirt and tears it off.

"Stop," I scream, my voice cracking as I attempt to cover myself.

Owen grabs my wrists and forces my arms down so he can tie them around the pole. Any attempts I make to break free are easily ignored, and I slam the back of my head against the pole as I struggle.

My fight is useless. Owen's people stand and watch as their leader rids me of my clothing, their faces void of emotion.

The people in Damien's pack would never let this happen.

"Damien—"

Owen strikes me again. My head swivels and my ear smashes against the pole. Blood seeps out of it and down my neck, warm and wet.

"Freya?" I try.

Damien didn't tell me what happened between her and Owen, but they were on good terms the last I heard. She may not like me, but I don't think she'd sit back and let this happen.

Owen smiles as I cry.

"She's not here," he says. "Your mate tried to pawn that whore off on me, but I refuse to taint my pack with her filth." His fingers tap against my throat. "You're the perfect one for me."

I shake my head. "I don't understand."

Owen seems to enjoy my confusion.

"I know this is a big adjustment, so I'll be gentle as you learn the rules," he says. Is this considered gentle? "You're to stay on this pole until your next bleed ends. You'll learn to be obedient in the meantime."

I gulp, my vision tunneling. Owen continues speaking, but I struggle to remain focused when my body's screaming in pain.

Owen grabs my hips and pushes me to the ground. My shoulders stretch painfully as my bare butt touches the dirt, but it's hard to worry about that as Owen's hands move to the insides of my thighs.

None of the beasts attempt to stop their leader from ripping out my menstrual cup. My thighs are wet and sticky as blood spills over them, and I struggle to breathe as Owen stands and steps back.

"You're going to learn quickly," he says.

He almost looks concerned as he grabs my chin and tilts my head to the side. He examines my mark before running a finger over the scar. I feel nothing but disgust as he touches it, but I stay silent.

"Did you consummate your bond?" he asks.

I try to look away, not wanting to answer.

Owen tightens his grip until I know I'm going to have small bruises from each of his fingertips. "I asked you a question."

I gulp, not sure why he's asking, before nodding. If he thinks Damien and I had sex, maybe he'll be too disgusted to touch me.

Owen frowns and steps away. "Then we'll need to break the bond first," he mutters. "Your body won't accept me until it's gone."

Chapter 24

DAMIEN

I LOOK AROUND, eyeing the beasts who have gathered for the hunt. They seem excited as they joke about the humans they hope to find tonight, their pride evident as they discuss how many they killed last year.

I clench my jaw as I listen to them make bets on who will get the most kills tonight.

I'm disgusted they all think it will be me.

Last year I put on a happy face, and I was up and conversing with my beasts. This year, I can't even manage that. I want to call this entire thing off and return home to Aine. I should've done so before she even asked.

A good mate would have.

I don't know why I didn't.

I restarted this tradition years ago, but much as changed since then. I'm no longer the lanky young man I was, and I know I can beat the beasts who would undoubtedly challenge me for my position.

My lips part to release a quiet groan as I try and fail to connect with Aine through the bond. I told Alex not to let Aine drink too much, but I'm not surprised he disobeyed my command.

He's mad at me for pairing Freya and Owen together, and he's even angrier with me for going ahead with the hunt.

One of the elders I've always struggled with takes a seat beside me, his thigh pressing against mine. Toby's one of the few who threatened to challenge me after my betrayal to Alex.

"You okay?" he asks.

I shrug, not exactly eager to explain myself to him. Everybody's already heard what happened between Aine and me, and I've heard enough opinions to last me a lifetime.

"The humans are weak," Toby says. He laughs and places a hand on my shoulder. I shrug it off. "We're doing the world a favor by keeping their numbers low. Your ancestors would be proud of you for putting your pack first. It's a decision your father was too weak to make."

I stand, uninterested in hearing another word.

My father was a good man. He did the best he could after my mom's and sister's deaths. He managed his grief, and he continued to be a present father and strong alpha for the pack.

Had my father been in my position, he would've called off the hunt before it was even asked of him.

What if Aine never forgives me? My mate is an enigma, always keeping me on my toes and challenging my opinions. I should be at home soundly asleep next to her, not getting ready to slaughter her kind.

Fuck.

I lock my hands behind my back and turn to face the group of hunters. They quiet, waiting for me to speak.

"No humans," I decide. This is going to enrage them, but I don't care. "If you come home smelling of a human, I'll tear out your throat and use your meat to keep us fed through the winter. You can hunt any other mammals."

My order is met with complete silence.

"Is this a joke?" It's Toby who speaks up.

I shake my head. "No."

Several seconds pass before a group of four men shift and disappear into the woods. They're the ones who enjoy a good hunt, and they probably weren't going to target humans, anyway.

Most others linger, waiting for me to admit I'm joking. I don't, and eventually they take off. They're annoyed, but they won't be a problem.

The men I once feared don't put up the fight they use to threaten, but I can tell by their tightly clenched fists and jaws that they're going to cause issues in the pack. Some will return smelling of human despite my order, and they'll find themselves disappointed when I follow through on my threat.

Well, most of it.

I have no interest in preserving their meat, but I sure as fuck will tear out their throat.

Six young men remain. They're challenging me, which is disappointing. Once I'm finished with them, I'll return to Aine. I'll apologize, and things will be better between us.

I eye my challengers.

I train with most of them daily, and none are ready for this fight. There are a select few members of the pack who can hold their own against me, but none of them chose to join the hunt.

Three men shift into their beast form. I hang my head.

They want to fight to the death, not submission.

The first beast lunges quickly. I already know his weakness. I sidestep and grab the fur at the back of his neck, and I slam his head into the ground until he stops moving.

I remain in my human form, hoping to intimidate the rest.

I don't want to kill my people, and I'm beyond relieved when one of my challengers leave and the two who shifted into their beast form turn back into their human one.

I can tell their hearts aren't in the fight as they lunge for me, but they're too proud to stand down. Someday I'll age out of my position and they'll be strong enough to win this challenge, but it's not today.

My body is slick with sweat and blood as I pin the last of my challengers to the ground and force him to submit. He whines as he touches his forehead to the ground and turns his head to expose his neck.

I release him, stepping back.

"Go home," I order.

He scrambles to stand and leave. The next challenge they attempt will be done in our beast forms, whether they want that.

I look around, ensuring there's nothing further for me to do, before beginning the journey home.

I'm sure Aine is already asleep, and I hope Alex put her in my bathroom as I requested. The humans always seem to get sick when they drink in excess, and I assume my fiery mate is no different.

The muscles in my thighs burn from how quickly I run home, and I can't stop from smiling as I enter my pack and shift back to my human form.

One of my men comes sprinting towards me, and he grabs my hand and pulls me back into the forest. He's out of breath, which is unusual. He's one of my best fighters, and he's staunchly against the hunt.

"Alex and the others left twenty minutes ago," he says.

What?

"We don't know when she was taken, but it wasn't long ago," he continues. "I'll stay here and watch over the pack." He pushes me in the direction of my brother's stale scent. "Fucking go!"

My world spins as I take off into the forest.

There's only one person my men would urge me so quickly to follow, and my fears are confirmed when I round the back of my house and smell Aine's blood.

I recognize Owen's, too.

I'm going to kill him.

My beast whines as we run atop Aine's bloody trail, and my panic grows as the scent thickens. I'm going to find her, and I'm going to rip apart every dirty beast inside Owen's sad excuse of a pack.

Chapter 25

AINE

OWEN'S BEASTS WON'T make eye contact with me. I cry and beg for their help, but they pretend not to notice. In the brief moments I do catch them looking, their gazes are full of contempt.

I don't know what I've ever done to earn such hatred.

My left eye's so swollen I can't see out of it, but I use what vision I do have to scan the tree line for Damien. I've been tied to this pole for over a day now, and I'm beginning to worry.

Owen seems to be on high alert, constantly pacing back and forth. His eyes occasionally flash to me, and I assume he intends to kill me if Damien arrives.

I stare at the back of his head, my breath hitching when he abruptly spins to look at me. His frown transforms into a smile as he notices my attention, and I look away before he gets any ideas. It's too late, though, and he excuses himself from the group of beasts he's speaking to and saunters over.

My heart pounds as he crouches by my feet.

"Look at me, Aine," he orders.

He grabs my cheeks, his grip painful as he forces me to look at him. I blink to try and clear my vision, but his image remains blurry and unfocused.

I can't tell if my lack of sight is a side effect of my swollen eye or a permanent condition caused by the hits I've recently taken to the head. I hope it's the first, but I wouldn't be surprised if it were permanent.

"I'm sorry," I say.

I don't know what I'm apologizing for.

Owen smiles. "Why are you sorry?"

I open my mouth to respond, but no sound emerges. I don't know what I've done, and I don't know what there is to apologize for.

Owen laughs as he senses my internal struggle, the noise loud and harsh. He taps his fingers against my cheek, the touch light before he shoves my head against the pole.

The back of my skull makes painful contact with the wood, and tears begin wetting my cheeks.

"We've discussed you not speaking," he says, forcing me to look up and meet his gaze again. "You keep making me punish you, Aine. I don't want to, but you're forcing my hand."

I try to pull out of his hold, but it's useless.

Owen squeezes my cheeks once more before bringing his hand to my thigh. His claws extend as he moves, the sharp nails scraping painfully against my exposed skin.

"If you stay quiet, I'll only have to do this once," he promises.

Then he slides a nail straight into the fleshy skin of my thigh, easily puncturing my muscle. My jaw drops in a silent scream, and I pant as I force myself to remain quiet. I don't want him to do this again.

An indescribable burn spreads along my thigh, my skin feeling like fire. Every inch of my body is telling me to cry out, but I follow Owen's orders and remain silent.

I'm covered in a cold sweat when he finally pulls his claw out of my leg. He offers soft assurances and praise, but they mean nothing to me.

Owen strokes my thigh. "We usually wait to do this, but you're doing so well. I think you're ready." He smears my blood around, drawing tiny designs with it.

I'm ready for what?

Owen stands and kicks my legs apart. I try to fight him, wanting to keep my thighs together, but he easily overpowers my attempts.

"I'm going to free you of your sins," Owen says. "We'll mark them in your thigh together."

I shake my head, not understanding what Owen means. He doesn't explain, and he looks excited as he pulls and tugs my limbs into the position he wants them.

"If you're good, I'll bring you clothes," he says.

My fighting ceases at the promise of clothing. I don't like how the beasts stare at me, their eyes lingering on my exposed breasts and thighs. My attempts to cover myself are useless as my hands are tied to the pole behind me, so I've taken to tucking my knees into my chest and crossing my ankles.

It's not effective, but it's the best I can do.

"I'm excited to hear your sins," Owen admits. "Tell me why you were sent to execution."

How does he know about that? Owen's smile teeters at my hesitation to answer, and with a loud sigh, he extends his claws and presses one into the skin next to the puncture wound he gave me earlier.

I shake my head and try to jerk away, but Owen's grip is too tight. I'm not going anywhere, and he knows it.

"Tell me why you were sent to execution," he repeats.

His tone leaves no room for argument, and I arch my back as he begins sinking his claw into me.

I cry. "I killed my husband."

The claw is removed, and before I can register what's happening, Owen grabs my other leg and cuts open the inside of it. It burns, and blood immediately begins to pour into the ground beneath me.

Owen lets me yank my leg free, but the relief doesn't last long. He wraps his arms around my waist, hugging me, and I feel disgusting as he runs his hands down my spine.

"You did so well. You're such a good girl," he whispers into my hair. "What else have you done?"

I shake my head, not wanting to answer. I don't want him to cut me again.

"Nothing," I say. "I haven't done anything."

Owen tuts, and my cries grow louder as he rips my leg away from my chest. No. My head pounds with the speed at which I shake it, but Owen pays it no mind.

I feel sick as I take in the sight of my thigh. The cut is long, and it's hard to see how deep it goes as it fills with blood. Is this what he meant when he said he would mark my sins in me?

"What else have you done, Aine?"

My head is empty. Owen's patience visibly thins, his lips flattening and eyes narrowing. I can't think. I need to give him something—anything.

"I forced my mark on Damien," I blurt out.

An abrupt laugh slips from Owen's throat, but he sobers quickly and tears open my skin again. He does it directly below the first slice, creating two parallel wounds.

I slam my head against the pole as I suck in a pained scream. The sting is unlike anything I've ever felt, and I'll never forget it.

Owen releases my leg and whispers more praises, but I block them out. I don't understand his game, and I don't like it.

"What else?" he asks.

I shake my head.

"Please," I beg. "What do you want with me?"

I thought he and Damien were friends. Did he discover Freya's true personality? Is this his way of getting back at Damien for setting him up with a woman he doesn't approve of.

Owen squeezes my cut, forcing more blood to pour out.

"What else?" he repeats.

I wrack my brain for something to admit to. Owen runs his nail up and down my leg in warning.

"I, uh—" I freeze as he sticks his nail's point into my kneecap. "Sometimes I steal food from the pantry."

It doesn't happen frequently, but I've taken a snack or two after unloading the wheelbarrow. Alex knows about it, and he pretends not to notice when I return to the garden with sticky fingers.

Owen cuts me.

He repeats this sick process until the sky grows dark.

The only breaks I receive are when one of his beasts interrupts to give an update on Damien. I've learned not to eavesdrop when my mate's name is brought up, and I turn away to show I'm not listening.

I hope Damien's coming, but given Owen's good spirits, I worry my assumptions are wrong. He should've been here by now.

Rain begins falling as I finish another round of confessions, and I glance toward the dark clouds swirling above. We're moments away from a downpour, but Owen doesn't seem to mind.

Will he untie and bring me inside to wait out the storm?

"This isn't ideal," he says, looking up.

If I weren't so afraid of his punishments, I'd ask about clothing. He promised he'd give me some once we were finished.

Owen releases me and stands. "I'll return when the rain has

stopped."

I open my mouth to protest, my eyes watering, but I stop myself before following through. He's not going to bring me anything.

Owen cocks his head to the side. "What?"

My mouth is dry, and my voice is hoarse when I finally find it.

"You said you'd bring me clothes."

Owen scoffs, which isn't surprising. He's going to leave me in the cold rain with no protection. Just as he did last night.

"I said no such thing," he says. He's lying.

I nod, watching out of the corner of my eye as he retreats into the woods. Only when I'm sure he's gone do I work up the courage to look at my legs.

The skin on my right thigh is covered in dirt and blood from where he punctured me, but it's the left that's torn to shreds. I giggle as I note that it looks like a serving ham, ready for the meat to be lifted and put on a fancy dinner plate.

My laughter only grows as the rain begins to come down in earnest, washing all my grime and blood away. I'm going to die out here. I'm going to bleed out and die tied to some stupid fucking pole that some deranged beast tied me to.

I bend forward, in absolute hysterics.

I should quiet before Owen or one of his men grow angry, but I'm unable to stop the loud shrieks that fall from my lips. I don't even know what I'm laughing at. I just know I'm laughing.

I continue my loud cackles even as Owen comes storming my way. His shoes splatter the newly formed patches of mud, some of the wet dirt even hitting me in the face as he comes to a halt directly next to my crumpled body.

I scream out in laughter, the noise loud and unforgiving as he raises his arm and swings.

It's bright the next time I find consciousness, the sun burning and reddening my sensitive skin. There are no beasts in sight, and I rest against the pole until I fall back to sleep.

My aching head is all I can think about the following day, and Owen cracks several jokes about it between beatings. I quickly realize my unconscious state is better than my waking one.

When the next day rolls around, I've given up hope of Damien coming to save me. Maybe he organized this entire thing with Owen to get rid of me.

There's an unpleasant chill to the air today, and I whimper as Owen casts a shadow over my face. The noise irritates my throat, and I spit up blood with a painful cough.

I'm surprised Owen hasn't killed me yet. I've been bleeding for days, and every bone in my body aches. I'm sure a few are broken.

Owen looks angry this morning. It's not a good sign.

He crouches, bringing himself to my level.

"Do you want me to kill you, Aine?" he asks.

Do I? I don't want to die, but I want this to be over. I'm exhausted, and death no longer feels so scary. I've been preparing for it for days.

I nod. "Please."

Owen smiles. He's proud of what he's doing to me, pleased he's gotten me begging for death.

"I can't do that," he coos. "I need you."

I can't fathom why. He straightens up and gives me the crazed look he always does when he's about to beat me, and I shut my eyes and wait for it to happen. He may not want to kill me, but he's going to. It's only a matter of time before my head hits the pole just a little too hard or he cuts me just a little too deep.

I wait for him to hit me, but nothing happens. My heart pounds as I open my eyes, needing to know what's happening.

Owen has moved away from me, and I stare at his back as he accepts a small object from one of his men. I crane my neck to see what it is, but I can't get a good view.

He's beaming when he turns back toward me.

"You're ready to move to the next level," he says.

He sets the object on the ground. Scissors. Why?

My question is answered as Owen begins bundling up my hair, pulling all the knotted pieces out of my face and off my shoulders. I let out a small whine. He's going to cut it off.

I squeeze my eyes shut again, not wanting to watch as Owen roughly cuts my hair. It's the last piece of myself he hasn't destroyed, and I don't want to see it removed.

"Such a good girl," Owen whispers between snips. "Look at your hair, Aine."

It physically hurts to pry open my eyes and look at the long strands lying on the ground. The pieces are uneven and blunt, and I can't imagine how my head must look. He purposefully did a poor job.

Owen places his fingers under my chin and urges me to look away from the ground and into his eyes.

"It looks good," he promises.

I hate myself for feeling comforted. What's wrong with me? I'm losing my mind. Owen's slowly tearing away and breaking everything I am, and I'm playing directly into his plans despite my awareness of it.

Owen pulls me into a hug, my cheek pressing against his chest. "He would never love you like this, but I don't mind."

I try to pull away, but Owen refuses to let me. I already know Damien would never love me like this, and I don't need the reminder.

"I think you look beautiful," Owen continues.

A smile forces its way to my lips. I don't want to feel

complimented by him, and I desperately wish for it to stop.

He rubs the back of my head, his touch the only comfort I have. My shoulders burn where they pull against the pole, but I ignore it.

Owen releases me after several minutes, and my face warms as he slides his hands to my cheeks. I avoid eye contact as he wipes away my tears, and he tuts when my crying only worsens.

I hate Owen, I know I do, but the touch feels so good.

"You're doing good, Aine," he says.

He leans forward and presses his lips to mine. I don't kiss him back, and I remain stiff despite knowing it's going to get me in trouble. I don't want to kiss him.

Owen pulls away, and I desperately look into the woods. I'm hoping to find Damien standing there, ready to rescue me, but all I see are Owen's beasts. There are four within my line of sight, and they all stare at me with outward disgust.

I'm growing familiar with seeing it.

"It's okay to want me," Owen says, drawing my attention. He strokes my cheeks. "I want you to kiss me back, Aine."

He returns his lips to mine, kissing me with more fervor. Despite my better thinking, I find myself shutting my eyes and moving my lips against his. He's going to punish me if I don't, and I can't handle any more of it.

Have Damien and I ever kissed? I struggle to remember as Owen grabs my hips and slides me toward him. It hurts, and I pull away with a loud cry as my shoulders stretch back.

Owen releases me, and I press myself against the pole.

"That was perfect," he says. "Did you like that, too?"

Owen waits patiently for my answer, and I hesitate before nodding. I feel disgusting for saying it, and I feel even worse for meaning it. Every touch I've felt these past few days has been painful, and the kiss *was* nice.

I truly liked it.

Owen strokes the side of my head and plays with the few uneven hairs that hang by my ear.

"*He'll* never want you again," he says.

I bite my bottom lip until I taste blood. I know he won't. I've seen the damage Owen's done to my body, and now I'm enjoying his kiss.

"You know that, don't you?" Owen continues.

My heart pounds.

"Say it," he orders.

"He'll never want me again," I whisper.

It feels like my heart is being torn out of my chest.

Chapter 26

DAMIEN

MY IRRITATION GROWS as another group of men return with no new leads. I don't understand how Owen managed to take Aine so far in such a short period of time, or how he managed to cover their scent so thoroughly.

We followed Aine's trail of blood for several hours, but even that has come to a stop. We've been searching in every direction from where her last blood was spilled, but that's leading to nothing but dead ends.

The forest is enormous, and we could travel for days in each direction before reaching any sort of civilization.

I know the general direction of Owen's pack, but I have no details. He's invited me to visit him several times since I took the alpha title, but I've never accepted. We have conflicting morals, and I had no desire to witness the monstrosity of his pack firsthand.

I regret that now.

My muscles burn as I shift into my human form. The men who just returned give a useless update, and I immediately send out a new group to continue the search.

All I need is a speck of blood or a hint of Aine's scent to continue the trail.

My men shift into their beast form and approach the pile of Aine's clothing Alex brought. They sift through it, taking large inhales of her scent before disappearing into the forest.

I pace, my head pounding. I'm feeling Aine's pain through the bond, and I'm growing increasingly worried. It wasn't too bad at first, but as the alcohol filtered out of her system, the intensity grew.

Alex approaches on my right. I ignore him.

"You should rest," he says.

Another wave of Aine's pain hits me, and I grab onto the nearest tree for stability. I'll sleep when Aine's safe.

Alex sighs. "Damien…"

My bond with Aine is dissolving. We never had sex, and our marks aren't yet permanent. I never concerned myself with fully completing our bond, I didn't feel there was any rush. We'd have sex eventually, and we spent enough time around one another that our bonds remained strong without it.

Both the physical and emotional distance is weakening them, though, and I'm sure the torture isn't helping.

I pull up my sleeve and shove my thumb into my mark, but I feel next to nothing. I press harder in a desperate attempt for something more, but there's no change. I hope Aine can feel it and knows I'm coming, and I continue forcing my nail into my mark until it's coated with blood.

It's only a matter of time before we find a trail. Owen did a good job covering his tracks, but there's got to be something he missed. We'll find it. We have to.

Chapter 27

AINE

OWEN LIKES MY silence. He says I'm allowed to speak when asked a direct question, but he prefers when I don't. When Owen asks something, he doesn't really care for the answer. He just wants to feel good about having asked it in the first place.

I can't remember the last time I spoke.

I stare at my legs while Owen speaks. I'm covered in so much dirt and blood that I can't see my skin underneath, and the leg muscles I once loved have been cut open and destroyed.

I was unaware just how quickly a human body could break down, and at this rate, I doubt I'll be alive by the time my next bleed comes around. I'd estimate I've been here for well over a week, but it's hard to know for sure. The days blend together, and when Owen doesn't visit me, I usually just sleep through them.

My lips curl as I think about my death.

It's only a matter of time.

Damien's not coming, and even if he were, he won't care to keep me. I'm too dirty. Dozens of beasts have seen my naked body on this pole. They scoff at the sight of my blood, and they laugh as I cry and try to hide the shame of my excrement.

Owen was kind enough to order a beast to clean up the worst of it, but no amount of scrubbing could thoroughly cleanse the small area surrounding me.

It's forever tainted.

I'm forever tainted.

Damien would turn and run for the hills if he ever saw me like this. I wonder if that's what happened. I'm sure he initially came looking for me, and I wouldn't be surprised if he took one glance at me and returned to his pack.

It wouldn't be hard for him to find somebody else to take my spot as his mate.

Owen sits beside me and clears his throat. I look over. He's clean and healthy, and he shouldn't be this close to me. My dirt is going to rub off on him.

He strokes my cheek, his touch soft.

"You're beautiful," he whispers.

I know he's lying, but I still find myself leaning into his touch. I want more of it.

"But you're losing too much weight," he continues. He pointedly looks down my frame. "I've sent one of my men to get food for you."

Did he really? I perk up, waiting for him to tell me it's a lie, but he looks earnest. He smiles down at me, and his hand slides to my neck.

I stiffen when his fingers trace over my mark.

"You lied about consummating your bond."

How does he know that? I gulp, panic rendering me motionless. Owen doesn't like when I lie to him.

The corners of his lips twitch upward as he breathes in the scent of my fear, his nostrils flaring. I forgot I told him that, and had I remembered, I would've come clean. My fear of Owen's punishments is greater than the preservation I have for the bond I share with Damien.

"I'm so happy," Owen says. "I never thought I'd get to see your beautiful skin without his mark."

Without his mark? I turn my head in a sad attempt to look at my neck. What does he mean by that? Is it gone? There's no way. Jenna made it sound like beasts mate for live, and Damien even said it's common for a beast to die soon after their mate does.

Owen chuckles, continuing to rub his thumb over the spot where Damien's mark is supposed to be.

"Unconsummated marks disappear," he explains. "The bond can always be broken, but the scar remains. A visual reminder of the man you promised to be with."

Owen's smile grows. "But yours is gone, my sweet girl. You're all mine."

My heart shatters. Every time I think I have nothing left, Owen finds something new to take away.

He slides his hand up my chest.

I feel nothing.

I am nothing.

When his hand travels to my waist, I instinctively press my thighs together. I don't want him touching me. I don't want him inside of me.

Owen slides his fingertips across the tops of my thighs before digging painfully into the flesh and forcing my legs apart. The beasts in the area stop and stare, their gazes heavy as they look over my exposed flesh.

I shake my head. I don't want this. If Owen's to have sex with me, I at least want it to be done in private. I want to face my shame in secret.

Owen stares between my thighs, and he lets out a long sigh before finally releasing me. I snap my legs back together and pull my knees to my chest.

Someday soon, he's going to do more than this. He's going to touch, and he's going to force.

"Look at me, Aine," Owen orders. My eyes grow wet as I look up, which seems to please him. "I love you."

My throat burns, and tears pour down my cheeks as I keep my jaw clamped shut. I won't tell him I love him. I won't do it.

Owen's expression sours as he realizes I'm not going to say it back, and I squeeze my eyes shut as he raises his arm. A second later, a burning pain spreads across my cheek. My head whips to the side and smacks into the pole.

Blood fills my mouth, and I drop my chin to my chest before looking back at Owen. He likes when I do that.

He hits me again, this time with more force. I'm a bit slower to recover, and already I feel my consciousness wavering. I don't stay awake for long these days.

Owen raises his arm again, but he lowers it when he realizes a beast is approaching us. The man carries a plate of mushed food, and Owen silently takes it.

"This is for you," he says, turning to me.

He scoops some of the mush up with his fingers and brings them to my lips. I wince, scared of what he's feeding me, but my hunger wins out and I open my mouth.

Owen places his fingers on my tongue, encouraging me to lick the food off them. I do, and I'm relieved the mush has no flavor as I force my throat to swallow. It's dry and painful, but I do it anyway. I'll take Owen handfeeding me over beating and fondling me any day of the week.

Time seems to pass slowly as he stuffs me full of food. I'm grateful it's warm and not covered in mold like the other dishes he's served me.

Owen is staring as he shoves the last bit in my mouth.

"Aren't you going to thank me?" he asks.

I open my mouth, but fear keeps me silent. I can't speak to him. If I talk, he's going to beat me. He always does.

"Thank me, Aine," Owen repeats.

I can't.

"Thank me before I'm forced to punish you."

He grabs my thigh, his nails digging into the skin. The muscle is already covered in tiny puncture wounds, dozens of them in various states of healing. It's his favorite form of punishment and, naturally, my least favorite.

I want to thank him, but my mouth and throat refuse to cooperate. I can't speak, and my cheeks grow wet as Owen begins to sink his nail into me. It tears easily through my flesh, sending fire throughout my entire leg.

I just want this to be over.

Owen disappears, his intimidating shadow hovering over me one moment and gone the next. I look up, confused as he sprints across the small field surrounding the pole. He's quick, and it's hard to keep up.

There's sudden frantic energy among the beasts in my immediate vicinity, the women rushing around as the men transform into their beast forms. Owen yells orders, his panic alarming.

I refuse to listen to the specific words he shouts, not wanting to get caught eavesdropping. What he does with his pack isn't any of my business. I know that now.

Even when the frantic energy grows and beasts begin to emerge from the trees, I keep my eyes averted. This is another one of Owen's tests.

The beasts that run in from the trees collide with Owen's men. They smash into one another with loud thuds, meeting head-on. Sharp teeth are quick to tear into the throats of one another, the large animals aiming to kill.

As foolish as I feel for even thinking it, I find myself looking around for Damien. I hope these aren't his men. I don't want him, or them, seeing me like this. He'll reject me after learning what Owen's done to me. I know he will.

He's nowhere to be seen, though. These aren't his men. Owen's probably just angered another nearby pack.

The beasts are vicious with one another, ripping flesh and bone with little to no hesitation. The attacking beasts are the better fighters, their movements calculated and assured as they circle and strike down Owen's men.

Owen's still in his human form yelling orders, but it's clear his fighters aren't listening as they scatter around with visible panic. A smile threatens to spread across my face, but I manage to refrain from showing any emotion.

I hope they kill me when they're done.

Owen continues to shout commands at his dying men, but when he realizes they aren't listening, he turns to me. He's angry, and his clothes rip off as he shifts into his beast form. It's a gruesome transformation, but I force myself to watch every broken bone and shed piece of skin.

I barely have enough time to register what's happening before he begins rushing toward me. I wait for the final blow, for him to trap me between his large jaws and snap my neck.

I'm excited for it, happy this torture is finally going to end.

Nothing happens, though. Beasts run in front of Owen, stopping him in his path. He easily tears through those standing in his way, his alpha strength proving to be too much for the others.

Owen's attention returns to me as the last beast blocking his way grows limp between his jaws. A grotesque mixture of blood and drool seeps from his mouth, and he drops the dead beast to the ground before stalking toward me.

He's so close, I can practically taste my death.

A beast slams into Owen, sending him sprawling in the dirt several feet from me. I'd recognize the white speck covered black fur anywhere. I spent hours staring at Damien's fur while he ran us to and from the human village.

A matching beast runs up alongside him, the two almost identical. It's Alex.

I can't help but feel disappointed. Owen was so close to killing me, to finally putting me out of my misery.

I don't deserve to be saved. Not anymore.

Alex shifts mid-run, his fur changing into skin as he skids to a stop by my feet. He looks frantic as he falls to his knees and begins untying my wrists. The movement burns my shoulders, but I ignore it.

Damien and Owen are still fighting. Owen continually lunges for Damien, but Damien easily sidesteps him. It doesn't look like Damien is trying to kill Owen, but I'm not quite sure.

Several of Owen's beasts run toward Alex and me, but they're quickly blocked by Damien's men. I don't understand why they're protecting me.

I thought he'd take one look at me and turn in the other direction. That's what Owen's men do when they see me. That's what Owen told me Damien and his beasts would do.

My arms are freed. I'm too weak to use them, and they fall limply by my sides. Then I begin to tip over, but Alex quickly grabs my shoulders and pulls me into his chest.

"We need to get out of here," he says, his voice low. "I'm going to pick you up and carry you. It's going to hurt, and I'm sorry for that."

He doesn't wait for a response before standing. He brings me with him, and my body feels like it's being set on fire as I'm removed from the ground. I cringe, my chest heaving, but I remain silent. This is nothing compared to the pain Owen gives.

Alex wraps his arm under my legs, holding me steady.

I've imagined this exact scenario hundreds, if not thousands, of times these last several days. Not once did I imagine I'd feel so much grief and disappointment when it did, though.

I'm dirtying Alex. I'm dirtying them all.

Alex turns and begins to sprint in the direction of the trees where Damien's men first emerged. They're still fighting, their attacks synchronized and efficient, but I see a few brought down amid the chaos.

They're dying for me. It's a wasted death, one I don't deserve.

I know I shouldn't, but I peer over Alex's shoulder in search of Damien. I spot him almost immediately near the pole where I was tied, his body shaking as he stalks toward Owen's retreating form.

Alex once told me a beast's fur won't grow around a mark, and my lip quivers as I realize Damien's forearm no longer holds my bite. Owen wasn't lying. Our bond truly has disappeared.

This is probably for the best. It will make leaving me easier.

Trees obscure my line of sight as Alex carries me into the dense forest, and he continues forward until the sounds of fighting are a mere memory. He's covered in blood by the time he finally stops and sets me on the ground.

I reach forward, desperate to wipe it off.

I've made him dirty.

Alex grabs my hands and gently pries them off his arms. He seems like he's on the verge of tears as he looks over my bare form, and his gaze lingers on my thighs before he clears his throat and looks away. So many of Owen's beasts have gawked and sneered at me these past several days, and Alex's quick glance barely registers.

"You're okay," he promises. His voice is soothing.

I want to cover myself and hide away. I'm ashamed of what

Owen did to me, and of how all of it is my fault. If I hadn't been so defiant, hadn't made Owen so angry, he wouldn't have been forced to hurt me.

This is my fault.

"Aine—" Alex exhales, his eyes damp. "I—"

His hand shakes as he lifts his arm and pushes his hair out of his eyes. He doesn't know what to say. I don't blame him. His attention darts to the right, and he moves to the side just as Damien appears through the trees.

He charges in my direction, shifting into his human form mid-step and skidding to a halt at my feet. His arms are wrapped around my waist and his face is buried in my neck before I can process what's happening.

What's he doing?

Fear spreads through my veins like wildfire as Damien continues to press his body against mine, his skin warm and coated with blood from the beasts he fought.

Owen promised that Damien would be disgusted with me. He said Damien would hate me, and he'd beat me if he ever saw how dirty I am. I believe it.

"Aine," Damien chokes out. He gasps into my hair, or at least what's left of it. "I was so scared."

He pulls back just enough that he can look at my body, his staring much more intense than Alex's quick glances were. I can't bring myself to watch his face, too ashamed to see the disgust I know lives on it.

I know he felt everything through the bond—at least until it faded. He felt me kissing Owen. He felt me being fondled by Owen. He felt Owen punishing me. He felt everything.

Alex stands and curls a hand around Damien's shoulder. Damien doesn't even seem to notice.

"I'll find her some clothes," Alex says.

Damien's shoulder is missing a sizable chunk of skin and muscle. It's not his only injury, and my chest burns as I note the number of cuts and bites he's endured. He fought because of me, and each scrape has my guilt mounting.

He shouldn't have come.

Damien reaches for me. I flinch, and he snaps his hand back to his chest as if he's been burned.

"We're going to take you home, okay?" he says. "You're safe now, Aine. I promise. You're safe with me."

I don't trust his motives. Damien's too intelligent to be tricked by the mate bond—Owen knew it and now I do, too. Damien will lure me into a sense of security and strike when I least expect it. Just like Owen promised he would.

Damien's pupils dilate, and he visibly hesitates with his hand in the air between us. It remains suspended as he struggles to determine what to do next, and with a quiet sigh, he drops it back to his thighs.

He doesn't know how to engage with me.

I don't know how to react.

The column of his throat twitches as he gulps, and he only moves when Alex approaches with an oversized shirt. I don't have enough strength to move my limbs, and I try not to look too petrified as Damien pulls the fabric over my head and helps ease my arms through the holes.

My frown deepens as I realize the shirt I'm being given belongs to Damien. I'm too dirty, and I'm going to ruin it.

My shoulders scream as I force my hands to rest in my lap, and I tug gently at the hem of Damien's shirt. I'm not strong enough to take it off myself, and I give Alex and Damien a desperate look as I pull at it.

I should say something, but I'm still too afraid to speak. The thought of even trying has my heart racing and my back breaking out into a cold sweat.

Damien and Alex glance at one another before shifting their attention to me.

Damien is the first to speak. "You don't want my shirt?"

I shake my head.

Alex clears his throat. "Do you want one of mine instead?"

I shake my head again. I don't deserve to wear anything.

A quiet rumbling emerges from Damien's chest, the low noise drawing my attention. Have I made him upset? Is he finally going to punish me? Damien has never physically hurt me, but I've also never put him in such a bad position.

What if his beasts now think he's a poor leader? He forced them into another alpha's land and made them fight for some damaged human. I may be Damien's mate, but our bond already dissipated. It would be easy for him to move on.

I open my mouth, needing to apologize, but I can't get the words out. Why can't I fucking speak?

Damien and Alex stare at me with clear worry, their nervousness apparent in their sideways glances with one another.

"Avia is coming with a transfusion kit," Alex says.

I don't want Damien's blood.

Before I can find a way to share that feeling, Damien pulls me back into his arms. I grow rigid as I'm pressed against his chest, and flames lick up my thighs as my cuts are stretched. I'm in more pain now than I was when Damien's beasts attacked me after my execution.

I didn't realize that was possible.

Damien quivers as he holds me, and he burrows his face into my neck before breathing in my scent. I'm embarrassed he's smelling me, my skin no doubt reeking at this point. I haven't been cleaned in days, and I know I'm covered in bile and excrement.

"I'm so sorry," Damien whispers.

What for?

He licks my neck, tasting the muddy skin with a content sigh. I don't know what to make of that, but my body makes the decision for me as my muscles instinctively relax.

My turmoiled thoughts continue, but I can't resist the temptation of comfort and safety Damien's arms bring.

He smells me again before cupping the nape of my neck and pulling back just enough to look me over. I've grown used to Owen's beasts staring at me, but I hate Damien seeing me like this. I'm disappointed in myself.

It's not until another person drops to their knees beside us that I work up the strength to look away from Damien. He tightens his grip to keep me in place as Avia grabs my arm and turns my wrist toward her.

I try to jerk away as Avia prepares my arm for a transfusion, my frantic actions causing Damien to pull me further onto his lap so he can better keep me still. My knees settle on either side of his thighs and my chest presses against his.

His thighs are slick with blood, most of it from the beasts he fought but some of it from me. It feels like all my cuts have reopened, and I'm soaking the ground and now Damien's lap.

He should be shoving me away, not trying to share his blood with me.

Damien holds my arm still, refusing to let me pull away.

"I'm so sorry," he chokes out. "I don't want to force you, but you're too weak to travel home like this."

Thick tears stream down my cheeks as Avia slides a needle in my arm, and she tapes it in place before doing the same to Damien. She moves quickly, and almost immediately, I feel the effects of Damien's blood taking place.

The hatred I feel for myself grows with each passing second, and the healing from his blood only adds fuel to the fire.

"You're going to be okay," Damien promises.

He presses soft kisses to the top of my head.

I wonder what he thinks about my hair.

He slides his hand to the nape of my neck, his thumb rubbing comforting circles against my skin as he whispers his quiet assurances. They only serve to make me feel worse. I'm undeserving of this kindness, and I'm waiting for things to turn. It's only a matter of time.

Several minutes pass in tense silence.

"Are you feeling better?" Damien eventually asks.

I nod. I've never felt so good, so healthy and strong, and I hate myself for it. I look down at my thighs. Most of the newer injuries seem to have healed without scars, but the ones from my first days here left little white spots behind.

Damien fingers the choppy ends of my hair as I stare at the tube pushing his blood into me. It's wider than the ones typically used, and I know more is being given to me than usual. Damien's giving me more blood than I need, probably at his expense.

Avia finally moves to remove the tubing, but Damien jerks out of her reach.

"Not yet," he snaps.

She sighs and reaches for him once more.

"Damien, you need—" she pauses when Damien moves away from her again, a loud, deep noise pouring from his chest.

I wait for his anger to be taken out on me. I don't understand why he's pretending to care, or why he's going to such lengths to have me healed. He's probably embarrassed for his beasts to see me in such a sad state. I imagine it's got to be quite humiliating for him. The strong alpha walking around with a weak, human mate who's covered in her own shit and can't even work up the courage to speak.

I'd be ashamed if I were in his position, too.

Avia continues to argue with Damien until finally, she gives up and leaves to help the other injured beasts. They trickle in from the direction of Owen's pack, their bodies visibly exhausted. Most seem to be relatively uninjured, but occasionally, one will return carrying an unmoving body.

My heart cries every time I see one, the guilt mounting. They probably have families back home, and they wasted their lives saving me. My time with Owen wasn't exactly enjoyable, but it wasn't so bad that anybody deserved to die over it. I was slowly learning how best to please and keep him happy. I was going to be fine.

"What's wrong with her?"

The question is whispered from somebody behind Damien. I don't recognize the feminine voice.

Alex orders them to leave, and Damien repeats the sentiment with slightly more colorful words. I watch the woman's retreating figure, not entirely understanding why she was yelled at. There *is* something wrong with me. It's easy to see.

Avia continues tending to the injured beasts, and after several more minutes, Damien finally removes the transfusion tubing from our arms and sets it aside. I feel strong, but Damien still takes it upon himself to lift me into his arms as he stands. My legs dangle toward the ground before he uses his free hand to grab my thighs and wrap them around his waist.

"I'll carry you home," he says.

I shake my head. I don't want him wasting his energy, and now that I have his blood, I'm more than capable of walking.

Damien hums when I try to pull away, his grip tightening.

"I'm going to carry you," he repeats.

I don't understand why. He's supposed to be angry and disgusted with me, not whatever this is.

Damien walks past his men, his chin held high despite their

stares. Some turn to look as we pass, but thankfully, most avert their gazes. They don't want to see me.

Damien kisses the top of my head.

"I'll never let this happen again," he promises.

I shrug, avoiding eye contact as I rest my head on his shoulder. I may not be in pain, but I'm still exhausted. I can't remember the last time I had any real sleep, and the few times I did find rest, Owen took it upon himself to wake me.

He hated when I slept, and I hope Damien doesn't get angry as I let my eyes slip shut for just a quick moment.

Chapter 28

AINE

DAMIEN CLEARS HIS throat.

It's the first noise he's made today.

"We're here," he says.

My eyelids are heavy as I pull my face from his chest and look around, eager to see if I recognize the woods that surround us.

Damien has been carrying me non-stop for the past two days, one of his arms wrapped under my thighs and the other holding the back of my head. He stops every few hours to shove barely cooked meat down my throat, but those are the only rests he's taken.

Beasts trot alongside us, their paces slow so they don't get too far ahead. Damien's faster in his beast form, but he refuses to shift. I fear it's because he feels the need to continue carrying me.

Even when his people have paused to sleep, Damien keeps moving. I don't understand why, and Avia has even gone as far as to stand in front of Damien to try and physically stop him from walking. Alex has done the same.

It only took one singular look for them to back away.

I've never felt so guilty, and the feeling continues to grow with each passing hour. Damien must be exhausted.

My throat runs dry when I spot the back of his house, the building larger than I remember. The beasts scatter as we enter the pack, everybody probably eager to return to their families.

Damien walks through his yard and pushes open the back door. I search for the blood I'm sure was spilled during my capture, but it seems everything has been cleaned up.

Even the area where Olivia laid is spotless.

I turn in search of her, my heart thumping loudly when I'm met with nothing but an empty house. Did Owen kill her? I remember feeling blood on her skin, but I never got to see if she was breathing before I was dragged outside.

"Let's get you cleaned up," Damien says. "Then we'll get some food in you."

He runs a hand down my spine, an action he does frequently. I no longer stiffen when he does.

I watch over Damien's shoulder as Alex follows us inside and runs upstairs. Damien lets out an annoyed huff as he carries me behind his hurried brother, his steps much more cautious.

Alex looks nervous as he pivots at the top of the landing and turns toward Olivia's room. So, she is alive? I perk up as he pushes open her bedroom door and steps inside, and I use Damien's shoulders for leverage as I try to catch a glimpse of her. There's a flash of a thin arm and the brief sound of her excited shout before the door slams shut behind him.

She's alive. Good.

I dig my fingers into Damien's shoulder as we enter his bedroom. It's the same as when I left, the sheets ripped off the bed and the objects on his dresser toppled over from when I tried to navigate my way out in the dark.

Damien carries me into the bathroom, and he hesitates before finally setting me on my feet. It's the first time I've been on them in days, minus the few short breaks to pee we've both taken, and I shift my weight from foot to foot as I get used to the feeling.

Damien frowns, looking upset when he notices the bundle of sheets in the corner of the room. His throat bobs as he gulps and scoops them up.

"I'll be right back."

I nod, turning just slightly so I can watch him leave. He haphazardly throws the sheets on his bed before pivoting and leaving the room altogether. I remain still, listening to the quiet creak of Olivia's door being opened.

Not wanting to get caught eavesdropping, I force myself to stop listening and move to the sink. My eyes are cast downward as I approach the large mirror that sits above it, and I take a moment to collect myself before lifting my head and looking.

My heart stops.

It's worse than I thought. I have no bruises or open wounds—thanks to Damien's blood—but it's clear I've been through hell. Dark bags sit underneath my eyes, the skin pulled downward like a child's drawing of the undead, and my lips are chapped and torn to shreds.

I refuse to let myself cry as I slide my gaze to my hair. Some spots are cut so short, you can see my scalp underneath, while other strands still fall below my shoulders. It's weighed down by grease and dirt, and I doubt any amount of washing will make it look better.

My hands shake as I finger the blunt ends.

It takes several more seconds for me to work up the courage to look at the spot that once held Damien's mark, and I let out a silent cry as I eye the unblemished skin. It's as smooth as the day I was born, not even a remnant of a scar remaining. My fingertips graze over the spot before pressing firmly down, searching for the pleasure it once brought.

There's nothing.

Damien steps into the room, and I drop my hands before he sees me mourning our broken bond. I can tell by his expression that he noticed, though. He glances between me and the mirror, and he lets out a quiet sigh as he moves to stand behind me.

I watch through the mirror reflection as he fiddles with the ends of my hair.

"Would you like to keep it like this?" he asks, his voice low as he touches the shortest strands. "Or we can cut it all and start fresh."

I purse my lips, thinking it over.

I've always taken pride in my hair, but there's no salvaging this. I open my mouth, prepared to ask him to cut it, but my throat closes before any sound emerges. Terror takes over, and I give up on speaking as I wordlessly point to the shortest pieces of my hair.

Damien cups my head. His touch is gentle, but I can't shake away the knowledge that he could easily crush my skull right now. It would take minimal effort.

We make brief eye contact through the mirror. He's still covered in dirt and dried blood from his fight with Owen's men, his dirty face matching mine. We both look awful.

Damien holds my gaze as he bends and kisses the top of my head, and he slides his hands down my arms before turning on the shower water and adjusting the temperature.

I remain where I am, too nervous to move.

When Damien turns to leave, I panic. I don't want to be left alone, and a quiet gasp slips from my throat. The sound is enough to stop Damien in his tracks, and he turns toward me with his eyebrows pulled tightly together.

I glance between him and the door, unsure how to ask him to stay. Thankfully, I don't need to.

"Do you want me to stay?" he asks.

I nod. Damien scares me, but the thought of being alone scares me more. Owen and his men are sure to come after me again, and I don't want to be alone when they do.

"I'm right here," Damien says.

He sits on the toilet seat, and he politely looks away as I strip out of his shirt and pull open the shower door. It's a kind gesture, but it's unnecessary. So many others have already seen me, and one more pair of eyes is nothing.

I step into the shower, letting the hot water hit my skin. My tight muscles relax for the first time in days. The water feels amazing, and the clear liquid turns brown the moment it touches my skin. My eyes follow the dirt as it trails down my stomach and past my legs before slowly spiraling down the drain between my feet.

Objectively, I knew my skin was covered in grime that could easily be washed off, but deep down, a fear that I'd always be filthy began to cement itself inside me. I turn away from the drain and look through the shower door for Damien. The texture on the glass obscures my vision and, in a panic, I push it open to make sure he's still here.

He looks up as I rip open the door, and I breathe out a sigh of relief. He hasn't moved. He's still here.

Damien clears his throat. "Are you okay?"

I remain silent, letting the question die between us. He hasn't acknowledged the fact that I haven't spoken, but I'm sure he's noticed. I'd be surprised if he hasn't.

I make no attempt to wash myself as I stand under the shower spray, too lost in my worries to do anything. It's only a matter of time before Damien snaps and abandons me as Owen promised he would.

Another minute passes before I find myself needing to search for Damien again. I rip open the door once more, beyond relieved when my wide eyes meet his confused ones.

He still hasn't moved.

"Do you want me to get in?" he asks.

I start to shake my head *no,* but I pause before rejecting his offer. It would be nice to have him here in case something goes wrong. What if Owen breaks in again? It's comforting having him close.

I nod.

Damien shows no emotion as he stands and approaches. He refused all suggestions from Alex and his beasts to put on clothing during the days he carried me home, simply stating they'd only slow him down.

I fail to see how putting on pants would slow him, but I don't question it.

Damien shoots me a nervous smile as he pulls open the shower door and steps inside, his movements slow in a clear attempt not to startle me. He navigates around the spray and sits on the small shower bench.

Feeling at ease now that we're in the same space, I decide to begin cleaning myself. I grab the body wash on the shelf, and I hold it toward Damien in an attempt to ask permission to use it.

Damien looks between me and the bottle before standing and taking it out of my hand. A small smile spreads across his lips as he leans over me to grab his loofah, and he presses a quick kiss to my temple as he pulls back.

"I'd love to wash you," he whispers.

I open my mouth, my cheeks flaming, but I shut it as he pops open the cap of the wash. That's not at all what I meant, and I'm horrified he thinks I've made such a needy request.

Owen would've punished me for this.

Damien looks happy.

I'm sure my face is beet red as Damien brings the sudsy loofah to my chest and begins cleaning my skin. He seems focused as he lifts my arms and maneuvers my body around with gentle nudges. Despite my initial nerves, I quickly find myself relaxing.

A wide smile I'm unable to control spreads across my face, and a hearty laugh bubbles up out of my throat as Damien abruptly sticks his pointer finger in my belly button to clean it out.

He freezes at the noise, his gaze snapping from my belly to my face as he takes in my reaction.

I slap my hands over my mouth, my eyes widening and pulse quickening. My laugh was too loud, and it wasn't attractive. It was a squawk.

Damien beams, looking awfully proud, before he begins to cackle. The stressed crinkles around his eyes disappear for the first time in days, giving him an almost boyish look.

"I didn't realize I was mated to a bird," he teases.

He twists his finger in my belly button before pulling it out altogether. My laughter fades, my attention captured by his words. He still considers us to be mates? I was under the impression he'd take the opportunity our lack of marks brings and finally leave me.

I look at his arm, unwanted tears filling my eyes as I confirm that my mark is gone. It was ugly and poorly executed, but I secretly liked it. I enjoyed the physical proof that he was mine.

Damien follows my line of sight.

"Are you upset your mark is gone?" he asks.

I nod. He already knows the answer is *yes*.

Damien frowns, and he swipes the loofah across my chest one last time before sitting on the small shower bench. It puts us at the same height, giving me a clear view as he tilts his head to the side and exposes his neck.

"Give me a new one," he says.

I don't move, unsure whether this is a trick. When I marked Damien for the first time, it was by force, and I know he wouldn't have allowed it otherwise. He's going to wait for me to get close, and then he's going to pull away and laugh in my face.

He doesn't really want me to mark him. There's no way.

Damien wraps an arm around my wrist, his grip light as he urges me closer. My thighs cage his as I'm pulled onto his lap, straddling him, and Damien continues until our bodies press together.

Then he winces.

"Fuck," he grunts. He reaches down and readjusts his manhood. "Sorry about that. I forgot for a moment that I have a penis."

I blink, my lips twitching. That was actually funny.

Damien releases himself and cups the back of my head, his fingers playing once more with my choppy hair. Then he guides my mouth to his neck, and we both grow tense as my lips make contact with his skin.

"I'm not going anywhere," he promises.

I open my mouth, still mentally preparing for him to pull away at the last minute and laugh at me. Owen once told me that I wasn't deserving of something so sacred, and that Damien must have been out of his mind when I sunk my dirty, flat teeth into him.

He said Damien must be relieved to see my mark leaving his skin. I'm not sure when I began believing the horrible things Owen said to me, but it feels like they're permanently ingrained in my head now.

Damien clears his throat, pulling me from my thoughts.

"Claim me, Aine."

I hesitate as I place the warm skin of his neck between my teeth. Why is he letting me do this? I pause, giving him one last chance to pull away, and I finally bite down when he doesn't.

Damien grunts, but he otherwise remains as still as a statue as I claim him as mine. Wetness from my eyes mixes with the shower water as his skin tears beneath my teeth and the metallic taste of his blood enters my mouth.

I pull away and spit it out, overwhelmed as a wave of emotion hits me all at once. There are so many, and it takes me several seconds to filter through them. Damien kept his emotions hidden before, and I anticipated the same now.

His terror mingles with my own as I pull back and look him in the eye. Why's he scared?

Despite what I know he's feeling, he appears calm as he turns his head to the side, displaying the already healed scar. It's not as clean as the mark he once gave me, but it looks arguably better than the one I placed on his arm.

All my teeth sunk into him this time, leaving behind a clear bite mark.

Damien's eyes meet mine as I tilt my head to the side, offering up my own neck. I want him to bite me back, and then I want to have sex so the scars always remain. I don't want to lose them again.

Damien uses his thumbs to rub soothing circles into my back, and I chew at the skin of my bottom lip as he leans in and buries his face into my neck. It was painful the first time he marked me, and I stiffen as I wait for the pain.

Instead of teeth, though, I'm met with Damien's soft lips.

His eyes shine as he kisses me and pulls back.

"I need to earn it," he says.

I frown. He *has* earned it.

He just doesn't want to mark me. Does he gain some sort of quick exit from our relationship if he doesn't bite me back? Maybe my mark won't last because I'm not a beast.

Damien cups my face, and I'm comforted by the feeling of fondness that courses through me. It's Damien's emotion, and he lets me feel it as he leans in and gives me a quick kiss.

"I'll never forgive myself for how I marked you the first time, and I want the second to be a memory you cherish." He releases a shaky breath before continuing. "I belong to you, but you don't belong to me until you want it. Until you decide I've earned it."

He laughs as he says the last part, his expression happy despite the anxiety I feel rushing through him. I can't imagine what's making him so anxious. It's probably my continued silence. I bet it's unnerving.

Damien clears his throat and gestures to his neck.

"Does it look good?" he asks.

I shrug, unsure what would be considered good. My bite isn't perfect, but it's significantly better than the one I initially put on his arm. He doesn't look mauled.

Damien waits, his patience unwavering. I need to say something, I know I do, and I clench my jaw before forcing my mouth open.

Terror bolts down my spine, and Damien seems to notice the change as he takes both his hands and runs them up each column of my back. His fingers dig into the muscle, massaging until I have no choice but to relax.

He doesn't say anything, and he continues his comforting touch as I struggle to work through my emotions. I may not trust that Damien's going to remain with me, but I don't think he'll hurt me as Owen has.

He's not going to hit me for speaking.

"It's okay," I choke out.

My voice is hoarse and barely audible, but Damien beams like he's won the lottery. He shuts his eyes, and his relief floods my system as he presses his forehead against mine.

"Thank you," he whispers.

Damien wraps his hands around my thighs as he stands, bringing me with him. He holds me, refusing to set me on my feet as he washes himself. It makes him terribly inefficient, but he doesn't seem to mind.

I loop my arms around his neck and my legs around his waist, relieved he can't see my face in this position. I need a moment to collect myself.

Several minutes pass in comfortable silence, the sound only broken when Damien shuts off the shower water and pushes open the glass door.

"I'll get my hair trimmers," he says. He sucks on his teeth as he searches for his next words. "You're going to look beautiful with short hair."

I don't believe him, not one bit, and I hold back tears as he sets me down and hands me a towel. I wrap it around my torso, and Damien loosely wraps one around his waist before beginning to dig through one of his bathroom drawers.

He lets his stream of consciousness flow from his lips, filling the awkward silence with words. I appreciate it, and I stare at my feet when he finds his trimmers and returns to me.

"Can you lean forward?" he asks.

I bend at the waist, and I squeeze my eyes shut as the cold metal touches the back of my head. Damien's pain hits me as he begins cutting off the remainder of my hair, and I hug my arms around myself while I wait for him to finish.

It's nice getting to feel Damien's emotions. I hated constantly having to guess how Owen felt and trying to anticipate his anger. I wasn't great at it, and I like not having to do the same thing with Damien.

Lips touch the newly exposed skin on the back of my head, but it doesn't improve my mood. I peek through my lashes and watch the remainder of my hair fall to the floor. My tears quickly join them.

Damien is efficient, and he quickly ushers me out of the

bathroom the moment he's finished. He leads me into his bedroom and toward his dresser, his large hands cupping my head the entire way.

"Do you want to see?" he asks.

Not really. I suck in a shaky breath, and with all the strength I can muster, I look into the mirror.

Damien catches my attention first. He stands directly behind me, and we lock eyes as he removes his hands from my head so I can see my hair.

"I left as much as I could," he says. "But the back was really short, and I assumed you wanted it to be even."

I did. Damien trimmed my hair almost to the skin, salvaging only about two inches. My head looks fuzzy, and I turn side to side as I run my fingers through the practically nonexistent strands.

It's not as bad as I feared it would be.

"You look beautiful," Damien says. He sounds earnest. "You have a good head shape."

I crack a smile, the reaction genuine.

Chapter 29

DAMIEN

AINE SEEMS UNSURE as she stares at the small plate of pasta I've set in front of her.

I hide my disappointment from the bond as I gesture for her to eat, not wanting her to get the wrong idea should she sense the emotion. The old Aine would've dug right in, and her sudden trepidation makes me want to rip Owen apart one more time.

"Are you not hungry?" I ask.

I know she is. I doubt Owen was feeding her enough, and she hardly ate during our journey home. I had to practically beg her to eat the meat my men caught and cooked.

Pasta is her favorite. I thought she would like it.

Aine jolts as I speak, and she shakes her head before grabbing her fork. I want to know what's she's thinking, but I know she's not going to be ready to share that for a long while. She's hesitant around me, clearly nervous of my reactions.

It reminds me of how she was when she first arrived here, which is a horrible realization to make. I may not have physically harmed her as Owen did, but I was no better. I went out of my way to humiliate her, not allowing Avia to use my blood to heal her and then forcing her to live in that dingy cabin. I was needlessly cruel, all because I was angry to have a human as a mate. I'm ashamed of myself.

Aine glances at me, no doubt feeling my emotions, and I hide them from our bond as Alex and Olivia tiptoe downstairs. They've been quiet, and they're careful not to make any sudden movements as they step into the kitchen and prepare some food for themselves.

Aine shoves a tiny bite of pasta into her mouth, and I take sick pleasure in the way the corners of her lips twitch upwards. She likes it.

"Your haircut looks good," Olivia says.

Aine fingers the short strands, her lips clamped firmly together. She briefly spoke to me, but it's clear she's not even going to attempt with Olivia.

I wrap my arms around Aine from behind and rest my chin on her head. She relaxes back against me, which I take as a good sign.

Alex turns toward me. "Olivia and I have something we want to tell you."

I hum, eyeing the overpriced granola he's openly stealing from my pantry. Alex is always eating my food, and it seems today is no exception.

"Olivia has agreed to move in with me," Alex continues.

That's a development I didn't expect. They've been friends for years, always sneaking around causing trouble. I've recently grown suspicious of their relationship, especially after Freya caught them together.

Alex clears his throat, his face turning red. "When I found her after…" He awkwardly pauses before continuing. "I thought she was dead, and it felt like my world was crumbling. I've asked her to be my chosen mate, and she accepted."

Surprise renders me silent, but it quickly turns to regret. I should've never gone after Olivia that day in my office, and I hope Alex doesn't hold it against me. I don't want him to think there's a pattern of me being intimate with his women. I don't want Aine to think that, either.

I turn toward my mate, wanting to see her reaction. She smiles, the expression slight but most definitely there. I love it.

"I'm happy for you," I tell Alex.

In truth, I'm jealous of him. He and Olivia have progressed further in the short time they've been together than Aine and I have in the months since her execution.

Alex's beast stopped recognizing Freya as his mate after the incident, but it still took him several years to move past it. His beast will never find another true mate, and I didn't even realize Alex was looking for a chosen one.

Aine's head bobs, the slight movement capturing my attention. She must be exhausted. She hasn't eaten nearly as much as I'd like, but I'll make her a large breakfast tomorrow. It's probably best for her to ease back into food, anyway.

My movements are sluggish as I scoop her in my arms. Aine jolts awake as I lift her, and the smell of her fear fills the room as she searches for the source of the touch.

She relaxes when she realizes it's me.

"I'm sorry," I say. I didn't mean to startle her.

I try not to dwell on her fear as I carry her upstairs. My beast urges me to place her in my bed, but I don't want to make her uncomfortable. She seems to be enjoying my presence, but I'm not going to push my luck.

Besides, it's important she learn to be comfortable by herself again. I love spending time with her, but I feel like I'm taking advantage—especially when she asks me to join her in the shower. The old Aine would've shooed me away.

Owen's hurt her in ways I can't imagine, and it's going to take a while for her to see beyond it.

It takes every ounce of willpower I have to bring Aine into her bedroom instead of my own. She's relaxed in my arms, and I squeeze her to my chest before pulling back her sheets and lowering her onto her mattress.

She almost immediately falls back asleep.

Old strands of her long hair stick to the sheets, the dark color standing out. I pick up all the ones I see, not wanting her to find them and get upset. She's sensitive about her haircut, and I don't want to surround her with reminders.

I continue grabbing the thin hairs, enjoying the sound of her heavy breathing. It grows deeper as I clean her hairbrush, and my beast urges me to get on the floor and sift through the rug for more.

My head is heavy as I get on all fours and begin searching, and only when I'm sure I have all the hair do I stand back up. I press a small kiss to Aine's forehead and pull the sheets to her neck, careful not to wake her.

I'm a little nervous she's going to wake up in a panic, so I keep both our bedroom doors open and turn on all the nightlights. If she wakes up, she'll be able to see into my room and know I'm close.

I haphazardly peel off my clothing and crawl into bed. The wooden frame creaks under my weight, and I don't bother getting under the sheets as I sprawl across the mattress. I make sure to angle myself so I can see across the hall into Aine's bedroom.

I'll speak to my men tomorrow about where they're keeping Owen. They were under strict orders to keep him out of Aine's vision and hearing as they dragged him to my pack, and I'll most enjoy torturing him until Aine's in a position to decide what she wants done with him.

I doubt there'll be much of him left by the time she's ready to make that decision, but I'll make sure to keep him alive until she is. I hope she lets me kill him, but I'll support her if she decides she wants to do it herself.

Aine jolts out of bed, and I force myself to remain still as she searches around trying to figure out where she is. The thundering of her heart quiets as she recognizes her bedroom, and I finally release the breath I've been holding as she sits up and looks for me. I kick with my foot and rustle my sheets to draw her attention.

I'm here, and she's safe.

Aine huffs when she sees me, and she quietly climbs out of bed. Her movements are cautious as she makes her way into my bedroom.

My affection warms our bond.

"I'm here," I whisper, hoping it doesn't frighten her. "Come lie down. You're safe with me."

The promise of safety seems to be what pushes Aine over the edge, and she scurries to my bed and burrows into my chest. I wish I knew what was going on in her head as I wrap my arms around her waist. I used to be able to feel all her emotions when she was marked, which drove me crazy most of the time. It was a near constant distraction, but it's a distraction I'd gladly take right now.

I'm happy to have her mark, but my beast isn't satisfied. I'm not, either. I'm desperate to sink my teeth into her skin, but I refuse to rush her into it.

I'm going to do better this time. She deserves it.

She seems to have forgotten the hunt, or at least, she's forgotten her anger. I feel like a small child who snuck my hand into the candy jar without being caught, but I don't deserve it.

I want her to be angry with me, and I want to plead for her forgiveness while she snubs and pushes me away. What if she's never comfortable enough around me to be angry again? I want her to be my equal, not some shell who's too afraid to speak up against me.

She just needs time.

I'm pulled from my thoughts as Aine sniffles and begins to cry, and I quietly shush her as I rub at the short hairs lining her scalp. They're soft under my fingertips, the stubby pieces moving easily underneath my hand.

"You're safe, Aine," I assure her. "You're safe."

Chapter 30

AINE

MOVEMENT STARTLES ME awake, and I panic as my brain takes a moment to process what's happening. I relax back into the soft mattress when I realize it's only Damien.

I refrain from smelling his sheets as he rolls out of bed and throws on some clothing, his attempt not to wake me endearing but poorly executed.

It's been three days, and not once has he managed to get up without waking me.

I panicked and slithered onto the floor the first morning I awoke in his bed, but now I don't feel that same fear. Damien's been exceptionally patient with me, and it's beginning to lull me into a false sense of security.

His lips brush my forehead before he leaves, probably to make me breakfast as he has every morning. I enjoy our routine, even if I feel guilty about how needy I've become. I follow him around all day, refusing to leave his side until it's time for bed.

I start every night in my own bedroom, but I always end up in Damien's. I don't know why I feel so compelled to be near him, but he doesn't seem to mind.

He doesn't even go to his office or the fighting fields, which is quite unlike him. I don't think I've ever seen Damien take time off work, and we're going on our fourth day of it.

I'm pretty sure we've completed every puzzle in existence at this point, and Damien's baked enough treats to give somebody a cavity.

A small part of me worries this is some elaborate ploy, but it's hard to imagine he'd be able to play the role of doting mate for so long if it weren't at least partly genuine.

I wait until Damien's left the room before pushing the sheets off myself and sitting up. I overheard Avia telling Damien that I should learn to be comfortable without him, and she suggested I start with the shower.

Damien agreed. I hate Avia.

Crippling fear pulsates through me every time Damien's not here to ensure a room is safe, and I do my best to ignore the negative emotions as I walk into my bedroom.

Praise seeps through our bond, Damien's excitement over me moving about quite evident as I go to my dresser and pick out an outfit. I've been putting this off, but it's time for me to shower.

I'm sure Damien doesn't enjoy having to sit on the toilet every time I decide to take one, and my naked body is probably quite unpleasant. I know it is to me.

My bottom lip wobbles as I hurry into Damien's bathroom. The sooner I get this over with, the sooner I can go downstairs. I feel too vulnerable in the shower, the loud water blocking my hearing and the door distorting my sight.

Somebody could break in, and I'd have no idea.

I remind myself that Damien's just downstairs as I turn on the shower and throw myself inside. My hands shake as I slam the door shut, and I begin washing as quickly as possible.

Once I'm clean, I can go downstairs.

My bond with Damien provides no comfort as tears begin rolling down my cheeks. I wrestle with the soap before getting the top open and pouring a large amount onto my loofah. My actions are messy and hectic, but I can't bring myself to care as I rush to finish.

Once I'm clean, I can go downstairs.

My chest begins to heave as I roughly scrub all the grime that's accumulated since yesterday's shower. I should've just skipped showering today. I haven't left the house, so it's not like I'm dirty.

Once I'm clean, I can go downstairs.

The skin on my arms turns red from the harsh rubbing, and my vision blurs as I struggle to keep my mind straight.

There's a quiet noise from just beyond the bathroom door, and I snap my head in that direction. I can't see through the glass, but fear prevents me from opening and checking. What if somebody attacked Damien and is now searching for me? Are they in the bathroom? Is it Owen? I know it is. I begin to hyperventilate as my thoughts go haywire, fully convinced Owen's standing in the room waiting to hurt me.

I slide down the shower wall, utterly defeated as I wait for Owen to burst through the door. He's here. He's here, and he's going to punish me. I bury my face into my knees with a loud sob, not wanting to see. I knew this would happen.

The sound of the door slamming open has me unable to breathe, and I flail as I'm pulled against a hard chest. I kick with my feet, trying to push Owen away, before trying to call for Damien.

Only silence leaves my lips.

"Aine!" The water is shut off. "Aine, open your eyes. It's me. It's just me." I shake my head and continue kicking. He's lying.

He's always lying. "Aine, please. You're safe. It's me."

Large hands run down my spine before cupping my skull. The touch is familiar, and I gasp as I open my eyes and realize it's Damien holding me. It's Damien. It's just Damien.

I sag against his chest, letting him pull me off the ground and onto his lap. His panic filters through our bond as he leans against the shower wall, his voice soothing as he whispers quiet assurances.

His clothing is soaked through, and guilt sets in as I realize I failed. He asked me to shower by myself, and I could barely make it two minutes before turning into a blubbering mess.

I'm disappointing.

"I'm so sorry. I should've never listened to Avia," Damien says between kisses to my temple. "You won't have to shower without me ever again if you don't want to. I won't push you again, I promise."

We remain on the floor until my cries turn into hiccups and my body no longer shakes. My lips rest against Damien's shoulder, and I gulp before opening my mouth.

"I'm sorry."

My whisper is inaudible to my ears, but I can tell Damien hears it. His fingers curl where they rest against my spine, fingertips grazing the bone before he leans back to look me in the eye.

His eyebrows are pulled tight as he scans me. Confusion and frustration hit me through our bond, a slight contradiction to the pain I see in his eyes.

"You have nothing to be sorry for." His tone leaves little room for argument as he wipes away the wetness on my cheeks. "I shouldn't have pushed you. This is my fault."

I don't believe that. I should've known nobody was here to take me. Damien already won, and Owen and his men are gone.

They aren't coming after me.

Tense silence stretches between Damien and me.

"Let's get you cleaned up," he eventually says.

Damien stands and sets me on my feet. He turns the water back on, and despite knowing it's irrational, I grow afraid that he's going to leave.

An audible sigh of relief slips from my throat when, instead, he begins pulling off his soaked clothing.

He's going to be joining me. Good.

Damien strips and steps back inside the shower. I remain still as he grabs the loofah off the floor and brings it to my shoulders. He keeps his eyes strictly on the parts he's washing, his movements much gentler than mine were.

A small part of me is embarrassed being naked in front of him, but after being exposed to Owen's entire pack, I no longer feel a strong sense of ownership over my body. Damien doesn't seem to mind being naked, and he spends most days parading around the house in his underwear.

I stare at his chest, my gaze gradually shifting to his shoulders and arms. It would be easy for him to pin me down and hurt me. He could do it before I even realized what was happening.

Despite that thought, I don't feel threatened.

Damien isn't going to hurt me.

I grab his wrist. He stills at the sudden touch, and his chest expands with breath as I take the loofah and bring it to his torso. My cheeks are warm, but I force myself to continue. Damien always washes me, and I want to return the favor. I've been meaning to do so for a while now, but I haven't been able to work up the courage to see it through.

Damien's unease filters through our bond as I begin washing him, the feeling painful. Does he not want this? Is he worried I'll dirty him?

Uncertainty and doubt win, and I drop my hand and hang my head. I should've known better than to think Damien would want me to wash him. He hasn't shown any romantic interest in me since the rescue.

"Aine…" Damien sighs.

I stare at his chest, avoiding his gaze until he places his fingers underneath my chin and softly guides my head up. He bites at his bottom lip, but I can't feel his emotions like I usually can.

He's hiding them from me.

"I like your touch," he says, his voice low. "It's hard being around you when we're naked, and I struggle to stop my physical reactions when you're touching me. I don't want to make you uncomfortable."

Is that true? I look down, wanting to see for myself. Damien's not entirely hard, but he's not soft, either.

I hold back a smile, happy I'm invoking this reaction out of him. I was under the impression he was no longer attracted to me. I stole looks the first few times we showered together, but after seeing only a soft, flaccid penis, I accepted he no longer wants me. It hurt, but I understood.

"Why do you look so shocked?" Damien asks.

Most of his questions are rhetorical, but after a moment of silence, I realize he wants a response. I shrug, not sure what to say.

Damien continues to stare, not accepting that as an answer. Eventually, I open my mouth to respond. Nothing comes out, but Damien is patient as I fight with myself and try to speak.

He's not going to hurt me. I'm safe.

"I thought—" I pause to clear my throat. "I thought you didn't want me anymore."

Damien's surprise courses through our bond at the same moment his jaw drops, and the sound of the water pouring from the showerhead is deafening as I wait for his response. I don't have to wait long for one, though, as Damien lets out an abrupt laugh.

"Aine, you're the most beautiful woman I've ever seen." He crouches until we're eye to eye. "I have to think about Alex's ugly mug whenever I'm near you so I don't get hard."

I'm sure my face is embarrassingly red as Damien's joking expression is replaced with a serious one.

"My little human," he says. "I may not have shown it properly when we first met, but I can assure you I always have and always will want you."

Damien grabs my wrist and pulls my hand toward his chest, silently asking me to continue cleaning him. I do, and by the time I finish, he's so hard it's got to hurt.

I can't look away, but when I reach for his length, he brushes me away. I try not to be offended as he grabs my hand and kisses my palm to soften the blow of his rejection.

"Not yet," he says. "Not until I've earned it."

I think he already has.

Damien doesn't budge, though, and eventually we leave the shower and head downstairs. Breakfast is already finished, and we eat in comfortable silence before moving to the half-finished puzzle on the coffee table.

We follow the same daily routine, and today is no different. The sun is setting before I know it, and Damien curls his body around me and plays with my fingers as we lie on the couch.

"Are you ready for bed?" he asks.

I nod, my eyes already drooping as we head upstairs. My exhaustion makes me malleable, and I don't bother pretending to sleep in my own bedroom as I walk directly into Damien's. He smiles, and I feel his excitement as I crawl into his bed and smoosh my body against his.

Damien squeezes my waist, holding me close until I fall asleep in his arms.

I feel like I've just shut my eyes when the sound of the front door opening snaps me awake. Damien's face is nestled in my neck, and he lets out a low groan before sitting up.

"It's just Alex and Olivia," he assures me.

I crawl out of bed and peek through the doorway, needing to see for myself. Sure enough, within seconds, the two stumble upstairs and barrel into Olivia's bedroom in a fit of hushed giggles. She holds his hand as she drags him around, a wide smile on her face as she pulls him from bedroom to bathroom and back once more.

They're packing her things.

Alex shushes her as she shoves her clothes into bags, his eyes darting to meet mine through the crack in the bedroom door. I hold eye contact for a second before looking away.

I'm not proud to be hiding in Damien's bedroom while Alex helps Olivia pack, especially after everything he did for me. Damien's only told me bits and pieces, but he's admitted that Alex blamed himself for my kidnapping and refused to eat or rest until I was found.

I want to speak to him, but I can't bring myself to leave Damien's room. He saw me tied to that pole, saw me covered in my own shit and vomit, and I'm too humiliated to face him.

Alex turns away, returning his attention to Olivia. I wonder what she thinks about all this. What has Alex told her? What are the other beasts saying about me? I'm sure they know.

Damien climbs out of bed and walks up behind me. His hands slide around my waist before he presses his body against mine.

"My nosy mate," he teases. He rests his chin on my head before pulling back and pressing a kiss to the tiny hairs on my scalp. "I told them to wait until you were asleep and to be quiet, but it appears they chose not to do either of those things."

I shrug. They're excited, and they're being relatively quiet.

I've been on high alert since Owen, and the old me would've slept straight through the noise.

Damien continues to hold me as I watch them pack Olivia's things, my lips curling as jealousy spreads through my veins. She and Alex look happy together, both grinning like lovesick fools. I want that.

"Should I tell them to leave?" Damien asks.

I shake my head. Olivia's been staying with Alex since my return, but her things are here. They need to pack them eventually.

Alex approaches Olivia from behind and wraps his arms around her, copying Damien and my's position. His mouth moves as he whispers, and her head bobs slightly to confirm whatever he's saying.

Then she glances toward Damien's bedroom.

I can't tell if she can see me through the crack, but I take a few steps back just in case. I don't want her knowing I'm spying on them.

My eyes widen as she pulls herself out of Alex's arms and walks in my direction. I back up another couple of steps, quickly growing panicked. Damien continues holding me as Olivia comes to a stop in front of the door and raises her fist. She knocks lightly, but the sound still feels deafening.

I don't want to talk to her. I don't want to face her.

Damien pulls me back another step, his movements slow and calming.

"It's okay, Aine," he whispers in my ear. "You don't have to go out there. She can't see you."

Olivia sets a small package on the ground. "I lost my hair a few years ago, and I know the breeze isn't always pleasant on the scalp. I made you a hat." She clears her throat before continuing. "I'm not great at knitting so there are a few snags, but Alex said they aren't that noticeable, so… yeah. I won't be offended if you don't like it."

Her eyes dart up to meet mine before returning to her feet. She shifts, her hands clasping together in front of her stomach before she rolls back on her heels and turns toward Alex.

He stands behind her, not bothering to pretend he can't see me peering out. I'm sure he can make out every detail of our forms with his enhanced eyesight, from Damien's arms around my waist to my fingers digging painfully into his wrists.

He looks away as Olivia returns to him.

"Alex told me she made and threw away four hats before he finally convinced her that one was good enough to give you," Damien whispers as Alex throws Olivia's bags over his shoulder and leads her downstairs.

"Why did she lose her hair?" I work up the courage to ask.

Damien hums. "Beasts don't like having unmated humans in the pack, and a few of the older men used to think it was funny to play little games with Olivia when I wasn't around."

He sighs, his guilt reaching me through the bond. I'm surprised by it, but I'm relieved it's the emotion he's feeling. I don't want him to be happy when he thinks about human cruelty.

I hope it means he's changing his views of us.

"I asked Alex to keep an eye on her when I wasn't around," Damien continues, his voice quiet. "Olivia couldn't get work done when she was harassed every time she ran an errand for me. They ended up forming a bit of a friendship, which Freya didn't like."

I'm not surprised. Freya isn't exactly a pleasant person.

"While Alex and I were in a meeting one day, she dragged Olivia to the training fields and shaved her head." Damien's arms tighten as his warm breath hits the top of my scalp. "Freya demanded Alex condemn Olivia in front of the pack. Alex hesitated, and I interjected and forced Freya to apologize."

Damien bends to grab the hat. It's made with bright blue yarn, and there's a large fuzzy green ball on the top. It's fun, and if I ever work up the courage to go outside, I'll be wearing it.

"I think that's why Olivia grew so attached to me," Damien continues. "I was the only person who stuck up for her, and it made her think I was her savior or some shit like that."

A long silence stretches as Damien waits to hear my response, his nerves distracting as they filter through me.

It explains Olivia's demeanor when we first met. I'd also be upset if the only man who's shown me kindness was suddenly throwing me to the side for his mate. She probably thought I'd be like Freya, forcing Damien to cast her aside for me.

I'm ashamed to realize that's precisely what happened. It was little things at first, like him giving me her favorite dress and shooing her away whenever I was near, but he almost always put my needs above hers.

I don't necessarily think Damien was wrong to put me first, but I understand why that would hurt Olivia.

"Do you feel differently about me after hearing that story?" Damien asks.

I shake my head. If anything, I'm relieved to hear he showed kindness to another human before I arrived. Damien relaxes, and a soft smile spreads across his lips as he sets the hat on the dresser.

"Good," he says. "Let's go back to bed."

He picks me up, and I laugh as I'm dropped in the center of the mattress. Damien's quick to join, and he pulls the sheets over us before curling his body around mine.

I'm asleep within minutes.

Chapter 31

AINE

DAMIEN SAUNTERS INTO the kitchen, his nonchalant stride inconsistent with the anxiety I feel coursing through our bond. I slow my chewing, waiting to hear what he has to say.

"So," he starts. "I've been thinking…"

He pauses, and I raise a brow. It's never good when he starts a sentence with, *I've been thinking.* The last time he said it, he followed it up with suggesting that I try showering by myself. It was a disaster.

Damien takes a seat on the barstool beside me, and I prod at my eggs. He made me three, paired with jam-covered toast and sausage. It's way more food than I can eat, but I already know he'll finish off what I leave behind.

He always does.

Damien clears his throat. "How would you feel about taking a walk to the garden today?"

I stiffen. I haven't left the house yet, and I honestly have no desire to. Damien's stepped outside to speak with Avia or Olivia a handful of times, but I never join him. It's safe inside.

Is this another one of Avia's suggestions? Damien promised

he wouldn't push me to do things I'm not comfortable with after the shower incident, and up until this point, he's remained true to his word. Why did he change his mind?

Damien rests his elbows on the counter and leans toward me. The action doesn't intimidate me as it once did.

"I'll be by your side the entire time," he promises.

I hesitate, reminding myself he's not going to hurt me, before shaking my head. I don't want to go. I want to stay inside, where it's safe.

Most of Damien's men saw me tied to that pole, and I'm not ready to face the hatred I know they hold for me. They probably think Damien's crazy for sticking by my side, no doubt wondering what he sees in me.

I know *I* think that.

Damien stands and walks around the counter. Sweat pebbles along the back of my neck as he takes my hands.

"Are you afraid somebody's going to hurt you?" he asks.

I shake my head. It's a fear, yes, but I'm comforted by the knowledge that Damien's already taken care of Owen and his men.

Damien hums. "Are you afraid I'll get distracted and leave you alone?"

I shake my head again.

"Is it because of your hair?"

I shake my head for the third time.

Damien's growing frustrated, I can feel it through the bond. He purses his lips and gives my hands a light squeeze, but he doesn't push.

I feel guilty for making this so hard for him. It's not my intention to be such a bother, and I'd stop in a heartbeat if I could. I haven't suffered any memory loss. I know this fear and mental paralysis is not who I was a month ago. The first few days back, I was so overwhelmed with my thoughts that I didn't realize just how much I've changed, but now I do. I borderline hated Damien, finding him crude and selfish. Now he's the only thing that keeps me safe.

Damien releases my hand and taps my temple to draw my attention. He's trying to be playful, but I'm too anxious to indulge.

"What's going on in that head of yours?" he asks.

This question isn't rhetorical. He's looking for an answer. I clear my throat, begging my brain to work the way I want it to. I need to speak.

My face grows red. "I'm embarrassed."

Owen mocked my feelings whenever he was able to detect them, and it's taken a lot of self-convincing to trust that Damien's not going to do the same.

Damien runs his thumb along my cheekbone, silently encouraging me to continue.

"What are you embarrassed about?" he asks.

I stare at my food, not wanting him to see the tears building in my waterline. "They saw me tied to the pole. They know what Owen did to me."

Damien slides his hand to my head, but I brush him away. I usually like when he touches my hair, but I find myself uninterested when it's paired with his pity.

"Most of the beasts were too busy fighting to get a good look at you," he says. "And I promise the few who did aren't judging. Nobody blames you for what happened." He clears his throat. "It wasn't your fault."

I shrug, still uncomfortable with the thought of seeing them.

"I think it'll be good for us to go outside and get fresh air. We can't hide inside forever," Damien continues. "Plus, I've heard the gardens are looking a bit rough without your magic touch. It's too much for Mia, Abby, and Alex to manage by themselves."

I force down a smile. I know Damien's just saying that to make me feel better, but it works. I spent a lot of time in the gardens, and I was proud of the work I did.

Damien cocks his head to the side.

"What do you say?" he asks.

He seems excited, and I drop my shoulders in defeat.

"You'll stay with me?" I ask, desperate to confirm he doesn't plan to drop me off and wander to the training fields.

I'm sure he's missing them. It sounds like Alex and Olivia have taken charge of the everyday tasks Damien once handled. Alex oversees the training, and Olivia manages the bureaucratic work.

"Do you miss working?" I ask.

Damien frowns, and his guilt travels down the bond. Why is he feeling guilty? For missing work? For being with me?

"I'm going to stick to you like glue," Damien says.

He ignores my second question, and he jumps up and walks to the other end of the kitchen before I have the opportunity to repeat it.

I frown, glaring at the back of his head before eating the last of my food and heading to the front door. The hat Olivia made me is sitting on the entryway table, and I shove it on my head before slipping on my shoes.

My palms grow sweaty as I mentally prepare to leave the house, and I'm still worried about how the beasts will treat me. I don't believe Damien's assurance that they aren't judging, but I at least hope they keep it to themselves.

Damien clearly misses his work, and it's selfish to keep him locked inside forever. He's already done so much for me, and I can't fathom asking him to stay indoors for the rest of his life.

Damien approaches and wraps an arm around my torso, his warm breath fanning over the top of my head as he hugs me. I'm sure he can smell my nerves and hear how hard my heart's beating, but he remains silent and holds me until the panic subsides and my hands stop shaking.

"My people hold so much respect for you," he says.

That's not true. I don't want to argue, though, so I nod as I pull out of his hug. Let's get this over with.

Damien continues to whisper encouragement as he opens the front door. I stare into the woods, hesitating, before sucking in a deep breath and stepping outside.

I grab Damien's arm for support, finding comfort in his touch as I make my way down the front steps. I'm unable to hear what he's saying over the thundering of my pulse, but the low timbre of his voice is still soothing.

I can do this.

Damien leads me in the direction of the garden, and we pause once we reach the halfway point.

"You're doing so well," he coos.

I glance around, wanting to make sure nobody's watching as I take a few calming breaths. This is harder than I thought it would be. We'll be at the gardens in only a few minutes.

"Are you okay?" Damien asks. "You've done so well, and we can go home whenever you want. Just say the word."

I'd love nothing more than to take him up on the offer, but I force myself to continue forward. Damien's done so much for me, and I'll be damned if I turn down the one request he's made.

My thoughts are jumbled and out of focus, unable to concentrate on anything and getting distracted by every slight noise. Damien keeps his arm wrapped around me as we walk, and he pulls me closer as we reach the last remaining trees that separate us from the open fields.

I can hear the beasts fighting, their loud snarls and clashing bodies audible from this distance. If I can hear them, they can most definitely hear me.

Every inch of my body screams for me to turn and run back, but I ignore the sensation and push forward. My eyes are cast downward as I break the barrier into the fields. Damien rubs my back and leads me in the direction of the garden, his voice low as he chats idly to keep me distracted.

"See how overgrown everything is?" he asks.

I look up, frowning as I realize he was telling the truth about the gardens. It's nothing too awful, but it's clear Mia and Abby are struggling to keep up.

If Alex has been working in the training fields, I doubt he's been much help. The watering and general maintenance has been done, but things are ready to be pruned and harvested.

I'm already here, so I might as well be useful. Damien makes a quiet noise in the back of his throat as I crouch down and inspect the carrots emerging from the ground.

"You don't have to do that," he says. "I wasn't bringing you here to work."

I shrug, working up the confidence to speak. "I want to."

Damien crouches beside me. He looks lost.

"What should I do?" he asks.

"Do you want gloves?"

"No." He chuckles. His amusement travels through our bond. "The gloves are for humans."

Damien reaches for an unripe carrot, and before I can stop him, he rips it out of the ground. The vegetable comes out short and deformed, and he grimaces and tries to shove it back into the dirt.

"Oops?"

I snort, pointing to one that's ripe. "You shouldn't pull them until they look like this," I say, showing him how the top of the carrot pops out of the soil.

Damien nods. "Noted."

He gently pats the leaves of the unripe carrot he just ruined before pulling the one I pointed out. It looks good, and I watch as he begins to search for more.

He quickly finds one, and he inspects it for a long minute before pulling it out of the ground. He turns toward me, looking for confirmation that it's ripe, and he lets out a loud cheer when I give a confirming nod.

The noise has me flicking my gaze toward the beasts, unable to prolong the inevitable any longer. I fully expect them to be glaring at Damien and me, but to my utter relief, most aren't paying us any attention.

Only a few are looking, but they don't seem angry.

Alex lifts his arm when he realizes he has my attention, and he waves wildly from across the fields. I find myself relaxing, and I feel a genuine smile spread across my lips as I timidly wave back.

Damien is silent as he watches us, but I can feel his anxiety. It mirrors mine, but it softens when he realizes I'm not upset. I was terrified the beasts would leer and judge as Owen's men did, but that isn't the case.

I turn toward Damien, my breath shallow.

"We're going to need the wheelbarrow."

Chapter 32

AINE

I WATCH DAMIEN and Avia from the bedroom window, a permanent frown etched on my face.

"She's having a bad day," Damien tells her.

I'm not having a bad day. I just don't want to do the things he wants me to do, and I don't appreciate him discussing my attitude with Avia.

Avia nods and writes something down in her notebook. I hate that stupid fucking book of hers. She's always making notes and telling Damien that I should do things I don't want to do. She's always judging.

Damien brings both hands to his head and rubs his temples. He seems stressed, no doubt an effect of my less-than-stellar attitude these past few days.

We had such a fantastic time working in the garden together. He laughed and smiled and seemed so happy as we moved through the rows.

His joy was an eye opener. It made me realize that I'm no good for him. Damien deserves to be with somebody who can make him feel like that all the time—not the once in a blue moon

I'm able to force myself to step foot out of the house.

I know he's confused by my recent attitude, but there's no way to explain why I'm being so mean. He'd only argue and try to convince me otherwise. He'd say he's happy as we are, but he'd be lying.

I think, after Owen, he feels obligated to protect me. He's with me out of obligation, and I need him to realize that.

"I don't know what to do," Damien continues. I've tried everything to cheer her up."

Avia makes another infuriating note. Then she brings her pen to her mouth and bites down on it. I bet it's rattling between her teeth. Damien hates that noise, but he doesn't comment on it.

"What about another trip to the gardens?" she asks. "It seems you both enjoyed that last time."

Damien throws his head back with a dry laugh. "I thought we had a great time, but she's been miserable since we returned. I thought maybe one of the beasts looked at her wrong, but Alex talked to them. It doesn't seem like anybody did anything that would upset her." His frustration grows as he speaks, the emotion pulsing through our bond. "Every time I ask if she wants to go, she shakes her head and refuses to explain why."

I clench my jaw, my guilt bubbling up as I hear Damien talk about his troubles. I thought he'd have given up by now. It's been almost four days of radio silence from me, and the only responses I do give are rejections.

Still, he sticks around, his resilience surprising me to my core.

Owen and Henry would've beaten me black and blue by now, but all Damien does is sigh quietly to himself and drop the subject.

This morning has been especially dreadful. He was in such a good mood when he woke, his voice loud as he bounced around the bedroom waiting for me to get dressed. He wanted to make me a special breakfast, something his mother made every year on his and Alex's birthday.

It killed me to pretend I hated it, refusing to put more than one bite in my mouth before getting up and making myself a bowl of cereal. Damien was visibly upset, but it wasn't enough to drive him away. Instead, he apologized and promised to stick to the basics from now on.

Later, when he asked if I'd like to do a puzzle, he was met with a *no*. That answer didn't change when he asked me to partake in three more activities with him.

Damien huffs. "I don't understand why she's so angry. She went from practically worshiping me to hating me at the drop of a hat."

My lip trembles at the hurt in his voice, and I step closer to the window. Avia, ever-so-vigilant, snaps her head in my direction. I duck below the window as her eyes meet mine, but I know I was too slow.

"Aine?" she shouts. "Do you want to join us?"

I consider refusing her request, but Damien's broken voice has me reeling. Instead, I find myself nodding and walking downstairs. Damien watches me like a hawk as I pull open the front door and walk down the porch steps.

Avia remains silent until I've come to a halt next to Damien. He rests his hand on the small of my back, but he drops it with a wince when I shake him off.

"I was hoping to talk to you today," Avia says, her voice chipper. She's pretending she didn't just catch me eavesdropping. "Jenna's been asking about you, and she wants to know if you'd like to come over for dinner."

She pauses to gauge my reaction, and an awkward silence stretches between us. "Or Jenna can come here. Whatever you'd prefer."

I grind my teeth as I think it over. I'd love to see Jenna, but I don't have anything to say to her. It would be awkward.

"No." Despite my nerves, my voice is firm. I've gotten good at saying that word these past few days.

"Are you sure? I think you—"

I cut her off. "No."

Damien hangs his head and gestures for me to go inside. It's an order I'm all too happy to follow.

"I told you she's having a bad day," he tells Avia as I walk away. "Try asking again in a few days, but don't tell Jenna that Aine rejected the invitation. I don't want her to feel guilty about it later."

Avia clears her throat. "I know. I'll tell Jenna I didn't have a chance to speak with Aine."

She excuses herself, and I listen from behind the door as Damien makes his way back to the house. He avoids eye contact as he steps inside and heads into the kitchen. He's walking on eggshells around me.

A painful mixture of his disappointment, confusion, and anger seeps through our bond, the painful emotions rendering me immobile as I watch him pour and drink a large glass of water.

He refills the cup before speaking.

"What do you want?" he asks.

He looks up, his stare intimidating as he waits for my answer. I feel warm under his gaze, the guilt of what I'm doing making me sweat.

I'm doing what needs to be done.

"Leave me," I say.

Damien's glass clatters as he slams it on the counter. "No."

I struggle to maintain eye contact as he storms toward me, and I grow rigid as he takes my face between his palms.

"Go away," I repeat.

Damien chuckles, but it's laced with pain.

"I'm not a dog. You can't shoo me away." He crouches until we're eye level. "I understand you're angry and hurt, but you need to understand that I'm not going to leave you. You can't drive me away."

My throat feels dry, and my head is beginning to ache. Damien needs to leave. He may not realize it, but I'm doing this for him.

"It's your fault *he* hurt me," I spit. "You made him angry, and he came after me because of it."

Damien recoils as if my words have physically hurt him. He opens his mouth to speak, to defend himself, but nothing comes out. My eyes water as I dig the knife in further.

"I will *never* forgive you, and I will *never* love you."

The pain that erupts throughout our bond has me struggling to breathe. I wish he'd shut off his emotions like before, blocking me out and keeping me at a distance. The Damien I first met would've left the moment I asked him to, all too excited to have an excuse not to be around me.

My voice is shaky as I continue.

"I hate you, and I want you to leave."

My heart crumbles as Damien's eyes grow glassy, filling with unshed tears. He looks horrified. I know how he feels. I feel it toward myself, but this must be done. I can't let him stay by my side any longer.

He deserves happiness. Something I can't give him.

"It's not going to work, Aine," Damien says. "I am not leaving." His palms are sweaty as he takes my hands. "Do you want me to step down and move us to the human village? I'll do it."

His voice takes on a desperate edge I've never heard before. It grows as he continues to offer things he thinks I may want. "Do you want a pet?" he asks. "We can't get a cat, but dogs don't have the same instincts. They usually aren't scared of us. I'll get you one."

Tears spill down my cheeks as he continues with his list. Why's he making this so hard?

I sob. "Why won't you leave me?"

Damien doesn't hesitate to give his answer. "Because I love you, Aine."

He seems so assured in his words, hardly reacting to them as he immediately continues listing the things he can buy for me. I'm frozen. He loves me?

I can tell he's genuine by the way the bond between us hums, and the revelation is paralyzing. Why does he love me? We hardly get along, and we barely know one another. It's preposterous to think he grew such strong feelings in such a short period of time.

"The bond makes you feel that way," I say, cutting off his ramblings.

Damien blinks, shaking his head. "That's not how the bond works. It makes me interested in you, and maybe even a bit obsessed with you, but it can't force me to love you."

"Those feelings are all my own," he continues. "I don't love you because some bond told me to. I love you because you're a brat who challenges and excites me. Who keeps me on my toes and forces me to be a better person."

Damien grabs my hips, and before I can tell what's happening, we're on the couch and I'm on his lap. I straddle him without thinking, continuing to reel from his words.

"I love you because you're my little human who threatens to touch your mark when I don't give you what you want, and you make sure the whole world knows when you're angry with me, and you're so, so resilient, and—"

I smash my lips against Damien's, effectively cutting off his rambling. I refuse to let myself overthink my actions as I wrap my arms around his neck and press my body against his. Damien tilts his head and deepens our kiss, his tongue slipping between my parted lips.

I struggle to form a coherent thought as I pull him closer, continuing until there's no space left between us. Damien seems to enjoy the action, a quiet groan seeping from his throat.

He loves me, and the admission breaks the last bit of resolve I had to push him away. I can feel that he means it, and I want it so fucking badly. All I've ever wanted was to be loved, and I grew to believe it would never happen after marrying Henry.

I thought it was impossible for somebody to feel such emotions about me, and while I suspected Damien felt something, I refused to even consider the possibility that it could be love.

I want more.

Damien grows hard as we kiss, his breaths deepening as I grind myself against him. He seems to enjoy it, and he lets out a quiet moan before grabbing my waist and stopping me.

I don't understand, and I hide my hurt as I pull away.

Damien's face and neck are flushed red, his eyes wide with shock. I'm sure my expression matches his. I didn't anticipate our conversation ending with me throwing myself at him.

"Aine, I—" Damien says, a ghost of a smile spreading across his lips.

I lean in, and Damien chuckles as I connect my lips with his again. He lets me take charge of the interaction, but his laughter quickly fades as I slide my hands into his hair and grip the strands at the base of his neck.

"Fuck," Damien groans.

He turns, laying me on my back before sliding himself between my thighs. I stare up at him, panting as he presses his erection against me. I'm desperate to feel him, and the emotions I've been holding in for weeks now are quickly tumbling out.

I drag my hands down his back, continuing until I reach the hem of his shirt. Damien buries his face into my neck, and he gasps as I slide my fingers against his bare skin. I want him, and I'm sure I'm making that abundantly clear as I wrap my legs around his waist and pull him flush against me.

Damien groans, his lips brushing the sensitive skin where my mark used to be. I wonder if he's thinking about biting me again. Does he fantasize about it the same way I do?

"Fuck," he says, pulling away. "We shouldn't be doing this."

I fail to hide my disappointment as he hovers over me, and I grudgingly remove my hands and unwrap my legs from around his waist. I was under the impression that him saying he loved me meant he'd also like to have sex with me. It's not as if the act is foreign to him.

Damien moves to the opposite end of the couch.

"I don't want to do anything you'll regret," he says.

My legs feel like jelly as I pull myself into a kneeling position. I'm not going to regret this, and I carefully inch forward and sit on Damien's lap.

He wraps his arms around me as I straddle him, and I swallow past the lump in my throat as his erection presses against my butt. I don't think I've ever wanted something as much as I want Damien right now, my need for him burning me from the inside out.

"I—" Damien pauses and clears his throat. "I know it's my fault Owen came after you. I called off the hunt, but I was too late. You were already gone, and I'm so ashamed I wasn't here to protect you."

My heart lurches, and I chew at my bottom lip to stop myself from crying. I don't even know where to start.

Damien gives me a moment to collect my thoughts.

"I didn't, I don't—" I eventually start. My eyes flutter shut as

I struggle to formulate the words in my head. "It's not your fault."

Damien nods, but I feel his doubt as if it were my own. I shake my head, eager for him to understand I don't honestly think anything that happened was his fault.

"Owen's a grown man, and his decisions were his alone," I continue. "I didn't mean what I said. I wanted to hurt you, but I know it wasn't your fault."

The weak smile that spreads across Damien's lips has me frantic. I should never have said those things to him, and I sit up straighter before cupping his face as he always does to me. His cheeks smoosh together, the sight cute.

"I only said that so you would leave," I shamefully admit. "I thought if I hurt you badly enough, you would."

Damien turns and kisses my palm. "I'm not going anywhere."

I believe him. I said the most hurtful things I could think of, and all he responded with was an admission of love. He didn't hurt me, or leave.

I want to be with Damien, and I don't want to fight it any longer. I want to feel his body on mine as he whispers confessions of love in my ear. I'm tired of living in fear because of what Owen and Henry did to me. I'm tired of feeling timid and ashamed of my needs.

Damien shifts as a comfortable silence stretches over us. His desire still courses through the bond, and I'm pleased with the knowledge of how badly he wants me.

His lust encourages me, and I lean in and connect our lips once more. He wants me just as badly as I want him, and I'll be damned if I wait a second longer. We deserve this.

Damien gently pushes me away.

My eyes water at the repeat rejections, the confidence I once felt crumbling. I don't understand why he doesn't want this. I can feel that he does. His arousal is seeping through our bond in rhythmic waves.

Damien presses his cheek against mine. "Emotions are running high right now, and I don't want to do something you'll grow to regret later."

Frustrated and borderline angry, I barely take a moment to think through my actions as I grab Damien's hand and rip it off my waist. He allows me to do so, seemingly not understanding my intentions as I guide his hand between my thighs.

I slide his fingers up the inside of my shorts.

"Aine," Damien whispers.

His voice is thick with lust, and he throws his head back with a moan as I move my underwear to the side and press his fingertips against my slick skin. His cock twitches below me, and he slides his fingers against my sex, spreading my arousal. I plant my palms into his shoulders as he touches me.

He slides his middle and ring finger down my slit before guiding them into me. There's a slight burn as he rocks them inside, filling me in a way I haven't felt in a long time.

It feels good, and I bite back a moan as the sound of my wetness fills the room.

"You have no fucking idea," Damien shifts, putting me on my back, "how much I want you."

His knees hit the ground with a quiet thud, but he hardly seems to care as he buries his face between my thighs. I pant as he teasingly bites the inside of my thigh at the same time he curls his fingers upward. They stretch me in the most delicious way, and I moan as he eases them out and roughly shoves them back in.

"I *need* you, Aine," he admits.

Damien pulls his fingers out of me, shifting his attention to my clit. He just barely touches the sensitive skin before gasping and ripping his hand back to his body.

"No," he grunts. He pushes my thigh away from his mouth.

"I'm not going to let you trick me."

There's a glint in his eye as he looks between my thighs, and he smiles before rising and crawling over top of me. My chest heaves as he brings his mouth to my ear, his lips grazing the skin.

"Don't be naughty, Aine," he says. "The next time you try to seduce me, I'm going to throw you over my lap and spank you."

He holds eye contact as he brings the fingers that were just inside me to his mouth, and he moans as he licks them. I'm beyond frazzled, and Damien clearly enjoys it as he pulls his fingers from his mouth and shuts my legs.

His devious smirk shifts into a serious expression.

"I want you to know that me telling you I love you doesn't mean I expect sex. I'll love you even if you aren't ready and want to wait. I fear that—" He gulps and looks away before continuing. "The pain I felt when *he* was hurting you was unfocused. I don't know specifically what he did, and if anything I ever do or say brings up bad memories, I hope you'll tell me."

I tilt my head to the side, unsure what he's getting at. It's clear he's speaking about more than just the general beatings, and my heart falls as I realize he's hinting at me being raped.

Damien's pain and guilt return as he brings up the incident, and I find myself eager to assure him I'm okay. Owen didn't go any further than removing my cup and grabbing my breasts.

"Damien," I say, waiting for him to look at me. I want him to know I'm speaking the truth. "I wasn't raped."

For a long few seconds, Damien has no reaction, but I can see the moment my words register. His body visibly relaxes, and relief floods our bond as he drops his forehead against mine. I didn't realize he thought these things happened to me. If I had, I would've assured him sooner.

The silence between us stretches as we struggle to rein in our emotions. Maybe Damien was right in saying we should wait before having sex.

Shyness takes over as I wait for Damien to tell me what to do next. Do we continue with our day as if nothing happened? Does he expect us to have a big heart-to-heart?

I'm not ready for a serious discussion. I need time to think before discussing with Damien how I feel. I know he loves me, and a part of me thinks I love him too, but I'm not sure. It's not exactly a feeling I've encountered before, and I don't want to say things I don't mean out of obligation.

Damien subtly adjusts his erection, his movements quick in an effort not to draw attention to them. His desire doesn't dissipate, the needy emotion continuing to pulse through our bond. His nostrils flare just before another wave hits me, and I clench my thighs together when I realize he's probably smelling my arousal.

"Would you like to go to the garden?" he asks.

He's tense, probably preparing for a rejection I'm not going to give.

Chapter 33

AINE

SEVERAL BIRDS CHIRP as Damien leads us to the garden, his hand wrapped tightly around mine. He gives my palm a firm squeeze at the halfway point, his excitement helping to urge me along.

I force myself to keep my head high as we cross the last row of trees that lead to the open field. I still can't bring myself to look at the beasts in the training field, but I'm taking baby steps.

Damien guides me to the garden, his movements confident as he pushes over the wheelbarrow and pops into the greenhouse to grab my gloves. I sit back and watch, loving how he remembered everything.

It feels awfully domestic, which is something I never imagined Damien would be able to pull off.

It's surprising how much he's changed since we met, slowly transforming from a monster I was terrified of to being the person who brings me the most comfort. If somebody told me six months ago that the man who left me to rot in a cabin would be the same one I'm looking at today, I'd have laughed in their faces.

If I didn't know any better, I'd say I've broken him.

Damien tosses my gloves at my head, smiling as they bounce off my forehead and fall into my lap. I shoot him a playful glare.

"Don't look at me like that," he jokes, squatting beside me and getting to work with the pruners. I admire at him for a long moment before slipping on my gloves.

I may have broken him, but he's still annoying.

We work efficiently, only pausing when Damien's unsure whether something's ready to be harvested. He's wrong most of the time, but I try not to let him feel bad about his poor instincts.

He's good at other things.

Damien moves to prune a main vine, and I grab his wrist to stop him.

"Not that one," I say.

He frowns, glancing between me and the vine. "Why not?"

"Because it'll kill the plant."

I release his wrist, and Damien pouts for a moment before muttering something under his breath. I'm sure it's directed at me, and I flick his thigh in mock anger.

I'm hesitant to tease him in front of so many eavesdropping beasts, so I keep my reaction muted.

The wheelbarrow quickly grows full, and I stand and dust off my pants once it does. I'm nervous to venture to the dining hall, but I refuse to let my fear win.

"We should take this to the pantry," I say.

Damien does a poor job hiding his shock, his eyes growing comically wide before he catches himself and lowers his lids.

"Are you sure?" he asks.

I nod, and Damien absolutely beams before walking over and kissing me. It's rough, and I melt into him as he cups the back of my head to hold me in place. He backs me up against the wheelbarrow, his hips pressing into mine.

Then there's a loud whistle. It's coming from the training

field, and I'm sure it's directed toward Damien and me.

I quickly grow rigid, anxiety and fear overshadowing the enjoyment I feel from Damien's touch. He continues to hold me, his lips sliding to my ear.

"You've done absolutely nothing wrong," he says between light kisses to my temple. "They're only joking. Nobody's upset we're kissing, and if anything, they're probably enjoying seeing me act like a lovesick pup."

I'm self-conscious about the fact that they can probably hear him, but his words are still reassuring. It speaks volumes that Damien's so quick to comfort me in front of his people.

He rubs my back until I've relaxed against him, my head finally dropping onto his chest with a quiet *thud*. I feel a lot of shame for still needing this coddling, but I'm grateful he offers it without making me feel too needy.

When Damien finally pulls away and grabs the wheelbarrow, I'm feeling much better.

"Are you sure you want to take this to the pantry?" he asks. "We can call it a day and leave it here. Somebody else will take it."

I shake my head, not wanting that. I'm not going to get better if I don't try. I want to live a normal life, and if that means getting better, then that's what I'll do. Especially since it doesn't seem like Damien intends to leave me anytime soon.

"I'm sure," I say.

Damien smiles and begins pushing the wheelbarrow down the worn path that leads to the dining hall. I follow closely behind, admiring his back. The muscles underneath his shirt flex with each of his steps, bringing up memories of how good his skin felt beneath my hands earlier today.

I'd be lying if I said I haven't been attracted to Damien since we first met, and now that he's close enough to have, I'm having trouble holding back.

He's within my grasp, and I want to taste him before something happens and he's untouchable again. I may not be able to say it with words just yet, but I want to show Damien how much he means to me.

A low rumble emerges from his chest as I continue to stare, the sound going straight to my sex. I'm sure he can smell my arousal, and I sigh as I shift my attention to his thighs. Henry would tire so quickly during sex, but I'm willing to bet Damien could go for hours if he wanted. He can probably take me in ways I can't even imagine.

My thoughts are so consuming, I hardly notice we've entered the pantry. Damien spins the moment we're both inside the small space, his body towering over mine as he pins me against the door.

"What're you thinking about?" he asks.

His pupils are fully expanded as he waits for my answer, the sight alone making my knees buckle.

"I want you," I admit. "I'm ready, Damien. I mean it."

Damien lifts me in one smooth motion, prompting me to wrap my legs around his waist. He practically purrs at my words, grinding himself against me.

"Then I'll take you home."

I shake my head as I reach between our bodies and cup him over his jeans. I don't want to wait. Damien is full of questions and doubt, his fear of pushing me too far very sweet but unnecessary. If we wait until we're home, he'll find another reason to postpone.

"I'm not some virginal maiden who needs you to romance me," I say. "I want to be with you *now*."

Damien places his hand over mine, stopping me from stroking the hard length hidden underneath the fabric of his pants. "Let me take you to our bed."

I shake my head, refusing.

By the time we get home, he'll have thought of a thousand different reasons why I may not be ready for this or how I'll regret our actions after the deed is done. I'm tired of letting my fear hold me back from being with him.

"I want you," I insist. "We've waited long enough."

Frustrated tears threaten to spill as Damien presses his forehead against mine. I can practically hear the internal battle he holds within himself, but when his hands slide to my thighs, I know I've won.

Damien carries me to the tiny counter in the corner of the room, and he pushes the items atop it into the sink so there's room for me to sit. The metal clangs as Damien knocks things around, but I hardly hear it over the blood rushing through my ears.

My mouth goes dry as he places me on the very edge of the counter, his arms wrapped tightly around my back so I remain pressed against him.

"You don't want me to romance you?" he teases.

He gathers my wrists in his left hand and holds them together behind my back. The action stretches my shoulders, and I stiffen as memories of being in this position rush through my mind.

Damien catches on immediately and adjusts. He releases my wrists, and he guides my hands to the front and places them on his hips. I'm happy he isn't commenting on it and ruining the mood.

Goosebumps pebble up along my arms as I dig my fingers into the soft skin at his waist.

"My human wants me to fuck her *now*," he continues. "Not a virginal maiden, she says." He brings his mouth to my ear, his breath warming the skin. "Exactly what part of me do you want?"

Damien looks at my body, and his hands wander down my sides before slipping underneath my shirt. I shiver, arching into him in a silent request for more.

His fingers tickle as they pass my ribcage, pausing momentarily to graze over the ribs that still show from when Owen starved me. Damien's been overfeeding me since returning, and I know the bones bother him. He doesn't stick around them for long, his interest quickly moving to the bottom of my breasts.

"Tell me what you want, Aine," Damien repeats, tracing the edge of my bra.

I feel like I'm on fire, and his desire for me is all-consuming as it seeps through the bond. He's making no effort to hold it back. He's probably doing it on purpose, pushing his feelings into me instead of letting them naturally filter through.

I tighten my thighs around his waist, beyond desperate as he finally reaches around and unhooks my bra. The tight material separates from my torso, making room for him to slide his hands underneath.

Damien cups me, his large palms easily covering the entirety of my chest. I hook my foot around the back of his thigh and pull him closer.

He moans. "So fucking perfect."

He follows up his words with a pinch to my nipple, and before I can react, he leans in and trails his tongue up the side of my neck. It feels amazing, and I'm all too aware this is the spot where he wants to mark me.

I have half a mind to ask him to do it, but something holds me back. I'm nervous. What if he doesn't want to?

"You haven't answered me," Damien says.

He pulls away, a lazy smirk spreading across his lips.

I wrack my brain, trying to remember what he asked. It's hard to think, let alone speak, when he's rolling my nipple between his fingers so softly. My cheeks grow warm as I recall him asking me to tell him exactly what part of him I want.

He already knows the answer to that, I've made it abundantly clear, but his grin tells me he enjoys hearing me say it.

"I want all of you," I say.

Damien shakes his head. "Be more specific."

I slip my eyes shut and rock my hips against his, desperate for him to continue touching me. His hands are still on my chest, but his movements are feather light and slow. I want more.

He pinches my nipple, the sudden pain jolting. I throw my head back with a cry. I can feel how badly he wants me through the bond, and my heart pounds as I grab Damien over his jeans. He hisses, and I run my hand over the hard length straining the material.

"I want *this*," I whisper, my cheeks flaming.

Damien grinds himself against my hand, his rhythmic movements foreshadowing how good he's going to make me feel. I need him inside me, and I tighten my grip to get the point across.

"Fuck," Damien sucks in a sharp breath. "Then take it."

He pulls my shirt over my head. My bra is quick to follow, and Damien throws both to the side. I work to undo his pants, eager to get him undressed. Damien helps, yanking off his shirt and dropping it on top of mine.

My hands shake as I eye his muscular chest, but my desperation to see him naked keeps me focused and moving. I lower his zipper, the noise cutting sharply through our loud breathing.

Damien grunts as I push his jeans and underwear down his thighs, finally freeing him. He's fully erect, and he takes a step back so he can finish removing his bottoms. I stare at his cock.

I've seen it before, but it's been a while. Damien's big, and I can't wait to have him inside me. I grab him as he kicks his underwear away, desperate to feel the silky skin in my palm.

He twitches as he steps between my thighs, and I take my time exploring him as he works on removing my bottoms. He's faster than me, and within only seconds, I'm being lifted so he can slide the material underneath my butt and down my legs.

I hiss as my bare skin touches the cool metal of the counter, my hand tightening around his shaft. Damien grunts and shoots me a warning look as I squeeze him.

I smile, happily taking in the sight of his darkened eyes and wet, bitten lips. He'll be okay.

"I love you," he says.

He leans in and connects his mouth with mine, and I release his cock so I can feel his torso instead. I want to explore him.

I press my palms flat against his pecs and drag them down his abs. The muscles shudder underneath me, expanding and contracting as Damien fights to stay still. I love it.

Damien gasps as I continue, sliding my hand over the trail of hair directly below his belly button.

"I've never done this," he confesses.

I pause, unsure what he means. It's no secret that Damien's been intimate with plenty of women. He's got quite a past, and it was confirmed when we saw those prostitutes in the human village.

"It's true," he continues. "I've never wanted a woman to explore me, to take their time and learn my body. I've never *made love* before."

His admission makes my heart clench. We're making love.

Damien grabs my hand and places it on his belly, spreading my fingers and slotting his in between. I giggle at his antics, enjoying the feeling of his stomach expanding with breath.

"You're the first woman to touch me here," he admits, dragging my hand to his neck. I curl my fingers around the column of his throat, and he pauses before moving my hand to his cheek. "Here, too."

My throat runs dry, and I wrap my legs around his waist as I run my thumb over his lips. His cheeks flush, and mine do the same as I reach out with my other hand and take hold of his cock.

He's so hard, and he claims my lips as I guide him to my entrance. His fingers curl where they rest against my thighs, his nails digging into the scarred skin. It's painfully familiar to what Owen did, and I instinctively tense before pushing the bad thoughts away.

Damien's not going to hurt me.

"I'm ready for you," I say.

The tip of his cock presses against me, the soft skin dipping into my folds before I pull back and drag him to my clit. I rub, using him to pleasure myself.

"Fuck me, Damien."

He moans. "Who knew my mate would be so dirty for me?" The question is rhetorical. "I'll fuck you here because that's what you want, but the next time I take you, I'll be picking the location."

I giggle as he swats my hand away and replaces it with his own, finally taking the lead.

Seeing his hand wrapped around himself has my stomach doing backflips, and I watch with a slack jaw as he presses his wide head against my entrance and drags his hand down his shaft, masturbating against me.

"I'm going to lay you on our bed and take my time tasting every sweet bit of you," he says, pushing an inch inside me before pulling back out and stroking himself again. "I won't even consider fucking you until you're begging."

He sinks the first inch of himself in again. I rock my hips, desperate for more, but Damien doesn't give it.

"Please," I gasp.

Damien smiles, finally easing more inside. "I love watching your pussy stretch around me."

He pulls out and pushes in again, continuing until he's buried entirely inside me. He moves slowly, giving me time to adjust as he rolls his hips and rocks in and out. If he's looking for discomfort, he's not going to find any.

His size is borderline painful, but I like it. I want to feel sore.

"Are you okay?" he eventually asks.

I blink a few times, struggling to focus when he's inside me.

"More," I gasp. I tilt my hips back until some of him slides out of me, and then I push forward and sink myself back down.

Damien's eyes are almost entirely black as he grabs my hips and finally begins to fuck me, his hips slamming into mine with each thrust. He watches himself disappearing into me, his loud moans mirroring my own as the sound of our fucking fills the room.

He presses his forehead against mine and smashes our lips together, immediately deepening the kiss. His tongue quickly finds its way into my mouth, muffling my moans.

My hips grow sore from the position, and Damien pulls out and picks me up when I try to readjust.

He huffs. "We wouldn't have to maneuver like this if you'd let me take you to our bed like a normal woman."

I laugh as he realigns himself and thrusts up into me.

"I don't think I'd be your mate if I wanted you to fuck me like normal women," I say. "You aren't a fan of those, from what I've heard."

Damien releases my thigh and cups my chin. "Don't talk about other women when I'm with you. You're the only one I love and want to be with. I don't care if you're adventurous or want me to fuck you in the same position for the rest of our lives."

He grunts, his hips slamming into mine before he continues. "I'm yours as much as you're mine, and I won't allow you to share me with another. Even in your mind."

His possessiveness is confusing. I understand him not wanting to hear about me being with other men, but to be so upset about an offhand comment regarding him being with other women has my mind reeling.

I like it, though. He's mine.

Heat spreads through me as Damien moans, his words slowly transforming into nothing more than incoherent gasps. He releases my chin and begins rubbing my clit, his other arm under my butt to hold me up.

It doesn't take long for my orgasm to build, the tension growing until I'm nothing more than a writhing mess in Damien's arms.

"Damien, I—" I stutter. "Oh!"

My body convulses as I clench around him, every muscle tightening as I cum. Damien continues to fuck me through it, his moans growing louder as he drives himself toward the same release.

I slump against his chest, going soft in his arms. He hardly seems to notice as he lays me back on the counter, my ass hovering off the edge as he drives himself into me at a pace I struggle to keep up with.

"I'm going to cum," he says, rolling his hips against mine. "I'm going to pull out, and I want you to finish me with your hand. Can you do that?"

I nod, desperate and excited to bring him to completion. I was hoping for him to cum inside me, but I push that desire to the back of my mind as he pulls out and shoves himself into my hands.

I wrap my fingers around his length and begin to stroke, desperate to make him cum. I know he's close when his eyes slam shut and his balls lift, the reaction accompanied by a loud grunt as he stills and begins to spill onto me.

His cum lands higher than anticipated, and I shriek and point him lower as the first bit hits my chin and neck. The rest lands on my belly, coating me before dribbling down his shaft.

Mesmerized, I continue to stroke until he shivers and pulls away. There's a comfortable silence as Damien works to catch his breath, but his worry and fear quickly begins to fill our bond.

"That was good," I say, eager to assure him of my feelings. I don't regret this.

Damien eyes the cum dripping down my chin, a smirk toying at the corners of his lips. I start to wipe at it, and he quickly grabs his shirt off the floor.

"I'll do it," he says.

His guilt hits like a ton of bricks as he begins wiping me clean.

"That day in my office... after everything with Olivia. I touched you, then I turned it into a joke. I knew you were upset, and I ignored it. I should've comforted you. I knew that's what you wanted."

I purse my lips.

"I'm sorry," Damien continues. "I'm really sorry, Aine."

I clear my throat. "You should have comforted me," I admit. I cup his chin, urging him to look at me. "And you're doing so now. You're giving me what I need, Damien. I promise."

Chapter 34

AINE

A HAND CLAMPING around my kneecap and pushing it straight has me shooting up in bed, my eyes darting sporadically around the dark room before landing on Damien's pained face. His eyebrows furrow together as he sucks in a breath, and he holds it for several seconds before slowly exhaling.

It takes me a minute to get my bearings straight, but once I do, I'm lunging forward and grabbing his cheeks.

"I'm so sorry." I gasp, moving my knee so it's no longer digging into his groin.

Damien huffs before rolling on top of me, his heavy body pushing mine into the mattress and practically suffocating me. I laugh and shove at his chest, glad I didn't harm him too much. It's not the first time I've accidentally kneed him in the balls while thrashing in my sleep.

"If you want to have children with me someday," he complains in my ear, "I'd recommend keeping your bony limbs away from my manhood."

I snort, my smile growing as he wraps his arm around my torso and rolls until I'm sprawled across his chest. I flail, trying to break free, but Damien wordlessly tightens his grip until I give up and let him hold me. I suppose I don't mind this.

He's been nothing but smiles and jokes since we finally had sex yesterday, his contentment heavy as it travels through our bond. It remained even when I made him disinfect the entire pantry.

Damien finally loosens his grip on me, and I slide off his chest and settle at his side. Our legs intertwine, and I rest my hand on his belly and my head on his shoulder.

"Are you sore?" he asks. "Because I am. I'm too old to have sex in pantries."

I roll my eyes, and Damien kisses my forehead.

"How are you feeling, though?" he pries.

I shrug, my cheeks warming. I thought he was over this, but I should've known better than to think he wouldn't ask.

Damien panicked when he saw my light spotting yesterday, and no number of assurances seem to be settling him. I've seen Damien's size, and it's been a long time since I had sex. I fully expected there to be a bit of blood.

Admittedly, I like that it hurts. The ache serves as a reminder that I had him inside me. I just wish Damien felt the same way.

"I'm okay, Damien," I assure him. "I enjoyed every second of what occurred between us."

Damien ignores my words, shoving his hand between my thighs so he can prod at me himself. His chubby fingers force their way between my legs and softly caress my swollen entrance.

I groan, squeezing my thighs around his hand before pushing him away.

"Stop that," I huff.

Damien clenches his jaw, hesitating, before pulling his hand back to his chest. "You can't demand me to stop caring for your health."

I frown. "I'm not asking you to stop caring for my health. I'm asking you to stop prodding at my sore vagina."

I push his wandering hands away once more.

Damien's annoyance barrels through our bond, but I refuse to give in. Me sharing my body with him doesn't mean he has permission to touch me whenever he wants. I imagine I'll be more comfortable around him in the future, but I'm not there yet.

I look at the ceiling, pretending not to notice Damien's watchful gaze. His stare feels heavy on my skin, weighing me into the mattress.

I think about the day ahead of us, and I force myself to keep a neutral expression as my thoughts and worries tumble together. How long does Damien plan to avoid work in lieu of taking care of me?

He says the pack understands and supports his absence, but with each passing day, my guilt grows. I'd be a fool not to see that Damien misses work. His eyes light up every time Alex or Olivia come around, and he's all too excited to step outside and be briefed on what's been happening.

He may love me, but he loves his job too.

Damien pokes my shoulder, and I crinkle my nose as I turn to look at my new burn. I didn't put on sunscreen before going to the garden yesterday.

"I forget how quickly your body filters through my blood," Damien says. "Avia can give you some after breakfast, and then we can finish working on our puzzle."

"Actually—" I pause and clear my throat before continuing. It's now or never. "I was wondering if you might want to go to your office and work today."

Damien's expression gives away nothing, but the bond screams shock. He remains silent as he takes in my words, his emotions filtering through an intense mixture of worry, stress, and relief. I try not to be offended at the relief, reminding myself that I'd feel the same way if I were in his position.

Damien sits up and leans against the headboard, still not speaking. Following his adjustment, I lift myself into a sitting position.

"What makes you say that?" he asks.

I shrug, not quite sure how to put my feelings into words.

"I've kept you away from it for too long."

Damien frowns, and I drop my gaze to my thighs. I thought he'd be happy about this.

"That's for me to decide," he says. "And I've decided I'll stay at home with you until you're comfortable being on your own."

Sighing, I shake my head and grab his hands. They're rough within mine, his callouses matured after years of fighting and training. Damien's eyes narrow as I run my thumb over his palm, the man clearly not trusting my motives.

"Damien—"

He cuts me off. "Aine."

I squeeze his hand and shoot him a glare, annoyed with the interruption. This is hard for me to do, and he's not making it any easier. Damien sucks in a laugh at my silent threat, his cheeks hollowing as he fights to keep a straight face.

"I'll be okay," I assure him. "Your office is just out back, and I know you can see the house through the windows. I trust you'll be watching me, and if I feel overwhelmed, I promise I'll come to you."

Damien remains silent, and he stares at the ceiling as he ponders my words. At least he's thinking it over. I try not to rush him as he mulls over my proposal, waiting patiently until he realizes this is an argument I'm going to win.

"I suppose I could do that," he eventually says. "But I'm not leaving you alone. Alex will stay at the house while I'm gone.

He's been bugging me about visiting, anyway, claiming I'm hoarding you."

I haven't spent time with Alex since the rescue. Other than the occasional *hello* and friendly wave, we haven't been around one another. I've been avoiding everybody, but I know I can't do that forever.

Not if I want to get better.

I suppose Alex is a good place to start. He's safe.

"I'm excited to see Alex," I say. "I miss him."

I turn and straddle Damien, wanting to feel close to him. He wordlessly wraps his arms around my waist and pulls me in for a hug. It lasts for half a second before he abruptly stands and carries me into the bathroom.

"Damien!" I gasp as he dips me backward so he can bend and turn on the shower. "What're you doing?"

He tightens his grip on my hips before pulling me in for a possessive kiss. My eyes flutter shut as his mouth travels to my neck, his tongue darting out to lick along the column of my throat before abruptly lifting and running from my cheek to my eyebrow.

I wince and pull away, opening my eyes to glare into the darkened ones of his beast. What's he doing? I wipe away his spit, worried he's going to attack my face with his tongue again.

I can tell he's hiding his emotions as I search the bond for them and come up empty-handed. Damien's never done that before, and I grimace before grabbing his chin and pulling his face toward me. I'm not sure if I'm supposed to return the favor, but I don't want to disappoint.

Damien leans closer without complaint, and his eyes grow comically wide as I lick his cheek. His stubble feels rough against my tongue, but I try to ignore it as I lick from his chin to his ear and then to his temple.

I try my best not to appear judgmental and grossed out as I

pull back and smile at Damien. That smile drops as I take in his confused expression and wet skin.

"My love," Damien says, holding back a laugh. He sets me on my feet. "My beast made me lick you because he was upset about your excitement to see Alex. It's a possessive reaction I'm not proud of, but I promise there's no expectation for you to lick me back."

Oh. I'm sure my face is a thousand shades of red, and I try to hide my regret as I roll my shoulders back and straighten my spine.

I clear my throat. "Well, how was I supposed to know that?"

My embarrassment is further fueled as Damien lets out the laugh he's been holding in. He clearly enjoys watching me squirm.

I spin on my heel and storm inside the warm shower. I leave the door open for Damien, worried he'll think he's genuinely upset me if I close it. Seeing the unspoken invitation, he quickly joins.

"I love you," he says.

He kisses the top of my head, the touch light, before grabbing our body soap and preparing to wash me. It's a daily ritual I've grown to enjoy, especially now that I get to return the favor when he's finished.

He takes his time cleaning me, enjoying the moment.

"Are you sure about me going to the office?" he asks.

I spin and kiss to his chest. "Yes, I'm sure."

Damien hums, not quite believing me, but he doesn't push the subject. We usually spend a long time in the showers, using them as an excuse to explore one another's bodies. I love seeing the way Damien's muscles shiver, or how his cock grows hard.

The need has been sated, though, at least for now. I'm too sore to even consider having sex right now, but I'm sure I'll feel differently in a day or two. It's only a matter of time before my desire for Damien demands action.

Damien wraps a towel around me once we finish showering,

and I let out a long sigh when he immediately begins rummaging through the first-aid kit he keeps in one of the drawers.

"Come here," Damien orders. He points to the toilet. "Sit."

I frown, already knowing what he wants. Every fiber of my being urges me to ignore his request and walk out of the room, but knowing how guilty he feels about hurting me yesterday, I comply.

Damien drops to his knees and spreads my thighs so he can drag an ointment-covered finger through my folds. I puff out my cheeks as he dips inside my entrance, already knowing his concern is unnecessary. I'm going to be fully healed within a day or so.

"You look much better than yesterday," Damien says, earning himself a sharp glare. He quickly backtracks. "Not that it's ever looked anything less than beautiful."

I snap my legs shut and stand the second he's finished. If it weren't for the concern I feel filtering through our bond, I'd reject his help.

"That's the only time I'm letting you do that," I say.

Damien lifts his hands in surrender as I tighten my towel around my torso and turn away. He chuckles and follows me into the bedroom, his footsteps fading as I open my closet and he goes for the dresser.

I'm scared to be without him today, but I push down my fear as I get dressed. I need to learn to be independent, and that's never going to happen if I allow Damien to keep serving as my crutch.

Despite his obvious attempts to hold it back, I feel his excitement as he gets changed, the emotion solidifying my decision. He's going to have fun today, and I'll get to see Alex.

There's nothing about that to be afraid of.

Damien keeps a watchful eye on me the entire morning, even as he cooks breakfast and yells out the back door for Alex to come over. I'm proud of myself for how convincing my smile is when

Alex finally saunters over.

The first thing I notice is the fresh mark on his neck.

He glances between me and Damien before slowly pulling open the back door and coming inside. Damien usually meets him outside, and it's clear he's confused with the change.

"Yes?" he asks.

"I'm going to my office," Damien says. He gestures to me. "You're going to hang out with Aine and keep her company."

It's a bit embarrassing having Alex as a babysitter, and I'm a little nervous he's going to be annoyed by it. Instead, though, he beams.

"Yeah?" he asks. He turns toward me. "Did Damien tell you I've been asking to see you?"

I give a half shrug, not wanting to lie but also not wanting to admit that he's here because I'm too scared to be left alone. I really am looking forward to seeing Alex, but it's not the main reason we invited him over.

"Don't touch Aine," Damien says. "And don't touch our puzzle."

Alex nods. I think this is the end of it, but Damien has more to say. He begins prematurely lecturing Alex, scolding him for several things he hasn't even done. I cross my arms over my chest, silently watching.

It's a good twenty minutes before Damien turns his back to Alex and approaches me.

"You can come visit anytime you want," he says. "I'll be back around lunch, and we can see how you're feeling before continuing the rest of the day."

I nod, gently urging him toward the back door. I wasn't expecting him to drag his departure out for this long, and I'm starting to feel bad for Alex.

"Shout if you want me," Damien continues. "I'll be listening."

"Yes, thank you," I say.

Damien doesn't move, and I give up on subtlety as I reach around him and open the back door. He looks between me and the exit with a frown, shuffling his feet. If I didn't know any better, I'd say he wants me to ask him to stay.

Alex, who hasn't spoken a word in almost ten minutes, steps forward and not-so-gently pushes Damien out of the house. Damien stumbles back a step, his lips turned down at the corners. I release the door and let it shut, wincing as his expression turns to shock as the glass pane comes between us.

Alex sighs. "About time."

I can see he's holding back a smile as he places his hands on my shoulders and turns me away from the door. Damien blinks, his left eye lowering into a wink.

"I was starting to think he'd never leave," Alex admits.

Damien disappears into his office.

I clear my throat. "I'm sorry I haven't seen you." I hope he can hear the sincerity in my tone. "I've been a bit of a hermit."

Alex sucks his bottom lip into his mouth, his eyebrows furrowing as he looks me from head to toe. I shift my weight from foot to foot before sitting on the island barstool. I hope he's not angry with me.

"Don't apologize," he says, sitting beside me. "How's everything with you and Damien? I've heard rumors, but I want to hear it from the source."

A few months ago, all I wanted was for somebody to ask me this. I wanted anybody to give me the opportunity to share just how poorly Damien was treating me. I had a whole speech prepared, a list of grievances I was eager to discuss.

I no longer feel that way.

"Well?" Alex asks when I don't respond.

"Damien's been kind," I admit. "I've been struggling, and

he's been very patient with me." It's impossible to stop a smile from lighting up my face. "He told me he loves me."

Alex hums, not sounding at all surprised. "I heard he's done much more than say he loves you."

I decide to play dumb. "I'm not sure what you're referring to."

I refuse to make eye contact with Alex as he dissolves into a fit of laughter. I don't think he's funny at all.

"I'm the only one who heard," he eventually admits. "I went to grab a snack from the pantry and quickly realized it was occupied. Don't worry, though. I stood outside like a good guard dog and made sure nobody else entered."

I'm going to die.

Alex happily continues. "And you should be thanking me, too, because a gaggle of teenagers decided they were going to sneak into the dining hall and steal some food. If it weren't for me, the entire pack would know every detail of your little escapade."

I drop my head into my hands. Damien was so against intimacy in the pantry, and I can't believe I practically bullied him into having sex there. His office, sure. The house, sure. The pantry where anybody could enter at any moment, absolutely not.

Alex continues laughing.

I huff. "It's not that funny."

"It is," Alex insists. "You're quite funny, Aine. Our parents would've loved you."

I pause, looking into Alex's eyes to see if he's lying. Damien told me one brief story about his parents when we were in the human village, but that's all I've ever heard of his family.

I assume it's a sore subject, so I don't bring it up, but I'm still curious. I want to know everything about Damien.

"Do you really think so?" I ask.

Damien's dislike of humans had to come somewhere, and the easiest answer is it being something passed through his parents.

Detesting an entire species is a learned behavior, and it makes sense it was Damien's family who made him believe we're too weak to be respected.

"Of course!" Alex says. "You're their son's mate. Of course they would've loved you."

"But I'm a human."

"What does that have to do with anything?"

I shrug, beginning to regret saying anything in the first place. "I assumed Damien got his hatred of humans from your parents."

Alex hums, tapping his fingers idly against the counter. I'd pay to know what's going on in his head, and I sit quietly as I wait for him to continue speaking.

I hope I haven't offended him.

Alex stands and walks toward the back door. He peers out it, staring at Damien's office. I'm desperate to know what he's thinking.

"Has Damien ever told you how our mom and sister died?"

I nod. "They drowned."

Alex clears his throat. "Beasts don't drown," he says. "Our mother was human, and our sister carried more of her traits than beast ones."

What? I have no response. Why didn't Damien ever mention that? I understand it's a sore subject, but this feels like a big thing to conveniently leave out. Does that mean that he and Alex are half-human? It has to.

"Damien loved our mother, but our sister was his world," Alex continues. "His attitude toward humans changed after she died. I know having you as a mate terrifies him, and so does the possibility of having human children like Jess. Beast genes are dominant, and most hybrid children will reject the human attributes and come out almost entirely beast, but there's always a risk."

I'm speechless, and I drag my fingers through my hair with a shaky exhale.

"Do you think that's why he pushed me away so hard?" I ask.

Alex shrugs. "I'd assume so, but you'll have to ask him."

"I wish he would've told me this." It explains so much.

Alex nods, continuing to stare out the back door. He seems off, his shoulders rounded forward and his eyes tired.

"What's wrong?" I ask.

"Nothing."

That's a lie if I've ever heard one. "Are you sure?"

Alex huffs. "Olivia's mad at me," he admits. "She asked if my beast misses Freya, and I hesitated. Our mates are everything to us, and even though mine no longer recognizes her as his mate, he still misses what we could've had. He'll grow to love Olivia with time, but I can't force it on him."

Freya's name leaves a bad taste in my mouth.

"I can see how that would make Olivia upset," I say.

I try to keep any judgment out of my tone. I wouldn't enjoy being a second choice, but I understand it's not something Alex can control.

I point to the mark on his neck. "At least you two are mated now. If that isn't a sign you've chosen her, I don't know what is."

Alex goes red and looks away. He avoids eye contact as he rubs at the back of his neck.

"What?" I ask.

Alex grimaces. "I haven't marked Olivia back, which is part of the reason why she's so upset. She thinks I'm leaving my options open."

"Are you?"

I was under the impression he was excited to claim Olivia, and I can't help but find it suspicious he's yet to do so. I shift in my seat, ready to lunge if he says he's contemplating getting back together with Freya.

"Of course not," Alex says. He sucks in a slow breath before continuing. "There's a traditional marking ceremony some beasts choose to do, and I'd like to have one. I want Olivia to have the same celebration the fated mates get."

His eyes grow glassy as he speaks, but I pretend not to notice. Alex looks down as he calms himself, and after a second his stiff posture slowly relaxes.

"The pack don't respect her as a mate, and I hope the ceremony will make them realize how serious our relationship is."

Alex shakes out his arms and turns away from the back door. I can tell the conversation is over and he wishes to move on, and I don't make a fuss as he leads me into the living room.

He politely ignores my occasional glances out the back door as he pulls out a deck of cards and begins explaining the rules of a game I've never heard of. It's simple enough, and much to Alex's annoyance, I seem to be better at it than him.

We rotate between three different games before settling on one he doesn't lose every time, and I have half a mind to start betting money.

Eventually, Alex looks at the back door and groans.

I already know why, and I beam as Damien comes bursting inside, his arms outstretched wide.

"Mate!" he shouts.

I jump off the couch, and Damien laughs as I barrel into him. Alex has been good company, but I've missed Damien. His excitement pours through the bond as he wraps his arms around my waist and pulls me in for a tight hug.

This day has dragged on forever without him by my side.

"I missed you," he says.

Alex grunts. "You were gone for less than four hours."

He's a sore loser. I've beaten him several times now, and this was the round he was finally going to win.

Damien lifts and swings me back and forth, causing my feet to dangle and hang by his shins.

"Don't be rude to me," he snaps at Alex.

They continue to bicker as Damien walks to the couch opposite Alex and plops down. I gasp at his sudden actions, spluttering as I sprawl unattractively across his lap. Damien mindlessly helps me adjust as he continues arguing with Alex, halting mid-sentence when he takes in my frustrated reaction.

"Oh, I'm sorry," he says, lowering his voice. "I'm overwhelming you. I forget your reaction time is slower than mine."

Alex snorts. "You're so fucking dense."

He mutters something else under his breath, probably something mean he wants only Damien to hear. Then he swipes the cards off the table.

I smile up at him. "Thanks for coming over today."

Alex blows me a kiss before leaving, and I ignore the jealousy I feel coming through Damien's bond as I lean against his chest. He doesn't even wait for Alex to be fully out the door before setting me on the couch and throwing himself on top of me.

"I missed you," he says, planting kisses all over my cheeks.

I giggle, enjoying this playful side of him. He hasn't been in this good of a mood since before Owen, and his happiness reinforces my decision to make him go to work. Damien continues to press wet kisses to my face, slowly moving inward toward my lips. He groans when he finally kisses me properly, the noise bringing heat to my skin.

His hips press between mine, rubbing against me before he pulls away with a cheeky grin. He's clearly proud of himself, and he sinks his teeth into his bottom lip as he watches me shift beneath him.

"We shouldn't do anything while you're recovering," he says. "I don't enjoy breaking my mate with my fat, giant, girthy, out-of-this-world, amazing cock."

I have no idea how to respond to that, and after a slight pause, I flick Damien's bicep. I secretly think those adjectives are true, but I'll be damned if I admit it out loud. I don't need Damien's ego growing any larger.

Damien sits up. "Did you have a good day?"

I nod, internally debating how best to bring up what Alex shared about their family. I want Damien to feel he can talk to me about these things. He's been there for me, and I want to do the same.

"I did," I say, clearing my throat. "I don't enjoy being away from you, but Alex kept me distracted. We had some interesting conversations."

I'm testing the waters. Damien takes the bait.

He cocks his head to the side before readjusting, getting comfortable and tossing my legs over his lap.

"Did you now?" he asks. "What about?"

I'm nervous. "He said your mother and sister were human."

Damien stills, and I wince at the sudden muting of his emotions. Sometimes he hides them from me, somehow blocking them from traveling through the bond, but never to this extent. I don't love that he's keeping me out, but I don't comment on it. Just because he let me mark him doesn't mean I'm entitled to feel everything of his.

Damien's lips twitch downward for just a moment before returning to their resting position, but it's all I needed to see to know he's not happy Alex told me this.

"That's true." His voice is low.

"Is that why you fought against the bond for so long?"

It takes a long time for Damien to answer. "I suppose that

would be correct."

I wait, urging him to say more, but Damien presses his lips together and gives a subtle shake of his head. He knows what I want, and he's pointedly denying it.

"Is that all you're going to say about it?" I ask.

Damien's chest deflates, and his fingers dig into my calf. There's no way he's surprised I'm looking to understand why he treated me the way he did when I first arrived.

His current behaviors don't excuse the past.

"I was, and still am, scared to lose you," Damien says. "I'll admit a lot of that fear stems from my mother and sister, but I don't..." Damien throws his head back and stares up at the ceiling. "I don't want to talk about this right now. I don't want to think about it."

His voice grows thick, and when I notice how upset he looks, I sit up and pull his head against my chest. I drag my fingers through his hair and press soft kisses to the top of his head, hoping to comfort him. He does this to me whenever I'm worked up.

"It's okay. We don't need to talk about it," I say. "I'd love to hear more about your family, but I can wait."

I take a deep breath, my heart pounding, before continuing.

"I love you," I say. "You know that, right?"

I was scared to say it for a while, scared to make myself so vulnerable. Telling Damien how I feel is like giving him a loaded weapon and hoping he doesn't turn it on me. Still, it doesn't make my emotions any less true.

I'm in love with him, and I suspect I've been for a while.

Damien's childish grin assures me he won't ever use my confession against me, and his timid nod makes my heart swell. He is good.

Chapter 35

DAMIEN

I'M SURE I look creepy with my face pressed against my dirty office window, but I don't care. I'm not proud to admit how often I find myself doing this, and I'm especially not proud of how many times Alex has caught me.

He's been kind enough not to say anything, but his judgmental looks are enough to have me sulking back to my chair. It never lasts long. The overwhelming urge to see Aine is too strong to ignore, and without fail, I quickly find myself returning to my dirty window.

I like looking at my mate, and I'm not going to apologize for it. Aine consumes my every waking thought, and being away from her physically pains me.

I see her shadow moving behind the kitchen window, and I straighten up as she flips on the light. I can't help but feel giddy as I watch her tear through our cupboards in search of food, her sporadic actions informing me she's still in her grumpy morning phase of the day.

I drop my forehead against my office window as I watch, grateful her human eyes can't see through the tint. Guilt eats at me for being unwilling to discuss my family's history with her, and I shut my eyes and knock my head against the glass as I struggle to find the words. She's not going to be happy with me.

After my mother and sister died, I lost all respect for humans. They're fragile, and when I met Aine, I couldn't see past it. I looked at her and saw my sister's bloated body and my mother's mangled frame. The current dragged them across so many rocks. They were indistinguishable by the time we found them.

My father's suicide only solidified my belief, cementing in me that humans aren't to be loved.

I thought Aine was a mistake, a punishment for being a bad alpha and allowing Freya on me. I thought my beast would eventually give up on Aine, that he'd realize how weak humans are and take a beast instead.

I can't admit this to Aine, but I won't lie to her.

She'd be crushed to learn how desperate I was to get away from her and how much I detested having a human as a mate. It feels like just yesterday I was convinced she was dead, tortured and murdered by Owen, and I can't risk losing her again.

She'll think my love is a lie, and she'll never believe me when I explain how my view of humans has changed. I love her gross sunburns and weak shoves and slow reflexes.

I want her. Only her.

She'll hate me.

I groan, watching as she continues puttering around the kitchen. My lips twitch as she takes advantage of my disappearance and pulls out the sugar cereal I keep hidden in the back of the pantry.

Sneaky fucking bugger.

She pours a giant bowl we both know will give her a stomachache, and I can't help but laugh when she spins around with the largest grin I've ever seen. She loves stealing it, finding pleasure in eating the one item I purposefully keep hidden from her. It's my absolute favorite, and I like to have it all to myself. Aine doesn't seem to care for that.

She disappears from my view, carrying her treasure to the living room to do whatever she does with Alex all day long. I appreciate him spending time with her, so I don't pry.

His constant teasing forces her to break out of her shell, and I hate to admit that being away from me is probably a good thing. I want her to understand that people respect and love her for her, not just because she's an extension of me.

I scan the house one last time, hoping she'll return, before turning back to my desk.

There's so much paperwork to get through, and my scouts haven't been able to find anything pointing to Freya's whereabouts. I know she told Owen where and when to capture Aine, the woman selling out my mate for her own benefit.

I'm going to kill her.

The sound of the back door opening draws my attention. Aine wanders outside with her lip pulled between her teeth, her hesitance visible as she glances at my office. I'm sure she knows I can see her.

I find myself holding my breath as I wait to see if she comes over. I want her to. She's more than welcome to pull me from work whenever she wants my attention.

I want her to *demand* it. Demand what's rightfully hers.

My smile grows as she straightens her spine and scampers across the lawn, and I force myself not to jump up and greet her at the door.

I take this time to tidy my desk instead. I've cleaned every time she's ever come to visit me, but historically I've pretended not to have even realized her arrival. I wanted her to feel I was calm and unaffected by her, but I wanted her to think I was calm and unaffected with a clean desk.

I'm not going to pretend this time. I'm too excited to do that, and I no longer want to hide my excitement to see my mate. I shove paperwork in random drawers as she greets Olivia and asks if I'm available.

"You're his mate, Aine. You don't need to ask," Olivia says. I like that answer. "Go right on in."

I sit and clasp my hands on top of my desk, and I struggle to hold back a smile as my nosy mate peeks her head inside. Her heart's hammering away in her chest, and I can see her holding back a laugh as she notes my waiting position.

"It's about time you came to visit," I say, gesturing for her to come in. "I was starting to think you never would."

Aine's face grows red, and I resist the urge to continue my teasing to see how deep I can get the color to turn. She steps inside with a quiet breath, her movements timid as she begins to approach. I push my chair back and spread my arms, wanting her to sit with me and not in one of the uncomfortable leather chairs on the other side of my desk.

Aine seems hesitant as her eyes dart between me and the empty chairs, her lips pursing as she thinks it over. I thought we were past this stage of her being anxious around me.

"What's wrong?" I ask.

My voice seems to pull Aine from her thoughts, and with a slight shake of her head, she hurries over and plops into my lap. I wrap my arms around her waist and pull her against me, trying and failing to ignore her hot breath brushing across the mark on my neck.

She shivers as she feels my body's response to her, and I'm sure if I sniff hard enough, I'll be able to scent her arousal.

"I asked Alex what happened to Owen," she blurts out. "He said to ask you."

I didn't expect this—at least not right now. I assumed Aine would eventually ask, but I haven't planned yet what I wanted to say. She's going to be pissed.

"I brought him back with us, and I had him tied up in the woods," I admit. Aine stiffens. "The plan was to keep him there until you were in a place to decide his outcome but, uh…" I'm unsure how to tell her what I've done. "I accidentally killed him shortly after we returned."

Aine's eyes grow wide. I don't need to mark her to know she's shocked, her scent and physical reaction giving me all the information she's yet to vocalize.

Owen's death *was* a genuine accident. I snuck out in the middle of the night to interrogate him, hoping if he told me what he did to Aine, it would help me understand her needs better. After only a minute of listening to him speak about the things he'd done, though, my hand was inside his chest and my fist was clenched around his heart.

I know it was supposed to be Aine's decision, and I feel horrible. Alex said she probably already thinks I killed him and won't be upset, but I'm not so sure about that.

Aine remains silent, her lack of reaction driving me insane.

I'm ready to drop to my knees and beg for forgiveness when she finally lets out a quiet grunt and slumps against my chest.

"Good," she says.

I'm sure she can feel my relief as I relax and curl around her, grateful to have been gifted a mate who's so forgiving. A comfortable silence stretches between us as I stroke her back and cup her scalp. Her hair's growing back quickly, the strands shooting straight out and giving her a fuzzy look.

I like it, even if she doesn't.

Her breath again washes over my mark, causing a pleasurable tingle to shoot down my spine. She must be doing it on purpose.

My gums ache with the desire to mark her back, wanting to claim her as my own, but I ignore the need.

When she's ready, she'll ask for it.

After several agonizing seconds, Aine turns to peer at the paperwork sitting neatly on my desk. She hums as she looks it over.

"What're you working on?" she asks.

I remain quiet as she reads, allowing her the opportunity to see for herself. Her eyebrows furrow as she makes sense of everything, her frown deepening as she spots Freya's name.

"I'm looking for Freya." I reach into my desk drawers to pull out the papers I shoved in there earlier.

Aine's lips purse as she looks them over, her hands shaky as she flips from page to page.

"Why?"

"She's going to answer for the things she's done."

I press a kiss to the side of Aine's head, hoping to help settle her racing heart. I'm never going to let anybody hurt her again.

Chapter 36

AINE

ALEX PACES THE length of the room, his frantic actions more than a little bit concerning. I knew he wouldn't take well to learning about Damien's search for Freya, but I didn't anticipate him barging into our bedroom in the middle of the night wanting to speak about it.

I'm also surprised it took him so long to learn. Olivia insisted on being the one to tell him, but that was almost a week ago. I was beginning to worry she'd never speak up and Damien would have to do it himself.

I curl up underneath the sheets, knowing this isn't my fight. Alex and I have been spending a lot of time together since Damien began working out of his office last week, and I don't want to get involved.

Damien sits up and pulls our comforter further over my shoulders, hiding them from the angry beast standing at the foot of our bed. The interruption startled me, but I'm proud of myself for not shriveling up as I would've when I first came back home.

"She's done nothing but torture our family for years," Damien says, rubbing the sleep out of his eyes. "She knew what Owen would do to Aine, and she didn't care. She *helped* him."

Damien just about shifted into his beast form when Alex came bursting into the room, and I run my hand down his back to try and calm his residual panic. I don't think he would've been able to hold back the transition if it were anybody but his brother.

Alex scoffs. "So you've decided to kill her?"

That captures my attention. I've been spending a lot of time with Damien in his office, at least an hour every day, and that's never once been mentioned.

I look at Damien, watching his jaw clench before he turns toward me. I thought something along the lines of a trial when he said she will answer for the things she's done, and I curse myself for not asking for more detail.

My cheeks puff out while I wait for Damien to confirm or deny Alex's accusation, and my annoyance grows when he doesn't immediately do either.

I raise my eyebrows, waiting, and I sit up when Damien releases a quiet sigh and nods.

"Yes," he admits. "I plan to kill her."

I grow tense, my muscles stiffening. He plans to kill her? I'm not sure how I feel about that. My instinct is to ask a million questions, but I don't want to do so in front of Alex.

He's clearly distraught over the idea, and I don't want to make things worse. He and Damien can sort through this themselves. Freya's done unspeakable things to both of them, not to mention the part she played in my kidnapping, and I won't stand in the way of Damien's retribution.

I wanted the same done to Owen.

"Does that upset you?" Damien's question is directed toward me, but it's Alex who answers.

"Yes!" he says. "This upsets me very much, Damien!"

Damien ignores him, and I run a hand down my face and tuck

my hair behind my ears. "I wish you would've been a bit more upfront about the details of your plan," I admit. "But no, I'm not upset. I understand why you want to do this."

Alex scoffs, and he flings his arms out to the sides before plopping onto the edge of our bed. Damien reacts instinctively, his foot shoving against Alex's thigh until the man falls off the mattress. He lands on the floor in a heap, but he pops back up a second later.

"You should return home to Olivia," Damien says. "She was okay with my plan, and I'm sure she's upset you left her alone to defend your true mate."

Alex's frown softens at the mention of Olivia, his eyes darting toward the door. I've recently come to learn that Damien and Olivia love to gossip with one another, and he's mentioned she's been expressing a lot of fears about Alex leaving her for Freya.

I'm sure this is only aggravating that insecurity.

I can't really blame Alex, though. He's in a tough position.

Alex shifts his attention to me. Damien leans over and lifts the sheet higher up my body, covering most of my neck, but I ignore him as I wait to see what Alex has to say. It was him and me against Damien for the longest time, and I can't help but feel I'm betraying him right now.

He must hate me.

My chin wobbles, and Alex's eyebrows furrow before he leans forward and pinches my toes through the sheets. It hurts, and I yank my knees to my chest.

"Stop that," he orders. "I don't like that."

I blink away my tears, and Alex lets out a booming groan before turning toward Damien. "We *will* be discussing this later," he says. "This conversation is far from over."

He's gone a second later, our bedroom door slamming shut behind him. Damien stares at the ceiling.

"You're worried," I say. I feel it through the bond.

"I'm not excited to kill Freya," Damien admits, "but she's made it more than clear she's willing to do whatever it takes to hurt us. I'm scared she's going to retaliate. She truly believed she was my mate, and her hatred for you runs deep."

I take his hand, hoping to bring comfort.

Damien sighs before continuing. "And now Alex is being, well, Alex."

Shame mingles with his fear, and I squeeze his hand before cupping his chin and pulling his lips toward mine. I don't usually take initiative like this, but Damien seems to enjoy it. Quiet rumbles emerge from his chest, and they grow louder as I deepen the kiss.

The rumbling continues, growing to an obnoxious level. It's distracting, and my lips twitch as I pull away.

"What is that?" I tease, poking his chest.

Damien shrugs. "I've never done it before."

I quite like it, and I press my ear to his sternum before realizing why it sounds so familiar.

I gasp. "You're purring!"

Damien smiles as I struggle to hold back my laughter, and the purring deepens as he takes notice of my approval. He sounds just like those cats I saw in the human village.

"I'll purr for you every day of the week if it makes you smile like that." Damien grabs my leg and throws it over his waist.

I roll my eyes at his not-so-subtle request, and I happily straddle his hips. My distraction helps to soothe the intense emotions rolling around inside his brain, and if I'm honest with myself, I've been looking for an excuse to get close with him for days now.

Damien's been ignoring my advances quite aggressively. He's convinced I'm still injured from sex the other day, and he refuses to touch me. I think he's being dramatic.

"Let me distract you," I say.

Damien runs his hands down my waist, and I subtly grind against him. He flips me before I can do anything else, putting me on my back and planting himself between my thighs. I'm naked, and he takes his sweet time admiring me, his pupils expanding as he scans my bare form.

"I need a distraction," he admits.

I arch my back, and Damien grabs my hips as I grind myself against his hardening cock. It feels good, and he helps guide my movements before eventually pulling away and taking hold of himself. I sink my teeth into my bottom lip, the action capturing my complete attention. Damien leans back so I can see better as he strokes his length, his motions slow and deliberate.

He moans. "Who knew my beautiful mate would love to watch me so much? I bet you're already wet."

He uses his free hand to feel for himself. I don't bother denying his accusation as he runs a thumb down my slit, teasing me. I'm always wet for him, my body eager to take him inside.

"Do you want me to touch you?" he asks.

I nod, wanting nothing more, but Damien gives only a disappointed *tsk* in response.

"Use your words, Aine."

"I want you to touch me," I whisper. I resist the urge to cover my face. "I want you to fuck me."

Damien's satisfaction is felt heavy through our bond.

"Good, baby girl." His grin is infectious as he applies more pressure to my slit, pushing forward until his thumb's slipping between my folds. My hips twitch, and his throat bobs as he finally begins to rub my clit.

Damien refuses to take his gaze off me, and his eyes burn holes into my skin as he takes stock of what I like. I love the attention, and I rock against him before reaching down and grabbing his hips.

Damien stiffens for a whisper of a second before relaxing, and I mentally curse Freya for ever hurting him. Damien does a great job hiding it, but I know it messes with him occasionally when I touch his waist or thighs.

"You make me happy," he blurts out.

My cheeks warm, but Damien doesn't look for a response as he sinks his finger into me and begins crawling down my torso. He presses wet kisses to my skin the entire way, and I clench around his fingers as his mouth gets dangerously close to my sex.

Damien chuckles. "None of that." He spreads my legs, preventing me from hiding. "I'm excited to put my mouth on you. It turns me on to make you feel good."

His eyes meet mine as he kisses the inside of my thigh, and he holds the eye contact as he shifts his attention to the slick skin between them. He's always teasing me, and I hold back a whine as he trails his lips up and down my thighs.

"I've never—" I start, my words ending in a choked moan when he finally connects his mouth to my sex.

My admission has him rearing back.

"Nobody's ever licked you before?"

I'm sure the reddening of my cheeks is answer enough, but Damien waits until I give a verbal response. He's making a habit of doing that.

"No," I admit.

Damien frowns. "I'm sorry *he* never treated you right," he says. He's referring to Henry. "But I am selfishly happy this will be a first for both of us."

It takes a second for those words to process. Damien's never done this before? My excitement grows, and Damien trails his teeth over the inside of my thigh before returning his mouth to my sex. His tongue is soft as he licks the entire length of me, and I instinctively flinch and knock my knee against his head.

Damien politely ignores the attack against his temple, and he smoothly cups my kneecap and guides it away as he begins making his purring noises again.

He eases in another finger, and his spit soaks the sheets below my butt as he flicks his tongue over my swollen flesh. The second finger provides a nice stretch, and I rock against him with a low, needy moan.

The vibrations from his purring only amplify the pleasure, and I can't stop myself from sinking my hands into his hair and rolling my hips. Damien stills, letting me ride his face as he works me with his fingers.

I'm faintly aware he's thrusting into the mattress as he licks me, finding his own pleasure as he gives me mine. He loops his free arm around my thigh and squeezes my flesh as I continue rubbing myself against his wet tongue, my movements quickening as my orgasm builds.

"I'm… Damien, I'm…" I cry, my thrusting sporadic.

I almost rip out his hair as my pleasure peaks, and I pant into the air and arch my back as I ride it out.

Damien licks me through my orgasm, stopping only after I grow sensitive and knock his head away with my thigh. He grins and crawls up my body as I catch my breath, his mouth and chin slick with my arousal.

I'm exhausted, and I relax into the mattress as Damien lines himself up with my entrance. He pauses when he notices my sleepy expression.

"Do you think you can cum again?" he asks.

I pause, not sure if I can, but my slight hesitation is all Damien needs to see to begin removing himself from me. That's not what I want, and I rush to pull him back.

Damien looks shocked as I wrap my legs around his waist, refusing to let him leave. His cock brushes against me as I bring my lips to his ear.

"I want you to fuck me," I whisper. "I need it."

Damien's eyes roll back, his mouth forming silent words before he lines himself up and sinks inside. He moves slowly, probably worried about injuring me again, and he stills when he bottoms out.

The stretch is amazing, and he gives me a second to adjust before beginning to thrust.

"You feel so good," Damien cries, shoving his face into my neck as he quickens his pace. "I love you so fucking much. I'm not going to last long, baby. You feel too good."

He curls his body around mine and resumes his purring. It's loud, but it's easily overshadowed by the sound of his balls smacking against my ass with each roll of his hips.

Damien's teeth graze against my neck before he clenches his jaw shut and throws his head back. His fucking is wild, borderline desperate, and it doesn't take long for him to reach the edge.

"Mine," Damien moans. He grabs my hips and guides them down with each of his thrusts. "You're mine. Mine, mine, mine."

He continues mumbling this to himself, only stopping when he begins to cum. He buries himself in deep, filling me with himself.

I rub his back, struggling to breathe under his heavy weight. It takes Damien a moment to collect himself, his cock occasionally twitching as he cums inside me. Once he realizes, he's quick to prop himself up on his elbows and make room for my lungs to expand.

I whisper soft praises into his shoulder.

Damien stops me almost immediately.

"I love you, baby," he mumbles. "But please stop calling me

a good boy. It doesn't do it for me."

I snort, and Damien grins and presses a sloppy kiss to my cheek. I enjoy the flush that covers his face, and I happily take in the sight. The red deepens.

"I usually last longer than that," Damien says.

I open my mouth to tease him about it, but I find myself distracted as his softening length falls out of me.

"You came inside me," I point out.

Damien grimaces, regret slipping through our bond. "I'm sorry. I didn't mean to. Pulling out has always been instinctual, but I don't have that drive with you. My beast wants me inside, and in the heat of the moment, I forgot. I'll be more careful next time."

I nod, appreciating the honesty. I'm not ready for a child right now. Damien doesn't seem to be, either, but this accident does bring up questions. I've never had the courage to address my concerns with Damien before, but I want to be prepared in case this happens again and I end up pregnant.

"I have a question for you," I say.

Damien hums. "Yes?"

"Will you be upset if I give you girls?" My words are a whisper, but I can tell Damien hears them by the way he grows stiff. He sits up.

"Aine, I only care that we have happy, healthy children," he promises. He opens our bond, letting me feel his honesty. "Male or female means nothing to me. We don't even believe in prediction healers here, and I'll be quite offended if you ask to go to one."

I relax, happy with that answer. "What if our children come out more human than beast? Like your sister."

Damien's anxiety spikes. He sits up further, and I quickly do the same. Why did that question make him so nervous?

"I need to talk to you about something," he says, taking my hands. "You asked the other day about my family and my treatment of you when we first met. I lied to you."

I cover myself with our comforter, not wanting my bare, flushed skin on display as he says whatever it is he's leading to. I already don't like this.

Damien waits for me to get adjusted before continuing. "I let you think I pushed you away because I was afraid of losing you. That's not the truth. I was disappointed you were a human because I thought it meant you were weak."

I open my mouth to speak, but Damien raises his hand to stop me. I suck in my cheeks and nod for him to carry on.

"I began to hate humans after my mom and sister died," he says, the tremor in his voice growing. "I thought they weren't deserving of love, and I was furious when we met. I was convinced my beast made a mistake, and I hoped I could sever the bond between us by being cruel."

It hurts to hear, but I'm not entirely surprised. I knew he thought little of me and hoped his beast would eventually give up and choose another mate.

"I don't feel that way anymore, Aine," Damien rushes to say. "I swear. The thought of losing you scares me, and I worry a lot about your safety, but I don't hate that you're a human. I love you, and I was stupid to think you were a mistake. I want you, and if I were given the option between you as a human and you as a beast, I'd still choose this you."

Damien leans forward to cup my cheeks, his desperation pouring through the bond. I place my hands over his, hoping to bring some comfort.

"I don't understand," I admit after a brief silence. "You were cruel to me because you were scared."

Damien shakes his head, flinching. "That's not true. I was

cruel because you're a human. Because I hated that about you. Not because I was scared."

I huff. "Yeah? And why did you hate humans?"

Damien refuses to make eye contact with me. "Because I didn't believe they should be loved."

Shame floods our bond, and I can tell he's not understanding what I'm getting at.

"And why was that?" I push.

"Aine, I—" Damien groans when I repeat my question. "My father was empty after my mom and sister died. They wouldn't have died if they weren't human."

"So, after they died, you watched your father grieve himself into death, and you grew a hatred of humans because of their fragility and the pain that caused," I say, trying to make sure I'm hearing him correctly.

Damien nods, and I squeeze his hands in what I hope is a comforting gesture.

"Damien, you were a child, and you were hurt. I understand you did what you thought you needed to do to protect yourself from feeling that again. That isn't to say I'm happy about it, and you definitely have some groveling to do for the way you treated me, but I'm not going to sit here and be angry."

Damien looks away as his eyes grow glassy, and I calmly wipe his cheeks before leaning in to kiss him.

"What's done is done, and I'm tired of dwelling on who you used to be," I say. "Right now, I'm looking at a man who loves and treats me better than I ever imagined somebody could. That's enough for me, and I'd appreciate it if you stopped trying to self-sabotage what we have."

I kiss Damien again before guiding him to lay on his back. He does, and I rest my cheek against his chest. His heart is pounding, and I listen to its rhythmic beat before continuing.

"You never answered my earlier question," I say. "What if our children come out more human than beast?"

Damien blinks once, twice, three times as he tries to make sense of the shift in conversation. He opens his mouth, probably to try and punish himself some more, but he snaps it shut when he takes notice of my pointed glare.

His lips twitch as he fights back a smile.

"The thought makes me uncomfortable," he admits. "I don't know how to interact with human children, and it'll be a learning curve." He pets my head and fingers the short hairs at the back of my neck. "But I'll love them just the same."

That's all I wanted to hear, and I let my eyes slip shut with a content sigh. I'm not ready for children, and I probably won't be for a long time, but I'm excited to have them with Damien. He's going to be an amazing dad.

We lay in silence until we fall back asleep, and when the sun finally streams through the windows and wakes us up, there's a noticeable lightness in Damien's demeanor. I didn't realize just how much he was being affected by what he perceived to be this giant secret.

Now we just need to figure out this Freya situation.

We don't speak her name as we get in the shower together, nor when we walk to Damien's office, but I can tell we're both thinking the same thing. He's been obsessing over finding her.

I'm starting to worry.

I follow him into his office and kneel next to his desk.

"You don't need to do this," Damien huffs. He's embarrassed, but I don't know why. It's such a silly think to be embarrassed about.

I get comfortable before beginning to pull out the files stuffed haphazardly in the drawers of his desk. I've always known Damien's a busy man, but I didn't realize just how much stuff he has on his plate until recently.

I think it would help him to be a bit more organized. He spends half his time searching for files and papers he's lost track of, and organizing for him makes me feel helpful.

"If you're looking for work, there are several things I think you'd enjoy doing more than this," Damien says. He mindlessly runs his fingers through my hair, his lips turned downward as I kneel by his feet and sort through loose papers. "The door across the hall leads to an empty office, and I can have it furnished for you."

Most of his papers are crinkled beyond belief, and I shoot him a silent glare every time I have to sit up and use the edge of his desk to straighten it.

"Like what?" I ask.

I love the garden, but I wouldn't complain about something that would keep me inside and safe with Damien. Plus, it's nearly impossible to work in the garden for any extended periods of time when the weather's hot and the sun's beating down on me.

My skin is just too sensitive, and I don't love the blood transfusions. I feel great afterwards, but it's a bit of a hassle and I need them more frequently when I'm outside.

"I have weekly meetings with Jenna to go over the clinic's needs, and with Alex for the kitchen," Damien says. "I also do a copious amount of inventory. We can start there if you'd like."

Meetings and inventory. Both sound like things I would enjoy, and I turn toward Damien with a cheesy grin. I'm ready to have some actual responsibility again. I'm ready to begin living my life again. I'm ready to heal.

"I'd love that," I admit.

Damien seems to mirror my joy as he knocks his leg against my shoulder, and I quickly kiss his knee.

"But I need to finish organizing your office, first," I say. "It's messy, and I don't know how you get anything done."

Damien's smile falls, and he gives me a glare before pointedly ignoring me and returning to work. I imagine he's thinking nasty things about me, but that's fine. He'll be thanking me once I'm finished.

We work in comfortable silence, but when his frustration seeps through our bond, I can tell he's begun his search for Freya. I ignore his occasional angry huff, but each one makes me worry. He's going to drain himself if he doesn't relax.

When his knee begins to bounce, I climb on his lap. Damien immediately wraps his arms around my waist, his stiff muscles softening.

Freya's hidden herself well, and I'm worried Damien will never find her, or be able to get past his paranoia and desperation to kill her. I still don't necessarily agree with his decision to kill her, but the beasts operate differently than humans. They don't honor life the way we do, their animal side seeing things through a different lens.

Damien lets out a muffled groan as he flips through files upon files of reports from when she lived here. On the corner of his desk is a pile of reported sightings from the past several years. I didn't realize he kept such a close eye on her after everything that happened, but it doesn't surprise me.

Damien can be a bit intense.

"We'll find her," I say, hoping he can't sense my doubt.

Damien's eyes shine as he looks at me, the expression shocking but frequent since his confession last night. I know he thinks of me as some sort of saint, but I think he's just too hard on himself. He's done so much to prove himself to me, and it's going to take more than one confession to drive me away.

He's stuck with me whether or not he likes it.

Annoyance seeps through the bond as he turns toward the

door, his eyes narrowing as it creaks open and Alex walks in. Alex closes the door behind him, his shoulders hunched and body tense as he lowers himself in the chair opposite Damien's desk.

I busy myself with paperwork, not wanting to intrude.

Alex clears his throat. "Tell me what she did to you."

Damien falls silent at Alex's request, his entire body freezing up. I peek over, trying to see if he wants me to leave, but he doesn't so much as look in my direction.

How could Alex ask this? He knows Damien doesn't like to think about that night, let alone speak the details. We know all we need to know.

A minute of tense silence passes, but when I move to get up and give them privacy, Damien grabs my waist and prevents me from leaving. I gulp, nodding to myself, before sinking back down on his lap. It looks like I'm staying.

"I don't want details, but I just—fuck, I can't get my beast to forget her," Alex admits. "You've never spoken about it, and he doubts she could betray us like that…"

Alex trails off, letting the rest of his unspoken sentence linger.

Does he think Damien slept with Freya by choice? My fingers curl and bend the sheets of paper I'm holding as blind rage courses through me. Damien would never do that, and both Alex and his beast should know that by now.

My anger toward Alex only grows as Damien clears his throat and buries his head in the back of my neck in a sad attempt to self-soothe. I can feel his pain, but the way it's muted tells me he's trying to keep it hidden.

"Alex," he whispers, begging.

Alex stands his ground. "You want to kill my true mate, and I need to know that your actions are justified."

He clears his throat when his voice grows rough. He looks uncomfortable, but apparently, that isn't enough to stop him from making his ridiculous demand. I know I'm not a beast, and I don't cherish the mate bonds the way they do, but this is still way out of line.

Damien kisses the back of my neck, and his shaky exhale warms the skin. "Freya helped me home after you left the party. I was struggling to move and talk, but I didn't think anything of it. I had too much to drink. She took off my clothes and helped me to bed, which wasn't unusual. Then she climbed on me."

Damien clears his throat and buries his face back into my neck, practically burrowing into my skin. He breathes in my scent before continuing.

"I was drugged," he says. "My body betrayed me, and I was too weak to push her off. She marked my thigh when I wouldn't stay hard, and she tried to—"

Alex interrupts. "Show me where she marked you."

I stiffen, my anger spiking. "Absolutely not," I spit. I'm done entertaining Alex. I understand he needs closure, but he's asking for too much. "Freya drugged and raped Damien, and he owes you nothing, least of all to show you his scars."

Damien's body curls around mine as I shout the words, his shame hitting me full force through our bond. I've seen the scar during our showers, and it's gruesome. She ripped out a large section of his skin, and I can only imagine the pain Damien feels having to see it every day.

Freya must have continued after marking Damien because the scar has never faded as our marks did, and I know that kills Damien. He's stuck with a permanent reminder of that night.

Alex's throat bobs, his eyes darting between Damien and me.

Damien grabs my waist and nudges me to stand, but I refuse to budge. He will not be showing Alex his scar. Not today, not ever. It's his body, and Alex doesn't get to make demands of it.

"She wanted me to finish inside her," Damien continues. "She was hoping to get pregnant. Alex, I didn't… I would never—"

Alex nods, a silent submission. Damien snaps his jaw shut with a quiet click.

"Freya's great-grandfather built a cabin about two hours south of here," Alex says. "It was a place we'd go to when we wanted to be alone, and I'm willing to bet that's where she is."

I try not to let my shock show as I absorb that information. Alex has known where Freya was this entire time and hasn't said anything? It's clear Damien's thinking the same thing as his anger funnels through the bond, and I place my hand on his in an attempt to calm him down.

"Thank you," Damien says after a brief pause. "I know this isn't easy for you."

Alex shrugs and turns to look out the large windows behind Damien's desk. I can practically feel the tension between them, and I wonder how this scenario would play out if they weren't brothers who shared so much love.

"My beast will recognize her death," Alex says. "Please make it quick."

Damien nods. I'm sure he intended to do that even if Alex hadn't asked. Alex and Freya will always have some sort of connection, and I know Damien would never purposefully prolong the pain Alex is sure to feel when Freya dies.

Alex teeters slightly, rocking back on his heels. "You remember that river Dad used to take us to?" He waits for Damien to nod before continuing. "The cabin is about three miles east of there."

Damien rubs the back of my hand as Alex shares a few more landmarks, then abruptly leaves. The door clicks shut behind him, and we both turn to watch him stomp across the back lawn and into our home.

"I want this to be over with," Damien admits.

I can tell there's more he wants to say, but I don't push him to speak. He doesn't like discussing his interactions with Freya, and I can feel how much self-hatred and anger are coursing through him right now. I'd feel the same way if somebody demanded I speak about what Owen or Henry did to me.

Damien peppers soft kisses along my neck, teasing the spot where he'll put his mark on me someday. I'm growing excited at the idea of it, and I've caught myself wanting to ask him to bite me several times these past few days.

"I didn't want anybody to know what she did to me," he finally admits after a long pause. "It makes me feel weak. If I can't protect myself, how can I protect my mate and my pack?"

I shake my head, immediately disagreeing with his statement.

Damien grunts as I spin and wrap my arms around his head. He doesn't fight my tight hug, and our bond hums as I press his face to my chest and squeeze his skull.

"You're not weak," I say. "Freya was your family, and nobody blames you for having had your guard down around her." I'm desperate for him to believe me. "Your people love and respect you."

I give Damien one last squeeze before climbing off his lap. Even without the bond, I can tell he's anxious. He's been looking tirelessly for Freya.

"Go on, then," I say, gesturing to the door. "I know you're dying to leave."

Damien hesitates, and I kiss his forehead before grabbing his hand and pulling him to his feet. He still doesn't seem eager, and despite my fears of being left alone, I lead him outside.

Owen is dead, and I can't live my entire life by Damien's side.

"Let me walk you to the garden," Damien says. "The beasts should be arriving for training soon, and they'll protect you."

I take his hand, letting him guide me there. I don't mind, and

I'm secretly relieved to be surrounded by beasts I trust while Damien's gone. I saw them fight Owen's men, and I know they're strong.

"Please stay here until I'm back," Damien pleads.

I planned to do so, even if he didn't ask.

There's enough work in the garden to keep me busy for several hours, and I hide my nerves behind a smile as Damien squeezes my arm and disappears into the woods.

Chapter 37

DAMIEN

I'M FAINTLY AWARE Alex is following me, his scent occasionally reaching my nose when the wind blows in the right direction. He knows I know, too, my frequent pauses to sniff and look around making it quite clear.

Still, he remains hidden until I reach the cabin. I ignore his approaching form as I crouch and peek through the trees, searching for any signs of life. I don't want Freya to see or hear me and run.

Alex's fur brushes mine as I circle the perimeter of the small building, continuing until I'm downwind and can smell her. She's in there, her scent thick as it merges with the wood of the cabin. I bury my paws into the dirt and plop onto my belly, waiting for the perfect opportunity to strike.

The last thing I need is to barrel in there, only to discover she's planned for my arrival and set up a defense for herself. Aine will kill me if I get myself hurt.

Alex follows suit, and I'm prepared to continue ignoring him when I notice him shifting into his human form. I turn to watch as he sits on his butt and leans against my side, his legs sprawled out in front of him.

"You remember when Dad forced us to learn how to swim after Mom and Jess died?" he asks.

I blow a tuft of air in his direction. Yes.

"He'd make us swim that fucking river until it grew dark. I'll never forget how you'd hold me up whenever he wasn't looking." Alex lets out a weak laugh before clearing his throat. "Even if it slowed you down and you could barely lift your arms the next day."

I wiggle my belly into the dirt, glad he didn't mention how I'd swallow so much water, I had to pause every ten minutes to puke. It had to be done, though. Alex has never been a strong swimmer, and Dad wouldn't let him out of the water until he completed his laps.

"I don't know how Dad never noticed," he says, poking me in the ribs. "I think he just assumed you and I were both shit swimmers."

Alex laughs as I grumble, the low noise emerging from my chest. I'm an excellent swimmer, but Alex slowed me down. If I knew what a nuisance he'd grow up to be, I'd have left him behind.

I glance at him before returning my gaze to the cabin. Just knowing Freya's in there has my blood boiling, and I smack my tail into the ground as I listen for any noises from her.

The painful tug in my heart grows as my adrenaline fades and the weight of what I'm about to do settles over me. I loved Freya as my sister for many years, and sometimes it's hard to ignore that fact.

"I never thanked you for that," Alex continues. "You always put me first, even at the end when Dad became angry." His voice cracks. "Freya's my responsibility, Damien. I can swim across the river by myself."

I rise and shift back to my human form. No words are exchanged as we sit next to one another, both of us staring at the cabin.

"That was a really smooth way of saying I'm going to kill my mate," Alex whispers. He's talking to fill the silence. I don't blame him. "I'm really good at metaphors."

He stands on shaky legs and begins walking toward the cabin.

I keep my eyes peeled in case Freya tries to run, and I'm beyond shocked when Alex knocks on the front door and she opens it a moment later with a smile. She pulls Alex in for a warm hug, and I step closer so I can better eavesdrop.

"I was starting to think you'd never come," Freya says, her words muffled as she speaks into Alex's shoulder. "I've missed you."

He doesn't respond, instead softly nudging her inside. I don't hate him for his kindness to her. My bond with Aine consumes me, and I couldn't imagine doing anything to harm her. The mistakes I made when we first met still haunt me, and even when things were as bad as they could be, killing her was never an option.

I refused to entertain it. It goes against everything we are, and Alex can't just turn that off. He's always been a good man, and despite Freya's betrayal, I know this is killing him.

I stare at the front door for a while before shifting back into my beast form and taking a lap of the cabin. There are no sounds from inside, even when hours pass and the sun begins to set. What's taking him so long?

I stopped by the clinic and asked Avia and Jenna to keep an eye on Aine while I was gone, but I still don't like to be away from her for too long. My human likes to put on a brave face, but I know she's scared.

Eventually I can't stop myself from approaching, and I'm

careful to keep quiet as I nudge open the cabin door with my head. I sneeze as the scent smacks me in the face, the cabin's interior an overwhelming mixture of bile, blood, and excrement.

My eyes land on Alex immediately. He's cradling Freya's head, bent over her body as his back heaves with sobs.

I don't hesitate to shift into my human form and crawl to him.

He looks up as I approach, his face red and covered in her blood. He looks feral, and I gently pull her head off his lap before urging him to move away. His hands are shaky as he scoots back a few feet, and I pull him into a hug before turning so he can no longer see her body.

It looks like he killed Freya quickly, a slice to her neck when she wasn't looking. I stare into her wide, lifeless eyes as I pull Alex to his feet and lead him outside. Sitting in here isn't good for him.

His bloody skin rubs against mine as we sit on the porch steps, and I hurry to shut the front door and trap the scent of death inside. Alex's gut-wrenching sobs gradually slow to occasional sniffles as the sun sets, the sky turning black before either of us works up the courage to speak.

I want to get home to Aine, and I hope she isn't still waiting in the garden for me. I have to trust that Avia and Jenna have taken care of her, though. Alex needs me right now, and I fear what he will do if I leave.

Avia is responsible.

Alex is the first to speak. "It's done."

I nod, having no words.

Alex continues. "I'm sorry I asked you to—"

I squeeze his wrist, stopping him. He has nothing to apologize for. Aine may not understand, but his beast needed to hear it. I'm not angry.

Chapter 38

AINE

DAMIEN SINKS INTO the mattress, the sudden distribution of weight causing me to roll over. I blink awake as I smush against a chest, and I can't help but from as I look up at Damien. What time is it?

The world beyond our window is black, and I stare at the moon before sitting up and peering down at Damien. It takes a moment for my eyes to adjust, and I use my hands to feel what I can't yet see.

I drag my fingers up Damien's damp chest, continuing until I reach his head. His hair's soaking wet, but I didn't hear the shower turn on.

"I used the bathroom in the hall," Damien says, grabbing my hand and bringing it to his lips.

I hum, sinking back into the sheets and resting my cheek against his chest. He was gone for so long today. I thought it would only be a few hours, and I tried waiting up for him, but eventually it grew so late I had no choice but to go to bed.

Avia and Jenna insisted on sleeping on the couch downstairs, both promising they were content waiting for Damien.

It was a comfort. I wouldn't have been able to fall asleep without the knowledge that Avia was downstairs. Damien must have sent them home while I was sleeping.

His emotions are muted.

Damien sucks in a shaky breath. "Alex came with me. He wanted to do it." He clears his throat when his voice cracks. "That's why it took so long."

"Is he okay?" I ask.

"No."

"Are *you* okay?"

It takes Damien a while to respond. "No."

It's not surprising to hear, and I pepper soft kisses to his chest until his breathing evens. I wait for him to speak up and start conversation, but he doesn't. We lay in silence, and after what feels like hours, Damien finally falls into a light rest. He must be exhausted.

It takes a week for Damien to fully open our bond again, and each day feels like torture. I refuse to acknowledge it, though, not wanting him to feel pressured. When he finally does open up to me, I'm overwhelmed with the amount of pain that filters through. He's mourning Freya's death, which is an odd feeling.

It takes two weeks for Alex to return to work. Things are off, but he puts on a brave face. Olivia is beyond patient with him, and they decide to postpone the marking ceremony until he's feeling better. I understand. I wouldn't want to celebrate the start of my life with somebody who is mourning the ending with another.

I know things are getting better during week three when I wake up one morning to Alex stealing food from our kitchen. He doesn't bother hiding his thievery, and he and Damien bicker for over an hour until grudgingly going their separate ways.

At six weeks, Alex and Olivia have set a date for their marking ceremony. Alex stops by Damien's office to tell us, and poor Olivia arrives twenty minutes later with a slight limp. I tease her for hours.

I watch Damien, obsessed with the way the muscles in his back flex as he follows Olivia through the woods. As if he can sense my gaze, he turns and smiles at me.

Olivia slows to a stop as we reach the spot where the marking ceremony is happening later today. Avia and Jenna are already here, the pair working quietly to place flowers around the alter Olivia and Alex will stand under.

"Are you sure you're okay with me leaving?" Damien asks.

It's tradition that Alex and Olivia will offer one another a fresh kill during the ceremony, and Damien has agreed to help Olivia catch something.

I nod. "I'll be here with Avia and Jenna."

The altar they've created is beautiful, a green vine and flower covered wooden arch set snugly between some of the largest oak trees within the pack. Olivia's worked hard to merge the human and beast traditions, and it looks incredible.

Damien doesn't look certain about leaving me, his eyebrows furrowed as he scans my figure. I know he's worried, but I'm truly okay. He and Olivia won't be gone for long, and I've got a long list of items to distract myself with.

"Go," I whisper, patting his butt. "I'll be here."

Damien hesitates.

"We'll be quick," he promises before shifting into his beast form. I'm continually shocked by how large he is, and I smile as he brushes against me.

His fur tickles.

"Go." I shoo him. "We don't have time to waste."

He and Olivia take off, and I busy myself with last-minute touches. The ceremony is in only a few hours, and there's a lot of work that needs to be finished.

Alex is nowhere to be seen. He left last night to hunt down his animal for Olivia, and he must be going after something big to be gone this long. I'm excited to see what it is.

Damien and Olivia return within an hour.

Olivia looks a bit pale, a dead bunny clutched tightly in her arms. She hurries to put the animal in the small cooler next to the altar, her hands shaking.

"I need to get ready," she says, slamming the cooler shut.

Damien trots toward me, his fur covered in blood. I jump and swat him away when he tries to rub himself on my arm. He doesn't get the hint.

"Go shower," I grunt, shoving at his snout.

Damien whines, trying to press his body against my legs before tucking his tail and leaving. I watch him walk away before turning toward Jenna.

"People will be arriving within the next hour or so," she warns. "I can handle it from here if you want to go home with Damien."

I shake my head. I've been outside in public several times now, but always with Damien and always at a distance. This is going to be my first time in close contact with the beasts.

I'm determined to do it with my chin held high.

"I'm okay," I say. "I'll get the chairs in place."

Almost everybody from the pack is expected to attend the ceremony, and the dining hall chairs were brought to the woods last night. I get to work setting them up.

I'm just finishing up with the first guests arrive. Insecurity runs rampant inside me, but I plaster a smile on my face as I welcome them. It's been years since Damien's pack held a marking ceremony, and everybody's so distracted with the excitement of it that they hardly pay me any attention. It's a huge relief.

Damien arrives and pulls me in for a punishing kiss.

"Come sit," he says.

I shake my head. "In a minute."

He huffs and takes a spot in the first row, and I can't help but smile when I catch him shooing away the few people who try to sit next to him. He's shameless in his desire to save me a seat.

I finish what I'm doing before joining Damien, happily sitting in the seat he saved. He immediately wraps an arm around my waist and pulls me into his side.

Alex and Olivia are the last to arrive, and I feel giddy as they make their way to the altar. Olivia's wearing white, and Alex even dressed up. I'm impressed.

I've been to plenty of human weddings before. I was a bride once myself, and the beginning of the ceremony follows the same template. It's sweet, and I rest my head against Damien's shoulder as a beast I'm not close with officiates.

He must be one of Alex's friends.

Eventually the time for the dead animal gifts arrives, and I sit up straighter as Avia brings out Olivia's cooler. Then she brings Alex's catch, and my eyes grow comically wide at the sheer size of the mountain lion she drags over. *Holy shit.*

I place my hand on Damien's knee, not wanting to miss a second of this.

Alex cuts a small piece of meat from the lion, and Olivia happily takes the bite Alex offers. He gives her a tiny piece, but I still hold back a wince as she chews. I don't want to imagine how gross it must taste.

After a few seconds, she turns and discreetly spits into a napkin. The raw meat will make her sick if she swallows, so the chewing is symbolic. Jenna sneaks up from behind and takes the napkin from Olivia.

I'm surprised Olivia agreed to participate in this particular tradition, but I assume it's to impress the beasts. She's hoping to win their approval today.

Olivia takes a moment to collect herself before grabbing her bunny. Alex grins like an excited child as she sets her offering on the small podium that sits beside her. Her jaw clenches as she grabs a knife, her hand visibly shaking.

Avia already cut the animal open for her, but Olivia still has to cut a chunk of meat out of the bunny.

Alex's smile wavers as Olivia hesitates, but it returns when she squares her shoulders and confidently cuts out a piece for him. I know how much she was dreading this, but she does well.

She offers the meat to Alex, and he eagerly bends and plops it into his mouth. I look away when he sucks her fingers in the process, and Damien infuriatingly lets out a quiet hoot.

He quiets when I elbow him in the side.

Alex moans. "Delicious."

Olivia rolls her eyes, a softness I rarely see taking over her features as she watches Alex. Next is the most exciting part, and I grab Damien's hand as Alex cups Olivia's chin. Blood smears over her cheek and jawline, but she ignores it and happily tilts her head to the side, exposing her neck.

I gulp, glancing at Damien as Alex brings his mouth to Olivia's neck. Damien's already watching me, his desire coursing through our bond.

The fact that he still hasn't marked me weighs heavy on my mind, and it's all I can think about as Alex sinks his teeth into Olivia's neck. Her face is turned away from us all, hiding her reaction, but her buckling knees show how intense it is. It was painful and overwhelming when Damien did it to me, and I imagine she's feeling something similar.

I begin to clap the second they pull away. There's silence before it picks up, the older, more traditional beasts who previously disapproved of their relationship congratulating them. I'm sure it will take some time for Olivia to be given their full respect, but this is a big step forward.

Alex and Olivia share a few words of promise before the ceremony is officially over and they disappear into the forest.

They'll be gone for several days to celebrate.

I turn to Damien. "That was amazing."

He nods, agreeing, before pulling me in for a hug. There's a large feast prepared in the dining hall, but Damien and I have already decided we're not going to go.

Today was a stretch for me, and I know I'll be overwhelmed if I go to the dinner. It's sure to be full of drunk, loud beasts, and I'm not ready.

"Put your feet on mine," Damien says.

I do, and a loud laugh bursts from my throat as he begins walking. He's in an uncharacteristically good mood as he brings us home with long strides that stretch my inner thighs.

"Did you have fun hunting with Olivia?" I ask as he stomps us through the forest.

We pass several beasts making their way to the dining hall, but thankfully, none try to make conversation beyond a polite greeting. I force myself to untuck my face from Damien's chest and smile, not wanting to appear off-putting.

"I didn't like leaving you, but I had a good time," he says.

I nod, agreeing. "I didn't enjoy you being gone, either."

We reach the house, and Damien silently carries us inside and onto the couch.

"I caught myself trying to push my emotions to you before remembering you can't feel them anymore," I admit, testing the waters.

Damien turns to face me fully, his eyes trailing over the spot that once held his mark. My heart feels like it's beating out of my chest as I sit up and straddle him. Damien's quick to grab my hips as I settle on his lap, his fingertips pressing into the exposed skin beneath my shirt.

"You never did teach me how to control it," I say. "It's not fair that you could hide your emotions, but I couldn't."

I slam my mouth shut as I realize I'm practically panting in his face, my excitement over our conversation overshadowing the nerves I feel.

"Do you want me to teach you?" Damien asks. "I think you quite enjoyed sharing with me your constant annoyance."

He brings a hand to my neck, his touch featherlight as he runs a finger along the side of my throat. He taps against the spot where his mark once sat.

I shrug, neither denying nor confirming his statement. That *was* a nice perk, especially when everything he did had me flustered and angry.

Damien gulps, and he looks at me with so much adoration that it makes me want to cry.

"I look forward to the day you ask me to mark you," he says.

I hum. "How do you want it to happen?"

I think he knows where this conversation is leading, but I'm enjoying it, nonetheless. After our first marking, I want this one to feel special.

"I'd like you to be sitting on top of me just like this, your belly pressed against mine and your body as relaxed as it is now," Damien says. "I don't want to make it sexual. Most beasts do, but I want ours to be about comfort."

Damien's eyes darken as he stares at my neck. "I'd love just to hold and feel your body on mine. Sometimes I feel like a piece of myself is missing, that when our bond died, a chunk of myself died with it. I feel empty if I think about it for too long."

The pain in his voice is nothing to the agony I feel coursing through our bond. I knew not marking me was hard for him, but he's kept the extent of it hidden.

He did it so I don't feel pressured, and as annoying as that is, I'm thankful. I'm ready for his mark now, but I know I wasn't then. I appreciate him urging me to wait.

I slide my fingers through the hair at the back of Damien's head, and I fail to contain my giddy smile as I guide his face toward my neck. His breath warms the spot that will hold his mark, and he lets out a quiet moan before kissing the area.

I shiver at the contact and further tilt back my head when he opens his mouth and runs his tongue up the column of my throat.

"Do it," I whisper, pushing softly on the back of his head.

Damien chuckles, ignoring me, before pulling back to look me in the eye. He's smiling.

"Ask me nicely," he orders.

I clench my thighs around his hips as I fight the impulse to follow his command. It takes everything in me to deny him.

"No," I say. "You need to ask me nicely. Better yet, you should beg."

Damien's face is back in my neck before I can process what's happening, his teeth nipping at the skin in warning. He may do many things I ask, but begging seems to be where he draws the line.

"My intelligent, dominating mate. Can I please mark you?" He groans, surprisingly giving in to my request. "Please let me feel you. It's all I've ever wanted. It's all I ever think about. How pretty you'd look with my mark."

His voice lowers into a whine I didn't even know was possible. "Please, Aine. Please let me mark you. I promise I'll make it so good."

His hips twitch beneath me, his cock hard despite how he said he doesn't want to make this sexual. I'd be lying if I said my desire for him wasn't borderline desperate right now.

"Good boy," I tease.

I shove his head back into my neck, obsessed with the way he continues to whimper and beg for my permission.

"Please." I gasp, unable to wait any longer.

I'm thrown onto my back the second the plea slips from my lips, and Damien grinds his cock between my thighs.

"Can I bite you hard?" he asks. "It'll hurt more, but our bond will be deeper."

I wrap my legs around his waist. "Do it as hard as you can."

Damien chuckles. We both know he'd kill me if he did that, but he knows what I mean. I can handle a bit of short-lived pain if it means our bond will be big and deep for the rest of my life.

His adorable purr starts up again as he searches for the spot where he wants his mark to live. I open my mouth to tease him, but all thoughts leave my mind when he finally sinks his teeth into me.

A burning pain immediately begins to spread, pulsating from my neck and down my shoulder. Damien's grip on me tightens as I instinctively try to move away, his chest lowering to press into mine and hold me still. *Fuck.*

I remember it hurting the first time, but it wasn't nearly this painful. I groan as Damien finally pulls away, his teeth leaving my neck. It still burns, and his purring grows louder as he licks the wound.

He grumbles as he pulls away to look at his work, and I relax on the couch as the burn begins to subside into a dull ache.

"You need more of my blood," he says. "It'll take a few hours to heal.

The bond shares Damien's delight as he looks down at me, his eyes continually darting to my neck. He struggles to hold back a smile as he waits for my reaction, his lips twitching every few seconds before finally spreading into a grin.

"I'd ask how you're feeling, but I don't really need to because I can feel it myself," he brags.

He sounds so proud of himself.

I'm eager for him to experience the bond as I have these past few weeks, and I try to push all my love and affection into him. Damien's eyes widen as he feels it, a subtle blush covering his cheeks.

Several minutes pass in blissful silence, only broken when Damien groans and rises.

"You're bloody," he says, pulling me into his arms. He holds me bridal style. "Let's get you cleaned up."

There's a noticeable bounce in his step as he carries me upstairs, his bliss outweighing all his other emotions. I love it.

Damien only sets me down so he can get the shower ready, and I wrap my arms around his waist as he adjusts the temperature. He lets me, his body soft and relaxed within my hold.

"I missed this," I admit as we step into the shower.

Damien agrees, and I lean against him as he washes my neck and chest. He takes special care not to injure the sensitive skin, which I appreciate.

There's no hurry to leave the shower, and we find excuses to linger until the water begins to run cold. Poor Damien's cock is so hard it must be painful, but he smoothly brushes away my attempts to soothe him.

"I'm being romantic," he huffs.

I'm pretty sure he's doing this more for my benefit than his.

He's trying to prove that he loves me for more than my body, but I already know that. Still, I play along.

"When do you plan to furnish my office?" I ask as we step out of the shower.

Damien hisses as he wraps his towel around his waist. I bet the fabric brushing against him feels good, and I chuckle as he pointedly avoids making eye contact with me.

"I don't know," he says. "Are you in a hurry?"

Damien smacks my butt.

"Get in bed," he orders. "I'll be right there."

He rushes downstairs, and I towel-dry my hair before sliding naked into bed. I tried my best to do things his way, but I'm desperate. My desire grows with each pump of my heart, and feeling Damien's arousal filter through our bond isn't helping.

I need him, and I lay back and touch myself while I wait for him to return. He comes back shortly with two books tucked under his arm, but when he steps inside the bedroom and sees my fingers playing with my clit, the books are quickly forgotten.

"Oh," he moans, ripping off his towel and climbing onto the bed. "Thank the fucking heavens. I really tried to make this romantic, but it's damn near impossible. My cock is going to fall off, Aine. It's so fucking desperate for you."

He's inside me within seconds, just the way I hoped.

Chapter 39

AINE

I TRY TO hide my excitement as Damien leads me out of his office. He's been complaining about my desire to have my own space all morning, and I smirk as he pushes open the door to the office he promised me.

It's empty and smells like cleaning product, but it's full of bright sun and promise. I resist the urge to scratch the healing mark on my neck as Damien places his hand on the small of my back and nudges me inside.

"We can put your desk there," he says, pointing to the wall directly opposite the door. "Then I can watch—" Damien pauses and clears his throat. "Then I can *see* you from my office."

I hold back a smile. "I don't think either of us will get much work done if you can *see* me from your office."

Damien kisses the top of my head, but doesn't respond.

I walk around the room, envisioning what it'll look like furnished. I'll probably put the desk where Damien suggested, even if it means losing some of our productivity. I like looking at him, and we can always close our doors if it becomes an issue.

"If you're comfortable, we can go shopping in the human

village next weekend," Damien says. "There are some stores there I think you'll like."

That sounds amazing.

"I'm thinking we can get some shelves to go here." Damien gestures to the long wall next to the door. "We can probably fit a small couch underneath them, too."

Damien circles the room and continues sharing his thoughts on furniture, and I'm surprised by how cohesive it is.

It looks like somebody's a bit of an interior designer.

Damien pauses when I approach and grab his face, his hands moving to my hips as I pull his head toward me and turn it left and right. His laughter's loud as he plays nice and lets me manhandle him, but I can see his confusion.

"What are you doing?" he finally gives in and asks.

I hum, holding back a smirk.

"I'm making sure you're still cute and fluffy."

"Am I?"

I shrug. "Not really."

The sheer delight that barrels into me has me blinking back tears, but it's the purring that tips them over the edge. I fucking love this man.

***

THE END

BONUS CONTENT

***

Looking for more of Aine?

Bonus chapters, original drafts, and current ongoing works can be found at: **patreon.com/inviwright**